FAKE GIRLS

For the 'real' Boris

978-0-6151-3682-0

FAKE GIRLS

Matthew Sloan

Afterhuman Press

1. Graves, bad luck, and fat men

I won the lottery. That's what I say when I'm at a party and someone asks me what I do for a living. And while they're still processing that, I quickly excuse myself to head for the booze table. Most people are only too happy to let me move on. Most people, unlucky themselves, don't like lucky people. Besides most people are really only waiting for you to stop moving your mouth so they can start talking about themselves and telling them you won a lottery tends to stop them dead in their tracks. What are they going to say to that?

Don't get me wrong. I'm not passing judgment. I'm just as self-absorbed as anyone. And who can blame any of us? Everyone's a mystery to themselves and one lifetime just isn't enough to figure it all out. I imagine that everyone dies asking more or less the same question: "What the hell was all that about?"

Maybe that's why we try to keep living as long as possible.

What do I really do for a living? This is what I do: I sit on a park bench and wait for someone to come sit next to me. It could be anyone: a jealous spouse, a suspicious business partner, a blackmail victim, a dirty politician (as opposed to what other kind?), the parent of a missing child, the lover of a missing person—or the loved one who wants to stay missing.

I sit on a park bench and wait for them to come.

And they do. You see, I provide a very valuable service.

What I do is solve problems.

Business is usually brisk. There is never a shortage of problems to go around.

Screwed to the back of the bench I'm sitting on right now is a little gold plaque dedicated to the memory of Edith and Ronald Kriefhoffen by their "loving family." All the benches in this part of the park have these little plaques on them dedicated to someone or other. I'm sitting on a tombstone, basically, with no body underneath it. I look around at all these memorial benches. I could be sitting in an empty graveyard. What I'm reminded of is how desperately we all want to matter, how fiercely we all want to be remembered. What I'm reminded of is that we don't really matter at all, how we won't really be remembered by anyone.

It's sad, when you think about all it entails, to be a human being.

In my line of work, I do a lot of waiting. When you do a lot of waiting, you have a lot of time to think. It's an occupational hazard, like getting black lung is for a miner.

While I wait for today's client, I feed the pigeons from a bag of leftover popcorn I bought for breakfast at Port Authority. Desperate and unashamed, the birds swarm around me like an impossible number of ex-wives. As I throw the stale kernels at them, I can only admire their enthusiastic celebration of voracious, opportunistic greed. Usually it's ten, fifteen years of life down the crapper before you get to see this side of the people in your life.

I know what you're thinking: *misogynist, misanthrope, malcontent, mental case.* But I don't have enough interest or passion left for any emotional investment as strong as that.

I don't hate human beings. Honestly, I don't. I just don't think I've ever actually met one.

Once a few years back, when I still thought of myself as quite the badass, I got into kind of a nasty situation that's not all that unusual in my line of work. The circumstances aren't really important. Suffice it to say, it was one of those affairs where you end up on your knees at three a.m. in an alley somewhere downtown, the barrel of a .32 automatic shoved rudely into your mouth, some really excited guy screaming something at you in Spanish. Everything is a mess, someone off to the side is going through your wallet, a pal of yours is sobbing for his mother, puke is everywhere, and you aren't sure whether that's blood or urine soaking the front of your pants. It's times like those when you're surprised, and later on, thoroughly appalled, to discover just what you'll do to stay alive. That's what this story, all stories, really, are about in the end. The kinds of things we do, day by day, to stay alive—even when there doesn't really seem to be much point to life at all.

He's big the guy who slides in next to me on the park bench this afternoon. He's more than big, he's obese, morbidly so, the kind of guy whose legs are foreshortened by all the fat hanging over his waistband. His stubby, meaty thighs are spread out to make room for that prodigious sack of a belly, plopped down there like he's expecting the birth of twin hippos, and he has that anatomically unique-to-fat men pouch of hard blubber under his exhausted belt that seems to make any kind of genitalia impossible. I'm about to tell this bloated wheezing bastard he has the wrong bench, that I'm waiting for someone and could he please go have his coronary on one of the other benches; he could even find one that doesn't have a plaque on it yet, and claim it for all eternity. I'm thinking, *This just can't be the guy I'm waiting to see* when from out of his wet fat mouth pop the magic words, "You Mr. Molloy?"

He sounded much fitter, much thinner on the phone. He also described himself as "of average build." You'd think this was a blind date the way he misled me. I'm not Molloy, by the way, that's not my real name, it's just the alias I'm using this afternoon, but I'm the guy he thinks I am, alright.

I nod. "Mr. Knott?"

"Who," he huffs, "else?"

He's sweating, and not lightly, from the exertion of walking here from wherever it is he came from, but it can't be any more than seventy-five degrees out. It's only the third day of summer and I'm thinking this guy isn't going to survive July. He swipes a handkerchief over his hammy red face, its features swallowed up by fat, distorted, smoothed over, so that he has that generic fat man look. I really don't mean to go on about it, I have nothing against the weight-challenged, in fact, I'm none too slim myself, but the amount of reality he's displacing for his existence, it seems excessive, it seems significant. I'm taking it personally. He's late, too, I should add.

"You're late," I say.

He checks the time, stretching his short chubby arm as far as it will go, which isn't far. But unless he's got some kind of inconceivably complicated optomological condition going on, he's not going to be able to see his watch no matter how hard he squints. It's on his other wrist. He grunts.

He says, "Subway fire," as if he's just saying that.

He takes out a pack of Camels, holds them towards me, his arm barely reaching across his chest. It's like he's wrapped up in a strait-jacket of meat. It must be horrible, I think, to be such a prisoner of yourself.

"Smoke?"

I hold up a hand. "No thanks. I don't smoke."

I try to say this as non-judgmentally as I can, even though, according to the anti-smoking lobby, anyway, armed with that cigarette between his fingers, he's practically as dangerous as any mass-murderer.

He lights up, hacks horribly, all phlegmy and loose, as if his lungs were liquefying, and then he blows some toxic bit of tissue from his mouth onto the pathway that I try not to look at, afraid that it might actually get up and walk away all by itself. After a while, he settles into a nice steady wheeze, like a failing air conditioner.

"Asthma," he explains, as if anyone asked.

I'm thinking, *Look at all the ways we try to kill ourselves, little by little, every day.* Yes, it's true, we'll do almost anything to stay alive; and yet, at the same time, we're killing ourselves all the while. It's so unbelievably fucked-up, like those mothers who love their kids so much they slowly poison them and then rush them to the emergency room again and again, (as if there were any other type of mother, right? Ha ha.) As I sit there thinking these thoughts, I'm noting the sweat rings under the fat guy's short-sleeved yellow shirt, a salty ring for each day. I'm noting the braided gold chain, circa 1977, around his thick, pink roast-beef of a neck, the pudgy little hands, carefully shaved and immacuately manicured.

"I represent a certain gentleman," he begins his spiel, violently swabbing his face with a handkerchief as if he were trying to wipe it off completely. He takes a gulp of air and continues his spiel by saying, "And this certain gentleman wants a certain matter looked into."

I don't say anything. This is all par for the course. The world is full of certain gentlemen who want certain matters looked into. If it weren't, I'd be working at Radio Shack hustling double-A batteries or living under a cardboard box down on Sixth Avenue. I wait patiently for the fat man to get around to the point.

He continues.

"The matter in question deals with a certain missing person."

"Did a certain gentleman call the police?" I offer.

"The police won't look for this missing person."

"I see." This is not surprising, of course. "Why not?"

"Only a few people know this person is missing. And the certain gentleman I represent is among them."

"And I'm supposed to find out what happened to this person?"

"Well," the fat man says, "there's more to it than that."

"Of course. How much more?"

"We want to know who she is."

"I don't understand. You want me to find a missing person and you don't know who she is?" I make a comical show of looking around in the leafy trees as if I were seeking out a hidden camera. "Is this some kind of joke?"

"I assure you it's no joke. There's nothing funny about this at all. In fact, its all very, very serious. The certain gentleman I represent met this missing person on the computer. They conducted a rather – erm torrid—online affair. And then one day, poof, she's gone."

"You mean they never met in real life?"

"I think you've hit the proverbial bulls-eye, Mr. Molloy."

"I'd like to meet this client of yours. Hear all this from the horse's mouth, so to speak."

The fat man briefly shakes his head. His waddle keeps shuddering an impressively long while afterwards.

"I'm afraid that's not possible. The certain gentleman I represent wishes to remain without a name, unknown, you know..." He looks stumped, like a fish suddenly deprived of its element.

"Anonymous," I say.

"Huh? Say again?"

"Anonymous," I repeat. "He wishes to remain anonymous. That's the word you're looking for."

Blank looks from both of us, but I'm guessing for entirely different reasons.

"Forget it," I say.

What I mean is to forget all of it, the whole thing, but the fat man thinks I just mean skip what I'd just said. So he goes on, explaining further, and he doesn't say anything he hasn't already said, which isn't much.

"This certain gentleman wants nothing for himself. If the lady in question does exist and has broken things off of her own free will, he understands. He just want to make sure she's okay. This certain gentleman is just doing his chivalrous duty, you might say. He believes in justice, in love, in those kinds of things."

The fat man gets points, in my book anyway, for saying all this with a reasonably straight face. I guess it's a reasonably straight face, unless any sardonic expression that might otherwise mar his impassive features have been totally obliterated by lard.

"Look Mr. Knott," I say, using what I'm certain is the fake name he gave me two days ago on a payphone near Columbus Circle. "This all sounds a little antic for my diet. I don't like to work through third-parties. I've had some bad experiences with that sort of thing in the past. It tends to bring out the worse in people. At worst, what you're describing has all the earmarks of invasion of privacy and harassment. At best, it sounds like a wild goose chase. Let me give you some free advice. More than likely, your employer has been had by someone pretending to be someone they aren't. There is probably no such person as the woman he seeks."

"Mr. Molloy," he starts, and I know immediately that this exchange of "misters" signals in reality a degeneration in the general cordiality of our conversation, "What is a real person anyway? The certain gentleman who I represent has fallen in love with her. Doesn't that make her real enough? What is the difference between invasion of privacy and the art of seduction? If this certain gentleman is concerned for her well-being, is it really harassment?"

I wasn't exactly in the mood for a philosophical discussion on the nature of being, ethics, or erotic love, so I say, "I'm sorry Mr. Knott. I'm not interested."

I get up. The fat man says, "You're making a terrible mistake. I assure you."

I shrug, "I've made plenty of those. It's no big deal. I'll no doubt survive to make others. But thanks all the same for the opportunity to make an ass of myself. Have a good day."

"You'll be hearing from me, Mr. Molloy."

He says this last thing to my back, as I'm walking away, purposely heading out of the park in the direction opposite from wherever it is I'm really heading, which is probably the nearest gym, the fat man having temporarily inspired me to finally start that cardioexercise regimen I've been putting off for the last twenty-five years. I'm fairly certain Mr. Knott meant me to understand what he'd just said as both a promise *and* a threat, which, when you stop and think about it, are often the only kinds of promises you can ever really count on anyone keeping.

2. Fast balls, fake girls, and mornings-after...

Sitting back, savoring a ten dollar beer-and-hot-dog-lunch, I'm watching the game unfold about a mile-and-a-half below me like a god in the cheap seats. It's a Wednesday afternoon, a two p.m. start, and Clemens is pitching against the Yankees. I like Clemens the way he is now, way past his prime: a big slab of a guy using brute intimidation even more than skill. He'll throw the ball at anyone's head and he lets everyone know it. To him, that's just a given and he acts as if he genuinely doesn't understand what the objection to his attitude could possibly be. He knows that during the short time that ball is in his hand, he's got the advantage. The moment he lets it go, he's a slave to fate just like anyone else. That one moment with the ball in our hand, it's all we ever get.

Today, though, Clemens is like most of us: he doesn't have a goddamn thing.

It's like that sometimes. No matter what you throw you up there, someone hits it back at you even harder.

Today the ball is flying all over the place, as if Yankee Stadium were a big old-fashioned pinball machine someone were making sing just this side of "tilt." The scoreboard is lighting up like a Macy's Christmas display, a row of crooked numbers. Clemens had given up seven runs and a dozen hits by the fourth inning when he's finally replaced by some sorry-ass reliever Houston has reserved to absorb the beating for the remainder of just such lost causes. But, to everyone's surprise, the Astros come back in the top of the eighth with an improbable bombardment of their own and win 12-10.

Too bad.

I took the Yanks and three so I don't cover and lose three hundred. I take the D-train back to Manhattan trying the whole time to catch the Mets on my walkman through a blizzard of static because I have two hundred on the Cardinals out at Shea. I'll lose that one, too, as it turns out, betting against the home team, it serves me right, I guess, and I steer myself into a basement bar in the East Village and pour a few pints of Guinness on my guilt and so its half-a-grand poorer and almost two a.m. when I finally head out to Brooklyn to keep my date with Meeah Soo.

I should admit right off that Meeah Soo is not like most girls, not like any girl at all, really, and yet she's more girl than most. She'll tell you so herself straight off, if you give her half the chance, because she's learned the hard way that most guys don't like any ambiguity or unnecessary anatomical surprises in this area. She's just off her shift at the strip club and we're having dinner at a dingy Chinese eatery under the highway, maybe two days after my already forgotten visit with the fat man. She's having the mu shu shrimp, only eating the shrimp, which aren't very populous in the mu shu here at Emperor Noodles.

Meeah likes when I take her out, even though I only take her out in those charmed hours long after it gets dark and long before it gets light. I only take her out when everyone still up are people just as mismatched as us, or too messed up to notice. I take her to dives like Emperor Noodles where no one speaks any English and you can get a whole meal with a small dish of pistachio ice cream for $3.95.

Meeah Soo is six-foot-one in her Rite Aid thigh-high fishnets even without the big white sissy platforms and she must weigh no more than one-fifteen soaking wet. She knows how many calories there are in a teaspoon of mustard. She knows the fat content of a raisin. If you're thinking, "eating disorder," then you're close. If you're thinking, "distorted body-image," you're on the right track. No one's image of her body could be more distorted than Meeah Soo's, and she's got all the scars to prove it. Most guys, they don't take her out at all. Most guys meet her in hotel rooms called "Rooms for Rent" and bring along a couple of 40s and sandwiches if they're romantics.

I'm always telling Meeah I'm sorry I can't take her out to regular places. She says, "I'm sorry I can't be more of a regular woman."

This is as close to true love as I've ever gotten: two people apologizing to each other for not being what the other wanted.

Meeah holds up and inspects a peanut-sized shrimp between her chopsticks to make sure it's not, in fact, a peanut, or an aborted mouse fetus, or something even less desirable. She shows me what she's got trapped between the tips of her chopsticks.

She says, "Does this look like a shrimp to you?"

I squint at whatever she's holding up, but before I can answer, she shrugs her shoulders, dips whatever it is in the sweet and sour sauce, and nibbles it delicately with her capped white teeth. Her dress is royal blue, one of those things that's off-the-shoulder, her big white sissy platforms must be four inches high, and her long press-on fingernails could make a visit to the toilet a life-threatening experience. She's wearing a blue silk scarf around her neck and she has big movie-star wax lips and her make-up is cracking a bit in all the places you'd expect it to crack if you've been pretending to smile at a bunch of groping perverts all night.

Meeah has an apartment she shares near a tin can factory with a friend and that's where we go after dinner. She checks her messages and they are mostly from married guys calling from cell phones. They all sound irritated and crabby, like guys with untended hard-ons tend to sound, irrationally expecting someone to be perpetually waiting on the other end of the line to help them with their situation, like mommy with a warm bottle, I suppose. I make myself at home on a couch that looks like the ghost of a couch because there is a white sheet covering it for some reason I probably don't want to know. I lean forward over a coffee-table covered with fashion and celebrity gossip tabloids. I pick up a copy of some cheesy rag with an article claiming that Jennifer Lopez has been dead for twelve years and a look-a-like has been performing for her ever since. That, I consider, would explain a lot. There is a story that Bigfoot is considering a run for Senate with the Democratic Party. That Oprah Winfrey is pregnant with an alien spawn that will populate Antartica in preparation for the Antichrist.

Meeah is still listening to her messages, an entire nursery of whining creeps. She looks at me, shrugs apologetically, and mouths, *I'm sorry*, as if she's forgotten that callers can't hear you on a message machine.

There are fabrics hanging from the walls that Meeah has hung to give the place atmosphere but mostly to hide the rotten spots where the wall has crumbled away like moldy cheese. There is a poster from years back of Cyndi Lauper in her "Girls Just Wanna Have Fun" incarnation. Right now I'm thinking two things:

1.) It's so sad to be a human being.

2.) How do we endure how sad it is to be a human being?

Meeah has finally gotten sick of listening to all that pent-up testosterone driven petulance. Or, maybe, the machine simply ran out of space for all the neglected hard penises in the world. She's mincing around the apartment, lighting candles and incense, and it's not easy to mince around on four-inch white plastic sissy heels. It takes lots and lots of practice; it takes dedication and devotion. It takes real athleticism. You'd be surprised. She asks me what I'm thinking about.

I say, "I'm thinking we really have to get out of that mess in the Middle East."

She pouts.

So I say, "Okay, okay. I'm thinking that you look very pretty tonight."

My heart, to use a well-worn euphemism for that flabby hunk of meat shuddering in my chest, is breaking when I say this.

Meeah smiles. She is putting the day-old flowers that I bought her earlier that evening from a subway station newstand in a plastic liter bottle of Pepsi One that she pulls out of the recycle pail. She fills the plastic bottle from the kitchen faucet and sits it on the table that stands between the kitchen and the dining area. Carnations, they probably are, or were, or that's what they're supposed to be. They are dyed all kinds of unearthly colors that are supposed to look better than the color carnations really are. I think the whole bouquet may actually be dead.

"They're so pretty," Meeah says, and the sad thing, of course, is that I know she really means this. "They're so lov-er-ly," she coos, and drops a little pill into the cloudy water so that they'll last a little longer. She says, "I don't have an aspirin, so I'm using a Premamin."

I smile when she says this. I'm thinking, *well, maybe they'll grow a nice set of knockers.*

At least, I hope I'm smiling when she says this, because if I'm not smiling I don't think I want to know what expression could be on my face.

"I'll be right back," Meeah says, and smiles right back.

At least, I hope that she's smiling, because if she's not smiling, I don't think I want to know what else that expression on her face could mean.

She goes off into the bathroom and flushes the toilet three times and curses and spits and something rattles around in the sink. I hear the shower go on, it sputters and spurts like a man with a bad prostate, squirting out a painful piss. I hear some gargling and hacking. I hear a staccato burst of sharp farts. A groan. I hear the angry buzz of an electric razor. These are the things you try not to hear. These are the things that you know go on behind the scenes all the time. These are the things people have to do to put themselves together, to reassemble the jigsaw, to put a face on to meet the faces that they meet. I pick up another tabloid and read the true-life confession of a desperate lover who sewed his dead beloved's head onto the body of a dolphin. You can't make these stories up. That's what they tell us, anyway.

"Miss me?" Meeah asks when she saunters back.

She's wearing a red silk kimono with some kind of poorly-sewn black embroidery of orchids, or maybe they're dragons, it's impossible to tell for sure, it's all unraveling. It's slit way up one leg, all the way to the hip, so you can see to the tops of Meeah's stay-up fishnets. It's supposed to be sexy, but it makes me feel like sobbing. Fact is, I did miss her. She must have been gone for about half an hour. I was starting to wonder what the hell had happened to her.

"Where's Treena T?" I ask. I'm looking apprehensively at the door, wondering if we're going to be alone tonight, or if Treena T will catch us in the midst of something sordid. Treena T is a bodybuilder and professional trainer when she's not acting in porn flicks with titles like *Love Muscle Babes*. She is terribly sweet, a real pussycat, but a little eerie, as any six-foot-five, two-hundred-twenty-five-pound muscle-bound guy with glued-on falsies, a black pixie wig, and a penchant for stiletto heels and knock-off Vera Wang gowns is bound to be. Believe it or not, there are two Treenas that could conceivably be coitus interrupting us here, but Treena T is Meeah's sometime roommate, the other one, Treena F. is in L.A., but how I know that I have no idea.

Meeah frowns. "She's in Jersey. Getting her cheeks done by some doc she met on the internet. But I haven't heard from her in, oh like, days…"

"She's getting her cheeks done *again?*"

"Yep."

Then something occurs to me. "Butt or face?"

"Face. She's getting what they did the last time fixed."

Jesus, I hope so, I'm thinking. I remember the last time I saw her, the resemblance her face had taken to a lopsided catcher's mitt resembling Dolly Parton was alarming and I've heard the resemblance did *not* go away when the swelling went down. These back-alley plastic surgeons were creating a race of cut-rate mutants in the underground sex industry. It was beginning to look like an X-rated version of *The Island of Dr. Moreau* out there. Anyway, all this sounds vaguely familiar to me, what Meeah just said, but then again, most things sound vaguely familiar to me lately. That's what happens when you've heard it all.

"I'm sorry," I say, "did you already tell me that at dinner?"

"I don't know," Meeah says, looking confused herself, and she gets up to retrieve two bottles of beer out of the fridge, and turns off the kitchenette light, although not necessarily in that order. She crosses the room in her big plastic sissy heels, lots of leg flashing along that slit in the kimono, and it's significant that neither of us turns on any of the other lights. She hands me the bottles, pretending she can't open them, and I open them. We sit on the couch for a while, drinking, not saying anything.

"I'll do that" Meeah says, because I'm bending sideways to take off my shoes, and she hands me her beer bottle with the lipstick smeared halfway down the neck as if she's been deep-throating it and slides silkily off the couch onto her knees. I drink out of her bottle because mine is already empty and I taste her fruit-flavored lipstick and it feels as if she's trying to undo my shoelaces, which would be a complete waste of time, because the shoes I'm wearing don't have laces. I take another long sip of the cold beer; Meeah, pretend little geisha girl that she is, always buys Sapporo, and by now she's slipping off my socks, and I'm vaguely worried about foot odor.

I take another pull of beer to distract myself.

Meeah's worked my pants down and she's licking me, making hmm-hmmming noises, and although I know her enthusiasm isn't entirely authentic, nothing is, I also know that it's not totally fake either, and that's something. I have my hands in her hair, but I'm not pulling too hard or messing around in there too much because I have no idea how much of her hair is real anymore and how much of it is extensions, and I don't want this to be another of those embarrassing moments we have to act like didn't happen.

Too much of all this is like that already.

"Hmmm-hmmmm," Meeah goes, and I'm amazed, as always, at how this all works, even though we might as well be reading from a script. It's all a little like your favorite dirty scene in a film you've watched fifty times before, and yet, somehow, it still works the fifty-first time, even though you know exactly what's coming, and when, maybe *because* you know exactly what's coming and when.

We end up in the bedroom after a while, which is to say, the corner of the one-room flat where the used futon is thrown on the floor beneath the satin comforter. There's some shouting coming up from the street, some garbage can racket, some bottles breaking, threats, curses, pleading, gasps of pain. As you might imagine, this isn't exactly a high-rent district Meeah Soo is living in, but the ugly-sounding commotion just seems to make being inside that much cozier. It makes you thankful to realize it'd probably take a stray bullet to get yourself capped up here, a one in a million shot. That kind of luck, good or bad, is rare.

I'm lying back on the futon mattress now and Meeah is on top of me, running her hands with the long painted nails over my chest, my stomach, and this is the time she'd be taking her clothes off, or I would be taking them off her, if she were any other girl. But aside from the red satin kimono with the wild orchids, or whatever, she still has on all the rest of it: the fur-trimmed bra, the leopard-print micro-mesh panties, the fishnet stockings, the big plastic sissy heels. Meeah is a bit like little Miss Invisible: she is the kind of girl that starts to disappear the more she takes off. Strange thing is, this is true of most girls more than you might realize. It's just a little truer of Meeah.

Sex seems like such a mystery when you consider what we're often driven to do just to make that connection, any connection. It seems inexplicable and I don't just mean what's going on now between Meeah and I, because what's going on now really isn't that much stranger than anything else, if you take the big perspective, if you look at it from the long range, like an alien, let's say, viewing this all from Alpha Centauri, or someplace far away like that. People will gladly acknowledge that we come into this world alone and leave it alone, but they generally never consider that we pass through it alone, too. That's what sex is really all about: a way to fool ourselves into believing we aren't utterly and eternally alone. After all, anything that causes us as many problems as sex can't possibly be all our fault, could it?

Meeah makes things easy, but, of course, it still isn't easy, it never is. There are all kinds of places to touch and not to touch, things to say and not to say, parts to see and not to see, to keep the illusion real. And so that's where we're at, as I'm touching her breasts, or where her breasts are beginning to be, or going to be, after a few more treatments. She's still got her panties on, the bra, the sissy heels, everything, and she's on her back now and moaning and squirming around because it's my turn to make her feel good, and I can't tell if it's really anything I'm doing or if she's just enjoying some movie version of herself that she runs in her head. Meeah's got this part of being a woman down pat. The fact that I'll be here with her while she watches this movie, that alone seems to make her feel good, that alone seems to be enough. I'm there to bear witness to her fiercely imagined femininity. Sex, like any other social interaction, is a performance.

"One day," she's always saying, "I'll have a pair of real breasts," but that's not true. "One day," she's always saying, "I'll have a real vagina," but that's not true either.

These are the kinds of little lies we tell ourselves all the time to make ourselves feel better. These are the kinds of lies we pretend to believe to make each other feel better. I have my hand on her silicone-filled bra, though, as if all this were true; I've slipped my hand inside her micro-mesh panties as if what she believes will one day happen already has.

Fact is, she seems even smaller and softer than she usually does and I'm reminded, yet again, of the cost of what she's doing to herself chemically, of the impotence, the inability to experience real sexual pleasure, not to mention the risk of permanent damage to her internal organs because none of what she's doing is being properly monitored by an endocrinologist, and I'm amazed as she comes, or pretends to come, bucking like the girl she wants to be against my hand with all these pretty little gasps and soft moans, of just how convincing she can be, if you don't think about any of it all too much, and it's not the first time or the last time that I'm making a real effort not to think about too much of anything at all.

You're not spending the night with a girl like Meeah Soo, that much you know going in. You're not spending the night if you have to brave a thermonuclear holocaust to get out of there before morning comes. It's kind of like being with a werewolf in reverse, except instead of the moon, it's all going to hell when the sun comes up, and

I'm not only talking about the need for a morning shave. You have to face up to a lot of harsh realities the morning after with a girl like Meeah Soo and those harsh realities are to be avoided at all costs.

So after we're done, I stumble around, pulling on my clothes, and Meeah Soo gathers the sheets around herself, knowing that I prefer she not walk me out, or kiss me at the door, or, for that matter, say much of anything at all. On the way to the door, I leave three twenties on the table near the dead carnations standing in the plastic Pepsi One bottle but neither one of us say anything about it because that's not what this is supposed to be about anyway. At least, we're both pretending that's not what this is about. Before you know it, I'm out of the housing complex and walking up a block of steaming manhole covers on a street that's looking less and less dangerous by the second in the graying morning light and instead just more and more sad and generically miserable than ever before.

3. Porn, aliases, and guilty consciences...

"Oh Christ," I mutter, cringing like a dog expecting the rolled newspaper, just like I always do whenever the phone rings, "what the hell can it be now?"

It's four in the afternoon and I'm trying to get some sleep because I'm driving the taxi tonight. I've had to pick up some part-time lately since business has taken a bit of a downturn.

Okay, "a bit of a downturn" isn't exactly accurate. Let me be perfectly frank: Business has ground to something just south of a screeching halt. I have no business. Basically, I'm doing nothing. I'm minding my own business, that's what I'm doing, and no one, including me, wants to be doing that.

What's happening to me lately is what tends to happen to people in my line of work when the last guy you worked for ends up disappearing off the face of the earth. Well, that's not entirely accurate either. It's even worse than that. Lately, the guy's been turning up all over the place, but only one piece at a time. The last I heard they'd found a hand in Albany, a partial torso in a landfill out on Staten Island. They tell me a kneecap made it all the way to San Francisco. At this rate, his family should have most of him back to celebrate Hanukkah.

Under the circumstances, you'd think I'd have jumped at the fat man's offer. You'd think that, but you'd be thinking wrong. You lose a lot of confidence in yourself when a client winds up scattered across the country like Osiris. Everyone else loses a lot of confidence in you, too. You try to learn from your mistakes and that case, as I recall, also began with a certain gentleman who could not be named. I swore to myself *never again* and here it was, again already.

It seemed like fate, alright. And just like everyone else, I was putting off fate as long as possible.

So here I am sitting on the couch, trying to remember who I am, where I am, why I am, head pounding, hung-over, afraid to stand up too fast, reluctant to stand up at all. And meanwhile the phone is still ringing. It's saying, *pick me up pick me up pick me up.*

I usually leave the damn thing unplugged and let the answering machine take the aggravation. Yes, the bad news comes all the same, it sits there waiting for you to plug the phone back in. Bad news will walk through the sun from the other side of the universe to make its way to you. But I figure you might as well keep it waiting as long as possible. You never know, the world really may end tomorrow. I know I'd be kicking myself all the way to the apocalypse if it did and I ended up doing anything that I could have put off for eternity.

Anyway, I like to deal with bad news only when I'm good and ready, and on my own terms. That's too say, when I'm not out of Zoloft and I've properly armed myself with a couple of six-packs or when I'm otherwise depressed enough to be reminded once again why it's not altogether a bad thing that senility awaits us, that we all have that appointment coming up with the Grim Reaper, that life doesn't go on forever.

True, too, that even though I forgot to unplug it, I don't have to answer the phone just because it's ringing. I could still let the machine pick it up. But knowing for sure that message is there, waiting for me, beep-beep-beeping, that's like Chinese water torture, that'll drive me nuts. So I pick up the phone just to get it over with, just to shut it up, getting ready to pretend my name is Malone if it's a bill collector, and Riley if it's practically anyone else.

"Yeah," I say, like someone peering around a dark corner, all set to pretend I'm not surprised no matter what, "Yeah?"

I've gotten to my feet to do this, of course, crossed the small cluttered room to my desk, a.k.a a badly-scarred card table where the phone sits, along with a laptop, an old goose-neck desk lamp with a broken goose-neck, various unpaid bills, dried up pens, paper cups from Starbucks, Dunkin Donuts, Borders, etc., and I've plopped down in a rolling office chair with a bum wheel rescued from a curb somewhere. It's sunny out: I can see every stain on the shades, every mummified fly-corpse on the window-sill. I'm still in my boxers, you get the grim picture.

No preamble, no intro, Johnny Nomad starts right in: "What the hell did you turn Mr. Flynn down for? He told me you turned him down. What the hell did you do that for? What the hell were you thinking?"

I've already figured out he's talking about Knott since that's the only person I've turned down in the last thirty-six hours and, thinking ahead to a long night in the taxi, I'm already beginning to wonder if maybe I shouldn't have turned him down, after all. I idly wonder if Mr. Flynn is the fat man's real name, although I doubt it is, anymore than Mr. Knott was.

"Calm down," I tell Johnny, "for crissakes calm down."

"I will not calm down," he says, "I cannot calm down," he then repeats what he just said in a rapidly escalating tone up the scale to sheer hysteria, as if determined to prove it to himself. "I will not calm down," he shrieks in an embarrassingly unmanly way, "I can't I can't I can't!"

"Okay, you've convinced me. You can't and won't calm down. I concede the point. So don't. Just tell me what the problem is. Tell me who Flynn is, or Knott, or whatever the hell his name is and why I shouldn't have turned him down."

"Meet me," Johnny sniffs, "meet me at the One World Café. Everything is *so* fucked up."

I say, "Okay, give me a half-hour. I've got to put my pants on." I take a look around on the couch, the floor, the top of the fridge. "Christ, better give me the whole hour. I've got to *find* my pants."

And when I hang up the phone I'm getting that wriggling-snakes-in-a-sack feeling that you get in the pit of your stomach when the last bus out of a town invaded by zombies pulls away from the depot and you really wish you were on it.

Waiting for a light to change on the corner of 23rd and Broadway, I suddenly have a feeling of déjà vu: three years ago, maybe, I was standing on this very same street corner. It was during one of those sudden summer rain storms, Biblical in intensity, that catch everyone by surprise, except for those Jamaican guys who appear out of nowhere to sell you a defective umbrella for five dollars each. I had retreated into the doorway of a Gap to wait out the storm and watched the lightning reach out through the sky with bony lethal fingers, feeling between the tops of the skyscrapers.

Although the lightning was miles away, with each clap of thunder, I saw everyone flinch, and, I admit it, me right along with them. Some atavistic instinct was at play no doubt, genetic memory from the caveman days, but I couldn't help feeling it was more than that, as if at the core of our very being each of us felt with the terror of superstitious certainty that of all the places the lightning could fall, of all the everywheres it could possibly strike, that lightning was God reaching down out of heaven to finger us in particular.

And that's when it hit me:

What the hell is it that we all feel so guilty about, anyway?

Three naked Japanese women are shooting each other with plastic water pistols on Johnny Nomad's computer when I arrive at the internet café. Oblivious to everyone around him, Johnny doesn't hear me coming, totally absorbed as he is in the internet porn sites he's cruising. He jumps about six inches when I tap his shoulder. These days we all jump about six inches when we feel a tap on the shoulder.

"Hey," I say.

"Shit," he says. "You scared me half to death."

Johnny Nomad isn't Johnny Nomad's real name, of course. That's only one of his screen names, but I met him online and that name seems more real than whatever his real name would be if he were ever to trust me enough to tell me his real name. I suspect that when we first met online, still unsure if I were a psycho or a cop, he gave me an alias, and never bothered to correct himself. I know that's what I did with regard to him. What you're talking about here is extreme mutual paranoia. You're also talking about taking sensible precautions. You're talking about two people who've shared everything but bodily fluids and birth certificates, and we've probably come close to sharing the former on a lonely virtual night or two, and still we don't feel comfortable giving each other our real names.

I point at the computer, all those wet Japanese cuties. "What's with the water pistols?"

He shrugs. "Foreigners. They think we do crap like that over here, I guess. Lord knows where they get the idea. Ratking hacked me the password to the three-hundred-seventy-five sites linked to this host. Something for everyone. A whole site devoted to women in high-heels crushing bugs and rodents. Wanna see?"

I grab his wrist as his fingers start to fly over the keyboard. "No thanks. Maybe another time. Anyway, shouldn't you be looking at this crap at home? You know, on your personal computer?"

Johnny Nomad shrugs. "Can't. Computer is on the fritz. A virus, I guess."

Johnny doesn't look too good. He never looks good, but today he's looking much worse than usual. He looks like a guy who's been awake in the same clothes too many days for no good reason. He looks like he's been living under a volcano, or in the waiting room of an oncologist waiting for his test results. He looks like he's lost a lot of something important, blood or air, something that you need to stay alive: money, perhaps.

I suggest we take a walk; and that's what we do, heading up Lexington Avenue, north, I think. Up the street we walk, going nowhere, because I find people more likely to tell you the truth if they feel they are walking away from it at the same time. Johnny, I notice, has picked up a limp from somewhere, but I can't tell if he's faking it or not, and I don't really have the time, patience, or interest to find out.

"What's this all about?" I ask.

The story goes something like this: the Yankees were having an unbelievable winning streak and Johnny kept betting against them. They'd be down by five runs in the ninth, two out, nobody up, and some weak grounder to second would go through someone's legs, a broken bat single would follow, a mix-up at first, a bad call, a raccoon loose in left field, a homerun, and before you knew it, the Yankees would win by three. Anyway, Johnny's regular online bookie couldn't carry his losses any longer so Johnny went surfing for another bookie. Enter Flynn, a.k.a. to me as Mr. Knott, real identity, unknown, and this guy was like sugar on a turd, making the shit go down all the easier, and while the Yankees kept winning, Johnny's losing streak continued, got worse, became a way of life. He was living in a house of cards and now he was way behind in the rent, and the big wind himself, Flynn, a.k.a Knott, had finally, inevitably, come around to blow it down.

"I figured I'd be able to scam this guy out of the payment. You know, like I usually do. I mean, it's the web, right? For all I knew, Flynn could be some wiseass thirteen-year-old computer geek. I figured, what's the worst that can happen, a few hundred spam emails for penile enlargement?"

"Jesus," I say, "why did you keep betting against the Yankees?"

Johnny looks stricken. "They have to lose sometime, don't they? Everyone does."

"That's the theory. What's this business he wants taken care of, anyway? Someone missing. Do you know anything about it?"

"No," Johnny says. "He just said he needed someone good and discrete. He also said something about unscrupulous."

"And I'm the first person that came to mind?"

Johnny shrugs. "Sorry dude. Listen, I admit I fucked up big time. He promises he'll discharge the debt if you take this on. I heard you could use the work. All you have to do is look into it: no strings attached. I'm into him for major money, man. Major money. I'm worried, I'll admit it. Frankly, this guy doesn't mess around. He sent me video files of the kind of work he does. And they don't look altered." Johnny shuddered. "People end up, you know, *disassembled*."

I stare out into what is supposed to be the distance. But I'm really looking at an ad for a new musical about the Jonestown Massacre pasted to the side of a cross-town bus parked at the curb two feet away. Last week, it was a comedy about Josef Stalin. It just goes to show you. If you only wait long enough, everything becomes a joke.

I say, "What the hell are you so scared of? I've seen Flynn, or Knott, or whatever the hell his name is. Just walk quickly up an incline. He'll have an embolism. The guy needs a moving ramp to step up to a urinal."

Johnny shakes his head. He looks very sad, very worried, very old, and suddenly very wise. "No," he says, "you got him all wrong. He's fast. Unbelievably fast. I'm telling you, man, he's cobra-fast. He's, shit, I'm pretty sure he's not even human."

"Yeah well," I say, "there's a lot of that going around nowadays."

"So you'll take the job. Tell me you'll take the job."

I tell him, "I'll see what I can do."

But I already know what I'm going to do. I mean, all considered, what choice do I really have?

4. Ecclesiastes, old people, and the 2 rules of life...

One of the handicaps I have which keep me from being a very good
taxi driver is that, like many native New Yorkers, I really don't have a
firm grasp of where the hell anything is in this city. On top of that, I
have an inherently awful sense of direction. You could probably call
me a geographical dyslexic (as well as a moral, spiritual, and
philosophical dyslexic). At any given point along a journey, if given a
choice between a right turn or a left turn, I can be sure of one
thing—I'll make the wrong turn. I defy even chance: I'm wrong
virtually all the time. Fact is, I suspect the only reason I got this job,
my one and only qualification, is that I can drive without a turban
and that seemed to amuse Mr. Sammy, my sadistic anti-American
Pakistani boss.

　　Every night, as I peer out my windshield, trying to remember
what comes first if you're heading east, Madison or Park, I'm amazed
how some guy just plopped down in the middle of this mess from
the remotest corner of Kurdistan, for instance, can find his way
unerringly to York or Bond, while I'm still having trouble locating the
Empire State Building in the same place from one night to the next.
Of course, that might be because my Afghani counterpart has spent
the last ten years studying terrorist maps of Manhattan in a desert
cave. But that's another story.

Idling at the light on 42nd and Broadway, the fare I'm ferrying towards Rockefeller Center via Port Authority is weakly tapping on the dividing glass between the front and back seats and saying something that sounds like she's asking me if the hotel they are staying at allows ironing. It takes me a while to realize that the older of the two women, and they are both as old as the origin of dice, is saying something about the theater we are momentarily stuck in front of, the Ford, which has been showing *The Lion King* for what seems like centuries now, as if it's the crowning achievement of Western theatrical art.

This is the street, 42nd, that was once famous as the sleaze strip of the world, the hangout of prostitutes and pushers, now the home of Mickey Mouse and Pikachu. This is what they used to call urban renewal, but what nowadays everyone recognizes as pathological denial.

I say something relatively neutral, like, "Yea, the Lion King."

Then I bear down on a rival taxi, cut him off for no good reason, and lean on the horn, scaring a bunch of teenagers caught in the crosswalk, who recover, give me the finger in unison, and beat on the hood of my cab with drunken fists.

Welcome to the cultural capital of the world.

Believe it or not, I make a few more wrong turns, race blindly up this or that street, and I end up in front of Rockefeller Center almost by accident, flags of all nations flapping, ice-skating rink if it were winter, the golden statue of Mercury, messenger of the gods, all that.

"Rockefeller Center," I announce, as amazed to see it sitting there as anyone.

The two old mummies climb out of the back seat in stages, unfolding themselves like those cheap plastic lounge chairs people use on the beach. I pull their improbably heavy tartan bags from the trunk, and even I've broken a light sweat. Each bag feels like it's packing a dozen bowling balls. How the hell are they going to manage these bags, I'm wondering, with real disinterest.

I watch them as I soften up a wad of chewing gum, moving slowly down the broad walkway towards the golden Mercury, who has no message from God, or anyone. There's really nowhere to go around here at this hour of the night. Did these two old dames really mean to stop here? They keep moving, dragging their luggage along behind them as if they were hiking up the side of a rocky ramble of snow and ice, an Everest of a sidewalk, but perfectly flat.

Old people, I'm thinking, *when exactly does that happen to you? When is it official?*

I'm thinking, at a certain point, what's the point? I mean, of course, there's never a point, but how obvious does it have to become? How hard does it have to be to put on your socks in the morning before you say, "Okay, that's it, I've eaten enough waffles. I've looked at enough junk mail. I'm ready to die."

Back in the cab, I head vaguely toward the upper east side, if that's where Lincoln Center is considered to be, and what I'm doing, basically, is cruising for a guy in a tuxedo standing next to a woman in a black evening dress, one of those black evening dresses that have those two crisscross bandoliers in front to cover her expensively upgraded tits. I can picture it like I'm a fortune-teller. These two will be standing there, waiting for a cab, which I'm conveniently driving, to whisk them back to their luxury hotel after they've spent four hundred bucks for orchestra seats at a performance of Mozart or Puccini, someone like that. The guy will still have a money clip thick with money, plenty for the big tip he'll peel off for yours truly, after he has me cruise through the park for an hour getting his money's worth in the back seat from his silicon escort.

That's the idea.

I go one for two, because there's a guy, but he's alone, not in a tux, but a very nice-looking Italian suit, good haircut, and shoes, that, as I see when he slides expertly into the back seat, look like they only walk on red carpets or the polished marble of high-class financial institutions.

I figure I know what he's looking for at this time of night. But I ask anyway, "Where to?"

He says, "Town Hall."

Hmm, I wasn't expecting that. Right off, I know this is going to be a challenge. I have, to put the best face on it, only the fuzziest notion where Town Hall is, but I figure, as usual, I'll head off in the general direction and ask some well-timed questions along the way. Glancing in the rearview, I'm thinking, this guy looks like a man-about-town. He looks like he knows where he's going. I shouldn't have trouble coaxing directions out of him. As it turns out, though, I needn't have concerned myself with the whereabouts of Town Hall because we aren't going there, anyway. He'd only been waiting for me to mosey aimlessly down some dark and desolate drive, like the one alongside the river I've just turned down, hopelessly lost, before he gets down to business.

"Make a left," he says.

I'm surprised at first because even I know that Town Hall isn't left of wherever it is we are.

"Are you sure?"

I look up and meet two of the hardest, coldest, most vacant eyes I've ever seen in my rearview. Looking into these eyes is like looking into a tunnel that's heading straight to the end of the universe.

There is a little column of cold air passing through the base of my skull. It's the track of the bullet I'm imagining will explode out of the gun he's pointing at my head if he decides to add just a few more ounces per square inch of pressure to the finger on the trigger, or we hit an unlucky pot hole, among other vagaries.

He says, "I'm sure."

Earlier this evening, driving around through Tribeca, I saw this bit of graffiti splashed in paint the color of blood on the concrete wall of a defunct parking garage:

Everything dies. Dare Everything.

Words to live by, I remember thinking at the time. The first precept pretty much no one has any problem obeying. But the second? That takes some balls to pull off.

Ecclesiastes once said, there's a time and a place for it all, and I'm sure hoping this isn't the time and the place to have my brain blown out of my forehead. So, I say, as nonchalantly as one can when you think you may be seeing your next thought splashed messily on the inside of your windshield at any second, "So where am I going, anyway?"

He says, "Go to the tunnel."

I'm guessing he means the Lincoln, because the Holland, even I know that must be clear across town.

I say, "I don't really go out of the five boroughs."

He says, "Tonight you do."

The gun at the back of my head has done wonders for my navigational skills, it's really cleared up priorities, no more daydreaming, I'm really focused; that gun has gotten me to pay attention to the here and now better than any course in meditation or self-hypnosis, that, and the fact that from the back seat, this guy is telling me, in minutest detail, every single move to make: merge left, pass that van, slow down, use exact change, exit here.

"Can you tell me what this is about," I ask about twenty minutes after we emerge on the Jersey side of the tunnel.

We're driving along the turnpike and I'm looking at all the surrounding swampland and thinking how easy they made it to dump a body out here.

"No," he says.

"If you want money, this really isn't necessary."

He says something, but not to me, and not in English, nor in any other language that I recognize, and a quick glance in the rearview confirms he's not talking on a cellphone, unless it's one of those subtle earpiece and wire jobs, only even more subtle and invisible than usual. I hope that's what it is, because otherwise he might (it makes me queasy to even consider) very well be talking to himself.

South, south, south, we go, the petrochemical plants dwindling away, IKEA in the rearview mirror, and the swamps opening up to marinas and green hills where the jeweled eyes of deer consider suicide by auto. I'm directed to take an exit just ahead and we're soon driving up a road along the ocean, at least I think we're by the ocean, there's a big long wall of gray rocks to our right separating us from something black and immense, closed-down fish restaurants and boat yards on our right, and lots and lots of sand all over the place.

"Off here," he says.

And I veer onto an access road, passed a big brown sign that announces we are entering the Gateway National Recreation Area. Part of the federal park service, the place is officially closed after sundown. But there are no barriers anywhere and we sail right through the booths usually manned by park service employees collecting admission fees, checking inspection stickers, forbidding this and that, monitoring everything. Where the hell is Big Brother now? Where is He, when you really need Him?

"Cut the lights," the guy behind me says.

It's eerie driving among the sand dunes in the moonlight, just me and this well-dressed guy in the back seat pointing a gun at my cerebellum. I'm hoping, now more than ever, for a bit of explanation. At the same time, I'm trying to figure out my odds of survival if I pull some kind of cop show antic. I'm trying to decide if I veer off the road and towards the side of a dune, jumping out of the moving car just before impact, what is the chance that I won't end up breaking my neck? Are my odds better or worse if I just do what he tells me? If I do exactly what this guy says every step of the way and he still ends up turning my head into a broken bowl of gray pudding I'm going to really be pissed off: at him, myself, God, everything.

"Look," I say, "I've really been pretty reasonable about all this. If you just tell me what you want…"

He says, "I want you to shut up and make that next right."

Rude, I'm thinking. Is that really necessary? But then, that's what a gun does for you: it finally lets you treat people the way you've always wanted to treat them. It lets you say whatever's really on your mind without worrying about the consequences.

I'm not crazy about where we are now: a dark little winding road between midget pine trees and rolling dunes covered with scrub and no view longer than twenty-five feet in front or back. I'm trying to think of all the people who could want me dead and really there are precious few who give that much of a damn about me one way or another. Maybe there's no one who could work up enough passion to have me killed. *No one who even wants me dead?* That's really a bit sad, I'm thinking. What have I been doing with my life?

And so it goes.

Our first instinct is always to find meaning in a tragic situation. It's human nature to try to make sense of things. And that's what I'm doing now. I'm trying to find meaning in why I may be about to have my head blown off. What's really terrifying to consider is that there is absolutely no meaning to it at all. All the jogging and racquet ball in the world and you still drop dead of a heart attack before you're fifty. All those goddamn pounds of bran flakes in the morning and you end up with a tumor the size of a shrunken head in your rectum. I've got to face facts. There may be no meaning at all in my getting killed out here in the middle of nowhere. It may just be one of those things. That's what no one really wants to consider: that everything is mercilessly random and there isn't a single goddamn thing you can do about any of it.

Any moment, now, I'm thinking, *any moment now I'm going to make my move.*

Yup, any moment.

Moments keep passing, and I keep following orders, and I'm still alive. Which is basically how we all live our lives, with or without a gun at the back of our head. Because let's face it, there's *always* a gun at the back of our head.

And because I want to keep living, and doing nothing is working so far, I continue to do nothing.

"Up ahead," he says.

Squinting, I can see the road ends in a great big wall of blackness that turns out to be the sky above a dead-end dune of sand held back by a log barricade, all of it indicative of a parking spot for fishermen, stargazers, and hitmen. I'm tensing up for my big move, although what it's going to be, I have no clue, but the first thing I do is turn off the ignition, and the sudden quiet is startlingly and sickeningly intimate, like a testicular exam. I'm getting the sense, though, that my kidnapper is not going to kill me, after all, at least not imminently, and I'm not exactly sure that I'm not just getting this sense because some sort of endorphins are flooding my brain to protect me from the certainty that he is, indeed, about to kill me. Brain chemistry, especially under these kinds of circumstances, is notoriously unreliable. I might be in shock: the kind of shock you see an antelope go into when it's brought down by a tiger.

He says, "Get out."

Right now, not a second later, I think, is the time to start running. The car is between us, the dunes along the impromptu parking lot are still about twenty yards of clear shooting space away, but it's dark, he may be taken by surprise, maybe he's not such a good shot, and even though I'm not lucky, I could get lucky tonight. But I don't run, I don't do a lot of things I probably should if you take things at face-value. I'm thinking something is up. I'm beginning to suspect there's more to this than meets the eye. At least I'm hoping there is because if there isn't, I'm done for. Basically what I'm doing is waiting to see what happens next.

"Move," he says, indicating with the gun where I have to go to find out what happens next.

So with me in front and him with the gun trained between my shoulder blades, we are marching down the beach, through the soft sand, towards the ocean, which I start to see, at least the foam on the curling waves, the crash and roll and sizzle and all that, and I can make out the beginnings of a figure seated in a canvas folding chair. His legs are genteely crossed at the knee and he's wearing a three-piece suit and a snap-brim hat, like a banker from the fifties, or an FBI agent from the same decade, and goddammit if he doesn't appear to be sitting there in the moonlight *fishing*.

5. Junk food, fishing, and looking for nada...

"Ho-ho," the fisherman says, and, at first, probably just like you, I think it's a fake laugh, but he reaches into a soft cooler by his chair and pulls out the packaged snack by that name, an artificially-flavored cake-roll injected with an alarmingly white chemical cream that seems to be giving off its own spectral light.

I say, "No thanks. I've already had my recommended daily allowance of carcinogens today. Who the hell are you?"

"Mr. Franklin," he says around a mouthful. He touches the brim of his snap-brim hat. "Nice to make your acquaintance."

"Well, Mr. Franklin, I can't say I'm too happy to make yours. In fact, I'm taking a really dim view of you right now."

He pushes the rest of the Ho-Ho into his pursed mouth, pressing it slowly into his face with his thumb, making it obscenely disappear, inch by gooey inch, popping his thumb from the tight orifice at the end of this performance with a loud wet *pop*! He licks his lips, licks his thumb, picks up Ho-Ho number two. Eyes it, eyes me.

"Oh really? Why's that?" he asks.

"How about kidnapping for starters? Being forced to drive here under threat of execution."

He carefully licks around the end of the second Ho-Ho, smacks his lips, and says, "Oh. That."

"Yeah. That."

"The night's young, Mr. Molloy. First impressions can be misleading. Perhaps I'll grow on you."

"I'd like to know what I'm doing out here," I glance around at the sand, the sea, the starry sky, most of it just a lot of blackness, "…in the middle of nowhere."

"We have some questions for you."

As my eyes become accustomed to the star light, I get a little better look at Mr. Franklin. He's in his late fifties, maybe even midway into his sixties, narrow-faced, baggy-eyed, sober-looking, thin as a weathered fence-post in a three-piece suit, gaunt, grey, a scarecrow with a bad heroin habit.

"*We?* Do you mind telling me who "we" are?"

"We are US. Think of US as Fate," he says, teasing the cream out of the tip of the Ho-Ho with a thin reptilian tongue, "unknowable, ineffable, unanswerable, inevitable. A real bitch. We make a demand, you fulfill it. Think of US this way, Mr. Molloy, and we will all be better off. I'm afraid you'll have to think of US this way in any event. I'm afraid there is simply no other way to think of US."

"Okaaaay…." I say, trying to decide if he's joking or not and deciding he's not. "But if you wanted to talk, couldn't you have just made an appointment like everyone else? This…" I wave my arms around to indicate, well, basically everything, "wasn't necessary."

Mr. Franklin leans momentarily forward and fastidiously flicks chocolate crumbs from what looks like his bank manager's suit, only more sinister because real bank managers gave up wearing this kind of suit decades ago.

He fixes me with his colorless eyes, "What *is* necessary, Mr. Molloy? If you strip away all that is unnecessary from a man's life, what are you left with? You are left with the instant that he ejaculates the seed that will conceive the children of the next generation. And, please note, only those ejaculates, not just any ejaculate. The rest of a man's life is just a commute to and from those moments."

This was not the time and place to argue metaphysics, not that if this were the time and place I'd have necessarily disagreed with Mr. Franklin, so I ignore what he just said and try to keep us focused on the business at hand, whatever it might be. In the meantime, I don't really want to see what's going on at the periphery of whatever's happening here. I don't want to get sidetracked. I know that there's a disaster lurking somewhere off to the side that's just waiting to happen. It's out there in the darkness, waiting to blindside me. But I don't want to think about that just yet. I'm not ready for it. First things first.

"You said you wanted to ask me some questions. What are they?"

"We understand that you've been contacted by a Mr. Knott."

As usual, I debate whether or not to lie, decide there's no reason to, at least not right now, and say, "Yes, that's true."

"We'd like to know what he wanted."

"He wanted me to find a woman."

"Really?"

Mr. Franklin leans back in the canvas chair, as if he were settling in to hear a good yarn. Problem is, of course, I don't have much more to tell him. I tell him as much.

"I turned him down. He had a problem telling me who he was working for. Just like you. And I have a problem with that."

"Mr. Knott is working for no one. He's working for himself. He has a fool for a client."

"What do you mean?"

"He's a lawyer. Well, he *was* an attorney. He's since been disbarred. With extreme prejudice."

"What for?"

"Erm…irregularities."

Ho-Ho number two, meanwhile, is in the process of disappearing, deep-throated in a snake-like manner so vulgarly identical to the previous Ho-Ho that it all smacks of ritual, or instant replay. When he finally finishes swallowing the cake-roll, he wipes his mouth fastidiously on a pocket handkerchief, and lifts the fishing pole out of the plastic holder planted beside his chair. He slowly, *very* slowly, reels in the line. This goes on quite a while, as you might imagine, and I find myself watching, with a certain amount of unavoidable suspense, to see if he's actually caught something. Neither of us says a word. Eventually he's got the dripping tackle up and I can see the large silver lure, bristling all over with cruel hooks and festooned with dangling Day-Glo rubber wiggly worms, smoldering phosphorescently in what little light there isn't.

"Nothing," he says, staring expressionless at the naked tackle.

He holds up the big metal lure, a red dot near the tip, supposedly an eye.

"Nothing," he says again. He peers disappointedly at the empty, dripping hooks. He looks up at me and says, "The ocean is depleted. What we have here is an exhausted planet, Mr. Molloy, a planet that is out of breath, out of energy, out of flounder, out of luck."

I notice for the first time that the grey pants are rolled up above his knees, his bare feet sunk in the sand, like bony claws. He has the skinniest calves I've ever seen. It's just one of those useless things you focus on, I guess, when you're scared shitless.

I say, "What does this have to do with anything, Mr. Franklin?"

He says, "Think globally, act locally."

"I'm not sure I understand."

"We want to retain your services, Mr. Molloy."

"My services?"

"Yes."

"Doing what?"

"We want you to find the woman Mr. Knott is looking for. But we want you to find her for us instead."

I'm not really sure how this offer is any different from the offer that the fat man offered me, except that Mr. Franklin is offering it to me at gunpoint, which, of course, makes it instantly more compelling.

"I'm a practical man," I say, "I like to deal in specifics. Can we get down to a few? Who's missing for instance? And why is everyone so interested in locating her?"

Honestly, I'm expecting more ring-around-the rosy nonsense, but Mr. Franklin begins promisingly.

"Her name is Nada Klone. Her real name is something else, of course. What she looks like, is, well…."

"Anyone's guess," I finish.

"No, actually. We have a photo. It will be provided."

"Mr. Knott said that no one knew what she looked like. That it wasn't even clear that she exists at all."

"Mr. Knott," Mr. Franklin interrupts himself and burps lightly into the back of his hand, "is a moron."

"Is she in some kind of trouble? I mean, Mr. Knott claimed the man he worked for was in love with her. Why do you guys want her?"

I was trying to get a grip on just what the deal was here: was this girl a victim, or a victimizer? By finding her, just who would I be helping—and who would I be hurting?

"She's an enigma," Mr. Franklin says with the straightest face you can imagine. He didn't seem to have any other kind. "A mystery, like the Mona Lisa, only she talks a lot dirtier."

"Do you have any idea what reason she'd have to disappear." And I'm thinking, *Is she trying to get away from you?*

"That's part of the mystery. You see, Nada Klone is the kind of girl who gets involved with a lot of interesting characters. The kind of girl that Nada Klone is, well, it allows her to move among some surprising levels of society, both high and low. There's just no telling where a girl like Nada Klone is going to turn up." He says this with a wink, "Nope, there's just no telling what kind of trouble a girl like Nada Klone may have gotten herself into. As for acquaintances, known hangouts, and the like, we've prepared a list. That, too, will be delivered to you. What do you say, Mr. Molloy. Have we a deal?"

I say what I always say. I say, "I can't make any promises."

Mr. Franklin regards me with his one-expression-fits-all face. He says, "Oh, that doesn't sound like the kind of overwhelming confidence and eager-to-please suck-up answer that we like, Mr. Molloy. Oh dear, not at all."

"I'm sorry, but it's the best I can do right now."

"Oh no," Mr. Franklin says matter-of-factly. "You can do better. I'm certain of it. I think this is the kind of case that will end up becoming an obsession. I think it's the kind of case that you will take to heart and make your very own. I predict," he says, putting his fingers to his forehead and squinting out of his cold lizard eyes as if seeing into a future that consisted of nothing but endless miles of uninhabited frozen tundra, "that it'll turn into a matter of life-and-death."

"I guess what you're saying is that I don't have a choice."

That's, I think, the very least of what he's saying, but I'm trying to put the best face on it, and even at that its looking butt-ugly.

"Choice?" Mr. Franklin repeats, as if he doesn't understand the word. "You're an amusing man, Mr. Molloy. Are you an amateur astronomer by any chance?"

I've lost him here. I say, "Huh?"

He's been looking up at the night-sky the entire time, ever since he gave up on trying to catch a fish, and now he's saying something about the Perseides, a meteor shower apparently scheduled for any moment now, but more or less, right now. He is pointing up into the black at something specific, a quadrant, as he puts it, and I'm following his grey skeletal finger, sighting along it like an arthritic gun barrel, basically to amuse him, but I don't see a damn thing, just black sky, a random scattering of shuddering pin-pricks.

He says, "Look just northwest of the Dipper."

I say, "The Dipper?"

If I look hard enough and connect the dots, I can imagine I see the Big Dipper just about anywhere. Right now, I'm looking just about anywhere.

He says, "There, there...Do you see it?"

"Yes," I say, seeing nothing.

Mr. Franklin looks pleased. He says, "Do you ever wonder at the bigness of it all, Mr. Molloy? The sheer immensity? Do you ever look up and think about the magnitude of possibilities? Do you ever have the feeling that there is something else looking back at you? A Great Spirit, perhaps, a Cosmic Intelligence? Is it likely, do you think, that it's really all just burning gases, explosions, and chemical reactions. Nothing more?"

There is something else, alright, but it's not coming from the heavens. It's approaching us down the beach from the north, a ramshackle beast, like a walking picket fence made of three uncoordinated black dogs. This is what's been happening off to the side that I've been trying not to think about. This is the catastrophe that's been waiting for me. The idea of running the hell out of here flashes briefly through my mind, but that seems ridiculous, I could certainly have been killed at any moment up to now if Mr. Franklin wished. As it is, I've got a queer feeling in my heart and it's for good reason: when I look down there's the red laser dot of a rifle scope jiggling on my sternum.

Mr. Franklin says warningly, "Steady there, Mr. Molloy. Steady."

This is not going to be good, I'm thinking. *Whatever this is, it's not going to be good at all.* I may actually be saying this aloud I'm thinking it so loudly and so insistently inside my thundering skull.

The shambling monstrosity coming towards me has resolved itself into something a little less nightmarish, but every bit as ominous. What's coming towards me now, it's clear, are two large men, both in natty black suits, and between them is a woman taller and bulkier than either of her muscle-bound companions and she's dressed in something black and slinky that's showing off little bits and glimpses of her impressive cleavage and thickly muscled legs. She is being held on either side by the two men, but it's not like she's being forced, it's more like she's being escorted, like she's drugged, maybe, or hypnotized, and it's her total lack of resistance that makes the whole thing seem even weirder and more disturbing than it should be.

The man on the beach chair interrupts my general confusion to say, "There may not by anyone in heaven watching, but we've been watching. We've been watching you for some time, Mr. Molloy."

"That's nice. I hope you were entertained. It's nice to know I've been fucking up my life for someone's amusement."

I'm trying to sound cool, and I'm cool alright, my blood is freezing in my veins and I'm saying all this through clenched jaws to keep my teeth from chattering. I'm trying to sound in control of myself, but right about now, I feel that falling to my knees and begging for mercy may soon be the most powerful survival strategy at my disposal. Right about now it's taking everything I have left to control my bladder and keep from squeaking out the words, *"Please, oh please just let me go."*

The hulking girl is on her knees now, on her knees on the wet sand and the pair of well-tailored apes have backed up a step or two behind her, and she's just kneeling there, her big paws at her sides, doing nothing. She's pulled her black evening dress up over her knees so she could kneel, and she's kneeling there, her square-jawed face calm and still and totally pale, her mascaraed eyes looking dull and spacey, but focused right on my face, as if I were a blank sheet of paper and she were faced with the world's worst case of writer's block.

Her hair, which is blonde and worn up, looks pretty good. I've never seen it this way before, even if it does show too much of her muscular neck. The last time I saw her she was sporting an unfortunate red perm, ala the early Nicole Kidman; the last time I saw her was at Meeah Soo's place, discussing cut-rate breast implants, because this was no girl, this was Trina T.

"Funny thing is," Mr. Franklin says, "I think you're beginning to see how all this involves you far more than you ever suspected. I think it's becoming obvious that there really are no innocent bystanders in the great big scheme of things."

"Mr. Franklin," I manage to say, "This is really a very bad idea." I'm not ashamed that my voice is cracking. I'm beyond any of that right now. "Mr. Franklin," I say, "Let's come to some kind of reasonable understanding."

The ocean breeze is picking up. One of the men, the one on the right, I think, has done something to Trina T's top so that one of her meaty shoulders is exposed, and also one small, chemically-enhanced breast that's growing out of the melting muscle around the nipple of her left pectoral. It's sort of hanging off her chest, like a white lemon. The horn of a tanker, miles and miles away at sea, on the edge of the horizon, only a row of seven shimmering lights, gives a few lonely toots.

It sounds like this: *"Toot...toot...toot."*

I say, "Why are you doing this? Why are you screwing with my mind?"

Mr. Franklin shrugs. "I can't help myself. What can I say? I'm an enabler." He pauses thoughtfully. "But I'm also a disabler."

What happens next I would like to forget. What happens next I would like to pretend never happened at all.

This is what happens next:

Behind Trina T, still kneeling on the sand, still half-exposed, still staring at me expressionlessly, like a cow at a fence, the two men in natty black suits have each produced a small silver pistol from somewhere, like they're both doing the identical card trick at the exact same time. Trina T slowly lifts her large hands, lifts her large, gnarled, broken fighter's hands slowly to her lopsided pug's face as if she were about to pray, because she knows what's coming next, and she modestly covers her eyes so that I can't see her disfigured expression when the small silver pistols talk to her.

Those pistols say, *"Pop pop...pop, pop, pop, pop, pop, pop."*

It's that simple gesture that I know right away will haunt me to my dying day. It's the way she lifts her helpless, busted-up hands with the French manicure to her face. That's what I will always remember, what I won't be able to forget, lying awake, staring at the shadows on a moonlit closet door at three a.m. for the rest of whatever is left of my life.

I would like to pretend this didn't happen, that somehow this was all staged. But there are things that happen to a human head when it is hit by half-a-dozen-or-so hollow point bullets of unknown caliber at close range. What I have just seen happen to Trina T's head is exactly what's supposed to happen. What happened is also a warning, I know, but a warning about what? A wave of nausea passes through me when I think that could easily be Meeah Soo lying there with a head like a smashed egg full of turkey chili. The temperature seems to have dropped about twenty degrees in the last ten seconds and another waves of nausea rolls through me and I realize it could be even worse: *that corpse lying there with the head turned inside out could easily be me.*

Trina T. is lying now, face down, on the wet sand, loose and boneless and beyond care and the two men step forward, as if they really needed to, and they point their palm-sized pistols down at the back of her already obliterated head and their guns once again say, *"Pop-pop-pop, pop, pop, pop."*

Mr. Franklin rubs his hands together with a flourish. He says, "Well, that's pretty much that then." He interlaces his long skeletal fingers and cracks his knuckles. He looks at me. He says, "Please Mr. Molloy, get a grip on yourself."

I'm bent over, hands-on-knees, closely inspecting the sand, being sick.

Mr. Franklin says, "Really, Mr. Molloy, this is most unbecoming."

I say, "Waaarrrgh, wralllghhhh." What I mean to say is: "Fuck you, Mr. Franklin."

He says, "Come, come now. We all have to die sometime. It's in the rule book."

When I'm done throwing up, when I'm done wiping the snot and tears and vomit from my face, when I'm done pushing myself up to an erect position, I look over at Mr. Franklin and whatever I was planning to say dissolves into a pathetic version of "Why did you do that?"

Mr. Franklin is pragmatic. "You needed to be motivated," he says. "But now I think you're finally coming round to the viewpoint that we're all in this together. I think you're beginning to experience the participatory nature of the cosmos."

I ask, "What the hell do you want from me?"

The men in the natty black suits are doing something to Trina T now, as if they hadn't done more than enough already; clothes are being ripped, limbs are being re-arranged. The whole thing is being made to look like something else. I'm not looking. I'm asking, for a fourth or fifth time, "What the hell do you want from me?"

You might say I'm getting hysterical. Yes, from Mr. Franklin's point of view, even motivated.

Cool as a cucumber, Mr. Franklin replies, "I want you to find out why she was killed."

"You killed her you son-of-a-bitch," I cry. "Just now!"

I'm crying out of rage and frustration. I'm crying out of fear. It's not just Mr. Franklin. It's not just the brutal, cold-blooded murder I've just witnessed. It's everything. It's a whole life of bullshit and lies and the frustration of dealing with other people boiling up to the surface, all of the stuff we usually keep festering out of sight.

"You killed her! I just saw you!"

Mr. Franklin has his bony hands on his bony knees and he looks like he's going to get up but instead he's just taking up this homey down-on-the-farm pose. He says, "That's now a matter for police inquiry."

He says this like he has insider information.

"What the hell's that supposed to mean?" I ask, as if I don't already know.

The ship, now so far out at sea it's invisible, calls out to shore. It goes, *"Toot...toot.........Toot?"*

I know what the emaciated bastard is talking about. I know only too well what he's talking about. My legs are shaking, my hands are shaking, my shoulders are shaking, my whole goddamn body is shaking. It's as if I'm shaking apart. Fact is, I don't know what's holding me together at this point. I feel like I'm going to be sick again, but that's impossible because there isn't anything left inside me to be rid of. I'm empty. I'm so totally empty I feel light-headed. I feel almost like laughing.

I am laughing.

Mr. Franklin is laughing, too.

He stops laughing.

He says, "You're a suspect, naturally. You're here, after all. Fibers, hair, footprints, DNA." He holds up a hand and counts off each of his points, one by one, on a skeletal finger. "Even your fingerprints will end up on the murder weapon." He holds up his other hand and he counts off those fingers, too. "Circumstances, opportunity, motive." He goes on. "History, physical evidence, prior connection with the victim, no credible alibi." Then he has to reuse the fingers of the first hand. "Eyewitnesses, photographs, times, and dates, past criminal record." He looks at me significantly, as if no one who'd used up that many fingers could possibly be innocent. "That's a lot of damn fingers Mr. Molloy."

"No one will believe it," I say, but the fact is, I can believe it, it's damn believable.

"Unless you find Nada Klone for us, whoever she is, wherever she is, dead or alive, you just killed her."

"I don't get it."

"No one else knows what Nada Klone looks like." He points to Trina T. "Unless you find her, we will arrange for that to be Nada Klone."

I'm not laughing anymore. I'm not crying. I'm just standing there feeling extremely drained and completely sorry for myself. I'm all of a sudden feeling just totally bummed out. I say about the only thing I can think of to say under the circumstances. I say, "Can I please go home now. *Please?*"

6. Bad dreams, paranoid delusions, and breakfast in hell...

It was all a dream. That's what's supposed to come after seeing the kind of thing I just got done seeing, but it's not a dream, because I haven't woken up; in fact, I can't get to sleep. I finally made it home sometime just before dawn; the guy who car-jacked me in front of Lincoln Center drove me back in my own cab and lord only knows where it is now, but I'm not worrying about that for the time being.

I stand in the dim hallway outside my apartment and put my key in the lock and I'm expecting the police to be there already, waiting for me when I open the door, but they aren't, not yet, anyway.

I take a quick look around the place; it's the kind of superficial look you take when you're already committed to a restaurant, for instance, seated, halfway through the fricassee, and you don't want to see the cockroach scurrying across the wall. It's the kind of look that says, I'm happy living alone, that lump in my armpit is just a swollen gland, sex isn't everything.

That's the kind of cursory look I'm taking now.

The place isn't tossed, that's for sure. It's not ransacked. As crappy as it looks, you can tell that much. But was that stack of books by the ratty armchair really toppled? That desk drawer, I don't remember it being partially open. The favorites list on my computer screen, I never leave that pulled down, do I? Even the cushions on the chairs don't seem quite right somehow. Maybe it's just my imagination. It's hard to say. Until something goes wrong, how much do we really notice of the places we spend our lives in, anyway?

Even taking me out of the equation, the apartment has the general feeling of a place that is being observed. I go to pull down all the shades but, of course, all the shades are already pulled down. I realize it's even worse than I thought. The sense of being watched is coming from *inside* the apartment; that is, if it's coming from anywhere at all.

Paranoia. I have a feeling it's going to be with me from now on like a newly developed sixth sense.

I'm making a silent vow: no matter what, I'm not saying a single word about anything in this place. For all I know, the tape recorders are running, hoping I'll incriminate myself. I'm thinking, *If you stub your toe, don't even say 'ouch'.*

But after that, as for a plan of action, I'm lost. What would be the sensible thing to do? *Think,* I'm thinking, *think.* If this were a movie, what would the audience be thinking the main character should do, instead of all the dumb irrational things he always ends up doing?

The answer, of course, is obvious. Right now is the time to call the police if I'm ever going to call them at all. Any delay whatsoever, and it's going to be too late; any dilly-dallying, and I'll end up looking guilty as hell. Any hesitation whatsoever and the very first question the police will ask me will be, *Why did you wait to call the police?*

But who's going to believe the story I have to tell them? To put your faith in the police, that's always a risky proposition.

When they finally show up, you are always the first person they suspect.

Lazy, just like the rest of us, cops don't want to work any harder than we do. I mean, if you can get away with loafing on the job, don't you? If you can ignore that file, transfer that call, stall that project...well, in short, why should the cops be any different? Why not just arrest the guy right at hand? Why go looking for trouble? If you really think that just because a lack of conscientiousness can send an innocent man to prison for twenty years is any more likely to get a cop off his ass, you don't know squat about human nature.

Anyway, there's always a chance that I won't be connected with any of this. So why complicate matters? Why take the chance? The upshot of all this treacherous cogitation is predictable: I do not pick up the phone. I do not dial 911.

Right from the start, I start doing everything wrong.

Asked to define his life and teaching, a famous Zen master said, *One mistake after another.*

That's my life, too.

One mistake after another. But without the enlightenment at the end.

What I do instead of calling the police is this: I go to the closet and take down a Nike sneaker box marked "Old Receipts" and remove a bottle from my Xanax stash. I shake out five or six 1 milligram pills, dry swallow them like the good panic disorder graduate I am, and sit down on the not-quite-right couch and wait for them to make me not care enough about anything to fall asleep for a few hours.

I need a discontinuity of consciousness really badly right about now.

I need an oasis of oblivion.

Two hours later, I'm improbably still awake. It's possible I've fallen asleep in the meantime, but if so, I don't remember. I don't remember sleeping and I don't remember waking up. I'm still sitting on the couch, trying to remind myself not to say anything. I'm wondering if the Xanax I took somehow lost it's potency sitting in the closet for however long it's been sitting in the closet. I'm wondering if they were even Xanax at all.

I'm waiting for a reaction from the pills, the police, the fat man, Mr. Franklin, something. But nothing happens.

I'm sitting there and I'm thinking, *I can't sleep anyway so I might as well wake up the rest of the way.* I'm thinking, *Let's go get some coffee.*

Two blocks away there's a twenty-four-hour coffee shop and that's where I go now, sitting in a booth by the window, my hands only shaking when I force myself to stop compulsively shredding my paper napkin.

I'm thinking, if I call the police now their second question will be asked all in italics and full of pretend disbelief and it will sound something like this, *And then you went where? To a coffee shop?*

The waitress arrives and I ask her for some coffee.

Then I ask for some eggs and toast.

Then I ask for some potatoes, some ham.

"Give me a side of pancakes too," I say.

For some reason, I'm suddenly, inexplicably, extremely hungry.

Maybe I'm just imagining it, but right before the waitress walks off to take the order at the next table, she gives me this little, *You're a murderer and I know it* look.

I blink and the look is gone.

I blink again.

I drain the first cup of coffee. A different waitress sleepwalks passed my table, pours me another, and I drink that one, and half a third one, too, before I slow down. I force myself to stop pulling apart what's left of my napkin for the fifteenth time. I wish I had a cigarette and I don't even smoke.

I'm keeping an eye on a TV that is sitting on top of an empty refrigerated case of what would probably be pie wedges if there were anything in there at all. I'm keeping my other eye on the door but since it's the only door I have no idea what I'm going to do if someone comes through it who means me harm. I don't see my face on the television, or the face of Trina T. I don't see the beach where she was killed. I don't see anything, really, except a row of boxes representing the weather for the next five days and there's a big bright smiling sun wearing dark glasses in each and every one.

It looks like some really sunny weather ahead!

Clanking my breakfast down in front of me, the waitress gives me this look that says, *So you think you got away with it, don't you?*

What she says out loud is, "Can I get you anything else?"

I say, "No."

I look down at the plates and I'm not exactly certain, but I'm pretty sure what I'm looking at is not quite what I ordered, but I've decided not to make a fuss about it. People in my position, they don't start arguments about the toast.

Whatever was going through my mind when I thought I was so hungry, that's not what's going through my mind anymore. I'm cutting things up with my fork but mainly just for show, mainly just to be doing something. There are a few other people in the coffee shop mostly hunched over coffee at the counter, staring up at the television, taking the occasional bite or sip of something or other. One other booth is occupied by someone behind a newspaper and another by four old men updating each other on who among their rapidly diminishing circle is dead, who is dying, and who is still clinging to life.

Are they all in on this together? Are they all plants? Is it really so unreasonable to suppose this is some kind of sting?

One of the old man says, "Frank passed."

Another says, "Oh no. Well, that's a shame."

"Who?" hoots a third.

"Yeah," the first old man says, "Woke up with diarrhea and feeling weak. Wife took him to the hospital. They sent him home with a bottle of Kaopectate. He died that night."

"Who?" says the third old man again.

A fourth old man, chewing eggs, weighs in. He says, "Quick at least."

"Nah," the second old man says, "He was sick for months."

"Who?"

If you loop this conversation back, change the names and physical ailments, splice it with talk about Atlantic City, politics, and the weather, and let it play continuously, then you know pretty much what it sounds like being old. What I'm listening to is the way our lives all end, and that's only if we're lucky, if we don't die much sooner. This is where you end up when you've worn out your welcome in the world.

The waitress comes back, wearing a wry look that says, *They're going to get you; you'll never get away with it, you know that, don't you? It's just a matter of time,* but what comes out of her mouth sounds more like, "Is everything okay?"

"Yes," I say. "Yes everything's okay. Why wouldn't it be?" I see the weird look on her face and enthusiastically add, "Thank you!"

After she leaves with the plates, still looking weird, I pick up the spoon and look at my reflection. Maybe I should have shaved before I left the apartment. I probably should have stepped into the shower. A change of clothes, I'm thinking, and I might not look quite so much like a guy who just shot a transsexual ex-fighter to death on a beach in Jersey less than five hours ago. What I'm doing is trying to figure out what someone who *hasn't* just shot a transsexual ex-fighter to death on a beach in Jersey less than five hours ago looks like. What I'm trying to do is remember what it's like to look innocent. I'm trying to think of what a good answer would be to the question, And then you did *what* after you left the coffee shop?, when the police finally show up to ask, which I'm figuring they will, oh about any minute now.

Back at the apartment, an e-mail tells me where the cab is. It's in a parking garage near Times Square. The e-mail is from an account I don't recognize. The subject line says: Your Cab is Here, Mr. Molloy. And the body of the text is the address of a parking garage near Times Square and instructions to look under the left front wheel well. The instructions also tell me to look in my wallet for the claim ticket. The instructions tell me to drive home carefully. They say, Have a Nice Day ☺.

I feel a bit sick seeing this e-mail. I know that whatever is going to happen, it's only just begun. I know that whoever is behind all this, they must know a lot about me. It's one thing being kidnapped and setup for murder. It's quite another to have your e-mail address hacked.

I find the claim ticket tucked between my driver's license and a spare ribbed black condom that's meant for Meeah Soo. Someone's been in my wallet, I think, as I stare numbly at the ticket, putting stuff there. I pat at my clothes, vaguely, not sure just what I'm looking for, but bugs come to mind, wires, hidden microphones, fake buttons, suspicious nodules.

I'm thinking about this again while I stand in the shower: my clothes from last night stuffed into the kitchen trash bin. I look suspiciously at my hands, my forearms, the insides of my elbows. Maybe there's a nanochip or something like that implanted under my skin. It's possible, isn't it? I check my fingernails, the backs of my knees. It occurs to me that I haven't literally looked between my toes in decades. There are so many places on my own body that would make excellent hiding places for whatever.

In jeans, t-shirt, and lightweight jacket, I hit the streets behind mirror aviator shades, going for that "just part of the scenery" look, an urban chameleon, one of ten thousand passersby, that kind of thing. I walk down the stairs into the subway, catch a train to Times Square, find the parking garage on 46th and Broadway, present my claim ticket.

The parking garage guy takes the ticket, stares at it, hands it to another guy who looks like his younger brother. They're both so strikingly good looking they could probably be pop stars in Bollywood or Nepal or wherever the hell they come from. The younger brother takes the ticket and disappears into the dark concrete esophagus of the garage. The older brother is staring at me as if he's waiting for me to say something, almost like he's daring me to start a conversation.

I say, "Was I the one who brought the car in?" I realize how suspicious this sounds, so I correct myself, "I mean, was I here when I came in before?" and I can sense immediately that I'm making the situation even worse. So I say, "Will twenty dollars cover it?"

He says, "Five hundred dollars."

He keeps staring at me.

Guided by the breakdown of prices per hour, half-hour, night, day, half-day etc. on the sign posted just over his right shoulder, five hundred dollars simply doesn't seem mathematically possible, but this doesn't seem the time to review our multiplication tables. I take out five crisp Ben Franklins that weren't in my wallet the night before, hand them over, and he stuffs them in his pocket without comment.

I consider that those five Franklins were put there precisely for this exchange.

"Keep the change," I say. "Ummm, by the way, was there anyone with me when I dropped the car off?"

He nods slowly. He nods, *No.* He's looking at me strangely. He's looking at me like he's trying to remember me for later and whatever he's going to remember about me is probably not going to be good. So I put my hand in front of my face and start fake-coughing and walk off a little ways to where the cab is going to come screeching its way out of the bowels of the parking garage in about ten seconds. I can already hear its tires squealing around the tight bends.

"Well," I say, "Well…"

I don't finish the sentence until I'm in the cab and I've driven all the way down to Second Avenue. Even then, I don't finish it.

7. Jiffy bags, urban warlords, and the rarest of all disasters

Pretending to be checking my tire pressure, I squat down beside the cab in a No Parking, No Standing, No Anything at Anytime zone right in front of a fire hydrant on Avenue C and feel around under the left front wheel well like the email told me to do. At first I don't feel anything. I don't feel anything the second or third time either. I'm thinking there must be a mistake. I'm thinking the guy at the parking garage got there first. I'm thinking the whole thing is some kind of a joke.

For the first time since last night, I'm beginning to experience a sense of relief. I'm beginning to think that maybe things are not quite as bad as I might have thought.

Then I feel it: it's a soft package all taped up. It takes some doing but I do it. I pull it free: a brown paper packing mailer that quietly explodes with all that carcinogenic confetti when I slide back into the front seat and open it.

Brushing the stuff off my lap, I shake out the contents of the envelope. It would be better to wait until I get some place private, until I get back to the apartment, for instance. I know this for a fact, but I open the envelope anyway.

I look out the windows, in the rearview, the side-view, all views. This wasn't the best place in the city to park: there are cars and trucks and sirens and passersby all over the damn place.

That I'm in trouble, I know that already, but how much trouble, it's just now becoming frighteningly clear. Inside the envelope this is what I find: a small silver palm-sized handgun and twenty-seven hundred dollars in twenties, tens, and fives.

The drive back to the Bronx is uneventful. Behind the wheel, I might as well be a zombie. There's this sort of rictus grin that I can feel stuck on my face like a cheap clip-on necktie. I'm paying tolls, making turns, looking both ways and things, but I have no idea how. It's amazing how one can live a life without giving any thought to it whatsoever.

At the garage, Mr. Sammy is extremely agitated. He is talking in Pakistani or Iranian or whatever his native tongue happens to be, but the only thing I understand is how close he came to calling the police to report a stolen taxi cab. He's tall, handsome like the parking garage guys, but older, fiercer, more distinguished-looking. Back wherever he came from, he was some kind of prince or multimillionaire warlord. He holds the tips of his elegant brown fingers about a quarter of a millimeter apart.

"This close," he says.

I point at the cab behind me like a moron. I smile. I say sunnily, "There it is. There's the cab."

I thank him for not calling the police. I thank him over and over. I don't seem to be making much of an impression on him, though. Then I remember the money. I take out about a thousand dollars in cash. The sight of the bills is helping matters, I can see that right away. I explain that I had a fare that wanted to go to Philadelphia and I hurry to cover his objections with another three hundred and seventy five dollars.

Mr. Sammy suddenly seems markedly less agitated. He seems, well, almost happy. He snaps his elegant fingers impatiently and I hand him the rest of the money. Now he seems almost overjoyed.

He is counting out the money I've just handed him, and when he's done, he counts it out again, and then once more. He's holding up a twenty as I babble on about something or other, hopelessly hoping to confuse him. Instead, he manages to confuse *me*: I shut up, looking at him looking at the twenty, examining the physiognomy of Andrew Jackson as if suspecting a mask, a fake nose, a celebrity look-a-like. Once again it occurs to me: the money was put in the wheel well for precisely this purpose. Everyone's being paid off…but for what?

After examining, sniffing, touching the tip of his tongue to the bill, Mr. Sammy seems satisfied that the money is authentic enough to exchange for grenade launchers, fake passports, season tickets for the Knicks. He cocks a handsome Egyptian--or whatever--eyebrow at me.

He says, "Next time you phone in."

He pinches the tips of his two brown fingers nearly together. "*This close.*"

He's smiling the whole time but his eyes are icy, cruel, self-satisfied. I imagine it's the look he'd give when ordering the liquidation of an entire mountain village.

He says, "Next time I call cops."

On the way home I buy the *Post*, the *Times*, the *Daily News*. I buy the *Star-Ledger*, the *Asbury Park Press*, the *Philadelphia Inquirer*. I buy the *Wall Street Journal*. I buy *El Diario*. I buy the *World Weekly News*. I'm looking for exactly what you think I'd be looking for under the circumstances. Instead, I find myself reading a story about nine miners who were rescued from a flooded mine somewhere in western Pennsylvania.

IT'S A MIRACLE, the headlines gush.

There are photographs of people holding up signs saying, *It's a Miracle, Thank you, God.*

Wives, mothers, sons, mining officials, people on the street, the governor of Pennsylvania, they're all singing God's praises, giving him all the credit, finding proof that someone up there is looking out for us. One of the miners is actually quoted as saying, "Someone up there was really looking out for us."

Of course, if the mine had collapsed and everyone had died under ten thousand tons of dirt, you'd never see headlines saying what a worthless, heartless son-of-a-bitch God was.

There'd be no television interviews with mournful survivors screaming curses and blaming the Almighty. There wouldn't be politicians publicly denouncing Jehovah as a corrupt bumbling incompetent and demanding his immediate impeachment. There'd be no criminal prosecution brought against the CEO of Heaven. They'd sue the mining company instead. Everyone would let the Creator off the hook, finding excuses, shrugging their collective shoulders, and saying things about the dead like, *Well, I guess it was just their time.*

They would say things like, *"No one knows God's will."*

They would say things like, *"The ways of God are mysterious."*

These are the kinds of things people say to feel better, to make themselves believe that there's some sense or order to all the senseless, disordered horror of our lives. It helps to believe that someone, somewhere is in control and all the moreso when everything is screaming out of control.

Funny thing is, no one really believes in God until something really good or something really bad happens. If you go into remission, you need someone to thank. If you don't, you need someone to comfort you.

What I'm thinking is that it's a pretty good gig being God, even aside from the omnipotence, omniscience, and immortality. Whenever you do something right, everybody is falling all over you with gratitude. If you're God, you just save someone once, and people are throwing themselves at your feet. They completely forget the other nine-hundred gazillion times you didn't do a goddamn thing and it all ended in some kind of horrendously senseless tragedy.

It's not hard to keep your good name, if you're God.

We should all be so lucky. We should all know even one-tenth of that kind of affirmation in our lives. We should all have this kind of margin of error in our jobs.

Being God, there's even less accountability to it than being a weatherman.

It was coming, I knew it, but my heart sinks all the same when I see it waiting on my computer: another email from Mr. Franklin. After some creepy "pleasantries," some cracks like "did you have a pleasant ride home?" and "you won't find any news in the papers…yet" which reinforces my paranoia that they're watching my every step, Franklin gets down to the business at hand. It's the promised list of places that Nada Klone has been and, dammit, it goes on and on and on, like the stock market page, only longer. This'll give you an idea how long it goes on: I've got my finger pressed on the page-down key and all the blood's run out of it and the nail has turned blue.

Just a cursory glance at this A to Z compendium of porn sites, X-rated blogs, chats, message board posts, and sex personals is enough to impress even a hardcore pervert such as myself. I mean, the most polymorphously perverse among us usually has a range on the spectrum of kink, but this Nada Klone went from one end of warped to the other, and then some. She added some new previously invisible colors to the porn rainbow. To judge by where she'd been, and been regularly, by what she'd done, and done often, she was that rarest of all rare breeds: she liked it *all.*

Girls, bondage, two men, three men, gangs of men, submission, men and women, whips, whipped cream, dominance, two women, three women, gangs of women, dogs, golden showers, brown showers, red showers, foot fetish, fur fetish, rubber fetish, did I say discipline?, leather, diapers, women and dogs, gangs of dogs, canned corn…in short, if you could imagine it, Nada was into it, and if you couldn't, she'd imagine it for you.

To read through this libidinal catalogue of excesses, so diverse, so debauched, so deviant they'd make a Roman Emperor blush, I could only conclude one thing: this was quite possibly the dirtiest girl to ever live. A girl, in other words, well worth knowing.

While I have the list printing out, knowing already I might run out of paper, toner, ink, and maybe even life itself before the list of

Nada Klone's perversions came to an end, I notice for the first time the attachment attached to the email and the simple file designation Mr. Franklin had given it: *Her.jpeg*.

I tap the cursor two or three times, wondering what kind of face this X-rated angel could possibly have and prepare myself for the inevitable: that whatever Nada Klone looked like she won't look like the image I've already formed of her in my mind's twisted eye. In other words, I prepare for disappointment.

It's like being on a blind date, I'm thinking, where you hope for the best and expect the worse and still you always end up surprised, but never in a good way.

This is one of those times, I'm thinking, as the image unfolds. I realize that my curiosity may have already led me to infect my computer with a virus. Right now hackers could be accessing my email, my credit card information, the bad poetry I wrote trying to get what's-her-name back. Right now my entire hard drive could be imploding, sucked into the void, but it's all worth it. Sometimes you have to take a chance.

It's worth it to know that Knott didn't have to threaten me, Johnny Nomad guilt trip me, nor Mr. Franklin frame me for murder. They were all wasting their time. If this girl was missing, I'd find her. If this girl were in trouble, I'd save her. If this girl needed a heart and a couple of lungs, I'd take off my shirt and get out the knife and scissors. Like everyone else in this ridiculous drama, I realize I need to find Nada Klone. In fact, I may need to find her more than anyone. I stare at the screen of my Toshiba laptop with my jaw unhinged. This was worse, far worse, than I could ever have imagined. This was that rarest of all disasters: it was love at first sight.

8. Megalomania, mass murder, and geek technology...

In the waiting room of Jimmy Ng's computer hospital on Sixth
Avenue, I'm sitting here waiting. All around me scared-looking
people are clutching laptops, palm pilots, memory sticks, Blackberrys,
hard-drives, boxes of compact discs. They've all come to Jimmy Ng's
hoping for a miracle. They're all looking for him to find a cure for a
fatal error message, a corrupted file, a missing directory, a total crash
of some sort or other.

   We're all sitting on hard orange seats, discarded office furniture
from circa 1970 or so. No one is looking at the old *Computer Shoppers*
on the table. The outdated issues of *Online, CompuWorld, Mac Today* go
unperused. Everyone's sweating it out over that lost novel they were
too lazy to back up, that quarterly report that got zapped, that
collection of adulterous email they were stupid enough to save on a
shared directory.

   Jimmy Ng's so hard to see because he has a reputation. He has
a reputation for doing the impossible.

   When everyone else says, *Sorry but that file's gone forever.* Jimmy
Ng rolls up his sleeves and says, "Let's see what we can do. Maybe it
got accidentally backed up on Wordpad." When everyone else says,
That's just a myth that everything on a hard drive can be retrieved. Jimmy Ng
puts on his glasses and says, "Everything on a hard drive can be
retrieved but only if you know where to look."

The other reason Jimmy Ng is so popular, why his waiting room is so full of worried-looking people, is that Jimmy Ng knows how to keep his mouth shut. You got a file of compromising photos with the family shepherd, Jimmy tactfully refers to it as "that problem with jpeg.k9luv." You have a chat log recorded where you're pretending to be watching your wife get it on with two well-hung black studs, he calls it "that matter concerning oreogrrl.doc."

You see, Jimmy Ng grew up under a totalitarian regime, so he knows a thing or to about the real value of freedom of expression. He knows how important it is to be able to write down your raunchy mother-in-law fantasies without fear of annihilating retribution. He's experienced pogroms and genocides so he knows the slippery slope it is between the socially disastrous disclosure of a construction worker's secret fantasy of taking his foreman's cock up the ass in full French maid's regalia and being arrested at three a.m., spirited away to an undisclosed location, and tortured to death because you've been reclassified as an "enemy-of-the-state" for teaching kids how to read.

As it turns out, though, it's not Jimmy Ng that I really need to see and that's just as well, because he's booked solid for months: CEO's, congressmen, celebrities, entrepreneurs, they all have representatives here with boxes and diskettes full of potential blockbuster trouble. Instead I need to see a guy Jimmy is supposed to know, if anyone could know this guy, a guy so legendary in hacker circles, his name is usually spoken in a whisper, if it absolutely must be spoken at all. I need to see—

It's finally my turn. Jimmy Ng stands in the doorway of his office and motions me impatiently inside, like he's called me two or three times already.

His "office" isn't much: it's really just the back room of the computer repair shop we're in. It's lined with shelves stacked with blank monitors, exposed motherboards, retired modems, antediluvian keyboards . It's like the land of lost toys in the Rudolph the Red-Nosed Reindeer cartoon. You can't help but feel sad for all this exhausted, outdated, unwanted hardware.

Ng says, "What up? What tlouble you?"

I tell him about the virus, about the frozen screen, the enigmatic symbol that's locked up my computer ever since I opened those files from Mr. Franklin. I tell him about the list of websites and my need for a digital dick to track them down. I don't tell him about the picture of Nada Klone. That's one thing I want to keep secret, all to myself. I'm ashamed. I don't want anyone to know how stupidly I caught this virus. I'm also scared to let anyone else see her. I want her all to myself. Believe me, it surprises me as much as it does you: but *I'm jealous.*

It's absurd, it's ridiculous, it's love alright.

Meanwhile Ng jump-starts my machine, watches it run through the obligatory scans, begins to access a shareware flight simulation program, and then everything goes blank a moment before the now eerily familiar symbol dominates the screen.

He says, "What the hell that?"

I say, "I don't know. What's it look like to you?"

Ng says, "A medical drawing of the entlance to a utelus? A new kind of non-schtick wok?" After a little preliminary tinkering, he says, "Lisren, cowbroy, you got plobrem. Velly big plobrem. Jimmy no can help with this."

I whisper, "I know. I was thinking" and I lowered my voice below a whisper, if that's possible, "Ratking…"

Jimmy nods. "He'd be the one."

I say, "Can you get me an appointment?"

"Ratkring don't like disturbance with real life."

"I'm not sure this is real life."

Ng seems to consider this a moment. Then he says, "I see what I can do. But it crost you."

"Cost me what?"

"Five gland."

"I don't know. That sounds a little…umm…steep for just scheduling an appointment."

Ng doesn't haggle. He cuts straight to the point, detours right around the bullshit. This comes from walking along dirt roads lined with mass graves open to the tropical heat and filled with entire generations. He leans forward among the broken speakers, printers, memory cards. He says, "You desplate?"

I can't lie. Well, of course I can. But with Jimmy Ng lying won't get me anywhere.

"Yes."

"Desplate men to desplate thrings. Five gland."

Fact is, I've got the cash. I got it just that morning via a FedEx envelope stuffed with cash. I count out the five grand and hand it over to Ng.

I say, "Okay. Where?"

He gives me an address in the Trump Tower. When I look surprised he says, "Ratkring, he like to rive rarge."

He's not kidding. He's not smiling. He's got the face on that he's always got on: it's the face of a boy who's seen his mathematician father roused out of bed in the middle of the night and summarily hung in the university quad as an example to anyone else tempted to criticize the government for taking over the newspapers. There's nothing funny about a world where that happens, he seems to be saying with that blank unreadable face, and there's nothing funny about this either.

Taking a cross town bus after that face-to-face with Jimmy Ng, I'm staring thoughtlessly at the chunky smear of Madison Avenue going by the window. *Maybe,* I'm thinking, *it's still not too late to go to the police.* Oh, who am I kidding? Can you imagine what they'd say now? You did what and what and then *what?* They'd never believe me. I decide never to think about going to the police again. Naturally, this thought is immediately followed by this one: *Oh why didn't I go to the police from the very start?*

I feel sick.

Someone takes the seat next to me, which is bad enough, but he's spilling over the edges, lumps of him pressing up against me. Dammit, it seems that lately I'm always drawing these fat-assed seat companions. It's as if the chubbos of the world are instinctively gravitating towards me. I guess this is my reward for all the cupcakes

I've denied myself, the extra slices of pizza I've resisted. The fattest guy on the bus sits next to me and takes advantage of the extra room. I'm about to give Fatso Rizzo here a warning elbow jab but he's got me overwhelmed with a landslide of his warm squishiness; it's like being buried alive under a ton of damp meat.

I'm about to turn, to shoot him a disapproving glance, when I hear him say, "Good afternoon Mr. Molloy."

It's Knott, of course.

I try to play it casual. I say, "How's tricks?"

He's got an inhaler in his palm and he inhales, as if he were trying to puff himself up with enough air to say whatever it is he has to say. When he's done sucking and gasping, he slips the inhaler back into the breast pocket of his pale yellow seersucker summer suit.

"So," he says, "I told you I'd be in touch."

"Yeah," I say, trying to yank my arm out from between us. It's like trying to pull the sword from the stone. "You sure are."

"I keep my promises."

"Whatever."

"Think anymore about what we talked about?"

"Some."

He nods. "And I'll bet you concluded that after further review you could use the work, after all. Am I right?"

I say, "Why yes, Mr. Knott, as a matter of fact you are."

"I usually am, Mr. Molloy. I usually am."

The bus hits a pothole and his huge body jiggles and undulates like a king-sized water bed has been propped beside me. "That certain gentleman I'm working for, he'll be very pleased."

I feel like telling him to cut it the fuck out, that I know damn well that he's not working for anyone, that he's working for himself. That this certain anonymous gentleman he's talking about is him.

Instead I say, "Do you know a guy named Mr. Franklin?"

Knott wipes his face of the momentary alarm that dented it. He plays it dumb, trying to turn his face into the equivalent of a stopped clock. I try winding up his works again. "Skinny guy. Real square. Dresses like an insurance salesman from hell."

Knott resumes animation. He inspects his manicure. He says, "Franklin, hmmm, doesn't ring an immediate bell. Common enough name, though. Why do you ask?"

"Just that he's been asking around for a missing woman, too."

Knott must have the most interesting cuticles in the world, because he suddenly can't seem to take his piggy little eyes off them. He says, "Is that so? Hmmm. Is that so? Interesting....hmmmm...."

I say, "Yeah, isn't now? The girl he's looking for is also from the internet. Her name is Nada Klone. That wouldn't happen to be the name of the girl you're looking for, is it?"

Mr. Knott looks up from his chubby chewed up fingers. His eyes appear, well, frantic. He says, with heat, "You must help me find her fast, Mr. Molloy. Whoever else is looking for her, those are the people we must beat. Those, people, Mr. Molloy, are the ones she's running from."

He's got his inhaler out again and he's puffing away at it, as if he were trying to inflate a life preserver on a rapidly sinking ship. His bulk is rumbling, trembling, shuddering. There is sweat running through his voluminous pink folds. He looks like he's having an asthma attack, a panic attack, a heart attack, and a Big Mac attack all at once. He looks so *overwrought*. He looks, and I hate to admit it, like he's telling the truth.

9. Trump, more Trump, and the King of Rats...

Maybe a million, maybe even two, that's how many times some
dumb-ass tourist has asked me how to get to the Trump Tower. Why
anyone would want to see that gaudy gold-plated turd of clueless
egoism except that they don't have anything so monumentally
tasteless in some place like Oak Ridge, Tennessee, or wherever, is
beyond me. Depending on where I am, I'm never really sure which
direction it's in, but every one of the million or two times I'm asked
where it is, I point off in whichever direction I'm pretty sure it's not
and say, "Go straight ahead. Just keep walking. You can't miss it,"
and then I pray for their sake that they do.

Anyway, here I am standing outside of it to finally see Ratking.
I'm looking at God only knows how many floors of this cheesy-
looking multi-mirrored dildo and it's even uglier and more
preposterous than I remember, which fascinates me, because that
seems impossible. Jesus, there are some kind of trees or shrubs
growing out of the middle of it all, so that it looks like the thing's
sprouting ear hairs. There's the big name Trump blazoned across the
front, as if you should possibly forget for even one single blessed
second the megalomaniac who planted this colossal pile of
compensatory claptrap smack in the center of Manhattan.

I imagine the architect who drew up the plans must have had
tears streaming down his face the whole time. As his pencil moved

across the graph paper and he betrayed every principle of taste and aesthetic held since the erection of Stonehenge, I'll bet he was silently begging the ghost of Frank Lloyd Wright, *Please, oh please, forgive me*...I imagine he's easily recognizable at any architectural convention: he's the one wearing the brown paper bag over his head.

The lobby isn't so bad if only because from inside this tasteless jewelry box of red carpets and gold-edged everything, you can't see the outside of the building at all. There are a bunch of shops selling the same crap you can buy anywhere else on earth for a fraction of the cost and they're staffed by snooty salespeople who'd be a lot more courteous if they were selling the same crap, cheaper, anywhere else on earth. This, apparently, is what the name *Trump* has come to signify on no matter what hotel, casino, or public toilet it happens to be slapped upon: *Pay up, sucker.*

It's surprisingly easy to gain access to one of the gold-plated elevators to Ratking's apartment. Basically, all I have to do is walk up to one, press the button, get on, and head upstairs to the 49th floor. There are some guys in suits walking around the lobby with earpieces in their ears but whatever they're listening to, it's not instructions to stop me, at least not yet, anyway. I'd have thought it would be a lot more difficult to gain access to a building where people are paying fifteen million dollars for an apartment full of stuff probably worth another twenty million. After all, I could be just some guy off the street; actually, I *am* just some guy off the street. Maybe I'm on camera, I think, looking up at the corners of this gilded hatbox of an elevator.

Anyway, while I wait to get to the 49th floor, this might be a good time to say a few background words about Ratking.

There are a lot of guys *like* Ratking, but only one Ratking, just like there are a lot of basketball players, but only one Michael Jordan, or a lot of a whole lot of all kinds of people, but only one that's the best at anything. The birth of the web bred a bunch of guys like Ratking back in the late nineties, but not really, because although a lot of guys do what Ratking does, Ratking does it at such an entirely elevated level that what he does becomes something different altogether.

Maybe the easiest way to explain it is to explain his nickname; people pick'em for a reason, you know, and Ratking is no exception. It's not what you think, either, it's not because he's got a weird thing for rodents or even because he's King of All Hackers; which he is; but it's a lot more than that. The real meaning of his nickname goes a bit deeper than that. You see, as any experienced exterminator will tell you, there are only so many rats that can infest a building, a critical mass of rats, you might say, and when this critical mass of rats is surpassed, when there are so many rats in the walls, under the floors, in the ceilings of a structure their tails have a tendency to become tangled. Picture it: hundreds, maybe even thousands of rats, their tails all knotted together. And these rats, all connected to one another, they start to move and feed and breed as one, they start to exist as one gigantic super-rat organism inside a building—they form *a rat-king*.

Creepy, isn't it?

Lots of people say the same thing about Ratking, too.

Creepy, isn't he?

They say he hasn't been out of his apartment since 1994. They say he doesn't need to go anywhere. He's already connected to everything. He can stay in the same place and be everywhere at once.

What does he do, exactly?

Well, it's not quite saying what he does just to say that he accesses information. It doesn't really do the trick to explain that he hacks into things. It would be misleading to say that he's a trafficker in corporate and governmental secrets. He does all these things, of course, but so much more. It would be damning with faint praise to merely call him an *uberhacker*. What Ratking is, that's not easy to say, but if you had to say something, maybe the best you could do was to call him a *cybermage*. He can walk through any firewall, open sesame to any password protected site, pass unseen without leaving a trace among even the most sensitive classified data. And I'm here to see him because, besides de-bugging my machine, I'm betting that he can track down Nada Klone from the abbreviated list of websites crammed into the pocket of my chinos.

Fortunately for the good guys, by which I mean the little guys like me, Ratking steals information exclusively from the rich and gives it to the poor. For all the fortunes he's pilfered, he is the Karl Marx of the digital revolution. A cyber Robin Hood.

The elevator says, "Bing-bing."

No time to say anymore.

We're here: the 49th floor.

Maybe I *am* on camera, I'm thinking, as I walk down the shiny hallway, a weird smear of Roman debauchery and art deco that makes you feel like you're headed for the slot machines no matter where you're going. I nod at some good-looking guy who might be Pierce Brosnan. I have a sudden paranoiac flash: maybe they, whoever "they" are, want me to be here. I wink back at a guy I think I saw on CNN last night. I hear muffled screaming.

It's Ratking himself who greets me at the door, which I guess really shouldn't surprise me, since it's his apartment door I'm knocking on, but somehow it does. He's wearing a Chicago Blackhawks hockey jersey, a pair of yellow FUBU05 ghetto shorts, and lime-green rubber shower sandals. It's an atrocious combo on so many levels, but, hey, I'm thinking, give the guy a break, he's just slumming it on an ordinary afternoon in his eleven million-dollar apartment. In his left hand is a cup of what smells like chai tea. In his right hand is the doorknob. In his mouth is a cigarette. He sticks his head out the door, looks quickly up and down the now empty hall and mutters impatiently, "Come in, come in. Don't malinger."

I step around him and he sticks his head out the door again. Then he slams it shut, engaging about forty-four different kinds of lock.

He mutters, "Chai?"

I say, "No thanks...wow."

What I'm amazed at is not how sumptuous and regal the place behind him is. I'm not oohing and aahing at the conspicuous consumption. What's got me flabbergasted is just how narrow, crappy, and cramped the apartment is. What room exists, and there isn't much, is pretty much filled up with a small student's desk, a cot, and a wastepaper basket. There's a stool. A clothes pole. In places I have to squeeze sideways to get passed the luxury of a folded-up folding chair. There's more extra space in a single occupant sleeping car on an Amtrak train. You could stretch out more comfortably inside the cell of a medieval monk. Maybe when I wasn't paying attention Stoicism became chic among Manhattan socialites. Maybe it's become fashionable for the super-rich to live like post-graduate Chaucer students or homeless crack whores. The only thing missing from this place that a total dump would have are the cockroaches and I'm suspecting they're only missing because there's no room for one to wriggle in here.

Ratking reads the surprise on my face. He explains, "Mr. Trump, he really likes to pack them in. I hear there are more spacious accommodations up above." He rubs his first two fingers against his thumb. "But they cost you. I think you have to be Pamela Lee Anderson. For my needs, this is quite sufficient."

Yeah, I'm thinking, if they could only slide this place out of the building when you die you wouldn't need to purchase a coffin: they could bury you in it. Maybe that's the idea. Maybe they just seal the room up when you croak. Maybe the whole place is really a giant mausoleum.

I hear a woman's voice coming from somewhere at the back of the apartment, but dammit if I can figure where she might be stashed in this shoe-box.

I say, "I'm not interrupting anything, am I?"

Ratking says, "No. That's just Veronika K."

I crook a questioning eyebrow.

"Cyber-mistress," Ratking says tersely. "The latest in virtual gynecology." Ratking presses the mute button on the remote he takes out of his pants pocket. "I'd introduce you, but I'm afraid she's a little indisposed at the moment. I'm still looking for a new custom skin for her. The one that came with her wouldn't accept tan-lines. Most disappointing."

We stand there regarding each other a moment. Neither one of us particularly likes what he sees. I see a guy about my height, my weight, my age. I see a guy who spends way too many hours of his life in front of a computer monitor. Speaking of which, that's all that's illuminating the place, about a dozen of them, softly glowing. There isn't a lamp or a window anywhere. And when you stop to think about it, why would there be?

Ratking elucidates: "I'm a techno-hermit. In ancient times, a man would have to sit in a cave and meditate for years to achieve a higher state of consciousness." He sweeps his hand to indicate the room full of flat screens, but he has to do it carefully or he'll knock something off a shelf. "This is my cave and these monitors are my thousand eyes of enlightenment. Through them, I can see into everything and everywhere."

Hmm, I'm thinking, *another megalomaniac.*

I clear my throat.

Ratking crushes out a cigarette, lights another. He mutters something.

"Huh?"

"Thirty-eight," he repeats.

"Huh?"

"The number of cigarettes I smoked today. I'm trying to quit."

"Doesn't sound like it's going too well."

"Death is inevitable," he says gloomily. "I'm only trying to throw a few speed-bumps in its way. Shall we get down to business?"

Bumping and grinding our way to the back of the apartment, we are passing more hardware, more monitors, more buttons, keys, and blinking lights than you'd expect to find on a state-of-the-art nuclear submarine. We squeeze passed something that looks like your standard desktop PC being anally raped by a two-headed toaster oven with mini-satellite dishes attached to the sides.

I point, "What the hell is that?"

Ratking eyes me suspiciously. "You wouldn't understand."

"Try me."

What follows is a bunch of techno gobbledygook that makes so little sense that I suspect he's just making fun of me. It sounds like he's reading a Microsoft user's manual backwards. He stops talking and I'm still staring at him like a pole-axed cow. He lights another cigarette. He disgustedly mutters, "Thirty-nine." Then he tries again. You see, for all his existential outlaw cool, Ratking is at heart a geek and, like all geeks, he's utterly incapable of not talking about his modified, souped-up hardware. Like all geeks with a captive audience, he can't help playing show-and-tell. So he's showing and telling, but this time he's doing it as if he were talking to a child, and not a very bright one at that. What I'm looking at, he explains, is a portable dial-up internet service that connects directly to the noosphere.

"And that's making it simple," Ratking says, drawing heavily on his cigarette. "That's idiot-talk."

"Huh?"

What I'm seeing, he explains further, is a broadband direct-link scanner that represents a node on the neural network of everyone's thoughts being communicated everywhere at once.

"And that's talking like a fool," Ratking says, smoking the life out of his thirty-ninth cigarette. If those cigarettes are killing him, he's returning the favor. "That's fairy-tale talk."

What this is, from what I can eventually gather, is a faster, better, more secure alternative to the internet and what the internet is only pretending to be in the meantime. What the internet is only pretending to be, this, apparently, is the real thing. This is the next BIG THING. This here is IT.

He explains that what he has is a machine that has direct instant access to the thoughts, dreams, fantasies of virtually anyone on the planet. It's like Google into the collective mind of Man. Once this thing's perfected, no one will be able to monitor or control information. No one will be able to stop communication. No one will have the power to monopolize and distort the truth. Everyone will be entitled to share their own reality. From that point on, you won't need dial-up or cable. You won't need radio waves. You won't need conversation. You'll be able to see and hear the thoughts right out of the thin air.

I say, "That's impossible."

He says, "Is it? Think about it. Why would it be impossible?"

And, really, now that he puts it that way, I don't know why it would be impossible, any more impossible than the internet itself, or traveling to the moon, or the light bulb, or a million other things just like that. It all seems fucking impossible when you really think about it. If the world ended tomorrow, for instance, I'd be hard-pressed to re-invent fire. If it were up to me, humanity would have to wait another eighty million years for the invention of the escalator.

"Ng told me about that virus you got. Nasty sounding. You got your machine?"

I hand it over.

"And those websites you want checked?"

I hand those over, too.

"Have a seat," he says, as if that's possible. "Make yourself at home. This make take a while."

"Where?" I look around. It would be like trying to sit down inside a motherboard.

But Ratking is already at the back of the place, which is to say, six feet away, running a diagnostic on my box, the plume of a fortieth cigarette rising above his head like the smoldering ruins of a sacked city.

I've fallen asleep against a stack of empty Gateway boxes when I sense someone hovering over me in a cloud of smoke. In my disoriented state, I have a vague fear that it's God, and for some reason he's burning. I sit up with a start and focus my eyes. Ratking is standing over me smoking a cigarette.

He says, "Well, I ran that list of sites you sent me and checked that photo against whatever's online: driver's license photos, corporate IDs, old high school yearbooks, etc. The names are written here." He hands me a book of matches.

"Names?" I say, climbing to my feet to look at the matchbook.

"Yeah. They aren't the same person. They are two different persons. Completely unconnected, from what I can gather."

"Nada Klone is *two* people?"

"Yup. A man and a woman."

"I didn't expect that."

Ratking stubs out his cigarette. "Is that a problem?"

"Well, I was kind of hoping it wouldn't be too complicated. How is that possible?"

He shrugs.

I put the matchbook in my pocket. What about my machine?"

He stubs out another smoke. "That I'll need to hold onto for the time being. Its very very sick."

"How sick?"

"Terminal."

"Then there's no hope then?"

"I didn't say that. But it's going to require some radical experimental treatment."

"What will that cost me?"

"I'll let you know."

"I'm not sure I like the sound of that. When is the bill due?"

"I'll let you know that, too. Don't worry."

I don't like the sound of that either.

He lights up a fresh coffin nail. "Sixty-three," he mutters.

Well, I'm thinking, watching him suck on that cigarette like a baby at the tit, maybe the Grim Reaper will pay him a visit before he gets around to collecting from me. I mean, why shouldn't mortality work in our favor once in a while?

"Okay," I say. "Thanks again. I'll show myself out."

And I do. Practically all I have to do is turn around.

10. Dirty talk, missing people, and birds of ill omen

The world has turned to egg shell, that's what life is like for me now. I'm afraid to make a move for fear that everything will shatter into a thousand pieces at any moment. I'm afraid to attract attention. Even worse, I'm afraid that, in spite of all my precautions, something awful is about to break in from the *outside*. It's like there's a big, shabby, egg-eating bird of ill omen sitting right outside my life waiting to peck its way in.

I'm trying to be Mr. Anonymous. But I'm already under surveillance. The signs are all there, they always are, if you look closely enough. The universe is on to me. I'm trespassing here and everyone seems to know it.

Cars are following me when I walk down the street, phones ring with no one on the other end, my ATM card stops working for no apparent reason, and then, for equally no apparent reason, starts working again as if nothing happened. Eyes watch me that extra beat on the subway, in stores, taking a short-cut through the park.

I don't dare say much to anyone for fear of making some awful gaffe, of committing a fatal slip of the tongue.

I'm trying to go unnoticed and yet I seem to be about as conspicuous as a goat anywhere a goat is especially not supposed to be. I don't tell anyone about this because if I don't tell anyone than none of this may really have happened: this is the kind of thinking I'm doing.

Call it magical thinking, call it delusional, call it incipient psychosis. I'm trying to be a practicing autistic. I'm trying to make my own reality and then live inside it.

I'm putting off the inevitable, sure . But we're all doing that anyway, if you really think about it.

It's coming: the cancer, the heart attack, the head-on collision. It's coming: the pneumonia, the renal shutdown, the carbon monoxide leak. There's a bullet flying in the air somewhere and it's got your name written all over it. Every year you pass the date they'll one day be chiseling on your tombstone. Let's face it. We're all not facing up to something or other.

Life, when you come right down to it, is nothing but putting off death.

There's a hush on the other side of my apartment door, the hush of those pretending not to be there. I don't open the door to make things easier for all of us. I don't want to unnecessarily embarrass anyone. I don't want to force anyone's hand. When I finally have to go out, they make it easier by pretending to be gone. But all of this is only for the time being.

It's all temporary.

What isn't?

Some guy named Buddha said something like this once, didn't he? He was considered a holy man, a real wise guy. Basically, I'm saying the same thing. But me, I'm just a bewildered asshole.

I've got that matchbook out that Ratking gave me with the identity of the real-life Nada Klone. I've got it out but I haven't opened it yet. Instead of opening it, I'm pushing it around on my desk with the tip of my finger. I pick it up, open it, and I strike one of the matches. I watch it burn down. I light the rest of the matches one by one, drop them onto a plate of stale crumbs, and watch them burn down, too. I accidentally set off the smoke alarm. Finally, unable to do anything else with the matchbook, I look at the names of the two Nada Klones written inside. The names, the addresses, the phone numbers, the email addys, the social security numbers. Ratking has very small handwriting.

I wonder how Mr. Knott will take it, Mr. Franklin, too, provided I tell them, when they learn that one-half of Nada Klone, the "brains" of the operation, so to speak, the one doing all the dirty talk, is some guy who lives across the river in Hoboken named Todd Sprocket.

As for me, well, I guess I should be relieved that the-love-of-my-life isn't the world's greatest cyber slut after all. That should give me a sense of relief, but somehow it doesn't. That the face of Nada Klone is the sister I didn't know Johnny Nomad had was only half of it, and not even the most troubling half. The other half has to do with *her* other half, namely her husband.

That a woman as beautiful as her would be already taken, I took for granted, but being my pre-destined soul mate since the beginning of time, I figured she could be re-taken by me. It was destiny, it was fate, it was a TV-movie-of-the-week in the making. But this is reality and reality has no happy ending. It was worse than I feared and I thought I had already feared the worst: the-love-of-my-life was a dentist's wife from Vail, Colorado. Just my luck. I never had a chance in hell. Do you have any idea what a dentist pulls down, per capita?

It'll all probably be for nothing, but it's time to visit Johnny Nomad, time to make him answer some hard, unpleasant, probably self-incriminating questions about exactly what he knows about all this that he hasn't told me. So I take the subway to where he lives in the Bronx, breaking the unspoken law of a virtual friendship such as ours, which is to say, I'm paying him an unannounced personal visit. I'm imposing my meat on his meat, as it were. I'm not imagining he's going to be very happy to see me and it's the reasons why that I'm interested in finding out. The way I figure it, if I drop him an e-mail or ring his cell, he's going to bolt, pretend he's off-line, be generally unavailable for comment. I'll get error messages, fatal flaw warnings, automated out-of-office replies.

The last thing I expect is that his whole building will be gone.

I've been to Johnny Nomad's a half-dozen or so times before; I've gotten drunk at his kitchen table, watched his TV, crapped in his crapper. The point is, I know where he lives. And right between this tall thin building made of bricks the color of poisoned blood and the tan one right beside it with its ground floor wrought iron railing and window boxes filled with dead geraniums, that's where Johnny Nomad's building is supposed to be.

Instead, there's just a thin strip of darkness that isn't even wide enough to call an alley. Instead there's a hairy-shouldered, heavy-set man on the stoop of the poisoned blood building next door. He's cutting the tip off a cheap El Producto cigar with a box cutter. He's wearing a wife-beater t-shirt and wide yellow suspenders and a pair of cargo shorts that show off two of the most horribly scarred knees I've ever seen. He's not looking at me in that way people have of not looking at you when they're been watching every move you're making.

He says, "Can I help you pal?"

It's not an invitation to help, not really; it's a last chance to get the hell out of the neighborhood in one piece if I don't have any legitimate business here, that's what it really is. He's protecting his stoop the way a guy within earshot of three or four buddies with aluminum baseball bats protects a stoop.

I ask him about the building, about Johnny Nomad's building, the building that isn't there.

He looks at me funny, like enough is enough, but I'm describing this non-existent building in such detail, with such conviction, I win him over long enough that he figures out what it is I'm looking for. He points with the box cutter to a square brown building with white cornices and a tall brick porch that looks like the prow of a sinking ship. It's across the street, about forty yards away from where it's supposed to be.

He says, "Is that the property you're talking about?"

"That's it," I say.

I know what he's thinking because I'm thinking it, too. That building looks nothing like the building I just described, not really, but that's the building where Johnny lives, I'm sure of it.

Until, that is, I cross the street and ring the bell and the landlord comes out. He's a short man with a goatee, probably Indian, who moves very slowly and smiles a lot, but not in a friendly way. I've never seen him before in my life but I know he's the landlord even before he smiles in that not-friendly way and sing-songs, "I'm the landlord. I can help you?"

I explain that I'm looking for Johnny Nomad, but I do it without mentioning Johnny by name, his real name, which I don't know anyway, and that leads to inevitable confusion.

I try to simplify matters. "I'm looking for the man in 3C."

He says, "I am the man in 3C."

I say, "There must be some mistake."

He says, "Oh no, no mistake."

He's all too eager to show me up the stairs, passed the old cat on the second landing, the big cheesy holes in the walls, the barred window with the view of a brick wall. He leads me passed the ceramic pot of dead roots, the sounds of *The Price is Right* behind a closed door, someone's unpicked-up copy of the *Post*.

He leads me down the hall to 3C, where he opens the chipped green door, and there is a kid in Spongebob underwear playing a video game with his little sister. There's a woman in a sari and dot wiping her hands on a checkered towel. There is the smell of lentils or dahl or something coming from the kitchen.

It's Johnny's apartment alright, I can still see the thousands of burn-marks they didn't have time to sand away from the thousands of joints he dropped on the floor where his computer desk used to be.

The man beside me smiles that not-friendly smile.

He says, "See, we are all very happy here."

Everything seems sort of okay for the next day or two. I buy some new pants at Old Navy. I see what I'd look like with my hair parted on the other side. I wash my pillowcases. This is the kind of everyday nonsense you have to put yourself through to get on with your life. These are the kinds of daily inanities that even when you're wanted for murder and the victim of a vast inexplicable conspiracy you still have to tend to. These are exactly the kind of things that most people omit in accounts such as this, but let me tell you, they go right on happening.

You'd think the need to buy stamps and to make a half dozen calls to straighten out your phone bill would be suspended when you were in the middle of being set up for a capital offense, but you'd be thinking wrong. You'd think trimming your toenails and soaking your bonsai would be two less things to worry about when friends went missing, along with the buildings they used to live in, but I'm telling you, *fat chance.*

All the stupid minutae of life goes on just the same as it always did, whether you're doing the nine to five thing, or dodging assassin's bullets.

Life is really mostly nothing but an unending avalanche of stupid minutae.

Two a.m. comes all the same no matter what you've got going on in your life and you'd better have something in the place to wipe your ass if you wake up needing to use the toilet. This I know for a fact.

Anyway, the Yankees win a weekend series against the A's, drop a Monday afternoon make-up game with the Twins, take a day off and then win two of three against the Indians. The Mets are on a seven game slide. When I tally it all up, I clear just over nine hundred dollars.

To celebrate, I put on my new pants. They are these khaki drawstring cargo kind of pants everyone seems to be wearing nowadays. These pants make it look as if we're all on a trek to discover a new continent. They have lots of pockets, flaps, buttons, zippers. These pants make it look as if we're all living in an occupied city, as if we're all part of some kind of urban military expedition. I wonder, maybe we are.

With these pants on, I head to the East Village.

Only one disconcerting thing happens during these two relatively idyllic days and this is the time it happens. I'm trying to work out my bets for the upcoming week but it seems that somehow the schedule I've been using all summer is suddenly all wrong. I have the Yankees playing in Detroit when they're in Boston, Seattle when they're in Texas, Anaheim when they aren't playing at all.

What the hell, I'm thinking, maybe the schedule I'm using is misprinted.

Standing at a Papaya King counter having a hot dog, I'm puzzling this out, comparing my schedule with some guy named Al, or Sal, or Hey Pal. Whatever his name, he's been scratching his sunburnt bald head trying to figure out what the hell I've been talking about for the last five minutes. He takes a look at my Yankee schedule, hands it back, looks at me a bit crooked.

I say, "Is the schedule wrong, or what?"

He says, "The schedule is fine. It's you that's screwed up."

"What the hell is that supposed to mean?"

"It means, you're looking at the third week in July."

I'm about to say something like, "Duh, where else would I be looking during the third week in July."

But before I can crack wise he shuts me up by saying, "Dude, we're in the second week of September." He looks me up and down. Then he says, "Cool pants."

11. Starbucks, blind dates, and big white lies...

Sipping a cappuccino something-or-other at the Starbucks on Park and 29th, I'm waiting for the aforementioned Mr. Sprocket to make his belated appearance. The way I'm reading time: he's already twenty-three minutes late. I start wondering if he's had a sudden change of heart, if he's had an attack of common sense. More than likely, I figure, he just wasn't as horny as he'd been at three a.m. the night before.

As it turns out, it's none of those things. He's actually here, but I don't see him and that may be because I'm looking for the wrong guy. What I mean is that the guy I'm looking for is tall and Sprocket is short; the guy I'm looking for has dark hair combed straight back Miami Vice-style and Sprocket has a dry mousy-brown flap-over like a dead Christmas grave blanket. The guy I'm looking for is fit, successful, tanned, dynamically outgoing, just like you'd expect a Wall Street mover and shaker to be. Sprocket is pot-bellied, disheveled, pallid, and every bit as shy and introverted as the forty-five-year-old Toys-R-Us stockroom clerk he actually turns out to be.

What I'm saying is that Sprocket was seriously misrepresenting how he really looked in the sex chat room where I tracked him down last night. He was "gilding the lily," as they say. He was softening the focus on how he looked, what he did, who he was. I guess you could say he was putting a positive spin on it all. But what you really ought to say is that he was lying through his teeth.

But there was another way to look at it, too.

You could also say that Sprocket was being truthful to his inner self. You could say that he was presenting himself as he really felt himself to be, as he might have been if fate hadn't trapped him inside the unattractive, decaying, middle-aged body of a total loser. The fiction he'd invented was who he'd be if he didn't have a crappy job, a crappy car, a crappy apartment, a crappy life. If reality hadn't gotten in the way, Sprocket would have been the cool, aggressive, slicked-back sexy romeo he was last night when he had me on my knees in that virtual gas station toilet. I'd had to move the romance along quickly because I was using a Wi-Fi connection at a crowded Barnes & Noble—and because I knew that I'd only get ten or fifteen minutes online at most before the rented machine I was using crashed.

I look at Sprocket again, probably the way no one else has ever taken the time to look at him before. Somewhere deep inside this bald, colorless, nervous little man was the seductive Don Juan I'd met the night before. More importantly, somewhere in there, too, was one-half of Nada Klone. This was the true magic of the internet. You could be not just whoever you wanted to be, but whoever you felt yourself to *really* be. No longer did you have to be trapped by the prison of your meat and bones. And who—if you really stop to think about it—was the real Sprocket anyway? Was it this unfortunate lump of flesh and teeth and hair sitting before me now—or the X-rated cast of sirens, femme-fatales, and lady-killers in his imagination whose escapades he acted out every night on the computer? The answer to these questions were all a bit more complicated than what might appear at first glance. And that's about all I have time for them at the moment because Sprocket, whoever the hell he really is, looks to me about to bolt.

As it is, I finally recognize him only because he's been darting urgent glances at every woman who walks in the door. He gives himself away by how he keeps looking at his Timex and carefully wiping his sweaty bald forehead with a napkin. He looks exactly like a man who's got a lot of explaining to do to a woman who'll be expecting him too look completely different than he does.

I'm not far from his table when Sprocket recognizes me as well. Maybe "recognizes" is the wrong word. I guess he can sense by the purposeful way I'm striding towards him that I am who he thinks I am: the guy he was having cybersex with until the crack of dawn.

His first reaction is understandable: he looks slightly sick. His second reaction is even more understandable: he looks like he wants to run for his life. But, to his credit, he realizes that would be awkward, rude, and probably impossible with me standing between his table and the exit. So he does the only sensible thing anyone can do under the circumstances. He cringes. He grimaces apologetically. He says, "Well you weren't exactly what I was expecting."

I'm thinking, *Well who the hell is?*

Still, I can see his point.

I'm supposed to be petite and I'm a rangy six-one. I'm supposed to be soft-spoken and submissive and I'm an obnoxious blabbermouth. I'm supposed to bear a striking resemblance to figure-skater Michelle Kwan and, well, the reality is, I just don't. The list of things that I'm supposed to be and the exact opposite things that I am goes on and on and on, but, perhaps, the one that's probably the hardest to get around is that Mr. Sprocket here was expecting me to be the girl of his dreams.

I scrape out the chair across from his, turn it backwards, and straddle it like a horse. I'm obviously overcompensating. But after the sexual shenanigans I indulged in with this guy last night, I could be the Terminator and it wouldn't be compensation enough. Awkward doesn't begin to describe how I'm feeling at this moment. Mortified does, but that's only a start. By now the foam has entirely melted off my cappuccino something-or-other and its cold, but I blow on it anyway.

"Yeah," I say, as tersely as you can say it. "Sorry. Disappointed?"

Sprocket shrugs philosophically. "Not really. I pretty much thought it would be something like this. You seemed too good to be true."

"I'm even worse than I look," I say, playing up the hard-guy role.

Sprocket glances down at his bottle of Tazo iced tea and I see the freckles on his bald pate. When he looks back up he says, "Still, you were pretty damn sexy."

I say, "Thanks. But don't get carried away."

Sprocket blushes. "I didn't mean…"

"Whatever," I say, somewhat unnerved. Still, I'm curious. "When you go to meet them, what do the women usually say when they see it's you instead of, you know, the guy you pretend to be?"

If Sprocket takes offense, he doesn't show it. He says, "I don't usually do this believe it or not. No, no," he hastily adds when he sees me roll my eyes. "I really don't. No fooling. This is rare for me. You really were good. I mean, *really good*. After all, I should know."

He's got a kind of smug look on his pasty face like he's proud or something.

"Listen bub," I say, "don't try to lube me up. I'm here for one reason and one reason only. And that's to talk about Nada Klone."

The double-take he does is almost classic—comic, too. So is his knee-jerk reply: "Who?"

"Don't mess with me, Mr. Sprocket."

Using his real name like that gets his attention lickety split, that snaps him right into sharp focus. He's sitting straight up now, ears pricked, and I'll give odds that the hairs at the back of his neck are bristling, too. Yup, I'd bet he'd tell you that if he were telling this story. I proceed to recite his address, his telephone number, his social security number, his license plate number, his bank account number, his lucky number. I'd tell him his cable TV account number, too, if even he would have recognized it. As it is, it would just be wasted on him. I tell him his mother's maiden name instead. Ratking really is frighteningly good at what he does.

He holds up his pudgy little hands. He says, "Okay okay. You've made your point. What are you, an identity thief?"

"No," I say, "But I could be. What I am is a guy whose doing a job he doesn't want to do. I'm a guy who's supposed to be finding you."

He says, "I kept my promise."

"What promise?"

"You know."

I suspect he's trying to addle me, and, frankly, that wouldn't be hard. I give him the stink-eye. I bluff and say, "Yeah, well there's some question if you really understood what we told you to do. Why don't you tell me? Let's see if you got it right."

He says, "I stopped being her."

"You stopped being who?"

"Nada. Nada Klone."

I say, "Well, that seems to be the problem."

Now he's giving me the stink-eye. He says, "What problem are you talking about? I thought the problem was to make her disappear. I thought that's what you people wanted. I thought you were with that guy."

We're both giving each other the stink-eye now. It's a stalemate of stink-eyes, a stink-eye stare-down, but he's going to break. I can sense it. The worry-lines carved into his forehead are collapsing.

"Listen mister," he says, "I don't want any trouble."

"I'm not who you think I am. By the way, who do you think I am?"

He looks like he's thinking over just what to tell me, how far he can trust me, how much he should fear me. After he completes these calculations, he says, "About two months ago, I got contacted by this guy who knew all kinds of real-life personal information about me. Just like you do. I figured maybe he was the webmaster of one of the sites where I appeared as Nada. Maybe he was able to trace my emails back to my IPS. Or followed a credit card trail. You never know. Maybe he hacked into my hard drive. Stuff like that happens no matter how careful you are. He had me meet him at the Metropolitan Museum of Art. At the Temple of Dendur. You know it?"

"Yeah," I say, "the fake Egyptian thing."

"Yeah...the fake Egyptian thing," Sprocket says. "I mean, I guess it's fake. Well, anyway, this guy meets me there. Good-looking, well-dressed, looks like....well, he looks exactly like the guy I pretended to look like last night with you. I figure a guy like that gets a lot of chicks, you know?" Sprocket grins sheepishly. "Anyway, he tells me to knock it off. No more Nada Klone. And he threatens to expose me if I didn't listen. It would be, you know, pretty embarrassing if people knew what I was up to on the computer at night. They might not be so understanding. There could be repercussions. I mean, it would be enough to kill my mother alone…"

"Did he say why he didn't want you to be Nada Klone anymore?"

"He said it was none of my business. I told him I hadn't done anything illegal. I mean, I made her up, right? Why shouldn't I be her? Nada didn't appear on any underage sex sites or anything like that. Nada was always about consensual sex. He said it didn't matter what I did or didn't do. He said it was part of an ongoing criminal investigation. He claimed to be some kind of internet cop."

"I don't suppose this guy had a name, did he?"

I'm saying this partly as a private joke with myself. I hardly expect a straight answer.

Sprocket says, "As a matter of fact, he did give me his name. He called himself Chambers."

"Chambers?"

"Yeah, Chambers. Do you know him?"

I repeat the name a few times to myself, listening for whether it rang any bells. I wish I could say my head was ringing like Nortre Dame on Sunday morning. But it wasn't: it was dead-silent.

"No," I say. "Never heard of him. What did he mean that he was an internet cop? Did he show you any identification? Was he NYPD or FBI? Homeland Security? CIA?"

Sprocket shakes his head. "No, he didn't show me anything. But, then again, he was threatening me, you know? Blackmailing me, essentially. So maybe he didn't think it was necessary. Listen, there is one other thing."

There's always "one other thing." I say, "Uhh-huh?"

Sprocket says, "This morning, before I left to meet you here, I started up my desktop and it was infected. A virus like you've never seen. Within fifteen minutes, my hard drive was shredded to ribbons. Nothing but gibberish. Complete meltdown."

"Bummer," I say, thinking of my own wrecked machine. "It happens. You have to be more careful."

"You don't understand. This is the *fifth* time it's happened. With five different computers."

"Maybe you're re-infecting it with an infected program, or visiting an infected site, or..." Sprocket is emphatically shaking his head "no" as I run through the standard list of possibilities. "Wait a minute, do you think maybe this Chambers guy was trying to trace this virus?"

"I think he was looking for Nada because..." Sprocket looks almost ashamed of what he's about to say. He says it anyway. "I know it sounds crazy. But I don't think I'm getting the virus from the internet. I think *I'm* infected."

"You're just paranoid," I say, but I'm feeling the flesh crawling around on my forearms. I'm thinking of that glitch and shut-down on the computer I was using at the Internet Café downtown, the freeze-up on the machine I used at the library, the two loaners I got from Jimmy Ng that locked me out with fatal error messages until, suspicious, he refused to loan me any more machines. Each and every computer I've used lately has ended up crashing with that same bizarre sign burned into the screen.

"Paranoid?" Sprocket cries, "Is it just paranoia when I've already been threatened by one guy and you're telling me you're working for another guy who wants to find me?"

"Two actually," I say, thinking aloud. "Two guys want to find you."

"Two?!" Sprocket looks worried like that gazelle with the limp they film on those nature shows that gets separated from the pack when the tigers leap out of the tall grasses. "What do they want?"

I say, "Well, I won't lie to you. One claims he's working for a guy who's in love with you. The other one," and I think of the ominous Mr. Franklin and try to put this in the most non-alarming way possible. The best I can come up with is this: "The other one is a lot more…ummm…ambiguous."

Sprocket says, "I don't like the sound of that."

I say, "To tell you the truth, if it were me, I wouldn't like the sound of it either."

"So what now?" He looks at me with big watery helpless-woodland-creature eyes, as if he were depending on me, or something. As if I had any real answers. For the first time in his life he's learning what every well-endowed thirteen-year-old girl knows: how creepy and potentially dangerous it is to be an object of desire.

If I were being honest, I'd tell Sprocket to get out of town, to go anywhere, to make himself a lot harder to find. But I've got Johnny Nomad to think about. I need to keep tabs on Sprocket. I need to know where I can find him if I need to hand him over. Mr. Knott has apparently gotten impatient and decided to prove his point by snatching J.N., or frightening him into hiding; that's my current theory. I figure it couldn't hurt to have a powwow with the fat man, smoke out his intentions. It seems absolutely preposterous to think so, but maybe they're honorable. I can't help it. I find myself laughing.

Sprocket says, "What's so funny?"

I say, "You really don't want to know." Then I say, "Let me talk to the guy who thinks he's in love with you first. Maybe he'll listen to reason. In the meantime, lay low, stay off-line."

Sprocket promises to do what I ask, but I know he's lying. We say goodbye. I walk up Park Avenue, wondering if I've managed to find out anything substantive. I'm not sure. I sort of doubt it.

Later, trying to sort this all out, I'm sitting in Wong's Noodle Shop down on Mott or Baxter, one of those narrow hectic Chinatown streets that all look exactly alike, each of them crammed with sidewalk shops selling the same paper lanterns, battery-operated frogs, roasted chickens, and fake Swiss Army watches. I'm eating one of the dinner specials at Wong's: beef and broccoli with all the fixings for $3.75. I'm checking the Yankee boxscore, jotting down averages, e.r.a.'s, fielding percentages, working out my betting strategy for the upcoming Baltimore series.

Looking up for a moment, I carry a few numbers in my head, and try to decide whether Mussina has anything left over this late in the season when I literally drop the grey piece of mystery meat I'm holding with my chopsticks. There, at the bottom of someone else's paper—some guy in a business suit eating pork lo mein at the next table save one—is the headline: **Suspect Sought in Missing Woman Case; Police Sift Computer Clues.**

But that's not what has me thinking, *Flight to Guatemala, pronto.*

Women are always going missing somewhere or other. People vanish into thin air every day. Dead bodies are turning up all the time. Police are always sifting through clues.

No, that's not what has me thinking, *Nembutals and plastic bag.*

What's got me thinking radical plastic surgery is the composite police artist sketch that's printed next to the article. It's the face in that sketch that I'm looking at that's looking directly back at me that has me completely spooked. The face in that picture, I'm thinking, *that looks an awful lot like me.*

I lay my trembling chopsticks down on my plate, nearly knocking over a bottle of low-sodium soy sauce, and pretend to take a sip of my tea, except I can't raise the cup more than two inches from the table without the tea inside sloshing all over my wrist since my hand is shaking so badly.

I'm trying to make out the name of the paper the businessman is reading because I checked the local papers this morning, as usual, and hadn't turned up a word about Trina T's murder. I had just been thinking how good I was beginning to feel, because, after all, it had been nearly two weeks since the incident at the beach, and I hadn't so much as been called in for an interrogatory beating, or given my first blackmail demand.

I'm trying to make out the name of the newspaper the businessman is reading without being too obvious about it, but that's not easy, not the way I'm forced to screw my face all up and peel my eyeballs. For crissakes, I must look like Quasimodo. Even so, from this distance, I still can't read the tiny print below the header of the page from which my possible face stares back at me.

Getting up to pretend to use the restroom, I pass the businessman's table, which happens to be in the opposite direction of the men's room. I pause halfway to the kitchen, make as if I've forgotten something, and walk back towards the restroom. I don't catch the name of the paper on the first pass, so I repeat the whole ludicrous exercise two more times. I've passed the guy's table more times in the last thirty seconds than the waiter has all evening and I decide I'd better sit back down before someone asks me to bring them a pu-pu platter.

I sit back down and wait for *him* to leave, figuring he'll leave the paper behind. But it's not going to be as easy as that.

Bastard, he's taking forever to finish that plate of pork lo mein. It's like he's eating it one goddamn noodle at a time. I nearly leap out of my seat to strangle him when he orders another pot of tea.

Sitting there, conspicuously doing nothing as I am, I'm forced to match him with a second pot of tea, also.

But he's drinking his, I'm just faking.

His bladder, as a result, gives in first. Off to the men's room, he leaves his newspaper behind. I realize just how lucky I am: if he'd had to take a dump he might have brought the damn paper in with him to do the word search. As he passes, I pretend to be examining the slip of paper I extracted from my fortune cookie twenty minutes ago. The slip of paper advises, *A wiseman listens more than he speaks.* I feel cheated. What kind of fortune is that? Was Confucius on vacation that day?

The businessman safely in the crapper, the waiter in the kitchen, the only other patrons, four drunken college kids, and an old man who looks like a homeless kung fu master otherwise occupied with his dumplings, I shove out from behind my table, grab the paper from the businessman's table, and head for the door.

Five minutes later, sitting at the counter of a Chinese bakery across the street, pretending to be eating a red bean curd bun, I don't know what to make of the banner at the top of the newspaper I'm looking at: if that's really me, then I have no idea how to explain what my picture is doing in the fucking *Denver Post*.

Among other things that don't make any sense, the *Denver Post* says this: the missing woman lives in Fort Collins, Colorado. She is the wife of a local dentist and community leader named, of all things, Dr. H. "Pop" Madsen. She is thirty-eight years old and belongs to the Ladies Auxillary. Her name is Norma Blake Madsen, which I already know from the info that Ratking gave me is the married name of Johnny Nomad's sister. The tiny inset photo where the story is continued on page nine looks a few years old. She's younger there, the hairstyle and make-up is all wrong, but I'd recognize that face anywhere even if she hadn't been named in the article—it's the face in the photo that Mr. Franklin sent me, the face of the-love-of-my-life.

    The article says that Norma has been missing for a couple of weeks, but that her husband just recently reported it to the police, hoping she'd come back on her own, not wanting to raise a fuss, not wanting to embarrass anyone. I'm wondering if Dr. H. "Pop" Madsen is the name of the certain man who was not supposed to be named, who would be nameless, who both Mr. Franklin and Mr. Knott went so far out of their way to refuse to name. And if so, why was it so big a secret since this guy is named right here in a newspaper with a circulation of, what, a few hundred thousand?

    I'm sitting there, staring out the window of the Chinese bakery, not even seeing whatever it is I'm looking at, when someone comes up behind me, and says, "Do you know the secret world?"

    I look up, and God only knows what expression I have on my face, but the waitress is trained to smile at anything. Her pretty face is tilted inquisitively to one side, and I notice, of all things, that she has really bad teeth, really bad, as if two or three of them right there in the front are almost totally rotten. She is holding a pair of clear plastic tongs which are poised, but holding nothing.

    She says it again, "Do you know the secret world?"

I'm thinking, *Jesus, this is weird. This is really weird, and it's really getting weirder by the second.*

But it all turns out to be a lot less weird than I thought, because what the waitress really seems to be saying refers to the bun I've just finished and now what she's saying sounds more like "Do you want more red bean curd?"

And then I wonder: that guy in Wong's Noodle Shop that I stole this paper from--was he an undercover detective? Is this newspaper a clue or a piece of incriminating evidence? Was that guy in the restaurant Dr. H. "Pop" Madsen himself? Is that even possible?

I hurry back to the restaurant but I'm not surprised to find the guy is gone. The waiter is gathering the dishes off the table where the man was sitting. He says, "You rook for man?"

I say, "Yes, did he leave already?"

He nods. He says, "He reeve fortune for you."

I look at the tiny strip of paper he hands me. Usually these things beat around the bush, talk in riddles, play it safe, but this one gets straight to the point. On the back of his fortune, in small, painstakingly neat calligraphy, the man has written: "Hop to it Mr. Molloy. Or you're dead."

Now that, I'm thinking, *is a fortune.*

12. Plastic cunts, twins, and performance anxiety...

Ten minutes ago I'm in bed with Meeah Soo and nothing is
happening. She's doing everything a girl like Meeah Soo can do, and
that's saying something, because a girl like Meeah Soo is almost ten
times more girl than any real girl you'll ever meet. She has to be, not
being a girl at all. Still, no matter what she does, it's not enough. She
looks up at me, panting lightly, her little puffy hormone titties
hanging down, dressed in nothing but a thong bikini, a fetish bustier,
and strappy stiletto sandals.

She says, "What's the matter, baby, you're not hard at all."

These words, in Meeah Soo's mouth, are tough to hear. These
words are tough to hear considering that her own chemically
shrunken little package is stiffer than mine. I can see her little bulge
inside the sheer pink triangle of her Paris Hilton-style-peek-a-boo
panties.

She says, "Is something bothering you?"

Alarmed, she touches her face.

"What is it? What's the matter? Do I need more beard
concealer?"

These are the kinds of things you go through when you're in a
relationship with a girl like Meeah Soo. I give her a kiss on her big
plastic sissy lips and pat her silicon enhanced ass. That ass, I'm
thinking, it cost a couple of thousand dollars. To be a girl like Meeah

Soo requires a real commitment. She's a girl with a vengeance. A guy has to respect a girl like that.

I slide out of bed.

I say, "It's not you. I've just got a lot on my mind."

I'm trying to reassure her, but I'm not feeling too sure about anything right now myself.

Ten minutes later, I'm sitting at the kitchen table. I'm staring at what's on my mind. To Meeah Soo, it looks like I'm just reading the paper, but what I'm doing is watching my life implode with the irresistible force of a black hole. What I'm doing is watching me become the target of a nationwide manhunt. I'm watching myself be set up for kidnapping and multiple murder.

Meeah Soo is still lying on the futon, pouting, flipping violently through a catalogue containing pictures of vaginas she can have made for herself. These catalogues actually exist: they have them for almost every part of the body, every part they've figured out how to make out of plastic, or extra fat harvested from wherever you have extra fat. She's slipped into a sheer pink peignoir because she still hasn't given up hope, and, looking at her walking towards me, I'm thinking, *It's too bad they can't make her new shoulders. It's too bad they can't make her new feet.*

I feel guilty thinking that.

I feel guilty all the time.

I feel guilty about everything.

So it almost makes sense that I feel guilty about a kidnapping and a murder I didn't commit.

I'm morbidly fascinated by this composite photo that may or may not be me. I'm wondering why two perfectly innocent women, well, a woman and a half, have been targeted for murder ostensibly to find Nada Klone, who doesn't really exist at all. Meanwhile, Meeah Soo is pouting, but she won't be pouting for long. That's one of the advantages of being with a girl like Meeah Soo. She won't deny you sex, nag you that you never take her to the movies, or complain about your friends. She won't carry on about your haircut, bring up something you said four years ago, or argue with you about who's turn it is to unload the dishwasher. It might sound mean, but the advantage of being with a girl like Meeah Soo is her massive insecurity. A girl like Meeah Soo knows she has to be better than any real girl. A girl like Meeah Soo simply doesn't have an option.

Meeah Soo bounces up from the futon with her vagina catalogues and comes sashaying over to where I'm still sitting hunched over the newspaper at the little kitchen table. She's got a catalogue of vaginas open and she's pointing out her favorites as if she were picking out a Honda. She wants to know if she should get the penile inversion or the more invasive and expense colon graft vaginoplasty.

"It says here they can take an eighteen to twenty centimeter section of my colon and transplant it into my neo vagina. It says I'll be able to self lubricate." She looks at me a little regretfully. "It says I'll be able to take up to eight inches.

She's slid the book under my chin, laid it right over the newspaper, and I'm looking at about a dozen or so graphic pictures of vaginas in various stages of construction. There are a variety of styles, too. This one has extra thick labia, that one exhibits a new kind of clitoral hood. Here is one using the original scrotal sack.

Meeah says, "I want you to like my new pussy." She adds, "After all, it'll be your pussy, too."

She says this flirtaciously in the seven-hundred-dollar voice she acquired with her latest trachea shaving.

"I'm sorry sweetheart, but I really can't look at all these vaginas right now. I have some problems of my own."

From between her eight-hundred-dollar lips, Meeah sticks out her undoctored, one-hundred-percent original and all-natural tongue. I show her the composite photograph. I ask her if it looks like anyone familiar. She knits her plucked and penciled eyebrows. She sucks her newly manicured forefinger. She's thinking.

I get to the point. I point to the newspaper. I say, "Does this look like me?"

Meeah makes her eyes go from the photo to my face, my face to the photo. She wrinkles a forehead it will cost three hundred dollars to grind down.

She says, "Well, your chin recedes much more." She looks at me appraisingly. "Your hair isn't as thick in the front." She sucks on her finger again. She says, "Your eyes are a lot more, oh what's the word, oogly-googly. Your eyebrows…"

I say, "Okay, okay, that's enough."

That this may be a picture of me, it's still a distinct possibility, but if it is, the news is even worse than I thought: the ugly mug shot is apparently a *flattering* picture of me.

Meeah Soo shrugs. She's studying her sunken belly. She says, "What are they saying you did, anyhow?"

"Murder a girl," I say.

"Hmmm," Meeah says. She stretches the already taut flesh of her stomach a scant half-millimeter. "Do I need a tummy tuck, do you think? They cost like three thousand dollars." She pinches shut her navel between two long scarlet fingernails. She contemplates it a while and then she looks back up and says, "You don't suppose they can turn an outie into an innie, do you?

I've spent so much time puzzling throughout my life how I was ever going to find the love-of-my-life that it never occurred to me that she would find me. Dammit, listen to me talk. I sound almost like a poet, like Neruda or Rumi or someone like that. Fact is, crap like this only happens in poetry, it doesn't happen in real life, and it especially doesn't happen to me, not exactly. I've been found, alright, but it isn't by the love-of-my-life, it only looks like her, it's her spitting image, in fact: its her perfect double.

But I figure, what the hell.

I figure, that's closer than most people get.

I figure, that's close enough.

Let me explain.

I'm smoking a morning cigarette (yes, I'm apparently smoking now; but just one or two, just to concentrate, I swear) on a park bench in Park Slope jotting down notes in a spiral notebook I bought at a twenty-four-hour Duane Reade about three hours ago. I'm hoping to get some kind of handle on this unhandleable case. Actually, I'd given up trying to get a handle on it, at least for this morning, and I'm simply staring blankly at the dirt between my shoes, smoking, watching ashes softly drop, when I hear a voice say, "It's *you*."

My first reaction is to immediately say, *"No it isn't. You've made a mistake."* I look up, get ready to say this, but the words stick in my throat. Instead I say, "It's you."

She says, "No it isn't. You've made a mistake."

I say, "The hell I have."

She says, "Who do you think I am?"

Her hair is all different, her eyes are hidden behind dark glasses, and that smile like a thousand suns all lighting up the world at the same time isn't turned on. But it's unmistakable. I'd recognize her anywhere. It's the love-of-my-life. "It's you," I say again, with emphasis. "It's Norma Blake Madsen."

She shakes her head, but on the horizontal. She says, "No. Everyone always says that. I'm not, though. I'm her twin sister, Naomi."

I peer at her closer. Could it be true? "The resemblance is uncanny," I say. "So you're Johnny Nomad's sister too?"

She nods. "Yes. That would make me his sister, too. Wouldn't it?"

I've only seen her head up to now, Norma's that is, in photos, but if I could have imagined a body to carry that head around, it would be the tight sexy body that I'm seeing now. Naomi Blake stares at me and I stare back at her and for fifteen seconds or so the total number of words we say to each other add up to exactly zero. It seems to me that no words are necessary for the way we are communicating during this incommunicable silence. *Love,* I'm thinking, *is like wireless: the hook-up is all happening invisibly and instantly.* Finally, though, someone has to say something and it's her. She says, "I'm hungry. What do you say? Do you want to buy me some breakfast? There's a coffee shop nearby. We can talk."

It feels like a Sunday, sitting here in the corner coffee shop with Naomi Blake. She's drinking coffee and I'm not, she's picking at a feta cheese omelet and I'm not, she's dabbing tears from the corners of her amazing eyes and I'm not. Across the street there's a big old dirty bridge that would look good if it were raining. Today, it's not even close to raining.

Naomi Blake has white blonde hair. When she takes off her sunglasses, she has emerald eyes. She has the kind of lips that look like they're about to kiss you even when she's not. Naomi Blake is wearing a short red leather jacket, faded jeans, and a cropped black t-shirt that says *nobody* in glitter across the front. She has a jingly bracelet on her left wrist made up of at least a dozen tiny chromium skulls. Every time she moves her hand the tiny skulls all bang together and make a kind of dissonant music.

She doesn't look like any dentist's wife I've ever seen. And, of course, that's because she isn't. "As I said," Naomi Blake says. "We're duplicates. Norma and I…copies, Xeroxes, we're twins."

Outside the window, passing on the sidewalk, an old woman is inching her way between somewhere and oblivion. She's stooped over so badly she looks like a walking question mark. *That is what happens if you live long enough.* I'm thinking, *that is what happens when you get old.* Your whole body takes the form of a question. Your whole body ends up asking, *Why?*

I look back at Naomi. I say, "What day is it?"

Naomi says, "Thursday."

"Really?"

She shrugs. "I guess."

She suddenly seems really suspicious about something. She says, "Just in case you try to figure it out, I don't live anywhere near here. I picked this place on purpose. I picked it because it's not even close to where I live."

I say, "It feels like Sunday."

She says, "Maybe it is."

The twin thing has me thrown for a loop. I'm stalling for time. There's always something eerie about twins. But then, as I've said more than once already, this whole thing doesn't make any sense. If you're talking about Norma Blake Madsen as a murder victim, it's not because she was an important person. If you're talking about her as the target of a carefully orchestrated conspiracy, she was eminently unkillable. But a woman is missing and a guy that looked like me was suspected of making her disappear. Now, this woman's twin sister had turned up in Brooklyn so at least that was a connection to New York. That didn't seem to be a heck of a lot to go on. Correction: that didn't seem to be much of anything to go on. Maybe it only seemed significant because nothing else seemed meaningful about any of this and I had to find significance in something. You know, like a Rohrshach blot.

I say, "How did you know it was me?"

"I saw you at Johnny's place. I've been keeping an eye out ever since he disappeared to see who showed up. And it was you."

"He was a good friend of mine."

"Funny, he never mentioned you."

"Well, he didn't really know my name."

Naomi gives me a funny look, and I think it's got to do with what I just said. Maybe it does. But it's also got to do with something more, as it turns out. "You know who you look like?" she says, and I know what's coming. "You look like the guy who's wanted in connection with my sister's disappearance. First, my sister, then my brother. What have you got against my family, anyway?"

"I don't have anything against your family. Fact is, I'm trying to find out what happened to them."

She suddenly looks worried. "Are you a cop?"

"No, nothing like that."

"Listen," she says, "if you're thinking of following me home and kidnapping me, forget it. If you plan on getting me alone and raping me, you're out of luck. This isn't even anywhere near where I live."

"Calm down. I'm not a cop or a rapist."

"Who the hell are you then?"

Like most spur of the moment lies, it's not a very good one, and, like all bad lies, it's going to require a furious cacophony of background lies to support it. But the necessity for that will come later. I tap my black spiral-bound notebook meaningfully. I say, "My name is Lucky Pozzo. I'm a true crime writer."

She says, "So you think there's been a crime?"

"Well, I'm not positive. But it doesn't seem unlikely."

She says, "I'm no author, but shouldn't you find out first before you begin writing?"

"You can't always wait around for the crime. This is a competitive field. I want to get ahead of the game. I want to learn a little about the possible victims first. You know, to make sure that they're the kind of victims that your average readers will care about. You'd be surprised at how unsympathetic even murdered people can be."

"That's disgusting. I'm glad I don't live anywhere close to this place. I wouldn't want it infected by your disgusting presence. You're a real vulture, you know that?"

"I agree. But do you think you could help me out, anyway? Can you tell me a little about your sister?"

She says, "What about the money?"

"What money?"

"For the book. Do I get a share of the royalties, or what?"

"Yeah, some. What day did you say it was, anyway?"

"Wednesday."

"Wednesday?"

She says, "I called in sick to work today."

I say, "Are you sick?"

"Not really. How much money can you give me for my story?"

She's still talking about her share of the fake book I'm pretending to be writing. She's talking about how much she'll get for selling her sister's personal story.

I say, "Five hundred."

She says, "That's not very much."

"It's an anthology. Your sister isn't the only victim in the book. It's a book full of victims. She'll have ten pages, maybe twelve tops. A lot depends on what happens."

She asks me some pretty astute questions about incentive payouts, royalties, book tours, advance copies. She makes some informed sounding queries about P&L's, advertising, returns, initial print runs. It's difficult to tell whether all this sounds so impressive because she really knows what she's talking about or because I don't.

I say, "My agent is handling all that."

"Who's your agent?"

"Vladimir Estragon."

I'm not happy about the name, but frankly I'm running out of them.

She says, "Maybe I know him. I use to be in sub rights at Dutton."

While she's flipping through her outdated mental rolodex trying to remember a fictional Vladimir Estragon, I try to get the conversation back on track. I try to get it even close to the track. I say, "When was the last time you talked to your sister?"

"Alive?"

That's an odd way to qualify the question, I'm thinking, and I'm making a special note of it. "Yes," I say. "Alive."

Naomi Blake is picking up her coffee cup, but it's just a nervous gesture. She puts it back down. On her wrist, the tiny chromium skulls are singing their weird unearthly tune. She's looking off to my right, in the direction of the kitchen, as if that's where the threat is coming from, ridiculous as that is.

"Look," she says. "I don't feel comfortable talking about this here." Suspiciously, she eyes a waitress passing with a plate of jiggly sunny-side up eggs and a side order of hash.

She says, "Let's go back to my place."

I say, "Where is your place?"

She says, "Don't worry. It's not far from here."

13. Psycho dentists, stuffed animals, and sex magick...

Right above the damn coffee shop, that's where Naomi Blake's apartment is, that's how close it is. She didn't even bother to choose a coffee shop a block or two away, nevertheless a subway stop or two. If her place had been any closer to the goddamn booth where we'd just been sitting, we'd still be in the goddamn coffee shop.

She has one of those apartments with old-fashioned molding along the walls and doorframes, like apartments built in the twenties or thirties, or whenever. The furnishings are all IKEA and wicker-style crap in brightly-colored Navajo-type patterns. On the walls are the usual homey plaques, mirrors, and mass produced paintings of flowers and elegantly reclining women that almost look enough like this or that artist's style to make you think they were actually painted by this or that artist.

Surprisingly, though, I'm spared the usual Georgia O'Keefe print. I'm spared the almost obligatory Gauguin.

All of it is pleasant and clean and perfectly typical of a woman's apartment. It's the kind of bright well-coordinated place that usually gets on any real man's nerves inside of a month. This just isn't the kind of place you can while away entire weekends munching potato chips in your boxer shorts. There's no room on the walls for your Jessica Alba calendar. The coffee table is no place for your *Leg Show* magazines, your empty beer cans, your used tissues; neither is the floor. Your favorite broken-in sneakers don't belong anywhere. It's the kind of place that makes you realize that men and women really have no business living inside the same box. You come to realize that if men and women were lab rats, they'd tear each other apart in a box like this before too long.

Maybe, we *are* lab rats. Maybe we're some higher intelligence's equivalent of the lab rat and the earth a giant rat maze with a piece of smelly cheese at the end. That would explain an awful lot that can't be explained. That would explain the viciousness and over-population of divorce courts, for one thing.

I'm sitting in a big soft purple armchair. On the coffee table there's a big coffee table book with classic photographs of Manhattan. Aside from the Empire State Building and a shot of the Fulton Street Fish Market in 1926, I don't recognize any of it.

A beat behind, Naomi says, "Sit down. Make yourself comfortable."

She disappears into the kitchenette, making a lot of noise with the cabinets. For all I know, she's stalling for time until the police get here. She calls out, "Can I get you anything?"

I picture her bent over in front of the fridge as she calls out the following list of items: "Applesauce, beef stroganoff, diet Pepsi, yogurt, fried rice, anything?"

It occurs to me she might be poisoning whatever it is she's eventually going to bring out.

She comes back into the room with a plate of macademia nut cookies and two glasses of water. She lays the plate and the glasses on the coffee table. She sits down across from me on the couch. She tucks her bare feet underneath her like a cat. She says, "I've been a nervous wreck for weeks. I hope I can trust you."

What Naomi tells me is that her twin sister was the best of mothers, the most devoted of wives, a peerless sibling. She gave her life to her stepkids, sacrificed her happiness to her demanding and negligent husband, put her own needs last whenever there was a list to put her needs on. She spoke no evil of anyone, wouldn't harm a fly, went to church on Sunday. To hear Naomi go on and on about her twin sister, it made you think that if there's a Hall of Great

Human Beings somewhere, then there must also be an empty plinth waiting for a bust of Norma Blake Madsen to be placed upon it.

There was just one little thing Norma Blake Madsen liked to do that nobody knew about. She just had this one tiny quirk that made her life a wee bit happier. So insignificant a thing, Naomi hardly thought it necessary to mention to anyone. One of those things that everybody does. You can't blame her, after all, married to that monster, H. "Pop" Madsen. Listening to this endless preamble, I take a sip from the glass without thinking. *Shit,* I think, *I shouldn't have done that,* but moving my tongue around my mouth, checking for burn sores, I decide the water tastes pretty normal, after all. Just like New York City tap water, more or less.

I finally interrupt. "So what is it that she did?"

She says, "My sister is only human. Please don't judge her."

I say, "He who is without sin…you know…"

"Yeah," Naomi says. "Ummm, okay."

"The point is, you can tell me."

"Norma liked to have sex on the internet."

"Well," I say, "that's not so bad. Lots of people do that."

"It's a little bit more than that," Naomi says.

"How much more?"

"It seems that my sister became…well, a little bit addicted."

A little bit might have been an understatement. Norma Blake Madsen had sex on the internet when everyone in the house was asleep. She did it during the day when the kids were at school. She did it while the laundry was in the spin cycle, the sauce was simmering on the stove, the kitchen floor was drying. She signed up for wireless so she could do it wherever there weren't wires. You could say that Norma Blake Madsen was addicted to cybersex if being addicted meant crawling out of bed at three a.m. to log on wildsex.com. If you dial up using your cell phone to make sexy talk with some sodomist from New Zealand while waiting for your pedicure, you might say she had a "bit" of a habit.

Naomi says, "Please don't judge her. She met a guy online who lives in Manhattan. They started an online relationship and it became more than…virtual. She came out here to stay sometimes when she was seeing him. He was married, too. It was true love."

I find myself reaching for the water glass again, but manage to stop myself. *Habit*, I think, *is a killer.*

"So," I say, "what's the problem? We've all been there. Seems a pretty commonplace situation to me."

"We don't have a Haroun in our life."

"A what?"

"Haroun, that's her husband. That's what the "H" stands for. He found out about the affair. He comes from Iran. Or Iraq," she stops to think a moment. "Maybe its Syria. You know, one of those places where the guys wear those checkered napkins on their heads and stone their wives if they're traveling across country to have sex with other men in hotel rooms."

Naomi Blake has a colorful fringe at the bottom of each leg of the faded blue jean bellbottoms that she's wearing. She's wearing purple toenail polish on her toenails. She is wearing a belly ring in the navel of her soft white belly. She is wearing a tattoo of a small black scorpion poised to strike inside her left thigh, but I'll see that later. She is wearing that smile that looks like she's kissing you even when she's not, and that doesn't go away completely even when she is. But I'll find that out later, too, but not that much later.

"My sister is only human," she says it again and there are tears glittering in her eyes. Twins, as I've heard a million times, feel everything the other one is feeling as if it were happening to them. She says, "Please don't judge her."

"Please don't judge me," Naomi Blake says. "I don't usually do this kind of thing."

I'm licking an aureole, a pierced navel, a purple toenail. I'm kissing an earlobe, an underarm, a mole on her ass. I'm really not thinking of judging her. But if I were thinking of something right now, that would probably be one of the last things I'd be thinking. I'm really not thinking of much of anything at the moment, and that's the best thing of all to be thinking.

She says, "My sister has a lot of problems. She is a good person, but she has one or two minor problems."

I'm nuzzling the inside of an elbow, a pinkie, the prickly hairs of her trimmed pubes. I'm tasting my own miserable salt-sea slime, old as creation itself, that I've deposited inside her a few minutes ago.

She shudders, and it's hard to tell if she's shuddering because she's turned on or just feeling creeped out the way some women feel after sex with a relative stranger, especially with someone as relatively strange as me. We're on her bed, in her bedroom, a bed piled high with comforters, with pillows, with bolsters, with stuffed animals. I've got my right elbow jabbed into a plush white tiger or puma, or something, something that looks endangered.

The lights are off and there's only one window in the room and that has bars over it, and you can't really see anything out of it anyway. I'm feeling grateful and mildly amazed like I always feel after I'm done. I'm feeling proud that the whole production came off without a hitch, well, with hardly a hitch. I'm flabbergasted that it all actually worked like it's supposed to, considering everything that can go wrong. I'm feeling that I've just been witness to a bit of magic. I'm feeling surprised that I was somehow able to pull this trick off one more time.

All in all, I'm reveling in wonder that my body actually worked like it's supposed to work, even after all these years, after all this mileage.

One day, I'll be an old man hunched on a park bench staring mindlessly at the tops of my Velcro shoes. One day, I too, will be crooked over in that perpetual osteo-question we all end up asking the cosmos, "*Why?*" One day my brain and all my thoughts will turn to an inert grey slush inside my skull, but that day's not today.

A part of me is actually contemplating trying again. But what I'm doing is pushing my luck and I know it. What I'm doing is playing straight red. Eventually, you're going to go bust.

I'm nibbling a shoulder, an ankle, a wrist. If I could, I'd nibble her adorable pituitary gland.

It's been a while since I've tasted a real live woman and I'm dimly remembering what all the commotion is about. I'm remembering why men run for president, go to the moon, invent a better mouse-trap, go through all that trouble breathing in and breathing out, just to do it all over again. I'm remembering why most people stand patiently on the corner every morning waiting for the traffic light to change instead of hurling themselves in front of the next bus and getting it all the hell over with once and for all.

To sum it up, I'm in love.

"Please stop," Naomi Blake says.

I've got two or three fingers in her ass. I have my tongue inside her.

She says, "Thank you very much. That was nice. Really. But it's enough now."

By that, I understand her to mean that we've squeezed about as much pleasure out of this particular moment as humanly possible. That now it's time to talk. That now the trouble and torture begins. That now the bill must be paid.

"Okay," I say, un-inserting myself.

I climb out from between her legs. I scooch my way pilloward where her pretty head is resting and closer to the story that is pouring out of it. This is what it sounds like:

"H. found out about Norma's affair. She told me that he was having her followed. She told me that H. was going to have her killed. She told me she was going to have to disappear for a while. She told me not to worry. But—I'm worried."

I say, "Did she have proof that her husband was planning to have her killed?"

"She told me that her lover told her."

"How did he know? Why didn't she go to the police?"

I ask this last question, by the way, fully aware of the irony. Someone could be saying the exact same thing to me and no doubt they will be, once the shit hits the fan, which should be any day now.

She says, "Same reason. Because it was a cop who told her."

"Huh?"

"The guy she was having the affair with. He's a cop."

"So why didn't he do something? Make an arrest?"

Naomi shrugs. "He was working undercover. He was married, too. It's complicated, you know? He told her to make herself scarce for awhile until he could figure something out. So she left. She ran away. She left it all behind. Her house, her friends, her lousy husband. She left her whole life behind."

"Where was she going? Do you know?"

"She was coming here first." There are tears running down Naomi's face when she says this. "She never made it. And then Johnny disappears. Who's next? *Me?*"

I say, "I think I might know who's got your brother. I think I might have something that he wants enough so that he'll give him back."

And I tell her about Mr. Knott and Nada Klone and the gambling debts and the grey little pot-bellied bald guy Sprocket who just might be the hottest woman in cyberworld. The fake girl that apparently Naomi's picture has been hijacked to represent.

"You've got to do it," Naomi says, "you've got to give this Mr. Knott the woman he loves. Even if it's not a woman."

"I'm not sure," I say.

"What's not to be sure about?"

"I'm not sure of…well, of his intentions."

Naomi says, "You've got to do it. You've got to." And the tears are really coming now, they're hammering out of her like rain on a roof. "You've got to help me. He's got half my family. You've got to save them. Who's more important to you anyway?"

And I'm thinking, put that way, she's got a point.

"This cop," I say, "did your sister ever tell you his name?"

Sniffing, sobbing, hiccupping, Naomi manages to burp it out, the name that is, and it's the first note in this otherwise discordant symphony of a case that seems to logically follow any other note, but how, exactly, it's impossible to say.

"Chambers," Norma's look-a-like twin says, tears now splashing onto her chest. I resist the temptation to lick a salty droplet hanging off her left nipple. "She said his name was Chambers." She shrugs. "But no one uses their real name on the internet, right?"

True, I'm thinking, but what are the odds that two people in the same case would be using the same fake name totally by chance? I'm no statistician, but the odds are pretty slim, I'd guess.

"So you'll help me, yes? You'll meet with this Mr. Knott? You'll give him the name and get my brother back?"

At some point during all this, she took hold of my manhood again. She's stroking it, tickling it, petting it, teasing it, coaxing it, and me along with it, trying to change my mind, both of them. She's performing that trick again. That magic show. That miracle. And, like Lazarus, it's rising from the dead. What can I say? How can I refuse? She's bending her head over my lap to whisper something down there. She mumbling the password to paradise. Because both of those minds, it's true, are one.

"Yes, yes, yes," I say. "Oh, oh, oh God yes!"

Whatever she's asking, that's the answer.

I'm not thinking of the consequences. I'm not considering the price to be paid. I'm not concerned with who gets hurt, betrayed, or left for dead. I haven't given any thought to the fact that if I find the love-of-my-life I'm going to have a lot of explaining to do. What I haven't quite perceived yet is the sticky situation I've put myself in. Maybe you figured it out before I did and maybe that's why you don't end up in these predicaments. Yup, that's it exactly. If I ever meet the love-of-my-life, she better be pretty open-minded, big-hearted, or kinky beyond all belief, preferably all three. She's going to have to be. Because oh-my-god, oh-my-god, oh-my-god-I'm so close, so close, so close….I'm fucking her twin sister! YESSSSS!

Waking up in my own bed the next day, I decide to sleep in until around noon. When I finally stand up, I'm still feeling temporarily okay about myself, still awash in endorphins, or whatever, from my roll among the stuffed animals with Naomi Blake the night before.

I'm feeling so good I do six or seven push-ups. I'm feeling so close to life-affirming I floss for the first time in ages, throw away some old eggs that have been in the fridge since God only knows when. For the first time since 1997, I'm almost glad I can't go online.

This, I decide, is a day for real life. So I get a bicycle tire repaired, I order some new checks. I take a tall hefty bag of whites to the laundry room.

I say "Hi" to a guy named Ned.

I go buy some carrots.

14. False faces, missing time, "Us," and "Them"...

What I haven't said is that during this whole time my apartment is
being "visited." It's an odd way to put it, but I can't think of a better
way.

Coming home, I find little things: a potato chip bag crumpled
on the window sill, muddy footprints just inside the door, the fresh
dampness of a dishrag. Every once in a while, they're more careless,
and the door is left unlocked or the phone is improperly set back in
its cradle.

I've taken to taping little notes around the place saying things
like, *Please remember to lock the door behind you. Please don't drink the milk
right out of the carton. Please pull the shower curtain ALL THE WAY closed.
Thank you!*, stuff like that.

Lately, it's gotten to the point where I almost feel like I'm living
with someone, like we're sharing the place, it's that much of a pain in
the ass.

Sometimes I find a shirt or a favorite pair of shoes missing, but
you get used to it, you just find something else to wear that day. You
live with a low-level hostile burn, but you adjust.

You make the best of it. You think, *Well it's better than living
alone.*

Where the hell *am* I going?

That's me asking myself what the guy in the back seat is screaming at me, something about wherever we are being nowhere close to Washington Square. I've been distracted all night, dropping people off in the wrong places all over the city, letting them out wherever we are when they start banging on the plastic partition. That's what the guy in the back seat is doing right now. He's banging on the partition with both fists, he's demanding to be let out.

What the hell *is* the matter with me? That's me again, asking myself the next question the guy in the back seat is screaming, a question I can't answer any better than the first.

How do I tell my unfortunate passenger that I'm having a hard time concentrating on something as relatively uninteresting as driving? How do I tell him I'm a bit preoccupied tonight. How do I tell him I'm desperately trying to remember what I did with the month of August?

Pulling over to the curb, I let the guy out of the cab. He's cursing and threatening and carrying on. He's stamping his feet, waving his hands, jabbing his forefinger at me.

He's so mad, he's flinging spittle in every direction, he's taking down my name, taking down my license number, taking down everything written outside and inside the cab. He's not acting like he's aware of it, but getting me fired from a job I hate anyway, that's about all he can do to me. You wouldn't know it by the way he's acting, but having no sense of direction is simply not punishable by lethal injection in the city of New York.

True enough, not knowing where you're going can get you killed, just like being in the wrong place at the wrong time. Fact is, it's both not knowing where I'm going and being in the wrong place at the wrong time that's gotten me into this situation in the first place, and it's about to get even worse.

Whatever my passenger is screaming at me now, a diatribe about me being an asshole, a lunatic, a motherfucker, it's all totally irrelevant, so I stamp on the accelerator like it's something ugly, and take off with his portfolio still on the back seat, but that's something I don't really notice until much later.

Anyway, here I am, riding around, going nowhere again. I'm waiting for the one fare that matters tonight. I check the dashboard clock. He's late. I'm suppose to get a call over the radio to go to such-and-such a corner at such-and-such a time and there Mr. Knott will be waiting for me to get the contact information for half of Nada Klone, aka, Todd Sprocket. Mr. Knott called me earlier in the afternoon while I was puzzling over the Dilbert calendar on my refrigerator, wondering why I hadn't noticed that I've been looking at the cartoon for the month of July for the last three months. In the background, over Mr. Knott's threats and ultimatums I could hear Johnny Nomad saying something as if he had a mouthful of socks.

I said, "Mr. Knott, is that Johnny Nomad I hear in the background?"

On the other end, I hear a chuckle, some chair scraping, and a short yelp.

"Say a few words Johnny," Mr. Knott said.

"Molloy? Is that you? [gasp, choke] Hey Molloy. Do what he says. [sob] Please. Do…"

I hear it again, but all in reverse: the short yelp, the chair scraping, and the chuckle.

"That'll be all Johnny," Mr. Knott said, and then more muffled gagging and the sound of someone talking through socks. "There you have it, Mr. Molloy."

"You kidnapped Johnny?"

"I haven't kidnapped him. You might say, I'm holding him for safekeeping. You know, until I get Nada Klone. I want her, Mr. Molloy. I want her now."

Don't ask, don't tell, and buyer beware; I suppose I could have omitted the whole truth, normally I would have, maybe I should have, but I didn't want to unpleasantly surprise a guy who'd proven every bit as mercurial and ominously hard to shake as Mr. Knott, especially if I didn't have to. So I told him about Sprocket, not all of it, but enough of it, the gist of it. As it turned out, Mr. Knott surprised *me*. That the cyber femme fatale who'd already caused so much trouble was just a pale dandruffy little stockroom clerk didn't seem to put Mr. Knott off at all. Instead, he replied to this news with considerable romantic passion.

"Do you understand what I'm trying to tell you," I feel compelled to clarify. "She's a *guy*."

"Have you ever been in love, Mr. Molloy? Have you? Does love change with the winds of circumstance? Does it fade when the grey years steal the first bloom of your beloved? Does love disappear because your destined soul-mate is a guy who counts boxes of Legos in the stockroom of ToyRUs?"

Well, that was good enough for me. I figured Mr. Knott has his own criminal reasons for getting hold of Sprocket, including using him to track down Norma Blake Madsen, but that was none of my business. I'd throw him Sprocket and take the head-start. Knott would return Johnny Nomad, and we'd all be that much closer to a happy ending.

So that's how I came to be driving around, waiting for his call, and playing a little mental game in the meantime. I'm trying to picture what pops into my head when I say the words *August fifteenth*.

This is what pops into my head: *Nothing.*

I'm thinking, Maybe I'm making too big a deal of all this.

I'm thinking, *How many times do you hear someone say, 'Where did the summer go?'* Seems to me every year people say, *'I can't believe it's Christmas already.'*

The day after Christmas they say, *'I can't believe Christmas is already over.'*

If you add up all the time I'm missing, a few days here and there, the weeks I can't remember, it adds up. I can't say I've gotten used to it any, but I'm trying not to look as upset and dumbfounded as I used to when I see the date on a newspaper or someone hands me back a check I've misdated.

I'm thinking, *I really need to start paying attention. I don't want to waste any more days.* I'm thinking, *This is my life I'm talking about. I can't afford to waste another second.* The next thing I know, it's Thursday.

It seems to me that I'm not alone either. It seems to me that no one can really account for their time. No one can satisfactorily answer the question, *What did you do on March fifth?*

Everyone seems to be walking around with a kind of amnesia. No one, it seems, can remember much of anything. There are these huge patches of missing time in everyone's brain, blank spaces, whole days, even weeks unaccounted for.

What happened to that year I was fourteen?

Everyone's walking around without an airtight alibi for anything. That's why when someone yells, *Hey!*, everyone turns around. That's why when someone yells, *Stop right there!*, a dozen people freeze.

Everyone's walking around feeling guilty about something.

Everyone's feeling like a suspect and there's a good reason for that.

Everyone is a suspect.

I turn onto Madison. I'm going sixty, seventy, eighty miles an hour. I'm going nowhere, but I'm going there really fast.

Right about now is when my radio starts squawking like a voodoo chicken someone stepped on. It's Mr. Sammy squawking.

This is what he squawks, "You wake up now. You wake up."

I say, "Yes I'm awake. I'm not sleeping, I'm wide awake."

He says, "You no good. You no good taxi driver. You slow down."

I lift my foot off the accelerator. My arms are trembling.

I'm going fifty, forty, thirty miles an hour. I'm still going nowhere, but I'm suddenly not in such a hurry anymore. Was I asleep? Have I been dreaming? I say, "Yes, I'm here. I'm on the job."

Mr. Sammy asks me if I can pick up a fare at Second Avenue and 63rd Street. Where I am, at the moment, I have no clue. This is what I tell him as I'm looking for the street signs.

Mr. Sammy says, "Don't worry. I know where you are. Pull over at the corner."

Logically speaking, I'm guessing there's a perfectly good and uncreepy explanation for how Mr. Sammy knows my exact location when not even I do, but I can't manage to talk myself into it at the moment. Sure enough, when I pull over to the curb there I am sitting at the corner between two green street signs.

One says, Second Avenue.

The other says, Sixty-third Street.

This is it, I think: the promised rendezvous with Mr. Knott.

Sure enough, when I pull over to the curb there's my fare waiting for me, but it's not exactly what I'm expecting. There are three guys waiting for me, two of them sort of propping up the other. And from the overall general lack of girth, from the fact that all three together wouldn't equal one of him, I can tell that none of them is Mr. Knott.

Stepping on the gas and driving away, that would be the smart thing to do. Instead, I look straight ahead through the windshield. One of the guys steps forward to open the door.

I say, "Where to gentleman?"

One of the two guys doing the propping slides his buddy into the back seat of the cab. Really, it's more like he unloads his buddy into the cab, shouldering him into the back seat like a box full of old stuffed owls. He's got thin blonde hair, the guy doing the loading, a wispy beard, and colorless eyes. The other looks almost exactly the same, only with red hair and no beard. They've both got the look of someone who looks really familiar but you can't figure out from where. They each look so much like no one they look pretty much like everyone, or maybe that's vice-versa.

The guy Mr. Blonde is loading back there has his chin on his chest, he's wearing a black stocking cap. He looks totally out of it.

Mr. Blonde is now whispering something into the unconscious man's ear, at least it looks like that's what he's doing. He looks like he's whispering something, maybe some kind of instructions, into the ear of his drunken companion, who's passed out cold.

Mr. Red, leaning into the cab, smiles at me, but it doesn't look like a smile. What it looks like is that something slimy and disagreeable has just slipped down his throat.

He says, "You take good care of our friend here." He points at the guy slumped in the back seat. "He's had a rough night."

He gives me an address up in the 100s I don't recognize at all. He tries to help me out. He says, "Morningside Heights."

If I have a look for "Even More Confused," I'm wearing it right now.

Climbing back out of the cab, the blonde guy stands, closes the door, and looks up and down the street. Apparently, whoever Mr. Blonde and Mr. Red are, they're not gracing me with their company tonight.

"Just get going," Mr. Red says, looking annoyed. "You'll be getting instructions soon enough."

He slaps the roof of the cab with his open palm like he's slapping the rump of a horse in an old-time western. I don't have to be told twice. Pulling away from the curb, I make a quick right at Fifth Avenue, glad to be on my way, and drive a few blocks before saying anything. I'm anxious to drop this guy off wherever he's going before the call from Mr. Knott comes in, because I'm still expecting it, and this guy's getting dumped off the minute it comes no matter where we are, no matter how fucked up he is. I have my window rolled down, my elbow on the door. On either side of us closed boutiques and whatnot are speeding passed. I decide to make a little strained chit-chat.

"So…hard day at the office?"

I glance into the rearview. He's nodding a little, the guy in the back, but that's really just the bad shocks and the manhole covers and potholes that I'm unerringly hitting. I say, "Your friends back there, they're a couple of odd ducks, ain't they?"

No answer.

I say, "You feeling alright?"

No answer.

I say, "You want me to pull over let me know. If you puke in this cab, I'll catch hell from my boss."

No answer. I look up again and notice for the first time that the guy's wearing a featureless white plastic mask along with the stocking cap. It alternately glows and vanishes as we speed under the streetlights.

I say, "What, are you back from a masquerade party or something?

No answer.

"Not feeling very chatty tonight, huh? You don't happen to know where you're going, do you?"

It's a curb I jump, (I hope), and the cab bounces violently and I glance up into the rearview to see how my passenger is taking it and he's taking it by pitching a bit to the side and throwing his head back. It's suddenly clear that I'm transporting a corpse just by the way he's keeled over. That's bad enough, as you can well imagine. What's even worse, is that I'm not really all that surprised to find myself in this predicament. But what's worst of all is that, in all the jostling around, the plastic mask has slipped off the dead guy's head and whosever corpse it is tossing around back there, *it doesn't have a goddamn face.*

Call it panicking, but I hit the gas with the general idea of putting everything as far behind me, as fast as possible. After running four red lights, jumping another curb, and starting the wrong way down a one-way street, I realize the clear flaw in my plan.

What I'm running away from, I'm actually carrying along with me in the back seat of the cab.

For a reason I don't want to acknowledge, I suddenly remember that last conversation with Johnny Nomad. I remember him talking about being afraid of Mr. Knott. I remember him saying how people dealing with Mr. Knott had a tendency to end up disassembled. I don't want to think that's Johnny in the back seat, but that's already a pointless wish because that's exactly what I'm thinking. I'm beginning to think that Mr. Knott has taken away my friend's face.

I slam on the brakes. I stop right in the middle of whatever street I'm on. I sit there and try to think of what I should do next. I'm sitting there and I'm trying not to look in the rearview at the guy in the back seat. I'm trying really hard not to remember what I've already seen: a head peeled like a purple grape with white squares of teeth embedded in it. I'm not doing too good a job not remembering because that's the image that keeps coming to mind.

In my chest, my heart is doing this thing where it's beating two times and then missing three or four beats entirely. It occurs to me that maybe I'm having some kind of heart attack but I have bigger problems than that at the moment. I'm drumming the steering wheel with my fingers, hyperventilating, and saying to myself, *Think, think, think.*

I'm saying things like, *What do I do now?* and *Don't panic!* And
then RUN RUN RUN!

I hear a calm voice like they say sometimes you can hear at the
moment you die. The voice of a dearly departed relative, or even
Jesus. Except this voice isn't coming from the end of a tunnel to
heaven, this voice is coming from the radio in the cab.

It's not Mr. Sammy's voice this time, either. It's an arid
monotone, like a thousand miles of Kansas wheatfields.

This time, it's Mr. Franklin.

The voice says, "First thing you want to do, Mr. Molloy, is get
out of the middle of a one-way street."

I say, "What are you doing on this radio, Mr. Franklin?"

He says, "First thing you want to do…"

He repeats what he said before. He repeats it in such a
deadening drone that I immediately feel a good deal calmer. Nothing
calms you down more than the same old thing. This still isn't normal
by a long shot, but it doesn't seem quite so much like a free-fall into
total chaos as it did ten seconds ago.

I put the car in gear, back out of the one-way street, and head
north on Madison, or Lexington or Fifth, whichever one of those
avenues heads north, what does it matter? I'm still driving way too
fast, which I don't even realize until Mr. Franklin mentions it.

He says, "Slow down, Mr. Molloy, this isn't the kind of
endeavor that will be helped by a head-on collision. Not yet,
anyway."

I say, "Mr. Franklin, can you please give me some idea what's
going on? What did you do with Mr. Sammy? Who the hell is that in
the back seat?"

"Those are not important questions right now, Mr. Molloy.
What's important is that you drive safely, that you observe the rules
and regulations of the road."

I can't stop shaking. I can't stop hyperventilating. I can't stop
thinking of that old Satchel Paige saying, "Don't look back because
whatever's back there might be gaining on you." There are horns
blaring all around me, pedestrians in the crosswalk pounding on the
cab, and I know it's only a matter of time before I attract the

attention of a traffic cop. I don't know what kind of ticket they write you for having a corpse in your back seat, but I'm guessing the fine is pretty steep. Like most concerns for our own survival, that thought sobers me right up.

"So where to Mr. Franklin?"

"That's better, Mr. Molloy. Now that's an important question."

He starts giving me instructions through the radio, telling me exactly where to go, where to turn, where not to turn. I'm doing whatever the radio says, whatever Mr. Franklin says. I want to get rid of the faceless fare in the back seat, and I want to be rid of him as soon as possible.

Where I end up is the front of an old luxury high-rise with a long green awning. There's a doorman and he's standing at the back door of the cab. He's wearing a flamboyantly tailored hotel uniform, like a rear admiral on the U.S.S. Flamingo. He's wearing white gloves. He's wearing a lavender kepi. He elegantly opens the cab door, pulls the faceless corpse out, props it up. I watch the doorman lead the dead man into the building, half-dragging him, really, hauling him along, sort of slung over his hip. The corpse's feet are dragging along behind it, losing a carpet slipper. The two of them disappear inside the luxury high-rise and I'm looking for a street number or name on the awning, the door, anywhere, but there's no street number or name that I can see. I look at the buildings on either side and I don't see any numbers on those buildings either. Halfway up the block there's a number—1230—on a townhouse, but it doesn't seem to have any logical numerical relation to the building four buildings up, 648. I have a sick feeling that if I come back here tomorrow, the street is going to look all different; if I come back here tomorrow, I'll never find the building the doorman dragged the corpse into again, that the building I'm looking at right now is going to be long gone.

Fifteen minutes later, driving across Central Park, I say, "Why, Mr. Franklin? What was the purpose of that?"

He says, "This was a second warning Mr. Molloy. You want to be a whole lot further along than you are. You really haven't gotten anywhere at all."

"It wasn't necessary," I say, and I think my eyes are tearing up when I say this. "You don't have to keep killing people to motivate me."

He says, "Oh, I don't know about that. You seem to have forgotten about US."

"US?"

"Oh yes. We're very disappointed in you."

"Who's US?"

"Me. US. Them. That's not really important right now. What matters is that we're *all* very disappointed in you."

15. Oedipus, two a.m., and barbecued meats...

This isn't a good idea, I know it already, but I'm on an Amtrak train
speeding out of the city on a bright, crisp, autumnal Saturday
morning, and I'm pretty damn certain that even as careful as I've
been, I'm still being followed. I'm not sure who it is or how many of
them there are, but I'll bet at least someone on this train is keeping an
eyeball glued to me.

Maybe it's the guy with the retro sideburns and the blue Nike
sports bag, or the distinguished looking business type in yellow Ping
golf shirt and steel brush cut. Maybe it's the young mother stoically
ignoring her two bickering brats behind a copy of *Women's Day*. If
they're smart, it's the leggy blonde girl in the UConn sweatshirt
dangling the flip-flop from her stubby brown toes while air-headedly
inspecting her nail art.

Most likely, though, it's the sharp-looking black dude at the
back of the car behind the black wraparound shades, head turned
towards the window, pretending to watch the coastline rip past. I can
hear the angry buzz of his hip-hopping Ipod from where I'm sitting,
my stomach churning, my left leg pumping, maniacally chewing gum,
and pretending to read a copy of *Skeptic* magazine. It's open on my
lap, the magazine that is, to an article about how otherwise intelligent
people get themselves to believe entirely unintelligent things. But

since I'm only pretending to be reading the article, I still don't know how that is.

This is a visit to my dad that I'm undertaking and I'm expecting it to be every bit as unpleasant as it always is, except maybe this time even a little more so.

What's different this time is that I'm packing a hot gun and I'm wanted for at least one homicide, another possible homicide, and a missing person or two. I've got nowhere to turn and I'm trailing surveillance.

I'm thinking back on that conversation on the cab radio with Mr. Franklin. I know dad would unreservedly agree with his assessment. All my life I've been a disappointment to someone. Yanked unwillingly out of the womb two weeks late, scrawny, screaming my head off, a red blob of a birthmark between my crossed eyes, I was instantly a disappointment to everyone gathered to greet me into the world and that was only the beginning. I was off and running from there.

Parents, teachers, friends, ex-wives, employers, I was a disappointment to all of them without exception; so being a disappointment to Mr. Franklin, that's not exactly a surprise, that's not late-breaking headline news. For me, being a disappointment is hardly worthy of mention; it's not so much an evaluation of my current performance, as it is a state of being.

For me, being a disappointment is a way of life.

If I weren't being a disappointment to someone somewhere, I don't think I'd be anything at all. If it were Mr. Franklin's intention to infect me with his misplaced confidence, I'm immune. He obviously hasn't done his research.

I'm disappointment incarnate. I could have advised him to grab himself a Webster's and look up the definition of *disappointment*. Well, of course you wouldn't find my picture there, but it should be there. It really should.

Maybe I'm in shock, I'm thinking, wondering if a general numbness to everything is a symptom of shock. If you've just given a ride to friend whose face has been peeled off like cellophane from a slice of processed American cheese, and you don't feel anything in particular, is that a symptom of shock? Looking at the half-burnt cigarette between my fingers, I'm wondering a bit where it came from. Yeah, I bought the pack of Camels back at the train station, it's not like I've forgotten, things aren't at that point yet, well, not entirely. But the question is, *Do I even really smoke?* The other question is, *If so, when did I start?*

Looking at the dead cigarette between my fingers, I'm put in mind of a hundred and fifty other things I seem to be that I have no memory of making a conscious choice about. Much of what I am, I had no hand in choosing at all. I mean, why do I like Coke over Pepsi, or drum solos, or the color blue? Come to think of it, I'm really not responsible for any of it.

Looking at this cigarette, I realize that's what a habit is. It's having a predilection for something you can't help. It's doing something over and over again without any choice in the matter. It may even be something you don't like doing, but that you can't stop doing all the same. Life is a habit, if you think of it that way. Life is a habit, and it's a pretty nasty one at that. We pick it up with that first fateful breath and we can't stop until it kills us.

While I'm thinking of nasty habits, I start thinking of Mr. Franklin and the ominous "Us" he mentioned. The problem with Mr. Franklin and the ominous "Us" being disappointed is not something to be treated quite so cavalierly as I seem to be treating it. I know that. It's not something to be poo-pooed the way I seem to be poo-pooing it. Mr. Franklin and the ominous "Us" have made it perfectly clear that they're not used to being disappointed. The message they've sent me loud and clear is that they don't take disappointment nearly as philosophically as I do, they don't take it as if they're expecting it, as if there's nothing to be done about it.

No, they've sent me an entirely different message. What they're saying is, *Do something about it.* They're saying, *We're not taking 'No' for an answer.*

To paraphrase what they're saying, you need to have your arm twisted sharply behind your back until all the tendons are about to snap. You need to have an Xacto knife pricking the soft, pulsing flesh just over your jugular.

I'm no Johnny Depp. I've never been in love with my face. But I'm not kidding myself, I don't want to lose it. As flawed as it is, I don't think I'm going to look any better with it peeled off my skull. Fact is, I don't think that's going to make anything any better, nosiree Bob.

They say that home is the place you go when you have nowhere else to go. The place they have to take you in when no one else will.

These are the kinds of things people say without taking people like my dad into account.

Home is someplace different every time I go there. This is the sixth home dad has had in the last nine years, and every new home is bigger and more ostentatious than the one before.

As I get out of the cab from the train station, I see that this one is made mostly of big brown river stones cemented all together and huge trapezoidal planes of smoked glass. There is a kind of useless turret, or something, mounted on the roof, and lots and lots of green lawn all around. I see a Range Rover parked outside the garage, a Hummer, two Mercedes, and a red Mazda Miata. There's a girl's pink bicycle with training wheels and silver streamers dangling from the hand-grips.

Greeting me at the door is a woman I've never seen before, but she looks pretty much like all the ones that came before her: blonde, polished, big-titted, tight-assed, and simmering with secret depravity. She looks so much like the others that I'm starting to wonder if they just come with the houses.

She smiles, but she smiles as if she's smiling at someone standing forty feet behind me.

And she probably is.

She says, "You must be…"

"Ben," I say, making up a name on the spot. "Yes, it's me, Ben."

She nods at that same someone forty feet behind me and says, "Of course. Come in, Ben. You're father is expecting you."

Inside, it looks just like you'd expect it would from the outside: like those pictures of immaculate rooms in magazines like *Town & Country* where you get the feeling that everything would be ruined if you actually spotted a real person inhabiting them. These are the rooms we are walking right by, rooms full of polished surfaces, books color-coordinated with the furniture, and things like humidors and mounted brown globes depicting the world in the sixteenth century.

In the kitchen we encounter a boy so blonde and motionless, blending in so perfectly with all the taupe tile and albino oak, that I nearly don't see him at all.

"That's your half-brother," my new step-mom says.

I'm not sure if she's talking to me or the eerie, fish-like little boy silently watching me, but I guess it really makes no difference. The creepy kid looks to be about eight going on fifty-five and I'm wondering where he's come from, if he's biological, or a half- brother through this or one of dad's other marriages, or just a child actor.

"Hi there," I say.

The little bastard takes off like a silverfish, disappearing along the wallboard into another room.

"Shy, is he?" I say to his supposed mother.

She smiles like she's smiling at the hired help. "Your father is waiting out back," she says and leads me through the French doors and out onto a flagstone patio the size of a 7-11 parking lot. At the other end, wearing an apron, standing in front of a large open bar-b-cue pit that looks like the doorway to Hell itself, is my dad. He's standing there forking some giant chunks of meat through a tower of fire they could see in the Auckland Islands, wherever the hell those are. As I approach, I try to find something familiar about my dad. The beard he's wearing, that's new. So is his nose, and whatever's been done to his eyes. The bald spot he's had for as long as I can remember, it's been entirely re-thatched.

He stabs at a thick shoulder of meat. The flames shoot a foot higher.

He doesn't even look up. He says, "Fucked up again, didn't you?"

He was never much of a father, so it's hard for him to be any less of one now, but you've got to hand it to him, he tries. He's still the same as I remember, even with all the new plastic surgery. Even though he doesn't look at all like he did the last time I saw him. Even though I'd be hard-pressed to pick him out of a line-up of two with him wearing the "Pick Me, I'm Your Dad" t-shirt. Fact is, he looks completely different every single time I see him. By now, I don't even know what he originally looked like. For all I know, this unrecognizable man standing here at the fire-pit behind this showcase home with his new wife and kid isn't really my dad at all.

"Hi to you, too, dad," I say.

"Well, you did fuck up, didn't you?"

"How can you tell?"

"What else is new? Besides, it's the only time you ever visit."

This is what it's like to have a father in the Witness Protection Program, or one who believes he's in the Witness Protection Program. Every family has its myths--this is one of the myths of mine. It doesn't make any difference how bad a guy you are, dad always said as we were growing up, just find someone worst and cut a deal. This is what it's like to have a dad who ratted out half the top Philadelphia crime bosses of his day, in exchange for immunity, that's his story anyway. Basically this is what it's like to have a dad who's a chronic, congenital, pathological liar and a childhood that, consequently, has as many holes in it as a bad alibi.

Dad says, "How's the cocksucker?"

That's my brother he's talking about. The brother who had the good sense to change his name and disown dad about twenty years ago.

"He still counting peas?"

"Beans."

"Huh?"

I say, "It's beans. They call accountants bean counters."

"Yeah...beans," he says. "That sounds like your brother, alright. Christ, does it really make a difference?"

"Angelo's fine. You're a grandfather again."

He grunts. "Congratulations me."

Dad tells me how a year ago this past August they took out another foot of his colon. "I'm running out of rope," he says. "Pretty soon, I'll be crapping out of my ears."

He jabs dejectedly at the burning lumps of meat. He says, "That's seventy-eight dollars worth of Argentinian beef you're looking at there. They graze on the rain-forest."

He asks me if I've had my pooper checked lately. He says, "Colon cancer can be hereditary. 85% of all colon cancer deaths can be prevented with early detection."

I say, "Is that really true? It seems like kind of a high success rate."

He shrugs and says, "Who the fuck knows?"

I get him up to speed on what's going on in my life. In the back of my mind, I'm still hoping he'll say something fatherly, reassure me that I'm over-reacting, that he's seen much worse. This is a guy, after all, that allegedly once fed business associates into wood-chippers, supervised their internment inside bridge abutments, watched them ground up into olive loaf. To hear him tell it, he's seen and heard and done it all. He waits until I've finished talking.

Then he says, "Son, that's got to be the single worse goddamn mess I've ever heard tell of in my entire goddamn fucked up life. I thought I'd seen and heard it all, but I ain't never seen or heard anything so fucked up as that. You, my boy, are really, and I mean really and royally, screwed up the ass."

"Jeez, dad, don't spare me the tough love..."

"Think hard. Have you been injected with anything lately? On the subway, standing at a street corner, minding your own business, did you suddenly feel a quick, sharp prick? I've heard shit like this is going on all the time now." He glances up at the clouds and whispers, "It's the government."

That's dad's paranoia talking. Along with the constant lying, he's also convinced everyone's out to get him: mom, me, my brother, the weatherman, the paper boy, everyone. Lying, egomania, and paranoia aren't dad's best traits, it's true, but they're just about the only one's he has. Take these away, and dad is pretty much not there at all.

I take out the newspaper story that I've been carrying around in my wallet for days now. It's getting kind of chewed-up looking, but you can still see the damning evidence. I ask him if he thinks the person in the police composite sketch looks like me.

He squints through the charred-meat smoke. He says, "The guy in the photo doesn't have your double-chin. You have much bushier eyebrows." He extends his arm to compensate for his nearsightedness, holds the picture next to my head, and looks from one to the other. He says, "Your ears stick out much more, like radar dishes, always did. I remember how all the kids use to make fun of you." He says something about how I should only look like the guy in the composite picture, that it looks like me without all the flaws, with about ten thousand dollars worth of top-rate plastic surgery. He offers to hook me up with a good hair transplant guy.

I snatch the clipping away, stuff it back in my wallet, and interrupt some unflattering comments about my teeth. I tell him I think I'm under surveillance.

He nods, peers up at the sky again, and says, "Someone is always watching. Remember that son."

How could I ever forget? This is what he's been telling me ever since I was a toddler. I'm getting the feeling that everything there was to learn from dad I learned by the time I was four. If I think of the labyrinth of complexes and neuroses he laid over me as a child, it's a wonder I can find my way from my bed to the bathroom in the morning. I'm not sure what I was expecting, but like usual, dad seems to have given me nothing and taken away what little I had.

Later, after a tense silent dinner with his new family, we're standing on the walkway out front, smoking ninety-dollar cigars. Dad's grown thoughtful, even philosophical, which means he's about to veer towards the suicidal. He's got a hose in this hand, splashing water on the perfect lawn.

"It doesn't need the water," he says, morosely.

"What do you mean?"

"The grass," he says, "is completely fake."

He tells me how much he hates his new life. It's even worse, he says, than his last five new lives. He hates the house, the lawn, the cars. He hates his fake wife, his fake job, his fake son.

"I didn't think it possible," he says, "but that creepy little son-of-a-bitch is an even bigger pansy than either you or your brother."

That's a keeper, I'm thinking, a real father and son moment.

He says, "I'm bored. Suburbia is poisoning me. The Feds knew just what they were doing sending me to this hell. It's a death sentence out here."

He tells me how he's organized a three-tier gambling operation among the other disaffected dads in the neighborhood. He's got a prostitution ring he runs out of his garage using all the bored, sex-starved soccer moms as talent. Right now, he's trying to set up an extortion and protection racket.

"You'd be surprised. People need protection out here," he mutters under his breath. "They have vendettas."

He waves the hose, wetting the plastic lawn.

"People out here," he says, "are all fucking bananas. They want to get back at each other for parking in front of their houses, stealing their recycling containers, not taking down their Christmas lights until April. I know a guy who wants a neighbor whacked for planting the same kind of red ornamental Japanese maple on their front lawn. There's a lot of untapped rage out here, a lot of hatred. You have no idea. It's dangerous. Christ, it's worse than the mob. These people, they'll kill each other over a fucking fence permit."

For the first time in my life, I'm thinking, *dad is losing it, he's getting old, he's not quite with it.* I feel a little sad, and I'm surprised to be feeling that way. Standing there, ranting in the setting sun, watering a plastic lawn with hardly any colon left, my old man looks somehow half-melted. You wait all your life to be able to beat your dad, the Oedipal thing and all, and then the day comes, and it's not a victory at all. It's only pitiful, and a little scary.

As it turns out, dad's not finished yet. Maybe this is his way of getting his revenge. What he's doing is giving me some fatherly advice. He says, "You're going to have to trust me on this one, son. I'm going against the conventional wisdom here. But if you want my advice, there's only one way to find out what the hell's going on. I think you should return to the scene of the crime."

Depressing as the ride out here was, it's even more depressing on the way back. Looking discretely at the passengers sharing my car, it seems to me that they are all the same people as on the ride out, only with costume changes. It's as if there are only four or five types of people in the world, and you just run into them over and over and over again.

I want to shout to my fellow passengers, "You're not fooling me one bit. I recognize you. I can see what you're doing!"

Instead, I pick up a copy of the *Hartford-Courant* someone left behind on the seat next to me and pretend to be reading the horoscopes. My act would be a lot more convincing if I weren't holding the paper upside-down, a fact I realize only forty-five minutes later when the train pulls into Grand Central.

When I get back to the apartment, there's an express mail envelope waiting for me. It contains $2900 and a typed message.

The typed message says: *Two a.m. Don't be late. This is your last chance.*

What's missing is what day at two a.m., where at two a.m., who I'm supposed to meet at two a.m., and why.

It's quite ingenious, I think. Whoever's behind this, they're trying to drive me crazy. I haven't a clue why they want to drive me crazy and maybe that's the real beauty of it. Maybe there's no reason at all. What better way to drive someone insane than to do it without any purpose whatsoever?

I check the envelope for a return address, something I might have missed.

Very funny, I think.

The return address, of course, is my own.

I guess I'm supposed to start suspecting me. I'm guess I'm supposed to start thinking I may be sending these messages to myself.

"That's very funny," I say.

I say it out loud to the empty apartment in case anyone is listening. I say it to whoever may be monitoring the bugs hidden inside the pencil erasers, between the bristles of an old toothbrush, in one of the holes of the colander under the sink.

I say, "That's very funny." I actually say the words out loud to the empty apartment: "Ha ha ha."

Call it thinking what I'm doing, wandering around, maybe it's Chelsea, at two a.m., in a steady drizzle. I'm calling it *thinking*, but a better word might be "desperation." I'm looking to keep that appointment with I don't know who and I don't know where. I'm wandering down where those crooked little leafy dark streets in the West Village are and I see some guy on a tall aluminum ladder at the corner of Morton or Bedford, or maybe it's Perry, one of those streets they leave off most of the tourist maps because it's too small and there's nothing on them to see. He's some kind of workman and he's standing there at the top of an aluminum ladder, at two a.m., in the rain.

As I get closer, I see he's got an electric portable something or other in his left hand and an unlit cigar stub clenched between his teeth.

The electric portable something or other goes......*zzzzzt*.

I'm standing at the foot of the ladder now, looking up, rain falling in my face like an old plate left out for a cat. I'm standing at the corner of something and something, who knows anymore.

I say, "What are you doing?"

The man looks down, grinning. The electric portable something or other goes.......*zzzzzt*......*zzzzzt*.

Rain is dripping off his pitted nose. He says, "What's it look like I'm doing, Einstein?"

I say, "You can't do that. People will notice."

He shrugs. He puts the sign for one street in place of the other. He says, "I change them back. Nobody notices. Some days it's one thing. Some days it's the other."

You can't see it tonight with the black clouds and rain and everything, but somewhere overhead the moon is hanging, dead and white, presumably having some kind of influence over all of this lunacy.

"That's simply crazy," I say. "What about the people who live here? They must notice."

He says, "Think about it. If you know where you are, do you ever read the signs?" He raises a thorny eyebrow. He grins again. The electric portable something or other goes......*zzzzzzt*.

It goes......*zzzzzzt*.

And I wonder, Is *this* a sign?

16. Litter, endangered species, and undercover cops...

Sand, sand, sand, and more sand. On the other side, ocean as far as the eye can see. It's overcast, the bottoms of my pants are wet and mucky, and it's all one monotonous trek to nowhere. That's not my life I'm talking about, but it could be. That's me returning to the scene of the crime, as dad suggested, to look for...what exactly? Believe it or not, that's a question I hadn't really considered up to this point. I have no idea what I'm looking for. Clues, I guess. Something that looks familiar, something that will jar a memory.

But so far, it's all just a lot of nothing.

So far, for all I can see, nothing at all may have happened here.

I'm not even sure exactly where on this long curving spit of beach it was that I saw Trina T murdered, but it seems to me it was more north than south, more east than west, more this way than that way of wherever I am, so that's where I'm walking. Seagulls stare at me balefully as I pass, hanging in the clammy air where the breakers curl over. Sandpipers, or whatever you call them, are scampering around. There are smashed shells everywhere. Fishing line, broken canvas chairs, rotting seaweed, plastic gallon jugs, tampon applicators, the occasional sneaker—it's all washed up here, festooning the beach like a festive garland of smelly crap.

Litter on this scale is really impressive.

To get an entire ocean this dirty, that's quite an accomplishment. That takes some doing. I don't know why we even fight it. It's a human accomplishment on a scale equal to building a pyramid or flying to the moon. To turn the planet into one big sloshing bowl of filth, maybe that's our species' true evolutionary purpose. Maybe humankind is supposed to go extinct along with everything else to make room for whatever comes next. Maybe there's a toxin eating slime smarter than Aristotle crawling its way out of the poisoned sea right now to populate the earth. Who are we to stand in the way of evolution? Who are we to say, *Evolution, but it stops right here! Evolution, but it's the human being to the end of time!*

What hubris!

As for the extinction of all the other species we take down the toilet with us, well, I have to admit, I'm not missing the Stegosaurus much on a day-to-day basis. Are you? So what if one less red-toed leaping flapdoodle leaps free across the pampas, what's it to me? What do I really care about the blue whale and the Bengal tiger? The only time I see a whale or a tiger anyway is on television. For all I know, maybe the real ones are all dead already.

These are the kinds of spiteful little homocentric thoughts I'm thinking when I walk straight into some tightly strung bailing wire.

The signs says, *Keep out!*

Under that not-so-friendly greeting, the sign says, *This area protected for migrating shore birds.*

I'm thinking, *What a perfect place to kill someone.*

Slipping under the wire, I step onto a stretch of beach that's exactly like the stretch of beach I've been walking on for the last hour. The only difference, they've scrubbed this part of the beach spotless to resemble the day of Creation. This has got to be the most pristine, most picturesque section of the whole goddamn eastern seaboard. And the only thing not allowed on it is a human being. Any pigeon or clam can hang out here, but it's against the law for me to set foot on this vacuumed patch of sand.

Sometimes you have to wonder how human beings even lasted this long. Sometimes you have to wonder if someone isn't just making all this up without paying attention. Maybe someone is—but that someone isn't me.

Poking around aimlessly, I'm looking at more nothing, only this is officially protected government nothing. I'm not really looking for any, but I don't see a single endangered migratory nesting shorebird that this beach is supposedly reserved for, not that I'd be likely to tell one from a fucking pigeon if I tripped over it while holding a copy of an *Audubon* guide.

Still—

I'm crouched down, peering into a big vacated snail shell when someone shouts out from someplace.

"Mr. Breen! Stop right there--"

That's not my name, of course, but I freeze anyway. I peer, flinching, over my shoulder into the leaden fog.

"Mr. Breem," the dunes say.

That's not my name, either, but the voice is close enough, it's close enough to be sure that whoever the dunes are talking to, they're undoubtedly talking to me. They have to be. I'm the only one here.

He's coming towards me, climbing over a piece of driftwood, coming through the long, dry dune grass. He's wearing a tie and the kind of sharp three-button suit all the celebrities are wearing this year. He's wearing dark shades. He's got his black hair slicked back and his handsome, chiseled face is perfectly tanned. He looks like that guy Sprocket was pretending to be when he described himself during that sex-chat on the computer.

He's holding out a little wallet. He's showing me a badge of some kind, but he snaps shut the wallet before I see what kind. He's saying "I'm Agent Chambers."

This is the scene of the crime I've come back to; it's the oldest cliché in the book.

I'm an idiot, I'm thinking. *I'm screwed. Thanks a pant-load Dad.*

I say, "What's the problem?" I shrug innocently. I look around. I say, "I didn't know." And I mean that as an answer to everything in general, whatever I might have done. Whatever question he asks, I've already decided: that's going to be my answer.

He says, "Do you know this area is restricted?"

I shrug, "I didn't know."

We stare at each other for a few seconds, saying nothing, as if trying to figure out if any of this makes any sense so far. I hear the rustle of the dune grass, the cry of a gull, the hoot-hoot of the wind in the mouth of an empty Rolling Rock bottle on the other side of the restricted area fence. Staring at me from behind his designer shades, Agent Chambers seems to come to some kind of internal decision. He seems to have decided to take me into his confidence, or to pretend to. He says, "You know very well that this isn't about protecting migratory birds."

This is a trick, I'm thinking. *He's just fishing.* If I just keep my mouth zipped, I can't give anything away.

He says, "I was out here the night that girl was murdered, Mr. Breen."

I'm not saying a word, my lips are zipped, but now it's not just a crafty strategy, now it's the result of total panic. Now it's a form of general paralysis. Like one of those lizards that pretends it's a stick, that's what I'm like right now.

He says, "Breem?"

I say, "Huh?"

He says, "What is it, anyway. Breem….with an M…or Breen…with an N?"

I say, "I don't know."

He shrugs his shoulders and beckons me with one of his perfectly tailored and monogrammed sleeves. "Either way, it doesn't matter. You'll want to come with me."

Without question or protest, I'm trudging dutifully after him over the dunes, through the dune grass, to the nearby parking lot. The whole time I feel like a schoolboy caught smoking by the janitor and heading for the principal's office. This is the image that flashes to mind, even though what I've been caught doing is capital murder.

He's got a beat-up red VW Cabriolet and I can't help but somehow feel a little surprised that he's driving around in something so small and crappy. He motions me around to the passenger side and I climb in, shut the door, and wait for him to do the same. The inside of the car smells moldy, it smells of old cardboard boxes in leaky basements, it smells like he's been driving around underwater.

He slides in next to me, reaches over, and snaps off the yakking scanner. He says, "We don't need any of that, do we?" He winks. "You never know when a radio transmits both ways, do you?"

Something, a lot of somethings, are tapping on the windshield and I look up and see its raining. I'm looking at the spattered windshield in a kind of imbecilic wonder. I'm really just stalling for time, but then, when aren't I?

Chambers smiles and tells me he's going to be level with me. He's going to give it to me straight. "There really isn't much time for fucking around the mulberry bush," he informs me.

He actually says, "Time is of the essence. Let's get down to the nitty gritty, shall we?"

The gist of it is this: Agent Chambers, or whatever the hell his name really is, has been keeping an eye on this beach. He's been doing it in a kind of unofficial capacity. He's been doing it pretty much on his own free time.

"Think of it," he says, "as a public service. First and foremost," he says, "I'm a public servant."

But the way he says this, the way he grins when he says it, causes you to remember that a hangman is a public servant, too. The agent pulls out a small pocket cassette recorder. He presses the red record button, records the time and date, and lays the recorder on the dashboard, so that it can record. He points out that he could have recorded all this in secret, that he didn't have to let me know that he had a tape recorder, that he wants to make a good-faith gesture. "I want to prove I'm a good egg," he says. "Do you appreciate that?"

"Yes," I say dutifully.

"Are you going to be a good egg, too?"

"Yes," I dutifully answer.

"Are you going to prove it?"

Dutifully I assure him, "Yes."

It's all well and good, I'm thinking, that he showed me the tape recorder, all very nice this talk of eggs. Maybe it proves something, maybe it doesn't. Fact is, the only voice on that tape is going to be his, because I have no intention of saying a goddamn thing outside of an absolutely unavoidable "yes," "no," or "I don't remember." He re-situates the tape recorder and tells me it's important to keep a record of these things.

"It's all being referenced," he says. "It's all being referenced for future reference." He shrugs apologetically. He says, "This is what I do."

He hasn't said anything about me being under arrest yet. I've been listening in particular for the words, *You're under arrest.* So far, he hasn't said them. He hasn't said much of anything of substance, come to think of it, and I'm wondering if that's because he doesn't know anything of substance. Does he know, for instance, that I've been to bed with Naomi Blake? Is he waiting for me to volunteer that information? If so, he's going to have to change the tape in that recorder a few million times.

The gist of it is this: there's been a lot of weird shit going down on this beach when no one's looking, a lot of questionable activity has been occurring here. He says, "You'd be surprised at what I've seen down here." He thinks about that for a second or two, winks in a way that causes a chill to run down my spine, and adds, "Well, then again, maybe you wouldn't."

What he's been doing is parking his car about three miles away and hiking to a place behind the dunes. He watches the beach, the ocean, the sky, the wind, the dunes. He watches the fishermen, the sand, the horizon, the ships at sea. He watches until dawn and then he goes home, changes, goes to work, and then he comes back here to watch some more.

I say, "It doesn't sound like you get much sleep."

He says, "I never sleep, Mr. Breen. There's no time for sleep. I have to keep at least one eye open at all times. I'm watching. You never know when something is going to happen. You never know when you're going to see something."

He watches every night, every single one of them. One of these nights was the night Trina T was *murdered.* The way he says *murdered* you can hear how he says it in italics.

"Really?" I say, "I wouldn't know anything about that." But this is last ditch, this is holding on with fingernails.

He says, "I saw what happened the night that girl was murdered. I saw you there. Mr. Breen."

"Then you know I didn't do anything wrong."

He says, "Do I?"

I say, "I don't know what you're talking about."

He says, "Don't you? Let me make it plain. Just as there are people who have an interest in shifting the blame for their crimes on someone else, the police have an interest in solving those crimes whether or not the person they catch actually committed the crime or not. Do you see how it all evens out in the end?"

I say, "Not really."

The gist of it is this: something smells bad. There's corruption here, there's rot in the air, there's a malignancy in the area, and there's corruption all around us and there's no telling how high it goes, how deep it goes, how far it goes. There's no telling how much is infected. There's no telling *who* is infected. This isn't the first time someone has disappeared on this beach. Chambers asks me if I have any idea what he's talking about.

I say, "No."

"Of course not," he says, with faux cheer. "No one does, do they? But I intend to find out."

All this time the rain is hammering the car, bouncing off the hood, thrumming on the roof, pouring down the windows, turning the world outside into a liquid with no form or sense at all.

He says, "Freaky, isn't it? You can't trust anyone. You can't even trust me."

Then he laughs. He claps me on the shoulder.

He says, "Nah, you can trust me."

He reaches in front of me and turns the scanner back on and it resumes squawking out codes for people having heart attacks, going berserk in malls, robbing cars, burning down warehouses, slipping in bathtubs, falling into really deep holes. Christ, what a lot of problems people get themselves into. Chambers points to the radio as a 611 or a 412 or *something* comes crackling through. He says, "I'm not answering that. Distractions." He says, "All distractions from what's *really* going on." He taps a well-manicured finger on my breastbone. He says, "Don't you be distracted."

The whole time I'm thinking, *This is the man who's having an affair with the love-of-my-life. This guy, sitting right beside me, is screwing around with Norma Blake Madsen.* And I'm screwing around with her twin-sister. Does he know that? Does he know I know that? What does that mean? He lights what I'm certain is a joint, inhales, hands it to me. I'm wondering if this is some kind of trick, if this is a set up of some sort. They've got me for first-degree murder and they're trying to entrap me on a misdemeanor pot charge? Does that make sense? Does anything?

By now I'm sweating under the armpits. I can feel the sweat trickling from under my arms, along my sides, dribbling down into the waistband of my boxers. I take the joint from his fingers, put it to my lips, and pretend to inhale. There's so much smoke right now inside the car, I don't have to take a hit to fill my lungs up with the pungent smoke.

What I'm thinking right now is: *Jesus Christ, I thought it was just me. But it's a lot worse. Everyone's crazy.*

The last thing Agent Chambers says to me before he drops me off at the Keyport bus station is this: "You're not alone, Mr. B." He turns from behind the wheel of the red VW Cabriolet, makes a pair of binoculars out of his fists and says, "I'm watching."

If this is some kind of clue, I don't get it. If he's got something to say, I wish he'd just come right out and say it.

He says, "Try to take succor in that fact. Try not to let it creep you out."

I stumble out of the red VW Cabriolet, gulping at the fresh air. I cross the parking lot where the bus back to Manhattan is already loading a line of ratty-looking commuters. With every step I take, I'm afraid Chambers is going to call me back. I'm afraid he's just waiting until I nearly make it to the bus to say what I've been afraid he'd say from the very beginning, *You're under arrest.*

Walking across that parking lot, it's like walking across a minefield, waiting to go boom with every step.

I board the bus and I'm still thinking something is going to go wrong. It's stopped raining at some point but it's just as gloomy as it was before. Sitting on a bus full of spies disguised as businessmen, old people, teenage girls, construction workers, I look out the window to where Agent Chambers is now leaning against the red VW Cabriolet, arms crossed. He's watching me. He does that thing with his fists again, making binoculars, peers through them. He's grinning, he's smoking his joint in broad daylight, he's mouthing the words, *"I'm watching."*

As the bus finally pulls away, I lean back in my seat. I put my head back, I close my eyes, I breathe a sigh of relief. I'm not under arrest, not yet, and I'm heading back to New York. Maybe it was a trick, maybe he was on the level. I'm thinking, *There are worse things than having a cop in your corner watching your every move.*

Wait a second, Am I crazy? No there aren't.

Anyway, all in all, I'm feeling surprisingly good about myself. But maybe that's because, in spite of myself, I've managed to get a contact high.

17. True love, parrots, and birth control...

"Barren," she says, "like the moon, nothing grows, nothing lives, it's impossible." What we are discussing are Naomi's chances of conception. We're discussing this after I roll off her for the second time tonight, staring at the ceiling, feeling like a deboned filet of something or other.

I just got done asking her if, well, we shouldn't be using some form of contraception. Asking this now while five million or so of my deadbeat spermatozoa are already loitering in her venusian tubing, I'm revealing my stupidity, but also much more than that. I'm revealing my total lack of faith in the laws of cause and effect. I'm living out my conviction of the total relativity of time. I'm also revealing my naivete that I can believe a single word she says. I'm revealing all of these things in equal measure, but it's my basic stupidity that I'm revealing most of all.

Naomi is lighting up one of the cigarettes she says she doesn't smoke. She seems so absolutely unconcerned about this conception thing that I start feeling reassured in spite of myself. I have to think that having a child with a loser like me who she basically just met and who, for all she knows, may be responsible for the disappearance of her sister and brother, has got to be the very last thing a girl like Naomi Blake wants. I figure she has to be pretty much on top of whatever needs to be done to make sure a disaster of this magnitude doesn't happen.

I guess I'm thinking she must have in place the contraceptive equivalants of the old Berlin Wall, complete with snipers and razor wire, standing guard over her fallopian whatevers. Star Wars defense systems, ICBM missiles, napalm, all that.

I'm not overly interested, but this barren thing she's mentioned seems like one of those conversation starters that require an answer. It seems like one of those lines of intimacy that need to be followed up on, one of those things "she'd like to talk about." What I'm saying, in other words, is that I recognize this is the price I have to pay for sleeping with her. More to the point, I know I'll be sorry, but asking her about this barrenness of hers is the price I'm going to have to pay if I expect to sleep with her in the future. It'll show my sensitivity, my empathy, how I care about her as a *person.*

Closing my eyes I ask, "What happened?" Gritting my teeth, I say, "Tell me everything."

She tells me about growing up in Chicago or someplace like that. She tells me things that sound vaguely like child abuse. She tells me of an unhappy marriage or two. There are a couple of miscarriages along the way. There are sharp pains in the belly. There are fibroids, cysts, possible tumors. There is the scraping of delicate reproductive organs. There is a car that stalls one night for no apparent reason on an abandoned stretch of state highway in rural Pennsylvania two days before Christmas 1996. There is a large circular shadow and a beam of piercing light from heaven to her navel. There is a doctor of "alternative medicine" who says he can perform a new kind of endoscopic surgery.

"He said he could make me fertile," she says. "He lied."

She tells me that right before they put her under, this doctor leaned forward and whispered what he was really going to do to her. She was in the process of passing out, so she doesn't remember exactly what he said. What's more, he'd been speaking the whole time in an entirely different language to the attending nurses, a weird language full of whirrs and clicks. But she understood him well enough when he told her what he was really about to do.

"What was he really about to do?" I can't help but ask, feeling like I'm sitting at a campfire ghost story.

"Deliver my first and only child."

"But I thought you said you couldn't have children?"

"It wasn't a human child. It was an *alien* delivery. Now I'm barren," she says, emptily. As proof, she points at the scar on her belly, a zipper line about four inches long. "I'm empty," she says. "They took it all out. So I can never conceive normally, that is to say, as a human woman, ever again. I'm barren."

Crazy, that's more like it, I'm thinking, looking at her serious, tear-stained profile in the gloom. She's a little bit kooky. But then, who isn't, right? She's a tad nuts, but probably not dangerously so. Maybe she's paranoid schizophrenic, but dammit, she sure is cute. And she fucks like a demon. And, well, her twin sister, the love-of-my-life is taken, so, you know, I can't be too-too picky. I can't expect perfection. I'm no Prince Charming myself, as everyone who sees that goddamn composite sketch seems determined to remind me. I'm lucky to get this much, I'm thinking.

There's not a lot of point trying to convince Naomi that she's delusional. These ideas crawl inside your head and before you know it, they're a part of you. They become part of the way you dress, make love, hold a fork, buckle up your safety belt. They're a part of the mythology you live by. Like everyone else, whatever Naomi Blake is, it's the result of everything that's wrong with her. Besides where would I begin to refute a story as ridiculous as the one she's just told me? I have my own ridiculous story I can't refute.

One thing I do know, it's time for me to get going. I know, for one thing, that after two orgasms my business here is pretty much complete, at least for another day or two, and if I hang out any longer, someone's bound to be disappointed. But for some reason, Naomi's hands are at work, fiddling around between my legs. When it dawns on me what she's expecting, I feel like saying, *"Oh come on you've got to be kidding."* I feel like giving her a crash course in the sad reality of the functioning of the human penis, at least the sad reality of the functioning of my own particular human penis, at this age and stage of the game.

Instead I say, "I really should be going."

"What's the hurry, big boy?" she murmurs playfully.

But there's no big boy in attendance in this bed.

I say, "Umm work...."

She coos, "All work and no play..."

She nibbles, "I'm in the mood for love..."

She sing-songs, "Let's get it on..."

The situation is getting pretty desperate. I mean the fact that there's nothing to conceal is getting harder to hide.

I say, "Seriously, I've really got to go..."

There's no way to make what Naomi says next follow what I've just said. How little it follows what I've just said, though, is so impressive in it's total lack of sequentiality that I find myself momentarily struck dumb. What she says is, "You don't find me attractive. You don't want me because I'm barren."

"That's just crazy," I say. And I mean this, rather literally. "You're crazy."

She shouts, "You don't want to penetrate me!"

"That's not true..."

She shrieks, "You find me revolting!"

I consider once again delivering that crash course in the sad reality of the functioning of my own particular human penis. But I'm convinced that such an explanation is more than I should have to admit to, more than our relationship demands, that kind of self-humiliation is beyond the call of duty, really.

So instead I say, "That's not true. It's the book," I say suddenly, desperate for an excuse, "the deadline for the outline is overdue and I've got a bitch of a writer's block."

It's not the best argument, but its the best I can come up with, and it's not convincing Naomi at all. She's on her stomach now, head in her arms, trembling violently, and sobbing. "If you found me attractive," she wails in response, "you'd penetrate me!"

What I should do is follow through on my plan to leave. I should tell her I'll call her later and then change my phone number. I should plan that long overdue re-location to the Nevada desert.

Instead I reach out and touch her shuddering shoulder blade. I say, "Come on. Let's do it."

"It's too late," she moans. "You're just saying that."

"No," I say, "I really want to."

She looks up at me and sniffs. "Really?"

I wonder if my smile is as shaky and insincere as it feels. Would that even be possible?

"Really," I say.

For the next forty-five minutes or so, Naomi is rubbing, pumping, tickling, sucking my poor overwrought penis. She's squeezing, coaxing, nibbling, scratching. She's doing everything but praying to the damn thing, and some of the dirty stuff she's whispering in my ear could be considered a kind of praying, if by prayer you mean begging for a miracle. She's twisting my nipples like she trying to get reception from China. She's wiggling a finger up my ass.

For my part, I'm fantasizing, visualizing, trying to conjure up every reason I ever found to have a hard-on. I'm going back into the archives, dusting off the old classics, flipping through the glossy centerfolds of my misspent boyhood. What I feel like I'm doing is trying to start a fire by rubbing two wet sticks together.

There's a point where I give up and start thinking about something else altogether. I'm basically ignoring Naomi and whatever she's doing at this point. I'm fantasizing about not being here at all. I'm thinking about anything that has to do with anything so long as it has nothing to do with sex.

By now, I'm starting to get sore, not to mention hungry, and I'm willing to say anything just to get it all to stop. That's the only way I can explain what I say next. What I say is, "I love you."

I'm just as surprised as she is when these words pop out of my mouth. Naomi seems so surprised, in fact, that she immediately stops torturing my poor limp penis. It seems that by merely saying these words she immediately stops expecting anything else from me altogether. To my utter relief, she curls up beside me. She lays her head on my chest. She contents herself with softly holding my genitals. I feel her breath across my bruised nipples. She sighs. She says, "I love you too." Then she says, "Oh...oh..."

What seems to be happening is beyond my comprehension.

What's happening is a miracle.

What seems to be happening is that I'm getting hard for no reason at all.

That's what *seems* to be happening, anyway.

I'm not exactly sure.

Fact is, I'm so stunned I don't feel anything at all.

Naomi says, "Norma was usually very careful. She wouldn't have gone to meet him if she wasn't sure she could trust him."

What we're doing is discussing her twin sister's decision to leave her husband and run off with Chambers. We're lying side-by-side in bed, post-coitus, a time, brief as it may be, when two human beings are about as close they're ever going to be. A time, when, within reason, you figure you have a pretty good chance of getting something that approximates the truth.

I shrug. "People think they can trust their spouses, brothers, business partners, priests, lawyers, employers, doctors. They think they can trust their own kids not to put them in the old age home, not to raid their retirement income, not to pull the plug. It's always a mistake. Everyone gets betrayed in the end. This was just a horny guy on the internet."

Naomi says, "Still..."

"Do you think she might have gone into hiding?"

"No," she says. "She wouldn't have just disappeared. She wouldn't want her loved ones to worry. She'd have gotten word back somehow."

"Her husband--what kind of a guy is Dr. H. "Pop" Madsen?"

Naomi's face folds down, like a fierce Kabuki mask. "A real prick."

"Would he really be the kind of prick to kill his wife?"

"He absolutely would be that kind of prick. I'm terrified of him. If he finds out where I am, he might come after me. Listen," she says, "I'm telling you all this because you're a writer. I'm telling you all this because I'm hoping you'll reconsider."

"Reconsider what."

"Your book. I'm hoping you'll decide to write a whole book about my sister. I think it will make fascinating reading. I really think it could be a bestseller."

Outside, presumably over that ugly bridge that would only look good if it were raining, I hear what sounds like a train clattering by.

I say, "I wouldn't expect too much. True crime isn't as hot or lucrative a genre as it used to be, you know. The audience is jaded. People are kind of burned out of possibilities. What can you do anymore that will shock anyone? Nowadays everyone is a cannibal killer. Nowadays everyone you meet has fed a lover or two into a woodchipper."

If there's even a shred of accuracy in anything I'm saying, it's purely accidental.

Naomi Blake is shrugging in the general late afternoon gloom shrouding the bed. She's lighting another cigarette. She's passing it to me.

She says, "So exactly how little are we talking about?"

Now it's me who's doing the shrugging. "I don't know."

She holds my penis and says, "How much can you give me right now?"

As my penis, doing an impression of James Brown, comes back in her hand for an improbable fourth time, I'm thinking of the latest Fed Ex envelope delivered to my apartment with the same enigmatic message to meet someone who isn't named somewhere unspecified at two a.m. Like all the other ones, I'm listed as the sender.

I say, "Four thousand in small bills. Tens and twenties."

She's nodding in the gloom. She says, "I'm sorry to be so mercenary. Please don't judge me. I need the money. I'm scared. I feel that it's really me they want. I can't tell you why. I don't know myself."

Egomaniacal as that sounds, I can't say I blame her. I can't even say it's not an idea that hasn't occurred to me. I mean, not that

she's the real target of all this, but that the real target is *me*. At the
same time, I'm thinking she has a perfectly good reason to be
paranoid. I'm thinking of how I just met Norma Blake Madsen's
lover on that beach and how I'm keeping it secret from a woman I
shouldn't be fucking in the first place because I'm in love with her
twin sister and how this is all eventually going to blow up in my face.
No wonder, I'm thinking, *that we're all paranoid.* There's a glass of water
on the bedside table. It's sitting on a little doily-type thing. I'm thirsty,
practically dehydrated, but I'm not drinking.

I take a look around the bedroom, at Naomi, at the glass of
water, at whatever the afternoon gloom will allow me to see. As great
as this all was, I know that if I had to sleep in this bedroom for the
rest of my life, one or the other of us would surely end up dead.
Maybe we'd both end up dead. We wouldn't survive. No one does.
Anytime you see a bedroom where a man and a woman have slept
together for a long time, you're looking at the scene of a crime.
You're looking at a place where someone has been murdered, or
soon will be.

Basically, you're looking at necrophilia.

That may be a dark view of love, but I guess it's better than
having no view of it at all.

"One more thing," Naomi Blake says, "Don't tell anyone about
us. If you tell anyone about us, I'll deny everything. I'll say you're
crazy. If you tell anyone about us, I'll say you just imagined the whole
thing."

Anticlimactically speaking, I'm feeling pretty good about myself. I'm
sitting in Naomi Blake's big purple chair basking in the cozy nuclear
afterglow of our quadruple-feature late afternoon lovefest. I'm
leaning forward over her coffee table book of Manhattan
photographs and I'm trying to place some silly-looking oblong
structure on long spidery legs resembling an upright egg comprised
of thousands of multi-colored lead glass windows. The caption reads
that it's been a famous city landmark since 1972. Of course, I've
never seen the preposterous looking thing in my life. And frankly, at

this point, I'm so proud of myself for what I accomplished in the bedroom, I don't care.

In the corner of the room, on a wood perch I haven't noticed before, is a large red-and-blue parrot. The perch is made of a twisted, natural-looking, sun-bleached branch of some kind. It has two tins attached: one for food, one for water. On the wall behind all this are explosive splatters of dried parrot shits. Aside from the fact that the bird is unnaturally still and quiet, I have no idea how I could have missed its presence on the way in.

The bird is cocking its head sideways, looking at me looking at it. I haven't seen anyone looking at me that intelligently in months. Come to think of it, I don't think I've ever seen anyone looking at me that intelligently.

I say, "Hi there."

The bird cocks it's head the other way. If I'm right, it's thinking something like, *Oh you look like just as big an idiot from this angle as the other.*

The bird says nothing.

I say, "Squawk!"

Naomi comes into the room holding two big mugs of steaming something. She puts one down on the coffee table in front of me, curls up on the couch opposite.

I say, "When did you get a parrot?"

She says, "Say what?"

"The parrot. When did you get it?"

"Oh," she says, "yesterday."

"That's odd."

"What's odd about it?"

"I don't know," I say, and I don't. But there's something odd about it, that's for sure. "You didn't mention you were thinking of getting a parrot."

"I bought it to keep me company. Living alone, it's nice to have something talking to you. Even if it's just repeating exactly what you say." She thinks about that for a moment. Then she adds, "Especially if its repeating exactly what you say. It's like living with someone exactly like you without using twice the toothpaste. It's like living by yourself without the loneliness."

Naomi has a bead on something here, I'm thinking. If she can just be happy with her parrot and leave it at that, she'll be okay. She'll pull through all of this better than most. Like the rest of us, though, I know she'll end up asking for more. We all do. I know she really doesn't have a prayer.

I say, "What's it's name?"

She says, "Ummmmm…..Max. With two x's."

"Hi Maxx," I say, using a parrot accent. "Hi there." I turn to Naomi. I say, "Doesn't it say anything?"

"Not yet. Not a peep."

She's holding her mug, letting the steam bathe her face, her eyes closed. She says, "Well it's a story to tell our grandkids."

"What is?"

"How we met."

Diplomatically, I let her comment slide. I don't want to shatter any fantasies, I don't want to lose my place on the perch. Besides, I think, she's barren, right, she just told me so in the bedroom, so what difference does it make? There won't be any grandkids. No need to rub it in. But I figure that my view on reproducing should only be a comfort to her. Like the parrot, I should know better. I should either repeat exactly what she says or say nothing.

"It's for the best, you know. You being barren and all. I never wanted children, anyway."

She says, "Why do you say that?"

"Why? Think about life. Think of how much pain there is, how much loss. Why purposely make another person just so they have to suffer through all that? What's the point? Why would I want to be responsible for putting someone through this pointless hell?"

"But life is beautiful. Love makes you happy."

I can't help but let a little reality sneak into this scene in spite of myself. I say, "Good grief, who ever told you that?"

"Don't I make you happy?"

"Yes," I say. "Yes."

I say "yes" like the parrot would say "yes."

"Oh yes," I squawk.

But it's too late. I can see it by the look on her face: a hard, impenetrable, closed look, like a porthole in a storm.

She says, "Aren't you going to drink you steaming mug of something?"

She doesn't actually say "steaming mug of something," but I'm not exactly sure what she calls what's in my mug. All I know is that I've had my mouth all over her, from head to toe, but I'm not putting my lips to this mug. I haven't seen her sipping hers, not that if she did sip hers, it would definitively prove a damn thing.

I say, "I'll sip it later. Thanks."

In the corner, on its perch, the parrot doesn't say anything, just like it hasn't been saying anything all along. It doesn't emit a single peep.

I figure its time to go. Actually, it was time to go twenty minutes ago. "I really think I should be going now."

Naomi doesn't object. She says, "I think I know what your problem is."

"Well, I'll stick around another minute or two for that. I've been trying to answer that question for decades. Have a hack at it, everyone else has."

"Your problem is that you're asking the wrong question. What you shouldn't be asking is *Why?* What you should ask yourself is, *Why not?*"

I'd consider that if I knew what the hell she was talking about. Instead I find myself staring at her robe. Up until this moment, I just sort of took it for granted because it's exactly the kind of thing women often take out to wear after being thoroughly fucked. It's some kind of red silk thing, cinched around the waist and all that, nothing unusual on that score, but it's covered in a repeating pattern of nonsense symbols that I suddenly recognize. It's the one on the screen of my infected computer.

FAKE GIRLS

18. Strike zones, organic vaginas, and good-bye...

"Cunt!," Meeah Soo is shrieking, "Don't lie to me. I can smell it on you!"

She shrieks something else and I'm guessing it's a variation of what she just shrieked, but I'm too busy ducking the shoe she's just thrown at my head to be certain. When Meeah Soo throws a shoe at you it's not just the usual hysterical girl gesture. When Meeah Soo throws a shoe it's an act of attempted murder. You see, Meeah Soo used to be a promising left-hander in the Philadelphia Phillies minor league farm system. A shoe, in Meeah Soo's large hand, is nothing short of a lethal weapon. The shoe Meeah Soo throws is a great big sissy platform covered in red spangles. So what Meeah Soo is essentially trying to do right now, whether she's really aware of it or not, is kill me.

"Cunt, cunt, cunt," Meeah Soo screeches, like a cat in a trap.

With her super-long sissy nails, she can't quite work the buckle on her other big spangled sissy platform, her fingers are trembling so badly, and that may have saved my life. She straightens up, sort of, one foot on a heel about three inches higher than the other, which is flat on the floor. I figure if she charges and I have to make a run for it, I'll at least have the advantage over the first several yards or so, because she's going to be hobbled like someone running in a three-legged race.

"What's the matter?" she howls, "Is my four hundred dollar mouth not good enough for you? Are my twelve hundred dollar tits not big enough? Is the twenty two hundred dollar self-lubricating neo-vagina that I'm getting made out of my own inverted intestines not hot and tight enough for you?"

Later on, I'll turn around and take a look at the wall behind me where her shoe has left a hole like the blast of an elephant gun that missed the elephant.

Right now, though, I'm just thankful to still have a head to duck. I'm thankful I can still think, that I haven't sustained a massive brain trauma. I'm hoping to keep my faculties a little longer, long enough to get the hell out of here in one piece, so I say, "Meeah, please, just listen…"

For the time being, she's not listening, which is just as well, because after asking her to listen I realize I really don't have anything to say. So she continues to holler obscenities. Other things are flying in my general direction, but none of them nearly so potentially lethal as her big red sissy platforms: pens, books, vibrators, unpaid bills, candle holders, breast forms, that kind of stuff. I get grazed by some of it, but most of it goes wide. As a pitcher, it's lucky for me that Meeah Soo's big problem was control. She couldn't find the strike zone as a top minor league prospect, and she can't find it as a hysterical pre-op transexual sissy.

She's still enumerating the expensive female body parts she bought to satisfy me like a real woman and I'm thinking how sad all of this really is. I don't volunteer the opinion that she isn't changing herself into a girl for me. I don't suggest that all the expensive surgery she whores herself out to pay for, the toxic drugs she gulps like candy, the horrendous collateral damage she may be doing to all her major internal organs--I don't suggest that none of this is really being done to make me happy.

The fake tits, fake lips, fake ass, fake brow, fake chin, fake pussy—she's doing it all for herself. Most of all, I don't provide the additional suspicion that all I am to her is part of the fantasy that she is a real girl. Or that if she could collect enough spare parts to pay someone to make the perfect man to love and adore her, she'd buy that, too.

Saying any of these things to Meeah Soo right now would be doing something really stupid. It's true, I'm doing something really stupid all the time. If nothing else, my life up to now has been a relentless chronicle of doing really stupid things, one right after another, as fast as humanly possible, and I suspect it will continue to be so, until I do the stupidest thing of all. But telling the truth to Meeah Soo right now would be stupid the way trying to lick a flame to see what fire tastes like would be stupid. It would be stupid like, well, like a whole bunch of stupid things just like that.

And I'm not *that* stupid, not yet, anyway.

Coming back to what Meeah Soo is actually saying now, I realize that she's moved into the "sobbing uncontrollably phase." She's run out of things to throw and knock over on her side of the room. She's run out of obscenities. She's run out of everything, including air to gulp. She seems to be hyperventilating and between hyperventilations, she wails, "Who is she? Tell me! Who the fuck is she? I want to know!"

Usually in these situations you hear of people saying something bone-headed like, *It's not what it seems.* Or, *This isn't what you're thinking.* They say stuff like, *You've got it all wrong.* Or, *This isn't about you at all.* What you think is that you wouldn't say something so lame in the same situation. But the fact is, there are only so many things you can really say. Fact is, there's really *nothing* to say. When you come right down to it, there's nothing but a handful of cliches to deal with the most important events in our lives. There's only so many ways, for instance, to say *I don't love you anymore.* Only so many ways to say, *You're not the one for me.*

There's only one way, really, to say: *Goodbye.*

On the way out, I notice that the shoe she threw at me has completely disappeared somewhere into the huge hole in the wall. A framed print of Gustav Klimt has fallen and the glass has shattered all over the floor. Somehow I want to tell Meeah Soo to be careful. I want to tell her not to cut her feet on the sharp shards of fractured glass, not to pick up the wrong guy, not to get herself killed. I want to start crying.

This is what love is, I think: for every two people who find it, one person loses it. For ever relationship started, another ends.

Already I hear tenants arguing from what sounds like every apartment in the building. All of them are howling away like dogs the way dogs do once one of them starts howling. All they needed was to hear one argument to remember everything they had to argue about, to remember how miserable they all were, how unfair everything is. What I realize is that basically nobody is happy. Basically everyone wants to start crying, everyone wants to start screaming. They just need an excuse.

"Leave then," Meeah Soo screams to my departing back. "Leave you fucking bastard. Just go, you impotent cock-sucking faggot."

I feel mad.

I feel sad.

I feel hurt.

Really, I don't know what to feel. I wish it didn't have to end this way. I want to say something to her; I want to give her some kind of answer that makes sense, that explains things, that makes things all better, but I have no answer to anything, nothing makes sense, nothing gets better. I don't know what to say.

So I let the door answer for me.

The door says, *Slam!*

Finding myself awake at three a.m., I'm sitting at the computer in one of the last remaining all-night internet café's that I haven't already been blacklisted from. I know I won't have much time before that damn virus pops up again and kicks me offline, so I have to work fast. I open my mail box and see two-hundred-twenty-seven new messages from Ratking. That's rather a lot of messages from someone famous for keeping mum. Each and every one of them has the same subject line: ***Urgent!*** That's a pretty dramatic subject line for someone with a reputation for hard-boiled cool. Something's not

right, you don't have to be a detective to sniff that out. I point at the
first message in the queue and hit the "delete" key. I hit the delete
key two-hundred-twenty-six times. That one time I don't hit it, I
leave one of the messages in my box.

I move the mouse which moves the little arrow to the button
marked "open." I press my finger.

The mouse goes, *"Click!"*

And there is Ratking's message on my computer screen.
Presumably, it's identical to the other two-hundred-twenty-six I've
deleted. What he writes, to boil it down to the essentials, is a lot of
talk about how he can't explain much in the email I've just opened
because people are now monitoring all his emails. He mentions *weird
shit*. He mentions *fatalities*. He uses the expression, *You wouldn't believe
it*, a whole lot. He drops in a few, *all fucked-ups*. He says the usual stuff
about me being in danger. I try to shrug off the words, *They're after
you!*

He wants to meet on a New York City tour bus. He adds that
it's not necessarily safer to talk on a New York city tour bus, but it'll
make whoever's following us feel ridiculous. He mentions Friday, the
downtown loop, evening. He says not to look for him because I
won't recognize him. He says he'll be wearing a disguise.

Then the screen goes black and everyone in the place starts
barking. Each and every computer, all sixteen of them, is frozen with
that damn enigmatic symbol on its monitor.

Infected, that's what my computer is, and that's what my life is.
Because it's not just my computer that's infected—*it's me*. Like
Sprocket said, it's as if the web itself is repulsing me from it's
immune system, as if a new virus protection software has been
developed to repel…me!…as if *I'm* the virus.

Something has snuck it's way into my system and now I'm
trying to figure out how to get it out. In the meantime, I can't access
my programs, can't open my email, can't even run a standard word
processor, just in case I'm inspired to write that true crime book I'm
pretending to write. I've got my address book online, my diary, my

banking. I've got my porn stored online. I can't shop for a pair of tube socks without computer access. I can't masturbate until I log-on.

It's not just that my life is on-line, it's that I have no life off-line.

And just when I think it can't get any worst is when it always does. I think of a truly frightening scenario. What if I've been infected by one of those bugs that attaches itself to your email and starts randomly sending files to everyone in my address book? What if my ex-wives start getting copies of my real federal income tax return for 2001? What if mom gets all my dominatrix incest porn?

This is the kind of radical honesty no one was meant to bear.

These are the kinds of things you only tell God, your shrink, or your hard-drive. These are the kinds of things that make us real, by which I mean, the things we have to hide about ourselves from everyone at all costs.

Over the next two days, and up until right now, I see that virus design, message, logo, whatever it is, turning up in the oddest places. Looking up from where I'm pissing in a Starbucks, I see some bored urinator has scratched it onto the wall in blue ballpoint pen while waiting for his bladder to empty. It's tattooed on the scrawny bicep of a girl tending bar in the Village; it's worked into the design of a manhole cover on Tenth Avenue; it's on dozens of posters plastered to a wall advertising an upcoming movie starring Britney Murphy. I think, *What's going on?* Is Hollywood co-opting my personal nightmares now. Am I only imagining things? Has it really come to that?

Whatever it means, I'm suddenly seeing this trademark everywhere: buses, soda cans, restaurant menus, book covers, newspapers, t-shirts. If it's the emblem of some new company, I never realized just how much of everything they own.

It's hard to believe, I'm thinking, *that I never noticed it before.* It's just not possible, is it, that there's been some kind of catastrophic financial coup, that some corporate mega-giant just bought up the whole world overnight.

And then I'm thinking, *Well, why not?*

We're all already owned in little pieces by the taxman, the lawman, the insurance man, the bossman. We're part-owned by our parents, our lovers, our kids. We've been taken over by our obsessions, our desires, our diseases. Almost noone retains a majority interest in themselves anymore. Just to survive, you have to sell off shares of yourself as you go along.

Maybe sometime in the night someone bought up all the pieces. Is that really so impossible?

Maybe we're now all owned by one giant entity. Maybe we finally have that long-dream-for single universal god?

19. Signs from God, tourists, and being nobody...

"Welcome to the Big Apple mon," the Jamaican guide shouts to us. He's trying to make himself heard over the screaming sirens, blaring horns, and whatnot of the surrounding stream of midtown traffic. Sitting on the top deck of the red double-decker tour bus, more or less as instructed, I'm only one of a handful of idiots up here. To tell the truth, I've always wanted to take one of these tours, but these aren't the circumstances I pictured when I pictured doing it. It might be all of twenty-two degrees today and it's prematurely snowing that special New York City snow, like dirty confetti, that makes everything look just that much dingier and grayer and more depressing than it did before.

Only a few hardy Czechs are up here with me and they are swathed in Siberian fur coats you could trek across Siberia in. I'm sitting here with no sign of Ratking in sight and I'm just beginning to think that the whole business, all those emails, were some kind of hoax or trap, after all. But I figure, while I'm waiting for the trap to be sprung, I'll take in the tour of Manhattan. I mean, what the hell, when will I have the opportunity to do this again; maybe I'll actually see some of the city for a change.

About five minutes after the bus pulls away from the curb, a guy of about forty in a black leather jacket slides into the seat next to mine. He's got blue eyes, close-cropped blonde hair, and a two-day's growth of beard. He looks a little like a cross between Kiefer Sutherland and Jean Genet, only much tougher, much cooler. I'll cut right to the chase and say it now: I've never laid eyes on this dude before in my life.

He says, "Hey Molloy." He says it with a German accent that doesn't sound at all made up. "I'm glad you made it."

I say, "Who the hell are you?"

"My name is Boris. But you know me as Ratking."

Turning the corner, the tour bus is trolling up towards Central Park and the guide, in English so broken it's not even English anymore, sounds like he's misidentifying what I happen to know for a fact is Columbus Circle. I look at the German tourist sitting next to me. I say, "Oh come on. You don't even look remotely like the guy I met in the Trump Tower."

"I told you I'd be in disguise. I lied, sort of. This isn't a disguise, but it might as well be. It's better than any disguise. It's really me."

The tour bus is picking up speed, making another squealing turn, we're now racing down Fifth Avenue. Over the microphone landmarks are being pointed out that we aren't even passing, that aren't in Manhattan at all. We're nowhere near the Flatiron Building, for crisssakes. The Sears Tower, that's in Chicago.

Up front, in their fur coats, the Czechs, like a group of excited bears, are snapping pictures of what they think is the Lincoln Memorial. Passing St. Patrick's Cathedral, I turn and say, "Did he just call that the Astrodome? This is insane. Who are you really?"

As loony as it all is, this probably authentic German guy is patiently trying to explain that his real name is Boris and that he really is the guy that I knew as Ratking. He patiently tries to explain that anyone can be anyone on the internet and the person I knew him as was just one of his myriad identities. Of course, I know all this as well as anyone, but he tells me, anyway.

"Who is anyone, after all? How well do you know even the people you know best? Each of us is so many people when all is said and done."

I say, "If you're really Ratking, prove it."

I'm sorry I asked. I'm warmed by embarrassment and squirming in my seat as he tells me some private stuff only Johnny Nomad would know and only Ratking would know if Johnny Nomad, that blabbermouth, told him. He shrugs, as if reading my mind, "Of course, that I know this stuff proves absolutely nothing. The information can easily be hacked. We are all subject to the same virus. True privacy is gone. Everyone knows everything…except, maybe, who we really are. In the end, you have to play it old-school. You have to rely on your gut instinct."

But all that said, the guy I'm looking at right this moment, he assures me, the guy sitting next to me now, that's really him, no shit, that's the real Ratking. He says, "It's really me. Boris."

I peer at him closely, squinting through the falling snowflakes, asking my gut if I can trust him. My gut does nothing but writhe with nervousness.

It's so cold up here on the top deck of the red double-decker tour bus with the wind and snow whipping over us that I'm having trouble concentrating. I'm having trouble feeling my feet. I say, "Can we go down below? I think my hair is freezing."

Boris says, "I think it's better if we stay up here. Fact is, I think they wanted me to find you. They put up obstacles they knew I could get around. It's all for show. They can hear us no matter where we go. But it'll be harder for them up here. If nothing else, we can always make their job a little harder."

"So I'm not crazy," I say. "There is an 'US.'"

"Well I can't vouch for your mental health, but yes, as far as I can tell, there is an US. Everything seems to indicate that."

But the really important thing, the thing everyone wants to know, that's the thing that Boris can't tell me. What he can't tell me is who "US" are. After years online, he doesn't have a clue. All he knows is that he's followed every link and they all ended in the same circuitous nowhere. Once he thought he could figure it out, but now he knows he can't. He's done, he says, he's retiring. He's logging off.

"You can't beat the house, not forever anyway. The odds catch up to all of us in the end."

Lord only knows what we're passing now, but, speaking of odds, I'll bet it's not even in the same hemisphere as whatever the tour guide is calling it. My face is so cold, it's frozen beyond all expression of disbelief. I can barely get my mouth to move. Still I manage to say it, "Suicide? You're killing yourself?"

Boris sighs, "Killing all my selves but this one. You can't be everyone forever. If you're going to live a life, you have to choose to be someone. I choose to be this."

"But is it really you?"

To my astonishment, he tells me he wants a wife and kids. He wants a little whitewashed cottage with a little garden in the little town where he really lives, somewhere in northern Germany. He tells me this is the life he wants to start living. He says he'll miss all the possibilities, but it's a dangerous fix he wants to kick once and for all.

"You get addicted," he says, "and then real-life isn't enough. All of a sudden a human being seems so puny and limited a thing. Your life seems so dull and—erm—lifeless."

He tells me he's not really looking forward to pushing a stroller through the German equivalent of a shopping mall on the weekends to shop for pillow shams and new shower curtain rings with the wife. Cutting the lawn, that's not what he's giving it all up for. But he does want to hug his kids goodnight. He does want to sleep with a real woman. You want to be a God and you can be a God online, but it's not real: it's better than real, that's the problem, but it's not real.

He says, "I can't do it anymore.

That's the United Nations we're passing, you asshole, I feel like screaming to the clearly tripping tour guide, but everyone seems to be just as happy thinking it's Monticello, or whatever the hell they're being told it is, and, really, just what the hell difference does it make, anyway? To Ratking I say, "For the love of Christ, can we please go below? I can't feel my nose."

Boris pulls out a cigarette. He says, "I need a smoke." He looks around for a sign. He says, "You can still smoke outside in Manhattan, can't you?"

He lights up, sucks on the cigarette, holds the smoke long enough to let the toxins saturate his lung cells. Twenty years from now, malignant tumors will grow there like mold spores. I'm seeing death being seeded in his tissues right now.

"How many is that?"

Ratking exhales. "Huh?"

"How many cigarettes?"

"Oh…well, I stopped counting."

"You're not trying to quit anymore?"

"I've given up giving up. Look," he concedes, "I'm making no fucking sense at all. I know that. Do you know the other day I finally finished Veronika K. I worked on her for five years and she was finally perfect. She has the blank stare of a Sphinx, the tits of a Playmate, and the amorality of an assassin. But do you know what happened when I put that final pixel into place? I don't want her anymore."

It's stupid, he explains, but for years, while he was building her, he'd fallen in love with this impossible woman of his imagination, like Dr. Frankenstein with his monster. Is it any wonder that no real woman could ever measure up? That love was always software, never flesh? Now he's telling me that he wants to find a real-life counterpart to Veronika K.

"She won't be perfect," Ratking concedes, "and she won't anticipate my every need and she'll make demands of her own and she won't go away when I turn off a switch…"

"And your point is?"

"She'll have the one thing I couldn't program. The one thing that maybe an imperfect woman *will* have. Maybe she'll love me back."

"That's quite a gamble," I say.

Boris smiles, "Yeah it is."

I shake my head. "I always thought I'd give up before you. You're a legend."

"Thou shalt not worship false idols. Because all idols are false. Listen, it's a lot like holding your breath, some can do it longer than others, that's all, but eventually we all have to come to the surface. Now it's your turn to stay under, to see if you can discover the secret.

Don't sell yourself short. You're pretty good at being nobody. Maybe you're even the real deal. Maybe you really *are* nobody."

"Jeez thanks. I think."

Hands thrust in my pockets, I'm so goddamn cold my teeth are rattling around in my skull like a box of Chiclets. The bus has turned around and we're now passing Central Park in the opposite direction, and it's now being variously described as the site of the first pilgrim landing, the last great Confederate offensive of the Civil War, and the assassination of President Richard Moby-Dick Nixon.

We pass the equestrian statue of General William Tecumseh Sherman.

"See there mon," the tour guide shouts, "Will Rogers!"

What Boris says about me being nobody, I've been hearing stuff like that ever since I was a little kid. Being nobody was supposed to be something to be avoided at all costs. From as far back as I can remember, being nobody was the worst thing you could possibly be. Under no circumstances should you be nobody. Just the opposite: you should try to be somebody, anybody, as quickly as possible. Parents, teachers, doctors, shrinks, bosses, cops, wives--they were all trying to get you to be somebody. But what I've always felt is that being nobody helps keep your options open. Being nobody keeps you mobile. It's what helps make you harder to define, harder to limit, harder to hit. Being nobody is the only way to be all the bodies you really are.

Boris lights up another cigarette. His chain-smoking is the only thing about him that I recognize. Bad habits, I guess, are one thing that carry over from one reality to another. We are passing the Cathedral of St. John the Divine where the Declaration of Independence, according to our guide, was signed by Edgar Allan Poe.

Boris says, "Whoever's behind this is big, as in omniscient, the puppet-master. Whoever's behind this is touching every thread on the web. There's no other way to explain how they can find us anywhere, everywhere, anytime at all. Whoever it is has been shadowing me the whole time I've been looking for Nada Klone. They've been looking over my shoulder."

I say, "Government?"

"Bigger. Someone who wants total control."

"And Nada Klone?"

Boris shrugs. His cigarette is getting damp. "Well, we know she's a composite. She was never meant to be real in the ordinary sense. The texts of Sprocket, the face of Norma Blake Madsen..."

"Like Veronika K?"

"Like that. But not exactly."

"So why all the deaths and disappearances?"

Boris shrugs again. "That part I don't quite understand. It seems totally unnecessary. Unless someone is trying to control *her*..."

"Is it US?"

Boris shrugs again. He says, "I hate to keep shrugging like an idiot, but I really don't know. Could be. Could be some entity named Chambers, who's been turning up all over the place. Could be someone else."

"Chambers? Did you say Chambers? Agent Chambers? The cop?"

"I don't know what he is, exactly. But whatever he is, he's no cop. At least not in the ordinary sense. Why? You've heard of the guy?"

"Maybe. Norma Blake Madsen seems to have been having an affair with some guy named Chambers before she disappeared. She met him on the internet. She thought he was a cop. I wonder if it could be the same guy?"

"Hard to say. It's one of those all-purpose names, you know? Unfortunately, I can't do much with my computer down. Can't get online even in an internet café for more than five minutes. It's like I'm carrying the infection with me."

I shiver and it's not because of the awning of icy slush hanging off my forehead. I say, "That virus, did it freeze up your screen, too?"

"Yeah."

"And that Egyptian-looking symbol?"

"To me it was like a sign from God, you know, telling me that I had to change my life. Before I came down with that virus, though, I connected Chambers to some kind of large online porn operation. I broke into the data base of subscribers. Some very recognizable names there, the kind you see in newspapers all the time, standing on the floor of the Senate, in the U.N., places like that. "

"Do you think he was stalking Norma?"

"If I may beg you pardon," Ratking says, "I don't think that can be true. From what I could see, that porn site was built around Nada Klone. She was featured there, and she looked to me to be an authentically willing participant. So if she were having an affair with him…"

"You're not trying to tell me what I think you're trying to tell me, are you?"

He says, "What do you think I'm trying to tell you?"

"That Nada Klone—Norma Blake Madsen—that she's in on it. That she and this guy Chambers are in cahoots in some kind of high-end international porn racket?"

He says, "I wouldn't say that. That would be making things a little too black and white. I think things are a lot greyer than that."

"How grey?"

"Very very grey."

As the bus skids around another corner, and we speed passed another half-dozen misnamed landmarks, I'm blowing on my numb, frozen hands and wondering if the New York I'm living in bears any resemblance to reality at all anymore.

You never die in cyberworld, you never get old, get sick, go bald, lose a kidney, and, even if you do, you can just log-off, crash an online identity, and start all over. You aren't limited by your age, your body, your sex, your job, your past, anything. You can be as many different people as you'd like, each one living out a separate, mutually exclusive life, each one pursuing it's own dreams, desires, and fantasies. You are limited by nothing but your own imagination and the number and variety of personalities that inhabit you.

That's the kind of thing that Ratking or Boris, or whoever he is, that's the kind of thing he's talking about. That's what Sprocket was talking about, Naomi Blake, too. That's the fix, the temptation, the thrill. It's the ability to live twenty-four lives at once, sitting at home, without changing out of your pajamas. It's all about having no limits. Having no limits means never having to make a choice between being a middle-aged bus driver in Baton Rouge and a teenage Japanese cheerleader, because everything is possible, everything is parallel.

Some experts might call this a symptom of a schizoid psychosis. Some spouses might call this infidelity and then call a good divorce lawyer. Some employers may call it an inappropriate utilization of company time and computer equipment. I prefer to call it the ultimate tool for the expansion of consciousness. I call it the technological equivalent of paradise. I call it the closest thing any of us are going to experience to being disembodied beings of pure spirit. You could, I guess, call it experiencing what it's like to be God, the closest thing to being immortal. Up to now I always thought of it that way. But now, I'm beginning to think of it all a little bit differently.

All of a sudden I'm starting to think of cyberworld not as the place you never die. Just the opposite. I'm starting to think of it as the most dangerous neighborhood ever invented.

I'm starting to think of it as the easiest place to get yourself killed, not just once, but each and every time you invent yourself anew.

20. Shop-lifting, bestsellers, and the perils of reading ...

Is it real or fake, the Temple of Dendur at the Metropolitan Museum
of Art? I've asked before and I guess I can ask again, but I never
seem able to remember the answer. I'm sitting on a bench in the big
airy room where the thing's been reconstructed or fabricated or
whatever. I'm staring into one of the shallow pools of water that
surround the temple at all the pennies and nickels and dimes visitors
have tossed into it to pay for wishes that won't come true.

What exactly I'm doing here, I can't say; just trying to soak up
vibrations, maybe, of a place where the person pretending to be Nada
Klone had met the man who was really screwing around with her.
I'm returning to the scene of another possible crime, of sorts. But
I'm also doing research.

All afternoon I've been wandering around one glass case after
another filled with shattered tablets, broken pots, assorted trinkets,
and other smashed-up crap of once-great civilizations. All this junk,
I'm thinking, that's all that's left of any of it, all the hate and love and
carrying-on that we do. It all ends up in a climate-controlled glass
case with a tag that says "Ox-cart shard VIIth Dynasty," or
something like that. What I'm looking for is the possible source of
the symbol that's heralded the virus popping up on all the computers
I've been using lately. I'm looking for it among shreds of mummy
cloth and broken tablets covered in hieroglyphs detailing things like

grain shipments and cattle sales in 1750 B.C. I'm lost in minutae, which is nothing new for me, but now I'm lost in minutae four thousand years old, which is.

I'm about to give up when I spot a small group of bored-looking seventh graders standing in front of a vacant sarcophagus. They're listening to an equally bored-looking museum curator, droning on and on about one of the Ramses. When she finishes, I wait for the kids to disperse and approach her with my sheet of notebook paper on which I've drawn the virus symbol. As it turns out, she explains there's a perfectly good reason I can't find what I'm looking for in the Egyptian section and that's because it isn't Egyptian at all.

"Sumerian," she says, and draws a line on my museum floor-plan to the correct section, a few thousand years way. "It's a rendering of the plant of immortality that the hero-king Gilgamesh plucked from the bottom of the sea."

"Oh really," I say, thinking, *Great, another piece of the puzzle that doesn't fit in anywhere.*

"Yes," the curator says. "Unfortunately, Gilgamesh fell asleep and a snake came along and ate the plant before he could bring eternal life to mankind."

"Bummer," I say. "Isn't that always the way?"

"Exactly," the curator says.

Something has been nagging at the back of my mind for some time now. It's something that, only now, walking among the display cases full of the junk of ancient Sumer, has gotten the attention of the front of my mind. It's not quite a thought, not exactly, more like the smoky form of an ominous suspicion.

I take out my cell phone and thumb the keypad and amble across the shiny floor to the side of a display case displaying the crushed-in helmet of some poor Mesopotamian bastard who looks like he probably didn't make it.

Naomi picks up on the sixth ring just like the answering machines does and she sounds so exactly like her recorded message that at first I think that's what it is.

"Hello," Naomi says. "Who's calling?"

"Hi," I say. "It's me."

"Where are you?"

"Sumer, circa 2,750 B.C."

"Oh."

"What's up?"

She hasn't been up to much, she tells me. The parrot's been shitting all over the wall, she suspects it's sick, it still doesn't say anything. The weather's miserable, she's not feeling so well herself, she has cramps, she's cut her hair, she's nauseous, she hates her life.

I say, "Do you think it's possible that your sister and Chambers were part of an online sex business? Does that at all sound like something she would do?"

"Is that something you really expect me to answer?"

"No. But if I did what would you say?"

She pauses and says, "I think I would have said I don't know. I think I would have said, She never told me."

"Well think about it."

"Okay."

"Did you ever meet Chambers, by the way?"

She pauses and says, "Umm…didn't you ask me that already?"

"I don't know. If I did, what would you have answered?"

"I would have said, not that I know of."

I say, "Is there anyone there with you?"

There's another pause on the line that, during peak hours, is going to cost me three dollars and twenty-five cents. Her hand is obviously over the receiver. You can hear what sounds like a lot of bumping around and whispering. When she takes her hand away she says, "No."

"Are you telling me the truth?"

"About what precisely?"

"About anything."

She thinks about that for a while. She says, "Yes."

"Can you expand on that?"
She says, "Not really." Then she says, "I have to get off."
"Naomi...wait..."
She's hung up.

Call me suspicious, but I think a pop visit to Naomi is perfectly in order. When I get there, she acts like nothing is wrong; she acts exactly like no one is hiding in the closet or has just snuck out the window and down the fire-escape to the sidewalk below. She acts so much like none of these things are happening that there's every reason to believe that they are.

On top of that, she seems to be trying to distract me. First, she asks me if I want some popcorn. Then she interrupts me to ask if I want some peanut butter. Maybe I want some ginger snaps? Some wine? Do I want to watch a movie? Do I want a clementine?

Finally she slides off the couch onto her knees, smiles, and opens her robe. She says, "I know what you want, you dirty boy..."

I don't want what she's doing now any more than I wanted a clementine or to watch *The Lord of the Rings*. I really want to talk. But what can I say now that she's started, now that she's got her head bobbing between my thighs? Fact is, you never know when something like this is going to happen again in your life. You never know if something like this will *ever* happen again. And you'll be kicking yourself all the way to the grave if it never does and you turned it down.

So you lay back and enjoy it while you can. You close your eyes, let your mind go blank, and figure all your problems will still be there later. You go into the bedroom. You take off her clothes and kiss her eyes, her nipples, her toes. You kiss her pussy, her mouth, her belly. You put yourself inside her. You grab her ass. You do the one good thing there is left to do in this world no matter how crummy everything else gets: you have an orgasm.

Later, on the couch again, she hands me another big steaming mug of something. She sits opposite me on her big purple chair and smiles. I start to mention Sprocket, ask another question about Chambers, but Naomi is having a different conversation.

"Someday," she says softly, "someday I really think I'd like to try having a child again. I've been thinking about it and I think I'd really like to get pregnant. I love children. I think I'd like to be a mother. That's what it's all about, after all."

The parrot starts squawking.

I'm looking from parrot to woman, from woman to parrot, and neither is making more sense than the other. I'm looking at Naomi but I could probably just as easily be looking at the parrot when I say, "I thought you said it was impossible for you to get pregnant?"

She sips her own big steaming mug of something…or she pretends to. I get the feeling it doesn't really make a difference whether she's drinking what's in the cup or not.

She says, "Well it's not technically impossible. Technically it's very possible."

I'm thinking, *Holy shit.*

The parrot is still squawking, it's been squawking the whole time, and it's only now that I actually hear what it's saying. Because it *is* saying something, after all. It's saying it in a parrot voice, so it's easy to miss the first few hundred or so times. But once you get used to the parrot voice it's not easy to miss at all. When you get used to the parrot voice you'd have to be working pretty damn hard *not* to hear what it's saying. You'd almost have to be in denial. What the parrot is saying is this: *Nada, nada, nada.*

"How odd," Naomi says.

The parrot shrieks, "Nada, nada, nada."

Eyes beady and black, it's staring right at me. "Nada, nada, nada," it screeches.

Naomi says, "How really odd. His old owner must have been a nihilist or something."

I'm trying not to show how freaked out I am, trying not to show how badly my hands are shaking.

Naomi says, "Careful honey. You're going to spill your mug of steaming something or other."

"Sorry," I mumble. "Sorry, but..." and I'm trying to change the subject, but not by much, from one disturbing topic to another, "where did you get that robe, anyway?"

Naomi looks down at herself self-consciously. She touches the silk of the robe whose pattern matches the Sumerian rendering of the plant of immortality which matches the symbol that's appeared on my infected computer, etc. A message, a clue...meaning, what? The woman I love is sitting there swathed in a robe covered with this alien script like the high priestess of a computer virus cult worshipped by gnostic hackers.

She says, "I don't know where I bought it. Odd Lot, maybe?" She frowns. "Why? Don't you like it?"

"That pattern. Do you know what it is?"

Naomi looks at the tiny repeated symbol as if she's seeing it for the first time. She says, "Paisely print? The head of Elvis?"

I don't say anything.

The parrot says, "Nada."

I don't say anything because the parrot is saying it all. I can't be sure because she supposedly looks just like her identical twin sister, but I think I'm really sitting here with Norma Blake Madsen. Which means I think I'm sitting here with Nada Klone.

The love-of-my-life.

Later that same day, I'm shrugging apologetically, grinning, throwing my hands up in the air, saying "Not me, not me," to no one in particular. What I'm doing at the time is walking out of the Barnes and Noble bookstore at Union Square when the alarm sounds. Turning around, I raise my arms in this comical, shrugging, palms-up, who-me gesture. I'm taking up the universal pose that basically says, *Oh come on now. I'm the last person...*

What I've been doing is research on writing. I figure that if I'm going to pretend to be a writer of bestselling true crime books, as I've been doing all along with Naomi, I should at least see what writing is all about. I've walked up and down the aisles and sales tables, had a cappuccino and lemon bar at the second floor café, scanned the bestseller shelves, and after half-an-hour concluded that I knew all I'd ever need to know about being a contemporary author. What I saw during that half-hour were books about fake love affairs, fake diets, fake celebrities. I saw books about fake politicians, fake scandals, fake histories. I saw books with fake confessions, books detailing fake crimes, books hawking fake cures for largely made-up problems. I saw that there wasn't much to writing a book at all: all you had to do was say what everyone wanted to hear, what everyone already knows, which isn't really a whole lot of anything at all.

As for the store alarm, I'm feeling pretty confident of my innocence. I'm pretty sure I haven't stolen anything from this store, not today, anyway. There's nothing here worth stealing. But the shrill *beep-beep-beep* is making me nervous. It sounds so damn sure that I've stolen something that it's starting to convince even me.

I fake a nonchalant yawn, an exasperated eye-roll, a conspiratorial smirk. But no one's taking my side. The other shoppers are looking askance at me in an embarrassed way, as if I've just pooped my pants. I'm already segregated, expelled, sectioned off from the herd like a sick animal left to be picked off by the wolves. Meanwhile, the security guards are walking purposefully towards me with serious expressions on their dead serious faces. It's the face that security guards everywhere wear. The face that says, *Come with us.*

When they reach me, one of them actually says, "Come with us."

I say, "This isn't necessary."

The other one says, "Come with us. "

They are touching my arms lightly, one on either side of me. The alarm has been de-activated. The whole place is as quiet as a snowy field when a snowy field is really quiet. I don't like the way they're barely touching me on the arms. The way they're barely touching me is the way they barely touch you when they know you know better than to resist. It's the way Gestapo agents lead you away. It's the way magicians get objects to levitate. We are walking back into the store and it's like they are moving me along whether I like it or not simply by the sheer force of their authoritative disapproval.

I say, "I didn't take anything. You can search me. It's against the law what you're doing. I can sue."

One of them says, "You don't want to do this here."

We're passing New Age, Self Help, Gay and Lesbian. We're passing Sports, Nature, Travel. At the back of the store, next to the Balinese Cooking section, there is an elevator I can't imagine I'd ever notice unless I were looking to make a Balinese dessert. Another security guard with a serious face is holding the elevator door open for us.

"Oh for crissakes," I say, "even if I stole something, isn't this a little over-dramatic?"

I'm acting as if the whole thing is ridiculous, but I'm starting to get a little nervous. I'm beginning to get a bad feeling about all this.

It's cold in the elevator, freezing cold. I'm shivering in my overcoat. I can see my own breath. The elevator stops so hard my jaws crunch together. I taste bitter crumbs of molar on my tongue. I say, "You guys are paying for those new fillings."

No one is laughing.

No one is smiling.

We are marching down a long gray hallway with framed prints of bestsellers gone by: Ayn Rand's *Atlas Shrugged*, Fitzgerald's *The Great Gatsby*, Hemingway's *The Sun Also Rises*, Margaret Mitchell's *Gone with the Wind*.

I say, "What is this, literary death row?"

No one is laughing.

No one is smiling.

We wheel to the right. We wheel to the left. We wheel to the right and then to the left. We pass a storage closet with a sink and a mop. We pass someone rolling a cart piled high with unsold books by some Nobel Prize winner or other. We walk into a room that's even colder than the elevator. There's a chair, and another chair. There's a table. On the table there's a copy of the latest Oprah Pick-of-the-Month. "So," I say, "it's torture then, is it?"

Someone says, "Wait here."

Then everyone leaves but me.

FAKE GIRLS

Everyone leaves so quickly that I don't even finish what I start to say. They leave so quickly that I don't even know what it is I start to say.

I say, Don't th…Shit…"

The door closes and I sit on one of the chairs. I get up and sit in the other chair. I get up again and sit back down in the first chair. I look around at the bare grey walls of the empty room. I pick up the Oprah Pick-of-the-Month. I think to myself, *I finally understand. This is why people read crap like this. They have nothing else to do with their lives.*

Time passes, like it always does, only I'm more aware of it. Flipping through the pages of the bestselling novel on the table, I see it's one of those books that are even more unbelievable than science fiction. It's one of those poignant, heartwarming stories that is supposed to reaffirm our faith in life but bears absolutely no resemblance to it. The hero and heroine in this book are acting in ways people never actually do in real life. That's to say, they are feeling and relating and being completely open and honest with each other. They are acting selflessly and nobly and doing all the other made-up crap you never really see anyone really doing. They are walking and talking the way we like to imagine human beings walking and talking, like we only wish they would; in other words, the way no real human being ever does.

Just once, I'm thinking, I'd like to have a conversation that makes as much sense as the page of made-up dialogue I'm reading. Just one time I'd like to meet someone who acts as logically and consistently from one scene to the next as the people in this novel are acting.

I'm wondering where the authors of these books get their ideas for human beings. I'm wondering how they dream up such imaginary creatures.

Books like these, I'm thinking, *are why people are so pissed off about their actual lives.* People read books like this and they feel like they're missing something. They feel like freaks. They feel like outsiders. They wonder why their own lives are so empty, pointless, and open-ended. They wonder why their lives are void of colorful characters, of meaning, of drama. They wonder why the only people they know are liars, cheats, fools, hypocrites, sociopaths. Where is the beginning, middle, and end? They wonder, Where is the climax? Where is the passion? Where is the drama? What the hell is the fucking point?

Just once I'd like one of these authors to tell the truth.

Just once I'd like to see one of them admit what a big, sloppy, incomprehensible mess life really is, peopled largely by halfwits, all behaving miserably.

I'd like to read a book like that.

I wish one existed.

Maybe we'd all feel a lot better.

Maybe we'd all stop expecting anything better.

Maybe then we'd be satisfied with life just as it is.

21. Miracles, lizards, and John Grisham...

Just at that moment, the two security guards from before, or two that look just as humorless, open the door, step into the room, and close the door behind them. With them is a tall, ascetic-looking man in a snap-brim hat and trench coat. In other words, Mr. Franklin. He's wearing a dour, sardonic expression, like an IRS auditor with very bad news about 1994. He's holding a pale-green folder. He says, "Good afternoon, Mr. Molloy."

I feel irrationally relieved by this professional civility, not to mention, he still doesn't seem to know my real name.

"Mr. Franklin, what's this all about? There must be some kind of mistake. They've got the wrong man."

He doesn't change expression. He only has the one, as I well remember. He opens the folder, checks it, looks up. He says, "There's never a mistake. You're the right man. Let's not make this difficult. Please empty your pockets."

I know that whatever this is about, it's not about what it seems to be about. It's not really about what's in my pockets, but I oblige him. Well there's the usual: wallet, coins, scraps of paper, toothpicks, pebbles picked up here and there, way too many keys to locks guarding things I've forgotten about, bits of lint. I'm happy to show this psycho accountant all of it: the expired Metrocards, the ATM receipts, bar napkins, a small pile of crap that all amounts to the average life of no one in particular.

I'm not faking my surprise when I pull the two thick paperbacks from the inside pockets of my overcoat. Well, maybe I'm faking it a little. The fact is, I'd begun to suspect something very much like this was going to happen all along. I say what's usually said in every circumstance even remotely like this one. "I have no idea how these got there. This must be some kind of set up."

I point to the two books on the table. "John Grisham and *The Big Illustrated Book of Sex Fetish*? Come on, you've got to be kidding."

There's an awkward pause. We're both looking at *The Big Illustrated Book of Sex Fetish.* Then I say, "Okay, you've got to be half-kidding."

I swear up and down that I didn't steal the books on the table, that I don't know what any of this is about. I swear on gods I don't believe in, mothers I haven't seen in years, children I never conceived, honor I don't have. Mr. Franklin listens to all of this with the patience of a toaster in a closed kitchen cabinet. He has the stillness of a robot that isn't switched on yet. When I'm finally out of air, he tells me that they've got me on video. They have film recording my every move in the store.

I say, "That's impossible. You can't film what didn't happen. "

Cool, he is, as the top of a pickle jar at the back of the fridge. He says, "They filmed Superman 3 and that didn't happen either, did it? Let's get down to the nitty-gritty shall we, Mr. Malone? I'm going to give you the straight skinny."

Mr. Franklin admits that he's not really concerned with my theft of the Grisham novel. He admits that they sell so many of the loathsome things that the theft of ten thousand here or there isn't going to make a dent in the profits. They sell so many of the goddamn things it can even pick up the slack for all the perverts that steal *The Big Illustrated Book of Sex Fetish*. Mr. Franklin admits that what this is really all about is something much, much bigger.

He says, "Mr. Molloy, we want to know what you know about Nada Klone. We eagerly await the tale of your progress."

I say, "There's not much to tell."

To one of the security guards standing behind me he says, "Make him remember everything immediately."

I sense one of them stepping towards me and I try to turn around. I try to say "Hey!" I try to stop the hydraulic hypodermic-thing that is pressed to my neck. What I hear is something that goes, *Phhhhht...*

I try to get up, but I'm forced back down in my chair by two heavy hands on my shoulders. I say, "You didn't have to do that ...this is all bullshit..."

Mr. Franklin says, "Calm down, Mr. Molloy. All you have to do is answer our questions."

I suggest that maybe later on I'll have something to say, but I don't right now. If he lets me go, I hint, I may learn a thing or two I can tell him.

Mr. Franklin sighs.

By this time, he's sitting in the chair opposite me. He's not smoking a cigarette, but he could be. He's not playing a harrowing game of mumbly- peg with a deadly Italian stiletto, but he could be doing that, too.

He says, "Let me show you something Mr. Molloy. Maybe this will make things clearer. Maybe it will shake you up a bit."

Reaching up, Mr. Franklin removes the archetypal snap-brim with both hands. He sets in on the table with exaggerated care. There's a head of thinning hair under the snap-brim, grayish comb over, not all that surprising, doesn't change a thing. Then, without another word, he reaches behind him, and, starting from the base of his scrawny neck, pulls his face from over the top of his head as if it were a mask. When he looks back up, well, I'm no herpetologist, but he looks like a komodo dragon, a skink, a brachiosaurus, something like that.

It's not what I'm expecting, but it's never been entirely out of the question, if I thought to ask myself such a question.

"We're an ancient race," Mr. Franklin says. "Far older than yours. We rule this planet. We built the pyramids. We set up the Stonehenge stones. We invented language, all that. Our bloodlines have run through every ruler since Ashrubanipal, and all the others before him too, right up to the current U.S. president, English royalty, etc. We don't intend that will change."

He's not really talking anymore, but mouthing words, and I'm hallucinating the rest. Whatever he's actually saying, I can't hear. Whatever brain-washing, truth-telling, mind-warping drug they've given me, it's going to make me say things I don't want to say if I don't fight it. Listening to Mr. Franklin's hypnotic, queer Midwestern twang, I feel vaguely sick to my stomach, like during a rectal exam. To keep my cool, I ask myself questions like, *Why do they keep it so cold in here? Don't reptiles like the heat? Didn't the Ice Age kill off the dinosaurs?*

As if inside a perfectly lucid dream, I say, "Listen Mr. Franklin. I know all about these cheap theatrical tactics. I've seen *Mission Impossible*. What you look like now, that could be a mask too. For all I know, your real human face is under that rubber lizard mask."

He knows the trick I know, but I'm explaining it so he knows I know: what you do is present a false front and then you dramatically reveal the "reality" behind the false front—only the so-called "reality" behind the false front is yet another false front, concealing the "real" reality. It only sounds complicated when you write it all out this way; in reality, it's very simple.

Behind the rubber lizard mask, Mr. Franklin merely blinks his eyes once, very slowly. If nothing else, I think I've communicated to him the depth of my skepticism. He seems to realize that no matter what the truth is, I'm not going to believe it. Fact is, if there's anything going to keep me sane through all this, it's simply that I don't believe anything at all. The government, the media, teachers, parents, wives, lovers—I've been lied to so many times by so many people I've trusted I can hardly be bothered listening to what anyone says. I simply assume everything is a lie. I don't even trust myself.

Taking a chance that, for at least ten seconds or so, I'm on an approximately equal footing here, I say, "So I guess we understand each other Mr. Franklin? I'd appreciate it if a gift certificate were issued for my trouble. Does this store happen to carry the new Britney Spears *Guide to Kierkegaard,* by any chance?"

No one is laughing.

No one is smiling.

Deadpan, Mr. Franklin has put back on his Mr. Franklin mask which is what allows him to look at me deadpan. He says, "You've got exactly three days to give us Nada Klone. If you don't, well, let's just say you'll face the consequences. So to speak." To one of the security guards standing behind me he says, "Make him forget everything again, immediately."

I sense one of them stepping forward. What I hear then is something that goes, *Phhhhhht....*again.

Then I don't remember any of what I just remembered, until I remember it two hours later. Of course, whatever they gave me, some sort of truth serum, I suspect, might have distorted what I think I just remembered. It strikes me that it's even possible that whatever I remember right now isn't anything like what really happened at all. Very possibly, what I'm remembering right now is just exactly what they want me to remember. You kind of have to figure they know what they're doing.

But then again, have you tried to call the paper-pushers at any government office lately? Have you ever tried to get a new driver's license at the DMV? Called customer service at your insurance company? Returned a pair of pants at a big department store? As hopeless as things are, there's always hope. Nowadays you place your last and only hope in the total incompetence of practically everyone.

"Pregnant," Naomi Kline is telling me, "I'm pregnant."

I'm not really surprised by this, not as much as you might think. Believe it or not, I've sort of seen this coming. I'm dunking a donut at the diner where we first met, something I don't ordinarily do, but I'm mechanically, numbly, doing it now. I had just finished telling her about my peculiar experience at the bookstore the day before when she blew away my little misadventure among the stacks with this apocalyptic non-sequiter. Compared to this news, discovering that the world is policed by government agents who pretend to be part of an age-old conspiracy run by an ancient race of extraterrestrial super-lizards hardly seems worth mentioning.

"It's a miracle," Naomi says, "I had no idea."

Yes, I'm thinking, *it's a miracle. You're bat-crazy, we have lots and lots of unprotected sex, and you've gotten pregnant.*

It's a miracle, all right.

"I hope you're not angry," she says.

She says this with her face glowing with the glow of impending motherhood.

I almost wish I could say I was angry, but I'm really not. I wish I could say I feel anything at all, but I really don't.

"Three months," she says, looking like she just created the world. "It's a girl."

She announces the due date like she's just discovered the cure for death. "I'm going to name her Maia. Maia with an i. Not the Maya with a 'y' because that means illusion. You're not saying anything," she says, as if she's just noticing. She looks at me like the answer to everything has just been found. "Say something," she says. "You're not mad, are you?"

I almost wish I could think of something to say, but I really can't. I just keep mechanically dunking my donut, over and over, like a donut-dunking machine, until the donut is so wet it's started to dissolve, until it's not even a donut anymore.

"No," I say, mechanically, "I'm not mad."

The bottom half of my donut falls off.

22. Chinatown, wiseguys, and little green turtles...

As it turns out, the Yankees got bounced in the first round of the playoffs weeks ago. This is a shame for a couple of reasons, but mainly because I've been betting heavily on them as lately as the day before yesterday. You'd think my bookie, being a sporting man and all, would have let on at some point. But no. Everyone, it seems, is scrambling for an edge. Everyone is taking whatever little advantage they can get. And my bookie, apparently, has been taking advantage of my temporary dementia.

I spend a largely wasted day in my underwear waiting for the rest of Mr. Franklin's drug to clear out of my system. I'm smoking cheap cigars and scanning the want ads. I'm drifting in and out of sleep. I'm making a half-assed attempt to hypnotize myself to a saner, slimmer, fitter, more prosperous new me.

I'm failing miserably.

I spend some time musing whether or not I'd given Mr. Franklin any useful information while I was under the influence of his mind-altering chemicals. If I had, I don't think he'd have turned me loose. I don't think he'd have bothered threatening me. I don't think he would have given me a deadline. He'd have taken the information and had me killed. For the first time in this case, I'm glad I don't know what the hell is going on. Ignorance may not be bliss, but this time confusion may have saved my ass.

At least for another three days.

Without my gambling winnings or my taxi driver job, I'm running dangerously low on funds. The fact is, I have no funds at all. None at all, that is, until Hank the Fed Ex man, hands me yet another airmail envelope. He squints at me hostilely as I sign the receipt. He's noticed the return addresses by now. He's recognized the handwriting. He doesn't appreciate walking up all these stairs to deliver a package I'm sending myself. Of course, it's way too complicated to tell him the truth. Besides, the truth sounds even nuttier.

Fact is , I don't even know the truth.

I tell him to wait a second, put the door between us, rip open the envelope. Inside there's eleven thousand dollars in tens, twenties, and fifties. Handing him four fifties, I thank him for any future troubles.

Hank seems a little happier then he did five seconds ago. He seems a little happier only in that particular way people seem a little happier when you give them two hundred bucks.

After thinking everything over, I decide to give Naomi Blake a call. I want to tell her that after thinking everything over, I've decided that maybe it's not such a bad idea to have a kid, after all. I'm beginning to warm up to the idea of getting a card on Father's Day, of having a son to grow up and hate my guts, a daughter to drive me insane with worry. Maybe its true, what the world really does need is a baby made especially by the two of us. Maybe, just maybe, that's what the world's been waiting for, what the world's been missing, what's been wrong with the world all along. I've got myself so worked up over the idea that I'm thinking of suggesting to Naomi that we take a ride out to IKEA that afternoon to shop for cribs; that we saunter over to F.A.O. Schwartz to stock up on stuffed bears; that we pay a visit to Babies'R'Us to buy a stroller. But when I finally get hold of Naomi, she sounds distant and cold and not herself at all. She tells me she's been thinking everything over, too, and she's decided that she can't have a relationship with me anymore, that she's not ready to have a relationship with anyone, that she doesn't even want to see me again.

I say, "What are you talking about?"

"This is goodbye."

"Are you serious? You can't possibly be serious."

She says, "Dead serious."

"Wait a second."

 "Goodbye."

She hangs up and then I hang up and I stare up at a cobweb on the ceiling for a long time. Then I get up and eat some almonds. I boil water for tea. I trim my toenails. I leave a message on Meeah Soo's answering machine to say I hope she's doing okay, I hope that there's no hard feelings between us. I try to find NPR on the radio for almost fifteen minutes but I can't. I don't take what Naomi said literally. I figure it's just the hormones talking. That it's just some kind of special lunacy you suffer when you're having a baby. You've got to expect a little insanity when you're growing a whole new human being inside your body to bring into this madcap world.

So here I am, on my usual nightly ramble. For some reason, I'm on Mott Street. That's where I find myself at this very moment, Mott and something. It's still early, only ten p.m. or so, and, as usual, I have absolutely no idea where I'm going, so I'm giving myself all the time in the world to get there. I'm using destiny as my map, that's one way of looking at it. You could say that I'm using fate as my guide. What it looks like, though, is that I'm just wandering around pointlessly. Anyone watching would say that I seem to be hopelessly lost. What I'm telling myself is that wherever I end up at two a.m., that's the place I should be.

That's right, I'm still searching for whoever wants me to meet him or her at two a.m. I'm looking for whoever is sending those Fed Ex envelopes stuffed with money to my apartment. Whoever is writing my name and return address in the little window marked "sender" in my own crimped, virtually illegible, and—so I thought—inimitable handwriting.

I'm still fairly certain that it's not me going to the bank, withdrawing random sums of money, stuffing envelopes, and sending them to myself. I'm still almost positive that I'm not rushing home and pretending to be surprised when I get the Fed Ex delivery the next morning. What I'm saying is that as best as I can tell, I'm not pounding the pavement sleeplessly night after night looking for me. From what I can determine, this isn't a Zen parable that I'm trying to fight my way out of.

What I'm waiting for is a nudge on the elbow, a confidential *Hey Mack*, a wink, a long *Psssssssst...* I look up and I'm on Division Street, I'm on Mott again, I'm on Pell. All the shops here are closed or closing up, steel curtains are coming down everywhere, padlocks are snapping shut.

Next to a pile of discarded cabbages, there's an old Chinese lady sitting on the curb beside a plastic bucket full of tiny green turtles. She says something in Chinese that I imagine must be something like, *Do you want to buy a tiny green turtle?*

Surprising myself I say, "Sure, let me have a turtle. I used to have one of these turtles as a kid. After two weeks or so they die and their eyes fall out. It's very educational."

Either she can't understand a single word I'm saying, she's totally disinterested, both, or she just has the good sense to pretend any or all of the above. So I say, "I thought they made selling these turtles illegal? I've broken the law, too, you know. Oh yes, I'm wanted for murder."

She's smiling, nodding, sending me on my way. She just wants my twenty bucks and me out of here and who can blame her for that? Besides, she doesn't need to attract any attention. She's selling illegal turtles, after all.

Twenty dollars lighter, I'm heading up Canal with a tiny green turtle in a small plastic tank with a tiny fake palm tree. I'm beginning to feel as if I could walk straight through walls. No one seems to notice me. For hours now I've been walking around the city and not a single person has said a word to me, except for the Chinese woman and I couldn't understand a word she said. Whoever I'm supposed to meet out here, they sure don't seem too anxious to meet me.

Okay, maybe it's not exactly true that no one but the Chinese woman has spoken to me. That's a slight exaggeration. Anyone lost

spots me from a mile off. People bumming money seem to see me
okay. This is what I hear, "Hey guy can you help me out with a few
bucks?" I hear, "Do you know where the Trump Tower is?"
Everyone who sees me wants some spare change. Everyone wants to
know where Houston Street is. But no one wants to reveal that
they're the one I'm supposed to meet. No one wants to tell me who
they are. I'm going to have to go to them, but where the hell are
they?

I look up and I'm on Mulberry, I'm on Elizabeth, and then I'm
somehow back on Mott for the third damn time. Where I'm at right
now is Little Italy. I've made my way down here on a hunch.
Standing at the curb fat guys in expensive suits are smoking fat, oily
cigars. They're talking to each other, or on cell phones, or both. They
start off talking in big friendly voices, saying things like, "Hey watcha
doin, where ya been?" and then two minutes later they are talking in
whispers and saying things like "Listen, watcha gonna do is dis…"
    What I'm doing is asking around if anyone knows anything
about a special girl, a girl who'll do anything, a girl named Nada
Klone. I'm asking about an operation run by a guy named Chambers.
Down here, I figure, I'm bound to find someone who knows
something about the kind of big bucks being pulled down by
shadowy X-rated websites. I'm bound to learn something about
something being traded in the black-market. Dad always said if you
want to catch a criminal go to where crime pays. But I'm not getting
any answers here either. What I'm getting is a lot of blank stares. I'm
getting a lot of disapproving glances to the left and right.
    There's always a sense down here that something is going on
behind-the-scenes, that everything is a front, that it's all being
manipulated. But tonight it's worse than ever. All over the place
three-hundred-pound wiseguys are sitting at little wooden tables,
delicately sipping espresso or cappuccino latte's from tiny cups with
their bejeweled pinkies out. They are eating itsy-bitsy pastries. Maybe
it's just my imagination, but they all seem to be watching me out of
the corners of their cold, dead eyes. Nobody here knows "nothin';

nobody here has any idea what I'm talking about. When I ask anything at all about Nada Klone they answer by saying things like, "I never heard nothin' about whatever it is you talkin' bout," or they say, "I remember a guy asked that once. Hey, Pauli, you remember that guy?" And Pauli says, "Yeah, I remember him. Didn't that guy trip on a stair and die?" And then they're laughing like the kind of guys who think it's funny when a head falls off.

I'm heading back towards Broadway when I notice I've picked up a pair of admirers: two big guys in dark suits right off the rack of the big man's shop and I guess the idea is that they're escorting me out of the neighborhood. I guess you could say that I've worn out my welcome. But that's not it, not quite, not exactly. No these guys actually want to deliver an invitation. What they tell me when they catch up to me at a crosswalk is that someone wants to talk to me. Someone waiting in the long black limo idling on the corner of Mulberry and something or other.

They say, "Let's go. Let's go right now."

I say, "Do I have to?"

They've already got me by the elbows. They're already wheeling me around, marching me back from whence I came.

I say, "Does it have to be right now?"

They say, "Do a pigeon got an ass?"

23. Family, tic-tacs, and the future of perversion...

The guy in the limo, I recognize him immediately, even if he isn't being taken into or out of a Federal courthouse, smirking, flanked by high-priced mob attorneys. It's Salvatore Ruffio, a.k.a. Uncle Sal, a midlevel gangster who used to play horseshoes with my dad in one of our many backyards. As it turns out, Dad never managed to turn over enough evidence to nail Uncle Sal himself, although many of Uncle Sal's "associates" ended up in the slam.

"Bygones be bygones, right sonny boy," he says, avuncularly, throwing a heavy, well-tailored arm around my shoulders when I slide into the coffin-like car. "That was business. This here is family."

He tightens the arm around my shoulders, gives me a shake.

When I think of all the "family" members that have been dredged out of the bottom of the East River, found in the weeds alongside the Jersey Turnpike, or who vanished altogether, I'm not as relieved to hear that we're "family" as you might at first think. Uncle Sal's face is so close to my face that I can smell his wintergreen Tic-Tac.

I look out the window at the street, at the people passing, and wish I were one once again one of them. What I'm thinking is that no one can see through the limo's heavily-tinted glass. You could make love to someone buck-naked in this car at noon on the corner of Fifth and Broadway. You could also kill someone in this car, same time, same place, buck-naked, if you wanted. Either way, no one would ever see a thing.

There isn't any plastic on the seats, though, to protect the expensive leather from my gushing bodily fluids, and I consider that a good sign. Uncle Sal is telling me that out of respect for my father, he is giving me a warning. That, too, I'm considering to be a good sign. That avuncular smile, that heavy arm around my shoulders, the fact that he's close enough to kiss me...I know enough to know that there's no way to take *these* as good signs.

His warning is this: I'd best leave things alone, I'd best forget about everything.

He says, "This business about Nada Klone I hear you asking about is none of your business. Capeesh?"

In spite of myself, I demur. "With all due respects, Uncle Sal, it is my business. She's special to me."

"Well now, that girl is special to a lot of men, son. Hey, don't tell me you've fallen for her. The whore with the heart of gold. That's the oldest cliché in the book, kid."

"She's not a whore..."

Uncle Sal gives me a shake. He says, "Harharharhar. They're all whores kid. Especially the ones that work for me."

"What do you mean she works for you? What the hell would you know about her anyway?"

"I know she's every man's secret fantasy."

"Did you know that she's the missing wife of a Colorado dentist? Did you know that she's the mother of my child?"

"No," he says, as if seriously considering it for a moment. "I didn't know that."

I tell him about Todd Sprocket. I show him the clipping in my wallet. He takes his arm from around my shoulders and I immediately feel seventy pounds lighter. He flicks on a reading light and stares at the crumpled newsprint for a while with the aid of a pair of bifocals.

"Well I'll be damned," he says.

He looks up at me, back at the picture, up at me. I know what's coming, or a variation of it, anyway.

"Man, have you aged badly."

"That's not the point."

"Have you considered Botox?"

"Uncle Sal, please."

He eyeballs me all over. "It says here that you took her."

"It wasn't me. I've been set up. I think you should know that there are a lot of people besides me looking for her."

He snorts. "Yeah, I know. She's one of the best little money-makers you ever saw. This one was practically minting it. To tell you the truth, I never suspected she was 100% for real. How could I? She was just too damn good to be true."

"I don't understand."

"We got to keep up with the times you know," he says, "just like everyone else." He waves at the street scene beyond the window. "STDs, abortion, police raids, women's rights advocates, neighborhood watch groups, profit-skimming pimps...not to mention the payoffs and hassles with the cops, the grandstanding politicians, the girls themselves...who needs that kind of bullshit, anymore? And if that wasn't bad enough, business is down. No one wants to get off their ass and cruise the streets for sex anymore. It's all going virtual these days. No one wants to roll the dice on a case of genital warts. The sense of adventure is gone. You can't even get someone to walk to the corner for a skin mag anymore. Who can be bothered to walk downtown for a blowjob? Guys rather sit in the office during their lunch hour and jack off to some chick flashing her nasties on the computer." He looks me up and down like a bad canoli. "Jesus Christ, whatsda fuck da matter with men these days?"

Uncle Sal tells me how he hired computer nerds to set up his online prostitution business. He says the syndicate has been moving away from flesh-on-flesh prostitution for years and is moving into cyberspace.

"I had to hire a team of IT geeks, cause I can't even load a video driver without crashing my whole fuckin system, you know?" He tells me how "the whole future of a multi-billion-dollar porn business is in the hands of a bunch of pimply nerds who never had a real piece of pussy in their pitiful lives. This Nada Klone character was one of a kind. A superstar of the genre. I came up with a knock-off of my own, not bad either, if I say so myself." He jabs me with an elbow. "Wrote some of the dialogue myself, heh heh. Too bad I lost her, goddammit."

"What do you mean you lost her?"

He tells me how he no sooner committed a major investment into this business than some guy started muscling in, stealing some of his girls.

"Well, maybe 'muscling' isn't the right word. Hacking them is more like it. Come to think of it, maybe 'girls' isn't the right word either, Anyway, this guy's got his own team of nerds. They steal the code, block access, and all of a sudden she's working exclusively for him."

"You mean there's a turf war on for cybersex? You can get that for free."

"Not like this you can't. You wanna see the future of perversion? I'll show ya."

He leans off me, opens up a compartment between the seats, and lifts out a device that looks something like…well, that thing I saw in Ratking's cramped apartment during that first meeting. Ratking called it one of the most revolutionary discoveries in human history, a harbinger of personal, political, and spiritual freedom. But I can see that just like everyone else, he sold out to the highest bidder. I can also see that like all of mankind's greatest accomplishments, if it can be exploited for sex, it will be, and, in this case, as I'm about to find out, whoever bought the patent and tech from Ratking has done exactly that. I guess I should feel betrayed, but Ratking warned me that there was a price to be paid, a bill to come due for his services, and I guess this is it.

Uncle Sal says, "Just look at dis baby. It's the latest…just a prototype, but imagine the possibilities." He strokes the mutated laptop almost lovingly. "Had to twist a few arms to get one of these, if you know what I mean. But it was worth it. Think of what you're about to see as the vinyl sex-doll of the 21st century. Once this tech goes mainstream, every guy with a modem will be able to live like a Roman Emperor. And I mean one of the bad ones. Once these babies become as common as Blackberries or Gameboys, you're going to see a sexual revolution that's gonna make Sodom and Gommorah look like Disnyeworld."

Uncle Sal starts hitting keys, connecting, and in a moment a woman, yes, a pixilated woman is constituted in the limo with us.

It's Nada Klone, of course. Well, not *her*, but an imitation, as imagined by a seventy-year-old gangster with a crudely filthy mind. She may not technically be here in the flesh, maybe not even in the spirit, but she's here somewhere in between. Like a fake Rolex you buy on 14th Street, she looks just close enough to the real thing to make you hope, *"Well, maybe it's for real..."*

Nada Klone 2.0 says, "Long time no see."

I say, "I'm not sure I'm even seeing you now. Are you really here?"

She looks around, "Of course, I am lover. Right here with you, ready for love."

NK2 is dressed for "work" in a kind of black lace-up corset with a matching choker collar that has a steel ring bolted to the front. She's wearing a pair of black latex capri pants, red stilettos, and elbow-length black latex gloves with about thirty-five or forty snaps from wrist to elbow. She's dressed like no one outside a triple X-rated porn fantasy would be dressed and I have a sneaking suspicion that's exactly what I'm looking at.

NK2 says, "I don't have a lot of time. How do you want to do this?"

Take away the platinum hair. Take away the blue-tinted mirrorshades. Take away the crimson lipstick, the black nail polish, all the fetish gear. Take away all that and add the sadness, the screwiness, the constant whining that I get an instant erection to fill the gaping, aching loneliness at the center of her and I'm looking at the spitting image of my dysfunctionally nymphomaniacal lover Naomi Blake, not to mention, the love-of-my-life, her missing identical twin sister, Norma Blake Madsen.

I say, "Are you Norma Blake Madsen? Are you the woman who's supposed to be missing in Colorado? Are you the woman I know as Naomi Blake?"

The expression "ghost of a smile" would be a good one for the expression playing on NK2's blood-red lips right now. It's a Mona Lisa smile, if Mona Lisa had just got done talking dirty. It's the default smile that she's programmed to give when you ask a question she hasn't been programmed to answer. Nada blows me an imaginary kiss and winks. She whispers huskily, "I can be whoever and whatever you want me to be. You can tell me your deepest fantasies and your darkest desires..."

She frowns and there's a flutter in the image.

I say, "Where are you?" I turn to Uncle Sal. I say, "Where is she?"

He hunts and pecks at the keyboard and Naomi-Norma-Nada comes back into focus.

I say, "Why are you dressed like that? Are you in trouble?"

"I *am* trouble," she winks conspiratorially. "I'm every man's secret fantasy. Tell me yours. Would you like a threesome, would you like to take me anally, do you want to tie me up?"

She suddenly looks confused again.

I say, "Tell me who you really are. Tell me if you're real."

She says, "Do you want to see me do it with a dog, do you want to kiss my boots, do you want to pee on me?"

I can't take my eyes off her, or what's pretending to be her, but I'm talking to Uncle Sal out of the corner of my mouth. "What the hell is going on here?"

"Ain't it obvious, Einstein?"

"Do you want me to make it with your girlfriend, do you want me to be your pony, do you want me to whip you?"

In these filthy ramblings, I'm recognizing the signature of my old pal, Todd Sprocket, as run through the twisted mind of Uncle Sal, and I'm trying hard not to think too much how closely this comes to having cybersex with the two of them. Sensing this is all coming to an end pretty soon, I try to fix Nada's ghostly pixilated image. It's already breaking up, flying apart like dandelion spores in an approaching hurricane, scattering in all directions at once. I say, "Don't leave. Don't go just yet...please." I know this isn't real, that she's not real, but I can't help but ask it anyway. Maybe it's a superstitious feeling, like shaking one of those fortune-telling plastic 8-balls. Or maybe it's because I can't ask her these things for real. I say, "Are you really pregnant? Are you really having our baby?" Maybe it's because I can't say it to her face that I say it to her image. I ask, "Do you love me?"

She says, "That will be $19.95. Amex, Visa, or Mastercard. Paypal is available."

I say, "Hold on...my credit cards are all maxed out...Uncle Sal..."

Uncle Sal is typing away furiously with this thick, furry fingers. But it's no use. Nada makes a totally screwed-up face. She waves her virtual finger no-no. She says, "Bad boy. I know what you're doing. I can't talk to you anymore."

I say, "Wait..."

She says, "I'm sorry lover. But this connection has been timed out."

In her place, that virus symbol, hangs in the air a moment, and then it, too dissolves.

"See," Uncle Sal grumbles beside me. "He's got her blocked. That motherfucker. He's exercising his copywright."

Thinking Chambers, I ask, "Do you know who owns her?"

"No," Uncle Sal says, looking at me disgustedly, like a waiter who brought him the wrong kind of rigatoni. "But when I heard you were asking around for Nada Klone, I figured maybe you might."

"I don't."

"You wouldn't lie to your Uncle Sal, would you?"

"No, of course not."

"I think you would."

About twenty minutes later, I'm leaning heavily against a cold railing on a pier at the South Street Seaport. I'm wheezing, squinting in pain, and spitting blood. I'm looking at the Brooklyn Bridge. It's all twinkly with lights, like a great big Christmas tree fallen over on it's side. *People jump from that thing*, I'm thinking, or they used to. *I can understand why*. I think I may have cracked a couple of ribs. That's what it feels like anyway: every time I breathe in, it feels like someone is stabbing me in the side with an ice-pick and rooting around in there for my heart.

I guess you could call what they gave me a "precautionary beating."

Uncle Sal had his driver bring me here to the river after that little virtual rendezvous with the knock-off Nada Klone. He turned towards me and said good-naturedly, "Now I'm going to have to have the crap beaten out of you. Out of respect for you father, I'm not going to have Fat Pauli put six in the back of your skull. But, out of the same respect, I can't let you go without breaking some bones. You capeesh, right?"

"No," I say, "I don't capeesh. I really do not capeesh at all."

Uncle Sal shrugs. He throws that heavy arm over my shoulders again: it feels like a hairy anaconda's draped there. Once again his face is too close to mine. He's in serious need of another Tic-Tac. He says, "No matter. Your old man will understand. It's for his benefit that I repay this debt of honor."

I ask if this is really necessary.

He gives me another avuncular shake. He assures me, "Oh yeah, it's really necessary."

Then the two big guys in the big man suits come around to the back and, um, escort me out of the car. They take me off a respectful distance to a spot where I've got a good view of the river and the bridge and then they waste no time beating me to the ground. They start kicking me once I'm on the ground and keep on kicking me until I stop trying to get up. Then they kick me a little bit more. Then they stomp on me. Then they get back into the car. I hear Uncle Sal call out from the back of the limo, "I'm doing you a favor, kid. Drop this Nada Klone shit. She's no good for you. No good for your health. And don't forget to tell your father I send my regards." Then they drive away and leave me there with my face in a grainy puddle of cold water.

I stay there for a while, curled up, not thinking much of anything, just feeling along my bottom jaw with my tongue to make sure all my teeth are still there. Then I crawl up onto my knees, grab the railing, and stand up, as previously mentioned. I promptly vomit into the river.

Through all this, I still somehow have the little plastic tank with the palm tree, but it's broken and empty. The tiny green turtle must have gotten out and crawled away.

It wasn't her, obviously, it wasn't. That's what I tell myself as I stagger along South Avenue. It was just an image, nothing more, not even that, a fake of a fake, a ghost. That's what I'm muttering out loud as I half-run, half-gimp it down Beekman. It's some kind of trick, a simulation, that's what I'm frightening passersby by shouting out as I bump my way up Pearl Street to the entrance of the Q-train to Brooklyn.

I know what I'm telling myself is true, is rational, is what's "real," but it doesn't make a damn bit of difference whatsoever.

If you've ever woken from a vivid dream of someone you loved and lost, you know what I'm talking about. If you ever ran across an old photograph of someone from happier times long past or heard a song that conjured up the memory of the long-lost love-of-your-life so real and poignant that it brought real tears to your eyes, then you know exactly what I'm feeling right now. You know it makes no difference that what I saw in the back of Uncle Sal's limo was just a copy of a simulacra of Norma Blake Madsen, or that she was little more than a digitalized ventriloquist's dummy for Todd Sprocket's XXX-rated computer sex scripts channeled through Uncle Sal's warped psychosexual pathology. You know why I'm racing to Naomi's apartment to see her, to hold her, to kiss her, to tell her I love her. What you know is that it makes no difference whether or not what I saw, dreamt, fantasized, or remembered was real...

What matters, all that matters, *is that the pain of missing her and the fear of losing her is all-too real.*

And if you're beginning to be as paranoid about everything as I am, given all that's gone on up to this point in the story, if you've begun to suspect the worst about practically everything, then you probably won't be surprised, just as I'm not surprised, to find that

Naomi Blake isn't home when I arrive at her apartment. Not only is she not home, but her home isn't ever her home anymore.

No big purple chair, no coffee table book of apocryphal Manhattan photographs, no crapping parrot named Maxx squawking out the word "nada" over and over again, ad nauseam. No, just two hard-looking black gangbangers, one tall, one short, in similar designer track suits standing guard at the door. The tall skinny one, his head braided in cornrows, exaggeratedly extends a long, wiry-muscled arm behind him, as if inviting me in.

He says, "You see any white ho livin' here, do ya, buster brown?"

The other guy, built like a stone bullfrog in a derby hat, grins malevolently and melodramatically widens his eyes. He flexes his gold-studded right hand and says mock-hopefully to his pal, "Do he? Do he?"

Behind them, the room looks like it belongs to an old black lady on a sitcom from the 80s: a worn flowered couch, a lamp with seashells in it, a plastic Jesus, *Divorce Court* on TV. Right on cue, a heavyset black woman in a housedress comes out of the kitchen wiping her hands in a dishrag as if she's strangling it. She looks over her half-glasses disapprovingly in the general direction of me. There's only one thing missing: the laugh-track.

She says, "Who that Chester? Somebody selling something?"

The tall one says, "He ain't got nothing to sell."

The squat one says, "He ain't nobody, ma."

The old lady says, "Tell him to go away. Ain't no business here."

The tall one says, "You heard her. Go away. You got no business here. Do ya?"

I take a look at the two scowling teenagers guarding the door, the sitcom apartment behind them, the disapproving black woman with the dead dishrag strangled in her hands. I figure I've got to agree. I've got no business here, nope, none at all.

24. Getting drunk, taking a leak, and all Hell breaks loose...

She's gone. Just like that. Oh, you know what I'm talking about. One day you're in love up to your eyeballs and the next day you're never going to see her again. Oh, you can say it's painful, but you know that's not quite it. Pain, that's a word for when you break your arm in four places or get cancer of the everything. No, pain's not quite the word for what you're feeling now. You know it's not. Pain isn't a big enough word to describe it. What you're feeling now is like someone came in the night while you slept and ripped the living heart right out of your chest and left a big empty hole at the center of you through which the cold wind of infinity is now blowing. Yeah, that's a little closer, except you've also got the nausea, the headache, the trouble breathing, all the things you might have if you were having a full-blown cardiac arrest that never ended.

   You go here, you go there, but nowhere is the place you want to be. You call and call and call and call. You get her answering machine. You hang up. You leave a message. You call and call and call some more. You make several trips to her apartment. You stand on the sidewalk and watch her window. You hang out in the neighborhood so you can pretend you just "bumped into her." You call and call and call some more. You leave a half-dozen more messages. Then you get a recording indicating that her phone has been disconnected altogether.

Yes, my friends, this is love. Well, a certain aspect of love—and let me tell you, like the scene of any catastrophe, it ain't pretty.

Maybe, I figure, Naomi had no choice but to go on the run. Those three days Franklin gave me were up, after all. Maybe her lover—or Norma's lover—came to collect her. Maybe Franklin had gotten to her. Maybe she needed my help. Maybe she got hit on the noggin and is wandering the city in a daze looking for me.

Maybe, maybe, maybe....a million maybes.

Maybe...she just didn't love you!

The most unthinkable "maybe" of them all.

Did you ever think of that?

Of course...almost all the time. It's the thought that has me thinking shotgun in the mouth, big toe on the trigger. It's got me wondering if it would even hurt to jump in front of the R-train. Drowning? I've read that if you can just overcome the aversion to take that first big gulp of ocean, it's actually quite pleasant.

Three suicidal days later, I'm still wandering around in the night looking for clues that don't seem to exist. I'm still searching for Naomi. I look up and I'm on Bowery. Then I'm on Delaney, Grand, Hester. I'm at St. Mark's Place. The head shops are still open, the Indian restaurants are still open. The tattoo and piercing parlors are still open. At the little sidewalk shops, black t-shirts are for sale with slogans like, *dead chic* and *zombification*. These t-shirts are waving in the breeze like flags of a nation without borders. They say stuff like, *alien nation* and *be vague*. At these same shops are tables with hundreds and hundreds of cheap rings with fake stones and fake symbols. There are necklaces and earrings with Celtic crosses, Egyptian ankhs, crucifixes, pentagrams, Nordic double-hammers, orphic snakes, lesbian scythes, all of it really, signifying a lot of nothing. Nobody believes in any of this shit anymore. None of it means anything, and maybe it never really did. It's just stuff to hang around your neck, dangle from your ears, decorate your fingers and toes. The only thing that seems to mean anything nowadays is that computer virus symbol: the plant of immortality from the Sumerian myth, *The Epic of Gilgamesh*. But what it means is anyone's guess.

Walking around, still limping, still bleeding a little from the gums from Uncle Sal's beating, I guess you could say I've given up hope. I feel like I'm wearing my own unique symbol, a flag signifying hopelessness. I feel pretty damn conspicuous in my inconspicuousness. I feel like a marked man that's been entirely forgotten. It's like someone is supposed to kill me but he slept late, got drunk, or just had something better to do. He'll get around to it later, but in the meantime, here I am. No one is paying me any attention at all. I might as well be the invisible man. No one hits me up for a quarter. No one even asks me for directions to the Trump Tower.

Looking up, I'm in a bar somewhere or other. I see a neon Budweiser sign. I see a Michelob Lite sign. I see a wall full of bottles filled to various levels with various poisons. I see a lot of empty glasses. I see an empty glass for every poor son-of-a-bitch on the face of the earth.

The bartender, he must have seen me, because I have one of those glasses filled with one of those poisons sitting right under my unshaved chin. The way I'm feeling right now, I'm guessing it's not the first second or even tenth glass of poison I've drunk tonight.

I'm guessing this isn't the first bar I've sat in either, and not the first night I've spent sitting in them. I'm guessing I've been poisoning myself for a long time now.

This is how they do it, I'm thinking. *They don't outright murder you. What they do is make the situation so intolerable you poison yourself in the end. This is the way the human race will be destroyed: we poison the earth, the air, the water, and, finally, ourselves. It's all one great big suicide we're watching.*

The way I'm feeling now, this is the way someone married eighteen years might feel. Someone working in the same office for twenty-five years might feel something similar. What you're trying hard not to realize is, *Way back when, I should have gone left, instead of right.* What you don't want to realize under any circumstances is, *This has all been one colossal mistake.* You never want to get to the point in the journey where you have to admit, *This isn't where I thought I was going, this isn't who I was supposed to be.* What you never want to hear yourself saying at the end--of an evening or a life—is something like this: *I have no fucking idea where I am. I have no fucking clue how I got here.*

And so I just keep walking. What else can you do? I look up and I'm on Canal, I'm on Vesey, I'm on Cortlandt. I'm down near where the World Trade Center used to be, I'm down near where City Hall is, where Wall Street has never stopped being. It's all dark here, it's all deserted, everything's closed up for the night.

I'm in a dance club for a little while. At least I think it's a dance club; if not, it might have been a brain seizure: there are flashing lights, pounding music, men and women frantically jerking about. I remember taking a blow to the side of the head, shouting at an Arab in a convenience store, a brief run through an alley. I remember staggering into a gas station near the Holland Tunnel begging someone for matches. I remember a long tearful conversation with Meaah Soo or my ex-wife or a volunteer at 1-800-SUICIDE, or maybe all three, or none. It's very possible I wasn't talking to anyone at all, or that I'd dialed the wrong number.

I seem to remember some poor bastard named Fred in Kew Gardens who gets woken up in the middle of the night to hear me complaining that no one loves me. I say, "Fred, I got no reason to live."

Fred says, "Who is this? Bill? Tim? Steve?"

I say, "I don't even know anymore."

Fred says, "I was sleeping. Is that you Dan?"

I say, "I haven't slept in weeks."

Fred says, "If this isn't Tony or Hank, you've got the wrong number."

I say, "I'm sorry Fred."

"If this is Harry, this isn't a good time. I suggest you call back at a decent hour."

"I'm sorry about everything."

"Good night."

Generally speaking, this is what you'd call a long dark night of the soul. Except, to be accurate, it's not just one miserable long dark night of the soul we're talking about here. We're talking a whole fucking bunch of 'em.

We're talking a long dark *life* of the soul.

But I keep walking. If you're not going to kill yourself, what else can you do? I'm on Sullivan, I'm on Thompson, I'm on Chambers. I'm on Bowery, I'm on Houston, I'm on Sutton.

Wait a minute….Did I say *Chambers?*

Chambers, Chambers, could Chambers have been the *street* where I was supposed to meet my mystery correspondent all this time? I'm racing across town inasmuch as you can call staggering drunkenly through the streets, vomiting at every corner, *racing.* I've got only the dimmest of memories where I saw Chambers Street, but that's where I'm heading now, heading there like a salmon heading up stream. But unlike the salmon, I'm hopelessly lost. I've got no instinct to find my way to wherever it is I'm supposed to go. On the corner of something and something, I see him: that guy on the ladder screwing around with the street signs.

"Phhzzzztttt, phhhzzzzzzzttt," the electric tool in his hands says.

"Hey," I say.

"Hey," I say again, because he can't hear me over what the tool is saying.

He looks down from the top of the ladder, grinning in the shadow of his hard-hat.

He says, "What's up chief?"

"Is this—"

I don't have to finish the sentence. Just to the left of his shoulder, I can see the street sign he's just bolted to the pole. There's no telling if it really is, or not, but it's what the sign says anyway:

Chambers Street

I've got a hunch. I check my watch. Wouldn't you know it? It's two a.m.

This is the street, I'm thinking, as I stumble down it, looking this way and that. This is the street, but there's nothing here, no one here, it's just a narrow little lane, dark, tree-lined, heading nowhere, like a thousand others. I'm almost to the end of it and nothing's happened. I'm about thirty yards from the end of it all and the only thing speaking to me is my bladder, all that poison I've swallowed tonight wants to exit my system and this is the street it's decided to do it on.

Fitting, I think.

So I find a dark crevice between two buildings, turn my back on the world, and unzip to do my business.

And it's then, right then, with the equipment in my hand watering a brownstone when, behind me, things take yet another sharp turn for the worse.

The trouble starts, as it so often does, with this ominous question, "Mr. Molloy?"

I jerk round, thinking I'm about to be arrested for public indecency or some sort of health code violation. I'm trying to think of some plausible excuse to be standing there with my meat tackle in hand. I'm trying to shut off the spigot, threatening to blow a gasket in my poor prostate.

There are three of them. They are dressed in black windbreakers, black shirts, black pants. They've got that big chunky generic look, like All-American football players from some beef and milk fed Christian university. They could just as easily be bouncers from a new club no one's ever heard of in NoHo, or security guards from a secret underground office complex at the United Nations. They could be storm-troopers for a radical wing of some neo-Nazi patriot movement or a paramilitary gay vanguard looking to shanghai straight men in a plot to overthrow heterosexuality. They could be any of these things, but I know they're not. They could be, but there's that gold logo emblazoned on the left breast of their black windbreakers, that Sumerian something-or-other, that virus symbol that's been popping up everywhere I go.

Dammit, I think, *it's a fucking trap.*

They're Franklin's men, no doubt of that now, and if there were any doubt it evaporates right away when the one in the middle says, "Mr. Franklin sent us to give you a message. 'Time's up.'"

They're coming towards me now, the three of them like three giant black blocks of a wall that's separating me from making a run for it. Because a run for it is about the only chance I have. That's right, fair reader, this isn't a movie, this isn't an adventure story, and I'm no more a hero than you are. I've got my pee hose in my hand, a few cracked ribs from the family reunion with Uncle Sal a few nights before, my heart is broken, and I'm halfway to Blottosville. There ain't no way I'm taking on these three gorillas.

But you know damn well I'm not going to buy the farm just yet. You know it, of course, because I'm telling you this story. You know I'm going to pull through to the end, that I'm going to escape these three muscular chunks of darkness. *How* is the real question. How does one escape such a hopeless situation?

Here's how.

The way I see it, there's negotiation, there's stalling for time, there's praying to God, and there's falling to my knees and outright begging these bastards for mercy. There are really no other options, none that I can see, anyway. I don't do any of these things, though. No, I don't end up doing anything at all. I don't say, "Look out behind you" or anything corny like that. I figure they won't believe me, anyway, and besides, it's better for me if they don't see what's coming, let them be unpleasantly surprised, like everyone else. That's my strategy. So I don't say a fucking thing. Instead, I watch, open-mouthed, speechless, as all hell breaks loose.

It's the guy on the left who doubles over first, grabbing his face as if he's been blinded, which I guess he has been, because he screams, *"Shit I can't see, I can't see!,"* and blood is glistening black between his fingers. The one in the middle turns like he's got whiplash and grabs his throat, making horrible choking sounds, unable to explain any further what's happened to him than to say, "grghlsshakkalth…," and the third has something in his hand, a Tasar, maybe, which is supposed to be for me, but it clatters harmlessly to the concrete, and he grabs the wrist of the hand that was just holding it like it's broken. Then the flesh on his face splits open and he's busy trying to hold that together. He's helped head first into a brick wall for his troubles and lands like a broken heap of midnight. The first guy, still staggering around blindly, takes an elbow on the crown of his skull like it weighed four thousand pounds, and the second—well—something happens to his spine to make it go crunch like a stack of wet crackers and I still cringe when I think about it.

Johnny Nomad was right, dammit. For a fat guy, he's fast, supernatural fast. Knott, that is. Because that's who it is, standing there, among all that goon wreckage, like a kung-fu hippopotamus, wheezing, sweating, consulting his inhaler, it's the fat man in all his fleshly excessive glory. He catches his breath. He looks me up and down somewhat disapprovingly. He says, "Zip up and make yourself decent, Mr. Molloy. We've got to talk."

These places are all supposed to be closed at this hour, but this one's not. You're not supposed to be smoking in Manhattan bars, but here you can. Gambling is against the law, but in this place it's cool—I'm talking about the after-hours Korean joint that Mr. Knott has led me to, shit-faced and stumbling, to explain how he managed to appear out of nowhere to save my sorry ass.

We've got our drinks in front of us, a group of drunken Koreans are singing *Sunshine Superman* on the karaoke, and Mr. Knott is holding forth with a long, whip-like stick of processed meat.

"What's that?" I say,

"It's the murder weapon. Have a bite."

"It looks like a Slim Jim."

"It is," Mr. Knott says, working a five-inch piece between his big jowls. "Helluva effective weapon as you witnessed back in that alley. Perfectly legal, too. And, as murder weapons go, pretty damn tasty." He shakes the gnawed-off end in my face and pontificates, "They can outlaw guns, knives, machetes, box cutters, but not smoked meats. Not yet anyway. Have a bite."

"No thanks," I say. To say I'm sickened by the sight and smell of the leathery thing is only part of it. The fact that it's wet with Mr. Knott's saliva and that it's just been used to beat three men to death is to say the rest. "I'm feeling a little queasy."

"That's not very considerate," Mr. Knott reflects, gnawing off another few inches, "all considered. You'd think you could help me eat the evidence since I just saved your life with it."

"I don't mean to be ungrateful," I gasp, grabbing the ends of the table as if I were on a ship in rough water, and waiting for the urge to hurl to pass. "By the way, how did you manage to pop out of nowhere?"

"Out of nowhere? I've been trying to set this meeting up for weeks."

"The FedEx packages?"

"Yup. Who did you think they were from?"

I shrug. "Me?"

Mr. Knott tsk-tsks. "What took you so long, anyway?"

"You send me a dozen FedEx packages and you never thought to add the place we were supposed to meet?"

"And have half a dozen government agencies waiting for us? I couldn't take the chance that your mail wasn't under surveillance. The only way to set up a safe meet nowadays is to be completely random. Or as close to completely random as possible. You're a detective, after all, aren't you? I figured you'd do a little deducing. Fact is, I never really trusted you Molloy. You're a sneak, a weasel, a look-after-yourself-first-and-fuck-everyone-else kind of guy. I could see that right off. That's, incidentally, precisely why I hired you. You can always depend on a man who looks out for himself. You can unerringly predict exactly what he'll do. It's like following the rats off a sinking ship. So I've been following you, watching your every move. When you made contact with Sprocket, I was watching. I wasn't going to wait around for you to play Cupid. I let you birddog Toddy down and then I swooped in myself to seal the deal."

"So you killed Sprocket, after all?"

"Oh heavens no! Toddy and I are very happy together. We're like two love birds."

"You're being sarcastic, right?"

"You must learn to look beyond mere appearances, Mr. Molloy. Beneath that flabby drab façade, Toddy is the sexiest little femme fatale this side of Salome. He's my Messalina, my Cleopatra, my Lolita, my Madonna, my Lilith, all rolled into one. Yes, Mr. Molloy, as improbable as it sounds, we're deeply in love. I owe you one Mr. Molloy, for leading me to the love-of-my-life."

This was information as nauseating to contemplate as Mr. Knott's lethal Slim Jim, and I tried not to contemplate it. I took another swallow of the poison in my glass. I gasped, "And Johnny Nomad?"

Mr. Knott looked a little bashful. "I'm afraid the news on that front isn't quite as good."

"How not quite as good?"

"Faceless."

I shuddered at the memory of the corpse in the back of my cab. That peeled grape head...

"You killed him for that gambling debt?"

"Not exactly. He owed me, so I had him work it off. I sent him to meet you that night you were supposed to give me Toddy's contact info, which I already had, by the way. But I wanted to see who was after me, who else was involved."

"US?"

"Yes, US."

"And just who are US?"

I try to keep the capitalization out of my tone. I try not to say US in italics. But it sounds like that anyway. It sounds like Mr. Knott is trying to do the same thing, but I wonder if I really did it as badly as he does it. I guess we're both trying not to sound paranoid, as if there's any point in that, when everyone seems to be out to get us. I take another big gulp of poison.

He says, "These guys are enemies of my old employer."

"The man who wished to remain anonyous?"

"Yeah," Mr. Knott says, with a little grin. "That guy."

I stick a fist in my chest, burp, and taste the after-burn of poison. When I don't keel over dead, I say, "Care to tell me who your old employer is?"

"He's a tireless purveyor of human pleasure, a fierce defender of First Amendment rights, a pioneer of information technology. If you put all that together and take out the bullshit, you get around to calling him what he really is. A pornographer."

I take another gulp of poison. I'm nearly completely poisoned by now. My poisoned brain is thinking about what Uncle Sal said. I ask Mr. Knott the very first question I ever asked him, the question that started this whole thing off in the first place.

"His name. What the fuck is his name?"

Mr. Knott says, "Chambers."

"Chambers?! There's like seven guys mixed up in this going by the name Chambers."

The fat man shrugs. "It's that kind of name."

"I met one who told me he was some kind of internet cop. He contacted me already. Toddy—Todd Sprocket told me he'd met him, too."

I stop short of saying he's Norma Blake Madsen's lover. I stop short of saying that Norma Blake Madsen is the other half of Nada Klone. I stop short of saying that Norma Blake Madsen has an identical twin sister who's my lover and who's now missing. I stop short of saying they are the same exact woman.

Mr. Knott laughs, "Ha ha ha," he says. "Mr. Chambers is no cop. He's the kind of guy that an internet cop, if such a thing even existed, would like to arrest."

"Please," I croak, barely able to keep my chin off the table. "Tell me how I can contact him?"

Mr. Knott could be joking. I don't know. I'm so poisoned now, so out of my mind, so blind-drunk I can't even see him, mountain of a man that he is.

He says, "Try looking in the phone book. You know, under Chambers."

This particular night ends the way all these nights end: on a subway car that I hope is the one that leads me somewhere within falling down distance of my neighborhood. Lately, I've begun to dread what I probably should have been dreading all along, sadly enough. I have begun to dread that when I climb out of the subway my building won't be there anymore, or someone else will be living in my apartment, a pair of secretaries from Smith Barney, maybe, or a family of acrobats from Beijing.

What I'm dreading is coming home one afternoon and finding some retired elevator repairman pretending that's not my television he's watching old *McGyver* reruns on, or my blue bowl he's eating fiber crisps out of. That it's not my fiber crisps he's eating.

Elbows on my knees, hands over my ears, I'm trying to hold my head as steady as possible as the train rumbles and bangs through the tunnel. Basically, I'm just trying to see straight. Basically I'm just trying not to throw up on my shoes. I'm trying to make it home alive one more morning, but who the hell knows why.

I'm thinking, *Maybe it's all just force of habit.*

Not exactly a zombie just yet, I'm aware enough of my surroundings to sense the mostly benign presence of the three other people in the subway car. In and out, they are sucking the trapped air along with me as we shuttle our way underground. They are disturbing the aether with their disturbing thoughts, unending ripples of hunger, boredom, frustration, sex, anxiety, sex, sex, and sex.

We're all going home, or someplace that'll have to do in the meantime; nobody wants any trouble; we've all seen too much of that for one night. I'm not a zombie just yet, I'm still in too much pain, and that's about the only way I can sense that I'm even alive at all.

25. Blackouts, fake-outs, and pretending to be normal...

The next thing I know I'm sitting in handcuffs on a hard bench beside a bunch of other handcuffed guys. We're all staring with great concentration at the tiled floor between our shoes, trying to look like we're patiently waiting for an apology for having been brought here by mistake, like we aren't all scared shitless, like we didn't do whatever it is they think we did. We're all in a police station somewhere, that's what it looks like to me.

Later on, I'll hear how I was spotted slamming the glass of an empty subway booth screaming for help. I'll hear of my jagged path of incoherent alarm through the early a.m. streets of Gramercy Park. They'll tell me of the commotion I raised in the lobby of the Carlton Hotel, the fright I put into the aged parishioners during morning mass at a church in the Village, the hullabaloo at Port Authority.

They tell me of some kookiness at the GW Bridge where, if you take out all the incoherent ranting and raving, as best as anyone can tell, I was threatening to jump.

The bruises on my shins, they'll tell me those happened when I fell off a stolen bicycle. The reason a couple of my teeth are loose, they claim that's due to the fall I took when I stumbled down the steps of the New York Public Library. You've got to expect a few lumps on the back of the skull, they tell me, when you faint dead away at the arresting officer's desk.

Later on, when I'm being—ahem—*questioned* for a second time, they'll fill me in on all these shenanigans.

I can't remember anything after that meeting with Mr. Knott except sitting on the subway heading home. That, a member of New York's finest is nice enough to explain with a calendar and a nightstick, was two days ago. "Blackout," I guess, is the technical term for what's happened to me. Letting your body go out on its own to experience the slings and arrows of outrageous fortune and then hearing all about it later—that's another way to put it. Not bad work if you can survive it. You pay for it sooner or later, though. The bill always comes back. And all indications are telling me that the bill is due now.

But, for the moment, I'm simply uncomfortably handcuffed and sitting on a hard wood bench between other uncomfortably handcuffed men. Like everyone else, I can taste blood in my mouth. I can taste fear. I'm wondering if I should have a lawyer present.

The man to my left says, "What they got you for?"

He looks like the prototype for every criminal to ever walk the face of the earth since the beginning of time. Just like we all do, if you look closely enough.

I say, "Murder."

He nods appreciatively. He says, "It always feels good to confess." He coughs up some blood onto his fist and contemplates it for a moment. Then he adds, "But only for a little while."

It's too late to say nothing. And that means it's too late for a lot of things. I'm being interviewed by a detective named Spurner or Stirner, something like that. He looks like an anguished literature professor listening to me give him a mangled interpretation of *David Copperfield*. He questions me like a dermatologist looking for suspicious moles. He has a maddeningly mild manner in spite of it all. He's excruciatingly patient as he asks me the same damn questions over and over and over again.

He asks me about the men in the alley. He asks me about the fat man I said saved my life. He asks me for my exact definition of the term "self-defense."

He says, "What exactly do you feel you need to defend yourself from, Mr...." He looks down at the papers on his desk. He says, "What did you say your real name was again?"

"Mercier."

He says, "Mercier," like he's not buying it for a second. "What is it you thought you saw again, Mr. Mercier?"

I don't remember all the stuff they tell me happened afterwards: the shouting, the crying, the disturbing of the peace. I don't remember all the psychotic and threatening behavior that supposedly got me picked up by a patrol car after some Lebanese donut dealer called 911. I don't even remember what I already told them about whatever I remember happening. The long and the short of it is that there are no victims of whatever I said occurred on Chambers Street. There are no witnesses. There are no reports of any occurrence that resemble in any way, shape, or form anything that I reported. To sum it up, my version of events bears no resemblance whatsoever to what is commonly agreed upon to be reality. It might as well have been a hallucination.

Detective Stirner says all this to me with a hint of confidentiality. He says it with a wink and a nod. He says, "You're lucky. *Nothing* happened."

I ask him to call Agent Chambers. "I think he's with the FBI. He'll vouch for me."

Detective Stirner looks disappointed; he looks like I completely misinterpreted the symbolism in *Billy Budd*. He looks like he just found a suspicious mole in an elbow fold.

With a great show of sadness, he says, "We already checked. There is currently no person with any federal law enforcement agency with the name of Chambers."

I say, "How odd. It's such a popular fake name."

The investigator gets serious. You can tell by the way his brow forms a corrugated "V." You can tell by the way he says, "This is serious, Mr. Mercier. You're lucky. Very, very lucky."

As usual, I'm confused. I don't feel very lucky. I never do. No matter how many times people tell me that I am.

"Nothing happened," Detective Stirner repeats. It's like a mantra or one of those slogans they use to sell cars on television. "*Nothing* happened. Am I correct?"

It's only slowly dawning on me now. Only at this moment do I begin to have some idea of what's going on here.

I've told the truth and everyone is pretending not to believe me.

"Yes," I say, "that's correct. Nothing happened."

"Excellent." And the detective really does look pleased, as if he were able to teach a particularly stupid dog a simple trick, after all. "Now we're getting somewhere."

I'm trying to pretend I'm perfectly normal. And this, apparently, is my last oral examination before graduation. Across from me, the shrink they want me to pretend I'm normal to before releasing me back onto the streets is so heavily doped-up on the Diazepine and Vicodin he's prescribing for himself that I can barely keep him awake. Meanwhile I'm trying to remember how to smile appropriately, nod meaningfully, look like I'm listening.

I'm not mentioning the reality-bending substances I suspect they put on the adhesive of the envelopes they give you to mail back your cable bill, the phantom injections you can receive without knowing it standing at a traffic light. I'm not mentioning the thought-control beams shot from invisible satellites that turn you into a witless zombie—a voracious unconscious consumer of Old Navy, reality TV shows, and two-party democracy.

Fact is, with one illegible scrawl on a piece of paper, the guy sitting across from me right now can send me packing to a city nut ward. If he doesn't like the way I answer the question, *Would you like a cup of coffee?*, that's it, I'm getting Thorazine injections and wearing a strait jacket for the next eight years. If he reads too much into a casual complaint about mass transportation, for instance, I could end up strapped down to a gurney in a room full of howling maniacs.

So I don't mention that buildings and people are disappearing in my life, the missing time, all the fake identities.

I make small-talk instead.

I say a lot of nothing.

I say, "I'm sorry for wasting everyone's time. Blah blah blah. I guess I just had a little too much to drink the last few nights. Har har har. I've learned my lesson. Blah blah blah. It won't happen again."

The doctor seems pleased with these answers. He says, "You didn't really see anything, did you? The police didn't really beat you, did they? You aren't being coerced to say anything, or omit anything, in any way, are you? The newspapers don't need to be involved, do they?"

I say, "Oh no, no, no, and no."

"Please say that into the tape recorder."

"No, no, no, no, and no."

I talk with insane enthusiasm about my job, my hobbies, my family. I mention the trees in the park, the hysterical new sitcoms, the joy of waking up each and every morning to a new day of the same old fucking inanities. I tell him there's nothing more than that in life and that this pointless nonsense is plenty good enough for me. I say, "I'm just happy to be alive. I love everything just exactly the way it is."

He nods, nodding almost off to sleep, and I take that for a good sign. I'm not saying anything to wake him completely up. Awake people, I've come to learn, are always extremely dangerous. As it is, I'm happy to see I'm boring this guy to death. He's scribbling something on a pad, rips a sheet off, hands it to me. It's a prescription for Xanax.

He says, "Take a pill three times a day. Go home."

"So everything's okay?"

"Well, not exactly. But as far as I'm concerned, you're pretending it is just about as well as can reasonably be expected."

Everyone seems to have lost interest in me by the time I get to the property desk to collect my things. I've never been so relieved to inspire so much general apathy. Everyone isn't looking at me, as if I don't even exist. They are looking right through me in such a way that, if I had a pineapple on my head, I get the sense they'd say, *Hey, look at that! A floating pineapple.* I'm hoping I'm not showing how happy I am about this, how ecstatic I am to be invisible again.

They give me back my keys, my change, my belt, an expired Metrocard, a handbill for a nude revue, all the worthless crap that was in my pockets. They give me back the small silver gun that killed Trina T.

I feel my blood turn to strawberry slush.

Sensing a trap, I point to the gun lying in the little plastic basket on the counter and say, "Don't you want to keep that? Isn't it illegal for me to carry that?"

The guy behind the bullet-proof glass at the high counter looks up from whatever he's looking down at on his desk. He says, "If that's illegal for you to have, then every ten-year-old in Manhattan is under arrest. I'll tell you one thing, though. You pull that on the wrong guy it don't make no difference if it's real or not. You'll get yourself capped same as if it was. You got no idea how many dead morons will pull a toy on you."

A toy, I'm thinking, *what does he mean a toy?* But now that I'm holding it, I know what he means. The thing's way too light and it's a completely phony color. I'm no expert in handguns, but looking at the label inscribed on the handle, I'm pretty sure that Playstation 2 doesn't make a line of lethal firearms. I grin at the desk sergeant sheepishly, as if I'd only been joking, mumble something about "that rascal nephew of mine," and stuff my pockets with the rest of my stuff. I want to get the hell out of the place as soon as possible before they can really find something I might have done wrong. Lord knows, it wouldn't take a Sherlock Holmes. The cop behind the counter slides a cell phone under the bullet-proof glass.

He says, "Don't forget your cell phone buddy."

I'm not asking any stupid questions. I'm not saying anything suspicious.

The one thing I'm definitely not going to do right now is tell him, *That's not my cell phone.*

I wave and bark out cheerily, "Thanks. Wouldn't know what I would have done without this! Have a good day. Goodbye."

I head for the exit. I'm waiting for them to come after me with handcuffs, dogs, stun-guns, pepper spray. I'm waiting for helicopters, SWAT teams, roadblocks. I'm waiting for the big flashlight. I'm waiting for someone to shout, *Hold it right there, asshole.*

But I'm through the front door and there's nothing waiting for me outside but sidewalks, dazed office workers, buildings, cabs, noise, and all the usual accoutrements of another incomprehensible grey morning.

Home sweet home is just as weird and unsettling as it always is lately, only maybe even more so. I make a lot of noise with the key. I clear my throat loudly a few times. I'm trying to give fair warning to my invisible roommate, trying to give him a chance to hide in the closet or jump out the window, or whatever it is he does if I come home unexpectedly.

If Franklin's men came back to the apartment for me, then they did it days ago. If they're still waiting for me, then maybe they'll listen to reason this time. If not, then I'm screwed. But one thing's for certain, I'm going back home. Like everyone else, I've accumulated a couple of decades worth of useless crap I can't just leave behind. That useless crap is my life and I'm going to take some of it with me even if it kills me!

When I open the door, the first thing I see is a lot of dirty dishes in the sink, the recliner is pulled out from the wall, and a game of solitaire seems to have been left unfinished on the coffee table. I look through the mail, which, by the way, seems to have already been opened. In the fridge most of the milk is gone again.

What's next? I'm thinking. *Dirty boxer shorts on the floor? Empty pizza boxes on the toilet?*

I call out sarcastically, "Hello? Anyone home?"

No one answers.

It's depressing as all hell, the entire situation, don't think it's not just because I don't say it is every ten minutes, but I'm depressed as all hell, all the time. And Naomi's disappearance has sent me spiraling to the bottom. Correct that, I'm not just at the bottom anymore, I'm tunneling under the bottom. Officially, I'm currently a miner in the subterranean depths of human despair.

I don't even pay attention to the empty can of Fresca on the radiator, the unfamiliar boots by the bookcase, the fact that the desk I'm sitting at isn't even in the same place where I left it. All in all, I'm just fairly surprised that the apartment is still here at all. By now, I kind of expected to be homeless. At the very least, I figured I'd come home and discover that I now lived in a thatched hut in Burma or in a duplex in some suburb outside of Kalamazoo.

On the window sill, I see the little plastic box I bought in Chinatown right before my bender two days ago. At least, I think it was two days ago. I've taken their word for it down at the police station. I haven't checked a newspaper lately. For all I know, it's February already. For all I know everyone is outside celebrating the Fourth of July.

I tap the plastic box with my finger.

There's a new turtle inside—it's simply inconceivable that the original turtle found his way home—along with a miniature green plastic palm tree. Who replaced it, and why, is anyone's guess. The turtle flinches back into his shell when my nail hits the plastic. The turtle's not happy. Pretty soon, I'm fairly certain, its eyes will fall out and it will die.

Just like we all do.

Anyway, I can't waste any more time on these morbid reflections. These intimations of mortality are just going to get me killed all the quicker. I've got to develop a hot foot. I've got to get the show on the road. I pull out a suitcase and start throwing stuff into it two-fisted like a circus clown. Plugging in the answering machine just for the hell of it, I listen to messages from debt collectors, debt consolidators, credit card companies, ex-wives, ex-wives' lawyers, Christian Scientists. There's a message from Meeah Soo. For an unlisted number, it sure seems to have found it's way onto everyone's speed-dial. The way it seems to me, there's hardly anyone at this point who *doesn't* have my number.

There are no messages from Naomi Blake, though. The only person I want to hear from doesn't call. The only reason to even have a phone…

Bending down again, I throw more crap into the suitcase and find myself holding the cell phone they mistakenly gave me at the police station. I'm wondering whether or not to pack it along with the rest of my worthless crap when it suddenly goes off in my hand like a premature ejaculation.

Beethoven's Ninth, the *Ode to Joy*, that's the ring tone. How cute.

It's bad news, I'm thinking, *when isn't it?*, and my first instinct is to pitch the phone, still ringing, straight into the toilet. Fact is, there's no such thing as a second or third instinct. There's just instinct and everything else is pretty much a mistake. Making a mistake, I answer.

On the other end the voice says, "Hey Chambers. Where you at? How you be?"

I say, "Who the hell is this?"

The voice says, "It's Joe. A friend of Tom's."

I say, "I don't know a single Tom."

Ignoring me, the voice says, "Dana is having a big New Year's Eve party. She's inviting the whole crew. If you can make it…"

Whoever it is on the other end is giving me an address on the upper East Side. Is it a code for another rendezvous, a joke, or a legitimate wrong number? Just in case, I write down the address on my driver's license, which is the only available piece of paper I can find at the moment. Well, I'm thinking, if nothing else, I've got somewhere to go to welcome in the year 2008. I won't have to face the new year alone. That's something to celebrate. If I still have a face to face it at all by then, that is.

Insanity, that's a pretty good explanation for what's going on with me lately and don't think it hasn't occurred to me either. Just the opposite: it's been occurring to me almost constantly since this business began. I'm leaving no stone unturned trying to explain what's happening and the probability that I'm going bonkers is one gigantic stone I've got to turn over no matter what wiggling psychoses I'm afraid to find underneath.

But however crazy I may be I'm not so crazy that I was going to admit how crazy I might be to that shrink the cops sent me to. I'm not so crazy that I don't know it's better to find your own private shrink to manage your insanity.

What I want is to let my lunacy leak out in drips and drabs in a comfortable, well-appointed office. I want to admit to bizarre behavior among potted ferns and muted aluminum-framed prints of mass-produced impressionistic seascapes. What I want is to walk home through Central Park after fifty minutes of tearful hand-holding with a fistful of those pretty pastel-colored prescription scrips. I want a medicine cabinet filled with small, but significant brown bottles. I want hundreds and hundreds of pills to make me feel sane.

So while I still have that cell phone in hand and the phone book I pulled out to look up Chambers Enterprises a few moments ago, I turn to "Psychiatrists" and start at the A's. I start at the Dr. Abels and dial my way through the yellow pages all the way down to the Dr. Zintermeyers.

At every number I dial, I get someone with an excuse why I can't go crazy in their office. I've got the wrong insurance, the wrong problem, the wrong referral. They aren't in practice, or they're out of practice, or they're currently over-practiced. They're Jungians, or Freudians, or Behaviorists, or they don't believe in therapy at all—it doesn't matter, they can't fit me in. I'm down in the Zurdyshenkos and running out of hope and alphabet when I think I've actually gotten through to a real-live doctor.

She says, "I'm sorry but I don't have evening or weekend appointments. I don't work on Wednesdays. I'm not in the city on Monday and Thursdays."

As she continues talking, I come to understand that she's not available on any day from nine to twelve, or from three to five on Friday or Tuesday. On other days there are bi-weekly groups, professional conferences, this or that workshop. One o'clock is forever impossible. There's her own therapy to consider, as well. I can hear her calculating time in her head. It's as if eternity itself is compressing. Her life isn't long enough. Maybe when I'm eighty-five there might be a slot open on Saturday afternoon at four-thirty-five. What is becoming clear is that there simply isn't time for me to go insane.

I say, "This is crazy. It would be easier for me to solve my own problems than schedule an appointment with you."

She says, "Sarcasm isn't appreciated Mr. Watt."

"Sorry Dr. Z. But maybe you can be so kind as to tell me when you *do* have time for me to go bonkers?"

"I'm afraid there just isn't time, Mr. Watt. I'm afraid there are just too many crazy people around to accommodate everyone."

"What the hell do people do then?"

"Generally, they just get crazier. You're still out there. You see what it's like. If it's special attention that you want, I suggest you do something special to merit it, to stand out a little from the maddening crowd. It's very competitive nowadays. If not, you can always get free treatment at a city facility. Have you considered breaking the law?"

I say, "Can I start by beating you to death Dr. Z.?"

She responds to my sublimated cry for help, not unpredictably, by slamming down the phone.

It sounds like this: *Bam!*

26. Bad news, the "real" Mr. Chambers, and 3.38 a.m.

"What took you so long?" Chambers asks. We're sitting at a flawless matte platinum conference table in the midtown Park Avenue headquarters of Chambers Enterprises. His secretary has just provided us with refreshments. Chambers is sipping a club soda. I'm having a black coffee. Needless to mention, I suppose, that this isn't the Chambers I met on the beach, Norma Blake Madsen's lover, the fake cop, in other words, not that I was really expecting it to be the same guy or anything. I say, "You were a difficult man to find. There are so many of you."

He says, "Why didn't you just look in the damn phone book. You know, under Chambers?"

"I just assumed it wasn't your real name."

"Yeah," he winks. "It is that kind of name, isn't it?

Chambers takes a sip of his club soda, but I don't dare touch the coffee. God only knows what it really is steaming away in that paper cup. He puts down his glass. He chuckles. He says, "The best place to hide nowadays is right out in the open. It's the very last place anyone looks," which reminds me of what Ratking told me that day on the top of that tour bus.

He's a good-looking guy, this Chambers, not in the same way that the other Chambers was good-looking, but older, grayer, more polished, like the guys in TV commercials who play doctors. He

looks the way the other Chambers will look in twenty-five years or
so, if he's got the right genes, takes care of himself, and has a good
plastic surgeon. Relaxed, charming, confident, he strikes me
immediately as a total charlatan. He reminds me of a televangelist or
an infomercial host. He could be selling you Jesus or food
processors, it really makes no difference. I'm suspicious from the
moment his secretary brings me in here for our one o'clock
appointment. He's wearing a sapphire pinkie ring, for crissakes. Who
can trust a guy like that? The possibility that it's not really Chambers,
that exists of course, it's always in the back of one's mind that
whoever you're talking to isn't who they say they are. That's a given,
that's an occupational hazard, that's just part of being human.

    "She's made contact with you," Chambers says. "You've talked
to Nada Klone." He says this matter-of-factly, as if he's getting it out
of the way, as if he's letting me know there's no point in wasting time
lying.

    The office is one of those offices that says: *This is a high-powered
guy.* A desk with no drawers and nothing on it, lots of steel and glass
all over the place, a big window with a view of some famous
landmark, everything voice-activated, including security, I'd guess.
There's art on the wall so fashionably minimal it practically isn't there
at all. There are plants that you'd never see growing outside in real
dirt anywhere. He's got a computer they haven't even invented yet.
Everything's consistent with him being the head of some vast semi-
secret global internet porn empire.

    I decide to play it totally naïve. I say, "Who?"

    He smiles, like in a movie. "Oh come on, Mr. Molloy. No need
to play dumb. I know you're smarter than that. Not much smarter,
perhaps, but smarter than *that.*"

    I say, "Okay, I've talked to her, alright. *Both halves of her.* I'm still
looking for the half that got away."

    Chambers says, "As am I, Mr. Molloy. Actually, I'm still
looking for both halves. That's why I had Mr. Knott hire you. But, as
I understand it, that fat bastard double-crossed me and cut his own
deal with you."

I squint my eyes, as if the man across the desk were a thousand light years away and I were trying to see him through a telescope. I say, "Who are you...*really*? And, please, none of that 'Who are any of us, really,' bullshit either."

He says, "I'm a dealer in identities, Mr. Molloy. Nada Klone belongs to me. I own her."

"How do you own a web personality?"

"I put her together, Mr. Molloy, virtual body and virtual soul. I gave her birth. I named her. You could call me the Henry Higgins of erotic personas. You can call me whatever the hell you want, but I've got a copyright on that identity. It's mine. *She's mine*."

"I'm no copyright lawyer, but I don't think you can own such things. These are real people you're talking about. You can't own real people."

As if he regrets it, Chambers says, "Slavery of real people ended in America in 1863. But the buying and selling of web personalities is a thriving business here in the twenty-first century. I own the web personality of Nada Klone. And, as I think you've come to learn, she's one wildly popular commodity. You see, I limit access to my little stable. I rent them out. And, if I want, I can sell my beauties outright. Then one and only one person has access to her. She's his very own slave-girl, mistress, dominatrix, whatever. Nada Klone is one valuable piece of digital ass."

Chambers stares at the bubbles in his tumbler of club soda for a while. He's staring at them like he's trying to decide whether to tell me something or not, but he's probably only pretending to be deciding whether to tell me something or not. A guy like him, he's got everything more or less already planned out ahead of time.

He says, "Do you want the truth Mr. Molloy? Do you *really* want the truth?"

I'm so stunned by the offer, I hardly know what to answer.

"Well...You know, sort of. I'm not expecting the moon or anything, but..."

He says, "I'm in love with her. I love Nada Klone. I know a pimp isn't supposed to love his product, but I do. I love everything I own, Mr. Molloy, that's why I own so much; but Nada is different. I love her like something you don't own. Do you know what I mean?"

I say, "You know, better than anyone, I would suppose, that she's basically just a figment of the imagination?"

"Does that really matter, do you think? She gives pleasure and she makes money and pleasure and money are more real than anything. Life wouldn't be worth living without them."

"What I meant to say was, what you love doesn't even exist. It's just an illusion."

"All the more tragic, don't you think?"

Chambers looks sad for a second or two, or wistful, or something like that. It's an expression we all get sometimes, we can feel it creeping over our face when we stop looking at all the TV screens and computer monitors. It's the expression we feel stealing over us when we turn off all the CD players and cell phones. It's the expression that reveals ourselves in spite of ourselves right before we order another drink or pop another anti-depressant or log back online. It's gone as fast as it appears and, in Chambers' case, I'm not sure I saw it in the first place.

He says, "What's love, anyway? Is it in the mind or in the flesh? Is it something that grows between two lovers over years of deepening intimacy or is it something that absorbs other entities during times of economic uncertainty and cautiously re-invests itself to return whopping dividends to shareholders when the market re-stabilizes? Do any of us really know, for sure?"

That's a question, I think we both know, isn't going to be answered right here and now, not by the two of us, anyway. It's the question Mr. Knott asked me, too, right at the beginning of this entire escapade. It's the mystery, apparently, that no one can answer.

"Well, we've got competition. There's this guy, Mr. Franklin. He seems to be looking for Nada Klone, too. And, let me tell you, he's willing to kill to get her. I hear he's a business competitor of yours."

Chambers makes a face like he just saw someone's booger floating in his club soda. He puts down his glass. "Franklin? That psychotic motherfucker? He's no business competitor. He's with the government."

"What government? That guy has broken more laws than Satan."

"No," Chambers says, "I'm Satan. Franklin is fighting for the forces of Light."

"You're telling me that Mr. Franklin is one of the good guys?"

"Oh yes. He's a good guy, alright. He's a good guy with a goddamn vengeance. He's a kind of colonel in a secret, parareligious branch of military intelligence. Using anti obscenity laws, trumped-up public hysteria over child abuse and Satanism, tenuous scientific studies linking porn and violence against women, they're trying to eliminate your right to wank off in front of your computer. They don't believe you should sit in the privacy of your own home and look at pictures of a girl taking it fore and aft by two well-hung black studs, they think it'll erode the foundations of this republic if you see pictures of lesbian toe-suckers, horny housewives and their pet retrievers, Japanese girls who vomit, panty-sniffers, pie-eaters, pissers, ass-kissers, you know, the whole wonderful spectrum of human desire."

"They want to control the internet?"

"You got it in one. It's the only thing they can't control. Not just yet, anyway."

"So it's Franklin who's the internet cop?"

"Well, if you can call someone who tortures, kills, and runs amok in total disregard for the law a cop," and here both Chambers and I share a significant moment of mutual understanding tinged with knowing amusement, "well, then you can call Mr. Franklin a cop. Fact is, Mr. Molloy, I do have a business competitor, but I don't know who he is. It's not your Uncle Sal, I can tell you that much. I'm afraid organized crime has left Sal Ruffio behind. It's not even Mr. Franklin. No, whoever took Nada Klone away from me is much more dangerous than that. I've take to calling him Mr. X. If I'm bad, then he's much worse than me. If Mr. Franklin is evil, then Mr. X is off the charts. I don't even know who this guy is, and I don't really want to know. Frankly, he scares me, Mr. Molloy, and I'm not a guy who scares. I'm far too rich and superficial for that."

I'm staring into the cold cup of coffee on Chambers' glass desk. I'm wondering, is my soul that black yet? If not, why not?

I look up. I say, "This guy, this Mr. X, what exactly does he do that's so bad? I mean, any worse than everything everyone else is doing?"

"I believe Mr. X is a collector."

"A collector?"

"An identity thief in the worst possible sense. A soul-stealer. An online stalker. I haven't told anyone this, but a few of my 'girls' have already gone missing. I'm afraid what we have here is a serial killer. And whoever he is he wants my Nada. Whoever he is, he's already cost me many millions and many pleasures and I'm determined that this time he won't have her."

Me, too, I'm thinking, feeling as if I were suddenly covered with ants.

Me fucking too.

"You must find her, Mr. Molloy."

"How?"

"Mr. X. You must find out who he is. Find X."

Great, I'm thinking, and algebra was always my least favorite subject.

Banging on the door is never good, and it's even less good I've come to learn over the years, when it happens at 3.38 a.m. My first thought is, *The secret police have finally come to get me.* And then I realize the US of A has no secret police, well, at least none anyone knows about. Of course, they do have police and they do secret things and until they come banging on your door at 3.38 a.m. you generally never know they exist.

But when they do come knocking, your heart starts beating so hard and so fast you figure maybe you just might not make it to the door anyway. Maybe you'll have a heart attack three steps across the floor and then everyone's problem with you, including, of course,

your own, will be solved once and for all. You always nurse this wild
hope for about two seconds that it's all a dream and then two
seconds later the banging starts again and you realize, goddammit,
you've never been so wide awake in your entire life.

I've crashed at Meeah Soo's place for the time being because
there really wasn't anywhere else I could think to go, which is how we
usually end up wherever we are, when you think about it. She was
reluctant to take me in at first, and that's being euphemistic. She was
contemptuous, disgusted, vindictive, imperious, emotionally
abusive—and who wouldn't be? But in the end she took me back
because, let's face it, she had nothing better going on at the moment
and because I swore on my life, crossing the heart I'm sure I don't
have anymore, that I was done with that "whore" Nada Klone.

I know what you're thinking, noble reader, I know what you're
thinking, because I'd be thinking it, too. But this is the way of the
world. I don't make up the rules; if I did, I'd have made them a lot
fairer, I assure you. But this is how the game was when they dealt me
in. Don't tell me you haven't done the same, or wouldn't, under
similar circumstances. Don't tell me you never took comfort with
someone just because they were the only one at hand or the only one
who'd have you. But, rest assured, I'm not a complete bastard. Meeah
Soo wouldn't let me be. She insisted I sleep on the couch.

Anyway, I'm stumbling, heading for the door, because going
out the window isn't an option without a fire-escape. Besides, the
secret police aren't stupid. They'll have men at the bottom of the
window. I have to be thinking they're thinking at least two or three
steps ahead of me, especially at 3.38 in the morning.

So I'm stumbling toward the door most of all just to make it
stop banging before Meeah wakes up, which isn't likely short of a
nuclear apocalypse on account of the Vicodin she took to ease the
pain of the electrolysis she'd had done that afternoon, and I'm
bumping into tables, TV-trays, folding chairs, piles of magazines and
sex-toy catalogues, whatever has been rearranged in the apartment
since the last time I was here, which was the night Meeah Soo threw
me out.

Shit, I'm muttering, as I nearly break my neck on an
unfortunately placed ab-roller. "Hold on goddammit!" I growl at the
door.

Fumbling with the doorknob because the lock's been changed,
I finally yell out, "Oh just kick the fucking thing in already, why don't
you?!"

In the corner, on the futon, beneath a pile of blankets, Meeah is
thankfully still snoring away.

Whoever's on the other side of the door seems intent on
knocking it down with their fists. That's going to take forever and
make lots more noise. So I reapply myself to the lock and manage to
get the door open.

Standing in the hallway is not a secret policeman, unless it's a
secret policeman dressed up in a fake Western Union uniform.

He says, "Mr. Murphy?"

Well, I'm thinking, that's in the ballpark, no use denying it.
"Sort of," I say.

"Telegram."

He hands me a piece of paper. He's grinning from ear to ear.
He says, "I hope it's not bad news."

Dad is dying, that's what the telegram says if you take out all the
unnecessary particulars. I'm to fly to Houston immediately, those are
the instructions if you take out all the stops and dashes and gobbley-
de-gook. I'm to go to Newark Airport, United Airlines Terminal 16.
A special bereavement ticket has been reserved for me under the
name of Camier. I'm to go immediately, the situation is touch-and-
go, the doctors say it's just a matter of hours.

Not so amazingly, when I get downstairs there's a cab waiting
at the curb. In a matter of minutes it's clear we're not heading to
Newark Airport, but to LaGuardia, but that's to be expected. That
the ticket isn't waiting for me at Terminal 16 should have been a
foregone conclusion all along. I know I won't be flying United when
I end up seated next to the window on a Northwestern flight. I'm
going to Denver, not Houston, but what's the difference, anyway?

My name on the ticket, by the way, is still Camier; well, that makes almost too much sense.

So in less than an hour after being woken up at 3.38 a.m. by the possibly fake Western Union secret police agent, I'm sitting in a coach-class window seat sipping a third-rate gin-and-tonic and staring out the window at an eternity of nothing.

Sitting next to me is some guy named Bart from Topeka. I know this because two minutes after take-off he says, "Hi. I'm Bart from Topeka."

For the next two hours he continuously interrupts my intense contemplation of nothing with talk of a design revolution in whatever that contraption is inside a toilet tank that makes it flush. I'm waiting for him to stop talking, but he never does, no one ever does. I'm listening to him drone on, the jet engines drone on, time drone on. I'm feeling sorry for myself and looking out at all that frozen blackness and thinking, *Here we are, all of us moving just under the speed of sound, but we aren't really going anyplace at all.*

27. Father, son, & make-believe...

Way up in the air, you start thinking about stuff in spite of yourself. Trapped for hours in a pressurized cabin hanging in the middle of nothingness with a bunch of other trapped idiots, useless junk floats across your mind. What I'm thinking about now is the woman I loved for the only three halfway decent months of what's turning out to be my miserable life. What really happened during those three months I have no clue. Of all of whatever happened, I'm not sure of a single goddamn thing.

All I know is that whatever happened changed me forever.

What I'm remembering is how I'd be inside her, staring down at her face, and it looked so beautiful that I was convinced I'd found the meaning of life. I felt at one with the movement of the earth, the oceans, the cycles of the stars, all that crap. I swore to myself that if I died at that moment I would die a happy man. The problem, of course, was that I didn't die at that moment; instead I kept on living too many more moments. I thought she was an angel, Aphrodite, god. Maybe if I had died right then like I wanted I'd have achieved the meaning of life, because later I found out virtually everything she ever told me was a sham. I never really understood a single word she said.

When she said, *I want you inside me,* what she really meant was, *I'm closing my eyes and pretending you're someone else.*

When she said, *I'll always be faithful to you,* what she really meant was, *until the moment I lose faith in you.*

When she said, *I love you* she meant you're *good enough for the time being.* When she said, *Pass the salt,* she meant *Is it supposed to rain tomorrow?*

When she said *fifteen,* she meant *four hundred and ten.* When she said *window,* she meant *sushi.*

It was like we were speaking two different languages. It's like I was hallucinating under the influence of testosterone and she was hallucinating under the influence of estragon. It's like we were both talking to ourselves.

When she said, *yes no yes yes yes no yes* what she meant was *yes yes no yes yes yes no yes yes no.*

Everything she said was, *Maybe.*

Everything she said was, *Maybe not.*

The only time she said anything that didn't mean something else was when she said, *Goodbye.*

The only time she told me the truth about anything was when she said, *We're through.*

I guess that's when the hypnotic trance was broken. When she left me, you could say the total mind control ended. That's when I noticed in retrospect a lot of things that anyone else would have seen weren't right from the very start. I remembered the hushed phone calls, the extra wine glass in the sink, the pair of shoes under the bed. I remembered that she looked okay in clothes but kind of lumpy when she was naked in the kitchen eating leftover Chinese chicken. I remembered her hair was thinning a little along the part. I remembered how she never shaved her armpits very carefully. When we were eating at the Renaissance Hotel one afternoon she had a long black hair growing out of her upper lip that she forgot to tweeze.

Yeah, baby, I'm talking about you. You know who you are. You were great at giving head, I'll grant you that. Thanks for all the bj's. About the only time you could stop lying was when my cock was stuffed halfway down your throat.

Sure, I know this is all petty and mean-spirited. Sure, I know it's kind of pitiful and sad. I know it's just sour grapes. But, hey, she didn't leave me any choice. Don't tell me you haven't said worse when the love-of-your-life dumps you. Besides, that's the good thing about getting to tell your own story: you get to say whatever you want. You get to get stuff off your chest. Have the last word. Besides, she should have had the decency to talk things over before just kicking me to the curb like that. She should have been a human being instead of whatever the hell kind of heartless, soul-killing, cocksucking, autonomic alien cyborg she turned out to be.

Let this be a warning to all you double-agents, aliens, adulterers, and advertisers out there: You shouldn't screw around with a...

And it's right then, thinking this thought as I'm floating around up there twenty-five thousand feet off the ground, that I start to consider actually writing the book I told Naomi Blake I'm writing. But the book I'm thinking of writing is not the book that up to now I've only been pretending to write, and it's not the book you're reading right now, although it started out that way. But I won't find out why that is until later, and neither will you.

No, I'm thinking, still in ignorance of so much, *you really shouldn't screw around with a writer.*

We'll do what nobody is supposed to do.

We'll do the most dangerous thing of all.

We'll tell the truth.

Two minutes later, of course, I have my face turned away from Bart and his incessant yakking. I'm looking at my reflection in the window of the plane and I'm watching the tears squiggling out of my eyes and I'm not sure because it's been a while but I think I'm really crying.

I'm remembering all the good things about Naomi and why I loved her with all my heart, body, and soul for almost four months. I'm wondering if maybe what she did wasn't even her fault. I'm wondering if maybe she were programmed to self-destruct just like so many of us. I'm wondering if maybe she couldn't help herself from hurting me, if she were just as much a victim of whoever and whatever as I was, but in a totally different way.

I'm thinking that for a little while we might have really been in love, that it couldn't have all been faked, not even her part of things, and I'm wondering if those moments of real love happened in spite of all the programming, or because of it. I'm sort of hoping it wasn't because of it because if it was than whoever or whatever is behind all of this is just too fucked up for words. But I'm also hoping the opposite. Do you understand what I'm saying? I'm sort of hoping she didn't love me, couldn't love me, because if she did, this is all too sad to endure.

I'm remembering how beautiful she was, how goddamn beautiful in spite of everything I just said, even because of what I just said. I'm remembering the last time I looked into her face and how the world looked all golden when I was seeing it with her.

I'm remembering how I always wanted to see the snowflakes falling in her eyelashes. And now I won't, not ever, because she left before the winter solstice could come.

What I realize at this moment is that even a writer can't get at the truth about anything, not really. All he can do, if he's honest, is tell you that he's lying. He's trying as hard as he can, but he doesn't really understand a fucking thing. All he can do is pretend he does. All he can do is lie and be upfront about his lying.

I'm crying and writing this on a damp cocktail napkin suspended by ten tons of airplane in the middle of empty space.

What I'm hoping is that this plane simply explodes to atoms in mid-air so I don't have to think about any of this anymore and I don't even realize that's what I'm thinking until the pilot touches us down safely at Denver International Airport, fragile as an oil pan full of trembling eggs, and I'm surprised at my disappointment at still being alive.

Landing in Colorado, I'm not expecting the car that's waiting for me to rush me to any hospital. I'm not really expecting to find dad in the ICU anywhere. I don't think I'm really going to see him dying peacefully with tubes running in and out of him, oxygen tanks standing sentinel, pretend family fake-sniffling into Kleenex. But then again, I'm really not expecting to be whisked to the top of a mountain at an exclusive Vail resort where dad is testing the packed powder on one of the most treacherous expert slopes, digging in his ski poles one at a time.

I've been through all this so many times before, but it's still a bit of a shock. The telegram is just a coded way of saying he's changing identities, he's switching residences, he's got to be re-hidden. I've seen these changes dozens of times but it always takes some getting used to. There's always a feeling of make-believe about it. There's always a lurking suspicion.

He's all duded up in a red metallic jumpsuit that fits him like a seal's skin fits a seal. He's wearing some kind of wraparound solarized ski visor that reflects everything, all the mountains and snow that are behind me. He looks tanner and fitter than he's ever looked. His jaw is squarer. His hair is thick and full and now it's what you'd probably call "a luxurious silver mane." The goddamn bastard looks like a movie star.

It seems to me I'm always asking the same question in the exact same way every time and everywhere I see him. "Dad?"

He says, "It's me alright, you little faggot."

"You look better and better every time you die."

"Dying can be good for you, son. A man gets bored with his life, he needs to die. It's invigorating. I'll get bored with all this soon enough, too, and then I'll die again. But right now, I'm feeling okay. The secret is all in the coming back. It gets a little easier after a while, the dying that is. Trust me."

Trusting dad has never been something I've ever once found to be a safe or wise life-decision. I've never found trusting dad to lead to anything good. But I need to trust dad now, even if I'm not sure it's really dad I'm talking to. Fact is, I'd probably feel a whole lot better if I could be sure it *wasn't* really dad I was talking to. Whoever this guy is, I'd trust him a lot more if I could be absolutely certain he was anybody *but* dad.

"Dad I need your advice. As much as things couldn't possibly have been more fucked up the last time we talked, they are even more fucked up now."

As I give him a quick update on what you already know, dad is checking the binding on his skis. He's making sure, I think, that no one has sabotaged his equipment before he takes off down the steep, zig-zagging slope. Some things never change. According to dad, there are assassins, apparently, everywhere.

He stands up, stamps his skis. He says, "Son do you really want my advice?"

I'm almost afraid to say it, but I say it anyway. I say it through a clenched jaw, "Yes, I really do."

He says, "Fake it."

What he says is, "Pretend you know what's going on. Set yourself up as an expert."

His advice consists chiefly of making a plausible enough case against someone, falsifying just enough evidence to make it seem logical, hand it all over to the highest ranking authority, collect the money, grab the freedom, and then simply disappear.

"Take on a new identity," he says. "It's easy. I've been doing it for years." The secret to survival, he says, is to be elusive. Don't let anyone ever know who you are. "Hell," he says, "if you can possibly help it, don't even know who you are yourself."

He tells me he can pull a few strings inside the Program. He has a few marks he can call in, a little finagling and fingering, a few people go to jail and, *voila*, I, too, can become an official federally protected witness. I can join the Witness Protection Program and be anyone and live anywhere I want. I can have a fake blonde wife like his new fake blonde wife Ingrid, Inga, Ina, or whatever the hell her name is now, just like he does. I, too, can have a weird little fake blonde son. Dad and I won't be able to contact each other anymore, well, not as father and son, anyway. But, as he says, that's a small sacrifice to make.

"Believe me," he says. "Family isn't everything. Usually it's just another disappointment you can do without. Give it up. What you get in return is complete safety. What you get is total anonymity. You get everyone off your goddamn back."

The way dad is making it sound, it all sounds way too easy. There's got to be a catch somewhere, I'm thinking, and it's not too hard to figure it out. I'm just drawing a temporary blank. I'm drawing a temporary blank, that's about to be filled in.

"All you have to do," he explains, "is rat everyone out."

I say, "But dad I don't have any information. There's no one I can rat out."

That's when dad confides in me the secret of his trade. He's passing on the essence of what he's culled from the experience of a lifetime. He's setting me on the right path, initiating me into the mysteries, imparting the wisdom of the elders. Like a medieval cobbler, he's handing me over the tools of the craft. What he's saying shocks the hell out of me, it freezes the marrow deep inside my bones. What he's telling me is that he doesn't know a goddamn thing either. He's an informant, all right, but he has no real information at all.

He says, "I just make it all up. I put the finger on people at random. All they want is someone to convict," he says. "It doesn't really matter who."

Somehow I try to convey the profundity of my shock over what I've just heard him admit. Staring at my father, I feel like I'm looking at a man I hardly even know. Of course, he *is* a man I hardly even know. He's a different man every goddamn time I see him. But listening to him now, this is a man I can hardly even *imagine*.

Seeing the simple-minded, open-mouthed expression on my shocked face, he says, "Oh grow up for crissakes, boy. Be a fucking man. The world isn't perfect."

Less futile it would be to try to talk the white out of the snow, the bull out of the bullshit, but still I feel the need to point out to dad the questionable moral dilemma his behavior poses for anyone with, well, a conscience operating above the level of a stone-cold sociopath. To his credit, dad listens to my naïve blustering patiently, turning only two or three times to make eyes at some passing ski bunny one-third his age, each of them inviting the wolfish leer he gives them with his perfect white-capped teeth.

"Listen little Miss Muffet," he says, turning back to me, "You think this is all gravy for me? You think I don't suffer? Do you really think I like living like this? Look around you. The snow is fake.

Those trees are fake, the trail is fake, even the goddamn mountain is fake. The whole goddamn world I'm living in is fake."

He lifts his ski poles, his feet with the skis attached to them.

"Shit," he says, "I can't even ski. But this is what I do," he says, "This is how I survive."

"This isn't exactly a life-affirming message, dad. This isn't showing a lot of integrity. This isn't making me feel any better."

Basically I'm saying that what he's telling me isn't what one wants to hear from one's father. I'm watching dad nonchalantly blow his nostrils clear into the snow, first one, then the other,. He wipes away the rest with the back of his expensive Gore-Tex heated ski glove. *Dammit*, I'm thinking, *he really is one helluva good-looking dude.* You'd never know he was riddled inside with cancer. You'd never know he had practically no intestine left.

He says, "What the hell do you want me to do, boy? Spoon feed you applesauce? Do you want me to wipe your ass for you?"

He spreads his arms out to indicate the fake snow, trees, ski-lodges, chalets, the whole pretend winterland panorama. He looks like Jesus with ski poles.

"This is the real world," he says. "This fake world right here is the real world. Take it or leave it. There are no happy endings." He says, "Even if you make it, even if you win, you end up dying. You end up lying in a hospital bed at seventy-five, all your insides eaten away, your panties full of poop. Where's the victory in that?"

Depression, they say, runs in families. Obsessive-compulsive disorder, panic attacks, bipolar disease, suicidal tendencies, they all have a genetic link, and I'm linked to them all. Maybe I don't bear any physical resemblance at all to any of the many men dad has been throughout my life, but I sure do share his sunny disposition on the utter pointlessness of it all.

He tells me what he can do for me. This, he tells me, is the best he can do. I don't think it's a coincidence, he lets on, that he's in Colorado of all places, do I? It's not a coincidence, do I think, that this is where Norma Blake Madsen was reported missing? If I had half a brain, he says, I'd have realized that none of this happened by chance. I'm not that much of a goddamn moron, am I? I don't see the need to incriminate myself so I leave his question unanswered. To tell the truth, I hadn't thought of it, but now that he mentions it, I guess it doesn't seem likely to be a coincidence that he's had me meet him in Colorado.

He tells me that he requested a new life here when it was time for a new life so he could do a little poking around. Poking around, he found a guy who might be able to help. When I ask why this guy would be willing to help me if he won't help the police, dad lifts a Gore-Tex warmed finger.

"If he doesn't, I put this finger on him. He does hard time for some unsolved murder or other, racketeering, white slavery, kidnapping, pedophilia, extortion, whatever the hell kind of nonsense I make up."

Grinning, I can't help but admire my old man for maybe the first time in my life. *God fucking dammit,* I'm thinking, *he really is one good-looking bad-ass motherfucker.*

"One last word of advice son," he says. "Keep running. Keep running until you can't possibly run anymore. Then stand on a corner one afternoon in broad daylight, push out your chest, and let them have a clear unobstructed shot at your heart."

Readjusting his polarized ski visor, dad shakes my hand. The world behind me is again reflected in a patina of fake gold. He stalks off to the edge of the perilous summit, digs his poles into the fake packed powder, bends his knees, and pushes himself off the edge of the fake mountain without so much as a backward glance. I watch him negotiating the treacherous trail, zig-zagging between the fake trees, fake rocks, fake bushes, the whole fake landscape. From what I can tell, he's pretending to ski like an expert.

Around a bend and it's copse of fake firs, he shushes out of sight and I know that's the last I'll see of him until the next time he croaks.

28. Cuckolds, contract killers, and hot tubs...

It's a two-car garage where I'm sitting, questioning the guy my old man threatened to finger. The guy's name, for some reason, is Pym, and I have no reason to doubt that. That's the name dad said to call him and he's answering to that name when I call him that. Of course, that's no reason to believe that's really his name either. If I've learned anything in this racket so far, it's that all names are suspect, any identity is little more than a working hypothesis.

Pym is a short, unassuming little guy in a flannel shirt and blue jeans. He's got a small, hard, pot-belly and a brown hair-fringe. He's the kind of guy you'd never look at twice even if he were the only guy in the landscape. That's what makes him so good at what he does: that's what makes him the best. He's sitting there in his garage on a metal stool in front of a lathe or a vise, something like that. What he's doing is working what he calls his "signature" into a shell casing.

He explains, "So they know it's me. So no one else tries to pick up the fee."

What Pym does, what he calls himself anyway, is a freelance photographer. That's what he puts down on his IRS forms at the end of the tax year. He puts this down in the line marked "occupation" because he can't really say what he's been doing all his adult life. He can't account for all the hundreds and hundreds of thousands of dollars he makes any other way.

Short, pot-bellied, unassuming, bald little Pym is a "semi-retired" contract killer, an assassin, a stone-cold murderer for the most powerful crime syndicate on earth: the U.S. government.

The two-car garage where we're sitting and having this conversation is on a leafy suburban side street that looks just like any other two-car garage on any other leafy suburban side street in America. It's exactly the kind of pegboard-lined two-car garage that I might have remembered my own dad sitting in building a birdhouse or fixing a wagon if we'd had a pegboard-lined two-car garage when I was a kid and dad did anything even remotely normal like build birdhouses or fix wagons. The only thing that might have been different is that mounted on brackets and hooks hanging from the pegboard of Pym's garage is every conceivable kind of handgun, rifle, pistol, grenade launcher, and assault weapon you can possibly imagine.

There are .22s. 38s, .44s. There are Brownings, Winchesters, Remingtons, and Walthers. There are machine guns, stun guns, shotguns, and Lugers. There are Glocks, Berettas, and Mossbergs. I can't accurately identify a single one of these weapons, of course, but there are so goddamn many of them on the walls of this place I'm just figuring that there's got to be one of everything. If you open a copy of *Guns & Ammo* and hold it up in front of your face, that's what the walls of this place look like.

Pym says, "You got questions? Ask'em."

He's a tough nut, Pym is, pot-belly, bald head, and all. He may be under my dad's finger, but he's not taking any bullshit off the likes of a pussy like me. That's the message he's sending, and it's coming through loud and clear.

I say, "I'm going to ask you a question and I want a complete answer. I don't want to feel like I'm pulling teeth. I don't want to play *Clue*, here. Got it?"

I'm not impressing a guy like this, it's stupid to even try. This is a guy that's been questioned by the best: CIA, FBI, Mossad, KGB, all the dudes who don't take "no" for an answer. This is a guy who's stared down the rifle sights at prime ministers, generalissimos, presidents, and presidentes. This is a guy who changes history with a pull of his finger.

Pym rolls his eyes. He says, "Oh, come on for, crissakes. Out with it."

I say, "Norma Blake Madsen. What the hell happened to her?"

Pym draws a long sigh. He's squinting at the bullet clutched in the metal jaws of the lathe or vise or whatever it is. He tries for a second or two more and then gives up putting his signature on the bullet intended for someone's heart. He sits back, places his pudgy little killer's hands on his pudgy little thighs. He says, "I was hired to shoot her. And let me tell you, it was the damnedest hit I ever did. Mad about this bitch, the fool was, and there she is hopping in and of the sack like it was a trampoline." Pym shakes his head disapprovingly. "*Love*."

"Who was the other guy?"

"A G-man, that's what my sources told me. But rogue, went a little off his lawman's oath, if you know what I mean."

"Who wanted you to shoot her? Her husband?"

I can feel the anger building up inside me, but I don't know at who—H. "Pop" Madsen for wanting to whack his wife; Norma for screwing another man, two if I count her husband as another man, and not counting all these others Pym is implying; Pym for planning to kill her; or myself for giving a damn.

"Cops wondered that too," Pym says. "It's always the husband they look at first. That's usually how it works. Killing a wife is cheaper than a divorce. But it wasn't the money with this one. Fact is, he didn't have any left. He had a bad snow problem even for Aspen. Cocaine, if you need it spelled out. The guy could have eliminated Antarctica with nothing but his nostrils. Where's a guy going under like that going to get the kind of money to pay a hit man like me, right? I'm expensive. I'm the best. Then, all of a sudden, he can pay me. He can pay the Columbians for his habit. He can even pay to upgrade the hot tub in his bathhouse. And it's the damndest thing because it's the first time in hitman history where a guy orders a hit on his wife and ends up richer than he was before the hit. No money comes out of his bank accounts, which is where the Feds look first, no houses are sold, no racehorses, no sportscars. Everyone's happy, which might be the first time that's ever happened, too. This is a fucked-up business, I'll grant you that, but it ain't that fucked up."

I'm trying to piece it all together, because it's a weird concept to bend my mind around. Pym is watching me, tilting his bald little head.

I say, "Because…"

Pym nods, as if to coax a slow child to a forgone conclusion. He nods as if to say, *That's right kid, come on.*

I say, "Because someone else paid the doctor to have his wife popped?"

Pym makes a gun with his hand. He sights along his forefinger, let's the thumb-hammer fall. He shoots me right in the heart.

He says, "Bulls-eye." Then, in case I don't get it, he spells it out for me. "B-U-L-L-S-E-Y-E.

I say, "Why would someone pay Madsen to pay you to kill his wife?"

"Madsen didn't want me to kill anyone."

"Huh? He didn't want you to shoot his wife?"

"Oh, he wanted me to shoot her alright."

He gets up from his stool and heads over to one of the pegboard-lined walls full of weapons. Already I'm feeling around in my jacket pocket for the toy gun. I'm not thinking that an expert marksmen like Pym would mistake it for a real gun, but I'm desperate enough to give it a try. I'm desperate enough to hope it may buy me two extra seconds to think of something better. I'm patting myself down like I've put myself under arrest, but it's no use, I'm coming up empty. The gun's missing. It's too late, anyway. Pym's already selected his weapon of choice. He's turning around.

I'm expecting the hitman to be holding an AK-47 or a Ruger Bearcat 22LR, something like that. What I'm not expecting is for him to turn around and say, "I shot her with this."

I'm not expecting him to say that while he's holding a top of the line Nikon 5100 digital camcorder in his stubby little assassin's hands.

I say, "You're telling me all you did was take her *picture?*"

Pym nods. "Thousands of them. Hundreds of hours of hot, horny, X-rated action. Inside hotel rooms, front seats of cars, movie theaters, state parks, in more sexual positions than the *Kama Sutra*."

I feel my ears redden. I manage to say, "But you're an assassin."

"Think about it. Who makes a better photographer than someone who fades into the background, than someone who can capture the light on a butterfly's wing from seventy-five yards away? You need roughly the same skill to catch a candid shot of Jude Law smooching with a fifty-dollar prostitute as to put a bullet into the head of the president of the United States from a Texas School Book Depository."

"But why? Why take pictures of her?"

Pym is pragmatic. "Why not? Someone offers me that much money for a money-shot, I take it. I don't ask questions."

"But if it wasn't Madsen who paid you, if he was only a front, who's money was it? Who paid you?"

Pym shrugs, "I don't know."

"Oh come on. You must." The wheels of paranoia were turning full-speed in my head. "CIA, FBI, NSA, NASA, Homeland Security, for crissakes? Just name a name. Is it Mr. Franklin?"

Pym says, "A guy this big don't have a name."

I say, "Everyone has a name. Even if it's a fake one."

Pym says, "Sorry kid. If this one has a name, I don't know it. If I did, I wouldn't tell you. Not even if your old man threatened to put the finger on me for the murder of Jesus H. Christ himself. This is a name you don't speak. Why don't you trying asking the man who hired me?"

It's difficult to know if Pym was telling me the truth or not: it's a little hard to totally trust a guy who shoots people from behind hedges for a living. But Pym didn't need to lie. All he'd done was take a few thousand X-rated photos of some guy's wife having multiple sex affairs.

I was driving my rented Buick down the better part of the best part of Aspen, through a neighborhood whose homes were so beautiful you couldn't see them at all because they were at the ends of driveways miles long, a neighborhood whose residents were so affluent the place looked positively uninhabited.

It was time to pay a visit to Dr. H. "Pop" Madsen. It was time to come face-to-face with the guy whose wife I've been fooling around with all this time, the guy whose wife may be having my baby, the guy whose wife I've fallen hopelessly in love with.

He's a bastard, pretty much like I figured he'd be. I pictured it all right down to the wafer-thin gold wristwatch and the professional manicure. He even looks the part: machine tan, expensively reconstructed hairline, smarmy grin. I didn't expect the rubber Adidas house sandals, though. I didn't expect the flaming USMC "Death Before Dishonor" skull tattoo on his hairy left pectoral. Most of all I didn't expect the broken-hearted look in the bastard's sad hound dog eyes. He's wearing a towel around his thickset middle-aged body and nothing else but the rubber sandals. He's got a cocktail in his right hand. You can tell by the disorganized look on his face that it's not his first. It's ten a.m.

What I did expect is the hostile attitude when he finds out why I'm here. He's been through his story with the police so many times and with such critical success he knows he doesn't have to convince the likes of me of anything. Hell, he doesn't even need to talk to the likes of me, a point he wastes no time in pointing out.

He slurs it all out in a boozy smear. "You've got a lot of balls coming here. Get the fuck out, asshole. I don't have to talk to the likes of you."

I say, "I think you're wrong. I think you do need to talk to me. What I think is that you'd better start doing a lot of talking to me and the first words better start coming out of your mouth right about now."

"And what makes you think that, fuckface? You know who you look like? You look just like the guy suspected of kidnapping my wife. I could call 911 and have you arrested in five minutes."

He's wobbling about on his thick hairy legs like an intoxicated bear.

I say, "So what's stopping you? Why don't you call the cops?"

I'm bluffing, of course, but it's got him clamming up for maybe ten seconds or so. We're standing in his sun room or solarium or whatever they call those places out back of what I'm sure is technically a mansion. The place is sweltering, full of sweaty tropical plants that look like expensive sex organs straight out of one of Meeah Soo's plastic surgery catalogues. Through the big windows all around us I can see the kind of picturesque mountains that people like Robert Redford and Cameron Diaz pretend to ski down in those photographs you see in *People* magazine. I think of dad's series of *Architectural Digest* homes and they look like hillbilly shacks compared to this joint. Being a dentist, apparently, is an even higher-paying gig than being in the Witness Protection Program. A few minutes ago, a frumpy Nicaraguan housekeeper guided me through this labyrinth of many rooms to get where we are now and she stands grimly ready to guide me right back out. She's gonna catch hell about believing the confusing rigmarole I used to get myself in here in the first place, but keeping the Third World illegally employed is not my problem.

My problem is that I've got about three more seconds to convince Madsen that he's the one who's got the problem and that problem is me. More exactly, that problem is what I know.

Truth is, however, I don't know much of anything. But I'm taking my inspiration from that little pep talk dad gave me on the slopes. I'm pretending to know something.

"Are you saying that you aren't fucking my wife?"

Madsen has asked exactly the question I've been hoping to avoid, the question that's kept me out of Colorado and a confrontation with the good doctor up to now. How the hell am I supposed to answer this question? I think it over and this is the best I can come up with: "I really don't know. Does she have an identical twin sister?"

He says, "Is that supposed to be funny?"

"It's not supposed to be, but maybe it is all the same. Are you telling me your wife didn't have a twin sister?"

"She has a gay brother she's not close to anymore. He lived in San Jose the last I knew. They weren't twins, but I guess they might have looked alike as any two siblings might, maybe you could confuse the two if he wore lots of make-up and a wig; maybe if he had tons of plastic surgery; maybe if he had a whole different fucking head grafted onto an entirely different body. Don't you think you'd know it if you'd been fucking a man or not, you nitwit?"

I do my best to ignore the sarcasm; besides, I wonder myself. Lately, I'm not so sure.

"Would your wife have contacted him after she left you? Maybe for a place to stay?"

He sighs. "The police already looked into that possibility. It's a dead-end."

"Do you have any pictures of your brother-in-law?"

He says, "Maybe from years ago…who the fuck knows? I haven't got time to stroll down memory lane. What the hell am I talking to you for, anyway?"

"You're talking to me because I know you had huge debts concerning all that coke you were hoovering up your nose holes. I know how all your debts got miraculously paid back all of a sudden."

The dentist seems unfazed, but he's listening. He says, "This is all old news, Mr. Molloy. The police have been over all this already. As you can see, I'm not under arrest; meanwhile, your picture is on a wanted poster. I see it every time I go down to the post office to buy stamps."

"That may be Dr. Madsen, but that might not be the case for long. You could be arrested at any moment, the way I figure. You see, I know someone paid you for your wife's life."

Madsen is fidgeting noticeably, but nothing too dramatic.

I say, "I know you were paid to let someone shoot her."

The dentist blanches the way I imagine one of his patients might blanch at the words *root canal*. He looks at me with a look that's a mix of something between rage, fake indifference, and just plain *I've taken about all of this shit that I'm going to take*.

"That's not true," he says, as if he knows it's all too true. "You're fucking crazy," he says, as if he suspects I'm perfectly sane.

I say, "I've talked to Pym."

I don't wait for him to say anything. I don't hang around long enough for him to have a chance to order me thrown out. Instead I turn and start walking toward the door of the glass solarium thing all by myself. I don't really know anymore more than I knew walking in, but I have a hunch that's all going to change before I make it to the liana bush by the doorway. That hunch pays off when I hear Dr. Madsen say, "Wait a minute, Molloy…Felicia," he turns to the housekeeper, still standing silently in attendance, "go clean a sink or something. Give us a little privacy." The housekeeper bustles off. Madsen says, "Please come back, Mr. Molloy. There's something we need to talk about."

"I'm listening."

"Not here. Let's have a soak. I've just had a new tub put in."

You end up in a lot of weird places in my line of work, and the place I am now is one of the weirdest of all. I'm sitting naked in a hot tub on the terrace with a guy whose wife I slept with and maybe even knocked up. We're sitting here almost knee-to-knee in a redwood box of steaming water and talking about the woman we're both obsessed with.

He says, "Look, you and I both know there's nothing against the law about having your wife's picture taken."

"We both know there's a bit more to it than that."

"How much more. What more, exactly?"

"To be perfectly honest, I don't know. But I do know that you wanted her killed at one point."

Dr. Madsen shrugs his furry shoulders. "So what? Maybe I did. What does that mean? Everyone has thoughts like that once in a while. I went a little crazy there for a time. I admit it. You would, too, if the woman you loved were fucking another man."

Hearing him talk about jealous rage and murder would be bad enough. But it's that much worse sitting naked in the same steamy broth with this guy.

He continues, "I changed my mind about killing her. That's the important thing. You pick up a gun in anger, you don't pull the trigger, you put it back down. What have you proven except that in the end you're not a killer? That, in the final analysis, you're not guilty of anything. That you're only human."

I say, "You're guilty of something."

He says, "You're guilty of fucking my wife, you bastard. Your face is on that composite poster identified as the guy she ran off. I should strangle you."

"So why are we sharing a bath instead? I'm sure you don't just want me clean before you choke me to death."

"Because you can't make your wife love you, Mr. Molloy. I realize that now. You can give her everything." He spreads his heavy, fur-covered, scarily tattooed arms. "You can give her all this, but if she doesn't want you, she doesn't want you. If I don't call the cops on you, if I don't beat you to death with my own bare hands, it's because I realize now it's pointless. It won't give me what I want. No one can. Especially not her. I just want to know that she's okay. I want to know what it is that you have that I don't. Call me curious. Call me an idiot. But I still love that bitch….I…"

And we're sitting out there in the steam and all, and there's water splashing up and bubbling, and it's easy to make a mistake, but I don't think there's really any mistaking it: Madsen is crying. He's wiping away the tears from his face with the back of a hairy paw, pretending he's got a splash of chlorine in his eyes, but he's crying. As much as I'd like to, I can't hate him anymore; well, not the way I'd like to. I can't hate this smarmy, rich, lovesick son-of-a-bitch anymore because take away the big house, the round-the-clock personal staff, the astronomical bank account, the stable of beautiful mistresses…and he's just like me, just another lonely, broken-hearted moron who's loved and lost.

He manages to collect himself and concludes, "If she ran off to be with you, there's not jackshit I can really do about it."

I say, "She didn't run off with me, Dr. Madsen."

He smiles ruefully. "Well it was someone who looks a helluva lot like you, then, I guess. Three witnesses came up with that composite. They say they saw Norma with a guy that looked like you shortly before she disappeared."

"I suspect those witnesses were phony. I didn't meet her until she was in New York. I'm being set up to take the fall."

"The fall for what?"

"It's a long story. I'm not even sure I understand the plot myself."

"The thing is, as much as I loved her, I couldn't go through this again."

"What do you mean, again?"

"Do you think you were the first? Don't flatter yourself. More like the fifty-first," he said, nonplussed. "But after a while, who's counting?"

I think of what Pym told me, what I've been trying not to believe. "Are you saying that your wife slept around?"

"Like George Washington."

"And you put up with it?"

"As well as I could, Mr. Molloy. We put up with a lot for love, don't we? Norma had a fidelity problem. You might say that she was incapable of it. She wasn't built for just one man."

"That didn't make you angry?"

"What the hell do you think? Of course it made me angry. But what sense did that make? How could I take it out on her? How could I blame her for something she had no control over? To blame her for being unfaithful would have been like blaming her for being unable to play the violin. It was simply a capacity that she didn't have. Fact is, there's something a little damaged about Norma."

"What do you mean, damaged?"

"I mean she's a little bit crazy, Mr. Molloy. Mildly schizo. A nymphomaniac, I think you could call her. It's not easy living with the insane. After a while, it tends to rub off on you. Norma had a hole inside her, Mr. Molloy, that no one man could fill, nor fifty. You could call it a lot of fancy names and throw away tens of thousands of dollars in psychotherapy to have someone give you all kinds of reasons and explanations, but at the end of the day, Norma is just a crazy slut."

Crazy enough, I'm wondering, to pretend to be her identical twin sister and start an affair with me? Madsen, I notice, is crying again.

"I tried Molloy. I tried everything. I gave her all I had but it wasn't good enough."

"So what made this time different than the other fifty?"

"This time she didn't come back. She always did before. The affairs I'd learned to live with, but not this, not her falling in *love* with another man. I couldn't take that. If she fucked around and loved me that would be one thing…but to fuck around on me and love someone else…"

"So, you were going to divorce her and the pictures were taken to use against her in court."

"No, I told you, I didn't order those pictures taken."

"Well if not you, who? Who would pay so much just for your wife's pictures?"

The dentist shrugs, "I wasn't asking a lot of questions. I needed the cash and they said Pym was a professional. Nothing funny, nothing sleazy. Tasteful porn. Norma ran out on me…I figured it was the least she could do. I figured she owed me that much. I'd had enough, Mr. Molloy. So I gave them access to Norma's computer. I let them go through her personal effects. I let them bug her car, her cell phone, her bathroom. I allowed them 24/7 access to whatever information they needed to track her illicit escapades. I cooperated in return for the cash and immunity to everything. You might say I betrayed her, but can you technically betray someone who's already betrayed you?"

"Who would be empowered to give you immunity to anything, let alone everything," I said, half-thinking out loud.

"I think it's best not to ask that kind of question."

"The FBI?"

"I'm not saying that."

"The CIA?"

"I'm not saying anything."

Madsen had stopped blubbering, but by now, *I* almost felt like crying.

"Hey, where are you going?" the dentist hiccupped. "Hey…"

He says this because I've just jumped out of the hot tub like a crab grabbed my balls. I'm jogging back through the solarium, my bare wet feet slapping the marble hallways, through rooms that look like museum galleries. I'm buck naked, dripping water from my wrinkled pink ass all over the hardwood floors and priceless Persian rugs. I barely notice the startled look on the housekeeper as I lunge passed her shouting, "Where are my clothes?"

I'm not sure exactly where I'm going just yet, it's true, but I'm going somewhere, I know that. I'm going somewhere, and like most places you go, I'm going to need my underwear when I get there.

What are the odds of that, I'm thinking, as I sit around the airport waiting for my flight home. Oh, I don't mean the FBI or something like it working a sting on the guy who's having an affair with Madsen's wife and a guy claiming to be with the FBI or something like it having an affair with her. I mean a guy in my predicament sympathizing with a bastard like Dr. H. "Pop" Madsen. The odds seem like they must be something like a billion to one. You'd have a better chance of hitting the lottery, by which I mean, you'd have no chance at all.

As it turns out, I have plenty of time to think thoughts like this. I'm sitting among a lot of grumpy passengers and all their lumpy carry-on luggage since all the eastbound flights have been delayed for one of the many bogus reasons they tell you they are delayed. For the eleventh time today, I take out the cell phone that desk cop at the police station gave me and punch in Naomi's number. On the other end of god-only-knows-where, the phone rings a whole bunch of times before disconnecting without any message at all.

Two hours later, as I head off to the gate where I think my flight may finally be boarding, I try not to get too discouraged about all of the many things I have to be discouraged about. I try, but as usual, it doesn't work.

29. Thanksgiving, suicide, and other emergencies...

By the time I get back to New York, I realize it must be nearly the
end of November. Man, how time flies. The weather's turned cold
and grey and blustery. Most of the leaves have fallen off the trees and
the ones that haven't are about to. Everyone's wearing a trench coat
and a scarf. Everyone's carrying an umbrella. Every once in a while
the sky spitefully spits little balls of frozen water at me.

I'm figuring it must be near Thanksgiving because there are a
lot of those stupid cardboard turkeys taped to store windows and
apartment doors. Even I buy one of these stupid cardboard turkeys
and I stick it on the nail in Meeah Soo's door where some past tenant
once hung something or other. What possesses me I don't know.
Some desperate last-ditch ploy for normalcy, I guess.

Since I've been away, Meeah Soo has been trying to spruce up
the joint—an end table here, a chaise lounge there, a new set of juice
tumblers. It's a mystery where she's getting the dough to do this until
she confesses that she's been opening up my mail, which the post
office has been forwarding here. On the new kitchen table there are
five more FedEx envelopes that made their way here yesterday that
she hasn't gotten around to opening, both addressed to me in my
own hand. If I add up all the checks, money orders, and gift
certificates inside, it adds up to something like $47,000. I now know
that this money is coming from Mr. Knott—the last of my finders

fee for locating his half of Nada Klone. I glance at those mailing labels that had baffled me so much not that long ago. What I also now know is that, among other things, Mr. Knott's apparently quite an accomplished forger.

What I'm doing is sitting at this new kitchen table as I do every morning lately. I've got a great big paper cup full of Starbucks coffee and I'm trying to start that true-crime book that I've been pretending to write. I sit here for hours trying to think of something to write, but I can't even think of a first sentence. I wonder if maybe I ought to masturbate to relax, unwind with a little Regis and Kelly, do some dishes, but all that seems like too much trouble, so I just sit and stare into space for long periods of time.

I guess you could say I was ruminating over the plot. You might say I was waiting for the muse to visit. But if you actually saw me, not being a professional writer yourself and therefore not knowing any better, you'd probably just say that I was staring into space and absently picking my nose.

"I don't want to live!" Meeah Soo is shrieking from behind the closed bathroom door, "I don't want to live!" I've only been back three days when she decides this. It's some kind of record, I think; usually my roommates last up to a week before driven either to manslaughter or self-annihilation. The fact is, Meeah not unreasonably thought my reappearance in her life meant that I'd come to my senses and decided to restart our relationship. To be honest, such an assumption wasn't just reasonable, it was probably inevitable. So was her reaction when I told her point-blank she was mistaken.

She shut herself up in the bathroom an hour earlier in her present hysterical state and I've been trying to talk her out even though I really think she'd be better off with professional help. I think she could call a hospital. I think she should call 1-800-SUICIDE. Frankly, I feel particularly ill-suited for this whole crisis because, at the moment, I personally don't have a real good grasp on what the point of life is either. My worst fears are confirmed when I half-heartedly mutter some inane platitude or other about the value of the little things and Meeah Soo wails as if I burned her with a red-hot poker.

"Oh god I hate my life!" she screams. "I hate it! I hate it! I hate it!" She sobs and kicks at the door. "Oh, why do I even bother to try. Why?! Why?!"

I really don't have a good answer to that question either. Why *do* we bother to try? I mean, the only answers that come to mind are, *What else are you going to do but try* and *I guess you never know what tomorrow will bring.* Those answers don't really satisfy anyone's existential angst, though, not really.

When Meeah Soo asks how is she ever going to find happiness when she's been born into the wrong body, the wrong gender, the wrong sexual orientation, what can I possibly say?

When she says that all she wants is to be a real woman, to be loved by a real man, to feel a baby growing inside her, what cacophony of rationalizations is going to smooth over the fact that she hates herself all the way down to her chromosomes?

Lamely I say, "No one is really who they want to be. Everyone really wants to be someone else."

Upon hearing these hideous clichés, Meeah Soo only shrieks louder, if that were even possible, and the way I'm flinching in the face of these unearthly decibels, it sure seems to be. I'm certain that she's doing her best to drown out whatever it is I'm saying to her, and really, I can't blame her. I'd like not to be listening to myself right now either. In fact, it would make it infinitely easier for me to convincingly say all the perfectly useless things you're supposed to say in these situations if I didn't have to hear myself saying them.

Behind the bathroom door, Meeah Soo could be doing anything. She could already be soaking in a bathtub full of red water and razor blades. She could be slipping into a barbituate coma. On the upside, for all I know, she could just as easily be sitting on the toilet taking a leisurely crap.

Realizing I'm not helping matters, I decide to get help myself. While Meeah continues sobbing and shouting and cursing and hating everyone and everything under the sun, I dial the suicide hotline. Holding the phone between my ear and shoulder, I'm trying to answer Meeah Soo and explain the situation to the volunteer or whoever it is on the other end of the line.

I say, "No it's not me. I'm not suicidal. At least, not right at the moment. It's my friend."

On the other end, whoever it is gives me a patronizing, "Okay I understand. Let's talk about your *friend.*"

Meeah Soo cries out, "Who is going to love me now. "Who? *Who?* WHO?"

I say, "Someone will love you honey. You're a beautiful human being."

The volunteer says, "Who are you talking to?"

I say, "That was my friend."

Into the phone, I'm trying to answer the volunteer's checklist of questions. I say, "I don't know if she's ever attempted suicide before. No, I can't see exactly what's she's doing right now. She's locked herself in the crapper."

I call out across the room, "You can put an ad in the personal columns in *New York Press.* Guys are always trying to meet transsexuals in there."

Meaah howls.

I'm considering kicking the door in, but I don't think it's necessary just yet. Though it might enable me to save her life, if this is a false alarm, kicking the door down is only going to cause a lot of unnecessary problems, like having to call the landlord for starters, and the inhibiting lack of privacy that will commence at the very next call of nature. We're all okay, I figure, so long as Meeah Soo is still screaming.

To the volunteer I say, "I don't know if she's been drinking or doing drugs." Towards the door I shout, "Meeah, have you been drinking or doing drugs? I mean, more than usual?"

"I don't want to look in the newspaper for love like a freak," she moans. "I don't want pity," she heaves great big drama-queen sighs of grief. "I don't want just desperate anonymous sex."

"Jesus, honey," I can't help but editorialize at this point, "what other kind is there?"

She wails, "I want love. *I want love!*"

I say, "Lot's of people meet people at the gym. Maybe you can join a book club."

The cry that Meeah emits now, even the volunteer on the other end of the phone asks, "What the hell was *that*. What the hell are you doing to that poor girl?"

I say, "I'm trying to help."

"For God's sake," the volunteer says, "Don't try so hard. You can't solve her problems. Just listen. Just be sympathetic."

Meeah sobs, "You were the only one who ever loved me. Now you're gone."

I say, "I'm right here Meeah. Honey, I'm standing right here outside the bathroom door." Answering the volunteer on the phone, I say, "I can't tell if she has the means to harm herself." To the door I ask, "Meeah, darling, do you have anything in there that can harm you? Oh," I say, as the volunteer rebukes me again, "I thought I was supposed to ask." I look back at the bathroom door in despair. "Never mind," I call out. "Nix that last question."

Realizing that any silence in these circumstances can be ominous and that Meeah has fallen silent for the last several seconds I say, "Meeah, baby, are you still okay in there?"

She says, "Who are you talking to out there?"

Looking into the phone receiver, I ask, "She wants to know who I'm talking to out here. Who am I supposed to be talking to?" Looking at the bathroom door again, I cheerfully say, "No one, honey."

Meeah shouts, "The fuck you aren't talking to anyone! I can hear you. I'm not deaf. Are you talking to *her*?" She growls, "Are you talking to that bitch while I'm in here killing myself, you two-timing, ass-humping bastard!?"

"Oh Jesus," I say, "oh for crissakes. Look," I shout into the phone, "I've got to get off. I've got a *real* problem on my hands now."

On the bathroom door, the knob is wiggling around so violently it looks like it's just going to fall off as Meeah Soo tries to unlock the lock.

"No," I say to the volunteer. "We don't need an ambulance. You've done more than enough. I'll handle it from here. Thank you for all your help. Yes, I'll call back to let you know how it all works out. Now I've really got to get off…I…*Holy* s*hit, she's coming out!"*

Hanging up the phone, I jump away from the bathroom just in a nick of time. Meeah Soo throws open the door with a bang and stands there framed by the bathroom light. She stands there in a short black kimono and stacked black platforms. She's got her hands on her hips and her make-up is all smudged by tears and snot. Her hair is in disarray and her long thin legs are spread wide and trembling like the rest of her is trembling with unadulterated fury. She is looking right at me and the look in her eyes is pure murder. In other words, right at this moment, Meeah Soo looks as much like a real woman as any real woman I've ever seen. Somehow seeing Meeah Soo looking like I'm seeing her now, as she's always wanted to be seen, somehow I know she's going to be okay.

"Get out," she says icily. "Get the hell out and don't ever come back."

Backing my way to the door in case I have to duck anything hurled towards me, I leave behind the latest batch of FedEx envelopes, the FedEx envelopes full of checks. I leave them on the new kitchen table on top of all those brochures for fake breasts, fake brows, fake chins, fake tits, fake cunts. I leave all that money and get the hell out of her life. I know that money can't take the place of loving Meeah Soo like a real woman, but maybe it will help buy her the illusion of love, at least for a little while. Christ, I hope so. It's the closest any of us ever get.

Far away at first, and then growing louder by the second, I hear the siren. I am in the back of a cab after leaving Meeah Soo's, so exhausted and emotionally wrecked by that whole scene that I've decided to spring the twenty bucks or so it'll cost to be driven back to Manhattan. Besides it's pouring rain and I couldn't find the subway station I usually take from her apartment. So I find myself in the back of a cheesy-smelling cab and I sort of recognize the driver as one of the drivers from the cab company.

I say, "Hey Manny, remember me? I used to drive for Mr. Sammy too."

The driver looks in the rearview, but not at me. He says, "My name ain't Manny and I don't know no Mr. Sammy"

"Okay. Have it your way."

Behind us, the siren is getting louder and louder. Turning around in the seat, I look out the back window and see an ambulance stuck in the traffic behind us. The lights on the ambulance are flashing wildly, blinking and strobing, like an ice cream truck in hell.

"Poor bastard. Well," I say to the driver, to myself, to no one really, "I guess however badly we're doing, we're not half as bad off as the poor son-of-a-bitch being carted off in that meat wagon."

In the front seat, the driver doesn't say a word and I'm thinking, *Oh fuck you,too, then*. Meanwhile the wipers are batting away helplessly at the hammering rain and the ever-louder siren feels like it's squeezing the brain right out of my ears. In spite of the traffic, the ambulance seems to be relentlessly creeping up on us.

I say, "Turn off at the next street. Let's just get away from that fucking siren. I can't stand it anymore."

What happens over the next several minutes grows creepier and creepier until I get that really creepy feeling that's become way too familiar to me by now. As I direct the driver to turn left, right, speed up, slow down, make a U-turn, whatever, that goddamn ambulance somehow ends up right behind us, siren piercing, lights madly flashing.

"What the hell hospital are they going to anyway? Get the hell out of their way."

The driver seems to be doing his best to lose the ambulance behind us, but no matter where he goes we're right in the path of an emergency.

He says, "I'm pulling over. I can't lose him."

The ambulance pulls up behind us at the curb. The inside of the cab is splashed with red light. I look at the driver's scarlet face and say, "What the fuck's going on?"

He says, "I think the emergency is *us*."

"That's crazy."

Behind us, the ambulance driver has cut off the sirens, but leaves on all the lights, syncopating the street like a scene from the last day on earth. From both sides of the ambulance, a burly paramedic jumps down to the street, and heads towards the cab, both of them bowed against the driving rain.

For a split second, it occurs to me that maybe I was wrong and I get a great big sucking feeling in the pit of my stomach. Maybe, it occurs to me for a split second, Meeah Soo tried to commit suicide, after all. But then I realize that the timing is all wrong. I just left her apartment. There hasn't been time for all that to happen, for her to commit suicide, for her body to be discovered, for the ambulance to get there, get behind me, and why would it be stopping me instead of rushing her to the hospital?

"Something is all wrong here. Something is really *really* all wrong. Get us out of here. Hit the gas! Do it now!"

For the first time, the driver doesn't obey. He just sits there in the front seat with his hands in clear view on top of the steering wheel and stares straight out the watery windshield. He waits for the paramedics to come up alongside the cab. He lets down all the electric windows at once and the weather instantly soaks my clothes.

On either side of the cab, at the rear windows between which I'm sitting, a paramedic is standing.

One of them says, "Come along, Mr. Molloy."

I say, "I'm not going anywhere. There's nothing the matter with me. I don't need an ambulance."

The other paramedic says, "You aren't well Mr. Molloy."

"I feel fine."

One says, "You're pulse is weak and erratic."

The other says, "You're having difficulty breathing."

"No," I say, "I'm okay, really."

"You are experiencing a crushing pain in the center of your chest."

"You've become disoriented."

I say, "I assure you I've never felt better."

But the fact is, I *am* feeling a bit short of breath all of a sudden…and there is a kind of deep prolonged pain in the center of my chest now that I think about it.

One says, "We need to bring you in for observation overnight."

The other says, "It's better to be safe than sorry."

Panting a little, I say, "You really should be out saving a life that really needs saving."

The paramedic on the street side of the cab opens the door.

He says, "Do you think you can manage on your own or shall we bring around the stretcher?"

Already drenched to the bone, a paramedic on each side of me, I'm hustled to the waiting, blinking ambulance. Squinting through the driving rain, I'm trying to make out the hospital we'll be going to so I can call someone, anyone, to get me the hell out of there before it's too late. What catches my attention instead is that there's no red cross on the side of the ambulance. There's no blue cross or blue shield, either. There's no gold caduceus. Instead it's that goddamn computer virus symbol.

Of course.

30. Bad news, selling out, and a 12-step cure...

You always wake up cold and alone and wondering where you are.
Taking stock of things, I seem to be in a hospital ward of some kind,
in a hospital bed, strapped into a hospital bed, really, in a hospital
recovery room with a lot of other patients, all of us shivering in the
lonely cold. *Uh-ho*, I'm thinking, *this is just the kind of thing I've been
hoping to avoid. This is my worst nightmare.* I'm wondering what they took
out of me. Or, maybe even worse, *what they might have put inside.* I'm
trying to sense where the wound is but I can't feel a thing, except, as
mentioned, cold and alone.

Eventually I notice there's something in my left hand that feels
like a tampon applicator with a button on top that's under my left
thumb. I can't tell if it's one of those things that releases a powerful
painkiller on demand for the terminally ill, or the call-button for
whatever nurse tends this shoddily-run hell, and it doesn't make a
goddamn difference. I'm pressing and pressing the button but
nothing feels any different and for a long time no one comes. Then,
finally, someone does get around to coming and, as usual, I'm sorry
they did.

She's supposed to be some kind of nurse, I guess, but she looks
more like a prison matron, and she shoves up the bars on the sides of
my bed with a forbidding final *click*. She unlocks the wheels I didn't
know were locked and gets me ready to roll. She's got the kind of

blank face that's seen too many radical colostomies. She's got the hard, looking-right-through-it-all stare of someone whose watched too many open heart surgeries, liver transplants, highly experimental and dubiously ethical procedures involving baboon tissue. She won't say a word, I know that right off, and if she did it would only be to tell me to be patient, that the doctor will explain everything in due time, that I must lie still and not shake around so much, that I don't want to tear anything.

Nevertheless, I give it a try. I say, "Can someone please tell me what's going on?"

Two orderlies, or security guards, or prison bulls—it really doesn't make any difference at this point, it's all the same mentality anyway, just different outfits—two of these kinds of guys take over from the nurse and push my bed out of the ward. Pushing my bed, they make the journey through the usual featureless corridors you'd expect. I'm pretty certain they're just going around in circles on purpose to disorient me. I'm pretty sure this place isn't really as big as they're pretending it is. Either that or they simply got lost.

I say it again, "Can someone please tell me what's going on?

Of what happened in the ambulance, I don't remember much of anything. I recall the usual blood pressure cuff, radio squawk, crinkle of white paper, tubing, circle of concerned faces, pipettes, all that stuff, all of it as familiar as any ambulance scene you've ever seen on TV. Maybe I did collapse, after all, I'm thinking. Maybe I really am sick. Looked at a certain way, maybe everything that's happened to me added together is really just a long list of symptoms of some disease or other. I just wish someone would tell me what it is. No, that's not true. I don't want to know what it is. What I really wish is that someone would just cure it without even having to tell me what I've got. What I wish is that someone would start off by telling me, *Well, now that you're all better we can tell you...*

I want someone to say, *It's nothing.* I want someone official to chuckle about the matter and say, *You're perfectly fine but for a while there, woo-hoo, you really had us going, you son of a gun, you...*

Seems to me that we don't so much come to a destination as that the orderlies just get bored pretending to be pushing me down the endless blind corridors. Seems to me someone wants a sandwich, or has to take a leak. There's mention of a much-needed cigarette; maybe it's just time to get back for the second half of the game I can hear playing in the break room. The door they suddenly wheel me left through, it seems almost entirely a random choice, it seems like they just picked the one they happened to be closest to when someone's bladder finally said, *Enough.*

Ratcheting up the bed so that I'm in a sitting position, there I'm left, strapped in, cold, alone. I'm in a room that looks a lot like that secret room in the Barnes and Noble where I was taken when they pretended I was stealing books. What I'm saying is that where I am looks like an interrogation room anywhere there's an interrogation room: windowless, grey, way too much artificial light that makes everything look even worse than it already is. The only thing missing is the glass of suspicious water, the ash tray, the pack of cigarettes with one last cigarette, and, of course, the empty matchbook.

This is where I'm at now, cold, alone, strapped in and two minutes from now I'm going to be looking back at this time and everything that came before it with a kind of dreamy nostalgia as "the good ole days."

It's always bad news when Mr. Franklin enters the room, that I've learned by now. Bad biopsy results, rejected car loans, pink slips— that's all Mr. Franklin's territory. He's in white shirtsleeves and vest, narrow tie, wire-rimmed glasses, and the ever-present snap-brim hat. Thin as ever, impossibly gaunt, expressionless, he's always the guy to deliver bad news because, well, lizard-cool, he has no feeling about it one way or another. He's a man in perpetual withdrawal from everything.

Mr. Franklin looks at me without looking at me. He speaks to me without speaking to me. He says, "I'm afraid its bad news, Mr. Molloy."

I'm wrong about there being nothing in the room but the hospital bed: there's also a little metal table-tray on wheels, but, to be perfectly accurate, I'm really only half wrong, because I think the little metal table tray on wheels has just been wheeled in by one of Mr. Franklin's assistants. On the little metal table tray Mr. Franklin has set his slim leather briefcase and now he thumbs open the locks and lifts the lid.

"Let's get down to business, then, shall we?"

Turning the open briefcase towards me, he lets me see the contents: row upon row of what look like sterilized steel surgical tools, each with a different size nib. Some are made for a wider line, others for a cut you hardly feel. There are tools for slicing, dicing, extracting, sawing, the curlicue flair.

Mr. Franklin looks up. Drily he says, "The tools of the trade."

His assistants have faded into the background, into the wall, like chameleons, but they're still there, in case they might be needed, all eyes and ears.

Mr. Franklin says, "Certainly by now you know something's terribly wrong, Mr. Molloy. This 'something' that you know, that's what I want you to tell me. You will cooperate eventually. Everyone does. There are injections and electric implants."

He indicates the open briefcase full of glittering unpleasantness. "There are things we can do with the teeth, the tongue, the delicate nerve endings on the lips. The asshole," Mr. Franklin philosophizes, "that is an entire playground of possibilities.

"There are the fingernails, of course, the eyeballs, the flesh just about anywhere after the epidermis is removed, need I even mention the testicles? I only have to whisper the word 'urethra' to see you squirm. The human body is made to feel pain, Mr. Molloy. The human body isn't made to keep secrets. It's just not made to resist authority."

I feel rotten, but I know that I'm not feeling nearly so rotten as I'm going to feel in a few minutes if Mr. Franklin starts working his bloody calligraphy into my flesh with that desk set from Hell he's got packed in his briefcase.

Still, I sense that he'd just as soon not be bothered overmuch with the tedious particulars. I feel I have a little bit of leverage. What I feel is that I haven't really got anything to lose but a lot of vital internal organs I'm probably going to lose to cancer and old age sooner or later anyway.

I say, "What's the deal. What can you offer?"

Mr. Franklin lays it out: a facility upstate, clean, quiet, top-of-the-line staff. Situated on about six hundred acres of rolling green hills, it has a view of the Hudson on a clear day. A high-functioning population culled predominately from the arts and sciences. No outright lunatics, mass murderers, sexual predators—the occasional original thinker, nothing more dangerous or annoying than that, but that's only to be expected.

"What I can promise is that your patience wont be tried by anyone thinking he's Jesus Christ," Mr. Franklin says. "No Napoleans or bald middle-aged guys in tube-tops and hot-pants who think they're Britney Spears. They're a well-behaved group of lunatics and perverts on the whole. Intelligent and nonviolent for the most part, always interesting, level-headed, even if they are completely insane."

So that's it, I'm thinking, *a mental hospital.* It may sound like one of those upscale Hollywood rehab centers the way Franklin is describing it, but that's just another word for "loony bin." He's making it sound innocuous, but I know what he's really talking about is a reconditioning facility. All in all, I'm thinking, it could have ended a whole lot worse. It doesn't sound like I'm going to have to endure a lot of forced butt-fucking in the shower, for instance. At least, not among such a nerdy-sounding population, not without half a fighting chance, anyway.

There are a few things I want to clear up before I agree.

"Lock down?"

He says, "Unnecessary."

"Rohrshach blots?"

"Just for laughs."

"Sensory deprivation?"

"Only upon request."

"Electro-chemical shock, surreptitious drug doping, slow poisoning, microwave thought control, bugging, constant video surveillance?"

He says, "Within reason. On the whole not much more than the average person living in the suburbs."

I say, "Limited internet access?"

Mr. Franklin shakes his head. "This is a program modeled on the traditional twelve-step addiction treatment philosophy. You're an addict, Mr. Molloy: an online junkie. The only way to kick the habit is to kick it absolutely. Total abstinence. Not so much as a single dial-up."

"That seems rather harsh."

"Trust me. It's the only way."

Professional that he is, Mr. Franklin can tell I'm close, really close. He moves in to seal the deal. "You have to understand, Mr. Molloy, if you're not one of US you're against US."

"Is everyone US?

"Practically."

"What's the point of all the struggle, then?"

"There isn't much of one. It's pretty pointless."

"Isn't there anyone who isn't US?"

Mr. Franklin says, "Not really. Just about everyone is one of US." He pauses for a moment. Accuracy, fanatical accuracy, is a virtue to someone like Mr. Franklin, the way it is to any honest accountant. He says, "Well, there are a few here or there who aren't one of US. They're alone though, sitting in front of computer monitors twenty hours a day. They're talking to machines, making love to machines. They're not living in the real world. They aren't talking to anyone but themselves. They're insane. They're sick. They're all where you're going, or soon will be. Many others are already getting better. You don't want to be one of the others. You want to be one of US, just like everyone else. We can all be US. That's the beauty of it."

In the midst of such a long speech, there's a chance for something to dawn on me. What dawns on me through the mental fog that is descending on me is this: "I'm not sure I want to be US."

Mr. Franklin says, "Trust me, you want to be US. If you're not US, you're nobody. And everybody has to be somebody."

Now there's something about that last statement that really bugs me on such an elemental level that I almost do the unthinkable: I almost disagree. There's a blind flash of something or other, and I almost tell Mr. Franklin to go fuck himself. I'm thinking about what Ratking said on that tour bus the last time I saw him, about how it was important to stay beneath the surface as long as possible. I'm thinking about how that was now finally all coming to an end. How I was selling out, just like we all do eventually, even a legend like Ratking, cashing in our chips when we get too tired, too lonely, too horny, too old, too scared. I'm thinking how very soon I'm not going to be no one anymore. How, from now on, I am going to be someone, just like everyone else. Who I'm going to be, I don't know, but that doesn't seem very important. Whoever I'm going to be, I'll get used to it soon enough. After all, I have a whole lifetime of it ahead of me. I'll get used to it alright, that's hardly the problem. Fact is, I suspect that before too long I'll get so used to whoever I'm going to be that I'll be bored to death of myself.

"What about that symbol I've been seeing all over the place. The one that first appeared on my computer?"

If he's growing impatient, Mr. Franklin doesn't show it. If he's ready to start carving the living hamstring out of the back of my thigh, he's not betraying his inclination. Mr. Franklin is the model of patience. He's the gold standard of method. He's the epitome of self-control. He's the living embodiment of efficient mechanical insanity.

He says, "Think of it as a non-denominational religious icon. Think of it as a meditation symbol. Think of it as the signpost that led you out of the darkness and into the light. Think of it, if it's any easier, as the logo of a powerful new anti-psychotic just approved by the FDA.

"We are curing you of Internet Addiction, of Virtual Catatonia. That's our goal, Mr. Molloy. To bring you back to the real world and real human beings. You've been living like an alien. You've forgotten your humanity."

I say, "That cockamamie story about the internet personalities being bought and sold, the missing buildings, the murders, all that....it's not true then?"

"Just a hallucination of yours, I'm afraid."

"But Mr. X--who is he?"

"Who?"

"Nada Klone?"

"Who?"

Well that's it then, I'm thinking. I'm satisfied. That about covers everything. I'm sure I'll remember something to ask later, but by then I'll hopefully already be long into some deep mental reprogramming that will soon cause me to forget this whole stupid fiasco.

"Okay. Let's do it."

Mr. Franklin says, "I knew you'd see your way to reason. In spite of all the nonsense you're a practical man, Mr. Molloy. There is just the formality of some papers to sign."

He produces a sheaf of official-looking documents full of the usual fine print, clauses, sub-clauses, attachments, amendments, provisos, conditions, and mediating circumstances. He suggests I read the document carefully before signing because by signing I'm agreeing to everything, but he knows I never will, that I can't possibly read this telephone book of footnotes in the thirty seconds he allots me. It's like when you sign a warranty agreement for a microwave or a cell phone plan. You're standing in the store with a line of impatient people behind you all wanting to buy the same crap and you can't possibly read the contract and you'd feel foolish even if you started trying. The damn thing could say anything within its many pages, its many paragraphs and paragraphs of miniscule terms the size of ant droppings. You could be signing away your liver. So I do what you always do: I pretend to scan the document quickly, grunt pointedly, and then I start to sign on the bottom line with the vicious-looking steel pen that Mr. Franklin has at the ready.

I hesitate for just a moment.

Lifting the lethal nib from the page a moment, I look up at Mr. Franklin. "What name should I use?"

He waves a long dry hand. He says, "Oh, any old thing will do."

When I'm done, Mr. Franklin takes the pen, folds the document, and locks it inside his traveling torture chamber of a briefcase. There's no handshaking or anything even remotely like that. But Mr. Franklin does say something to mark the event: the concession, or truce, or unconditional surrender, whatever it is.

"Welcome," he says, somewhat ominously it seems to me. "Soon, you'll be one of US."

31. Meds, feds, and the great escape...

Being a committed lunatic isn't such a bad gig. You get three squares a day whether you're hungry or not. You get meds at regular intervals whether they make you feel better or not. You see the same old sitcoms on the TV in the lounge whether you think they're funny or not. You go to sleep and wake up on a schedule that has nothing to do with whether you're tired or rested. You play checkers, you have meaningless conversations, you cry, you walk around aimlessly, you scream, you despair, you jerk-off, you sit in a chair all by yourself and stare into space.

All in all, it's not that much different from life outside and the more of it I'm experiencing the more I'm starting to think that this *is* life on the outside. Mr. Franklin, it seems, has kept his promise with his customary vengeance: *This is real life.*

I've been enjoying this real life for I don't know how long by now. Months, maybe? Years? Who knows? Time seems to have stopped, or it's going by so fast it doesn't seem to be moving at all. Well, maybe *enjoying* isn't quite the right word. Maybe it's more a word like *enduring.* Perhaps you could stay *tolerating.* I keep coming up with words like *coping, bearing, putting up with, gritting my teeth,* that sort of thing. More often than not, you could just say that for mercifully long periods of time I completely forget that I'm alive at all.

The phrase, *Well it can always be worse* seems to come up again and again. As in, it could always be worse, I might have leprosy. Or, it could always be worse, I could he impaled on a railroad spike.

I'm always thinking up ways that it could be worse. But lately, it's getting harder and harder. It's really exhausting my creativity.

Warts, avalanches, drill-press accidents, all kinds of things involving objects getting stuck in my eye, the list of ways my life can be worse, and probably will get worse, just goes on and on and on. This, my therapist tells me, is called being thankful for the little things.

"This," she says, "is called appreciating the precious gift of life."

So that's pretty much how it's going; if I had to write a postcard about this place I'd say something like, *Real life—it's great! I never want to die. Weather's terrific. Wish you were here!* And then I'd put a stamp on it and send it to my worse enemy. That's why I'm open to suggestion when one day, while browsing through the library's incomplete collection of old *Reader's Digests*, a large man in a shabby green bathrobe comes up beside me and says, "Pssssst....Mr. Molloy?"

And on more levels than I'd like to admit, I find myself asking, "Are you talking to me?"

He says, "I think I'm talking to you. It's you, isn't it?"

These are the kinds of trick questions I'd thought to be done with once and for all the moment I signed the papers to commit myself as an official madman. For once in my miserable life of questioning and second-guessing myself, I hoped to finally be finished with asking the most pointless question in a whole list of pointless questions: *Who am I?*

This big, shambling, sort of unkempt looking man, white beard, thin white hair in spiky disarray, looks me up and down with equal distaste. He says, "It's always hard to tell. We change in here so quickly."

Weakly, I suggest, "We are US?"

If this big slab of a buffoon hears me, he doesn't show it. He holds out his large paw like a trained polar bear. He says, "You don't recognize me. I figured they'd get you in here sooner or later. I've been waiting. I'm working under cover. Deep under cover."

I look at him with an expression just about as blankly as you might expect.

He leans close enough for me to smell last night's poisoned turkey loaf on his breath. He whispers, "It's me. It's Agent Chambers."

"Agent *Chambers?*"

He grins, "The one and only."

Over the next dozen days or so, I can't seem to get away from the guy. He corners me after meals, after therapeutic yoga, after interpretive self-portrait class, after nap time. He tells me all about the resistance, the anti-programming, the coming rebellion, the advent of a new society of enlightened nomadic beings.

I say, "I just want to enjoy pizza night on Thursday. I'm looking forward to the bowling trip this weekend. Aren't they showing *Pirates of the Caribbean* tonight in the lounge?"

Agent Chambers says, "Wake up, man. That's all a con. They're putting you into deep hypnosis with all that crap. Do you really think that's what it means to be *alive?* I mean, how many fucking episodes of *Law & Order* can a sane person watch, anyway?"

Hearing this kind of talk, considering where I am, really isn't so surprising. But hearing it come from the mouth of a guy whose presumably an undercover FBI agent and not a mental patient blitzed out by psychotropic drugs and bombarded by psychotherapeutic re-conditioning 24/7 as I am—well, that kind of stone-cold-sober insanity is really impressive. You'd have to figure the guy was truly committed to his craziness to hang onto it through the sort of mind-numbing propagandistic normality programs we're subjected to literally nonstop, morning, noon, and night.

He explains, "I'm here to rescue you, Mr. Molloy."

"I really don't think I want to be rescued. But thank you very much all the same."

"Nonsense. We all want to be rescued."

No, he's wrong about that. We don't all want to be rescued. It's a lot of trouble being rescued. I'd rather paste collages from pictures cut out of old pet magazines with rounded safety scissors during Arts and Crafts hour. But I can't help but listen to Agent Chambers' heretical rap. In spite of the ping-pong tournaments, the wheelchair races, the endless games of tic-tac-toe that end in ties, I find his subversive rancor strangely addictive. Maybe what he's saying is crazy, but at least it's interesting in the way that, say, yet another episode of the *West Wing* isn't. What the hell good is reality, anyway, if you can hardly sit through it without falling asleep?

I know it's wrong but soon I'm sneaking off to meet Chambers in the laundry room, drifting over to the fence for a private tete-a-tete during co-ed kickball, listening to his crackpot theories about missing people, government conspiracies, and roving assassins whenever there's a break during Quiet Hour. That what he's saying interests me at all, I know, from the hours and hours of therapy that I've already endured, is a danger sign. The very fact that I'm even listening to his paranoid delusional outbursts with something like an open mind is a warning sign of incipient psychosis and total breakdown.

I'm courting trouble, after all the trouble I've already had, and I can't help myself. We're in the cafeteria, eating the grey loaf, when I say, "You don't even look like the guy who met me on the beach that day."

"That," he says, predictably enough, "is because that wasn't me. The agency dispatched someone to impersonate me when I dropped out of circulation. The idea was to see who contacted the fake me and follow up the leads to the real me and eliminate everyone along the way."

"Mr. Franklin?"

"Exactly."

"Mr. Franklin is part of the FBI?"

"Oh no. Mr. Franklin is part of a shadow-FBI, a powerful agency that does all the things that the real FBI would do if doing those things were legal in a constitutional democracy. If this weren't a free country with a Declaration of Independence and a Bill of Rights, Mr. Franklin would be the real FBI, although you'd probably then call it something like the Gestapo. Every government needs it's Mr. Franklins. Mr. Franklin is a necessary evil. You see, Mr. Franklin is a crackdown artist. He cracks down on what needs cracking down on. He's the most dangerous kind of agent of all. A do-gooder."

"And he thinks the internet is destroying our country?"

"He believes it's an addiction, yes. The way drugs are an addiction, alcohol, pornography, dream-machines—any mind-altering, mind-expanding technology, and, most recently, that includes the internet. It's dangerous, they say. Too much freedom is dangerous; it's destabilizing. Freedom needs to be regulated, doled out like spoonfuls of medicine, like tablets of psychopharmecueticals, by government licensed professionals. But that's not why Mr. Franklin has been dispatched. He thinks that's why he's been dispatched, but its not the real reason. Mr. Franklin thinks he's the right-hand of the shadow organization he represents, but he's not. He's really the left hand. Because the people he works for, they operate by sleight of hand. They don't do anything straightforward."

"You're not being very straightforward either," I say. "If he's not trying to stamp out internet addiction and return us all to real life, what is he doing?"

"He's trying to stop *me*." Oh, Christ, I'm thinking, another paranoid who thinks this is all about him. "Mr. Franklin doesn't know it, but he's leading those he works for straight to me."

"And why would he be doing that?"

"Because of what I've uncovered in the course of what started out as a pretty routine investigation. I was working a missing persons case—people disappearing from internet chatrooms. That's how I met Norma Blake Madsen."

Norma—the sound of her name brings back a pang that I'd learned to ignore with deep-breathing, mantra-chanting, and heavy doses of Welbutrin, Luvox and Zyprexa. Well, almost ignore. I feel a cold tear trickle down my cheek.

"We got to chatting pretty regularly, serious stuff after a while, not just sex-fantasies, and she told me about her marital problems. We eventually met and began an affair. I wish I could say it was part of my undercover duties, but I can't. Well, her husband found out, as they usually do sooner or later. Oh, I don't mean that he found out about the affair with me. No, he was three or four affairs behind. Norma, you see, was pretty prolific in the infidelity department. She was, you might say, fidelity-challenged. Anyway, her husband hired someone to kill her, changed his mind, changed it again, and changed it back again. In case you lost track, he decided not to kill her. I was following the whole thing from behind the scenes. I advised her to take off, hide herself away in an apartment I sublet from an exotic dancer of my acquaintance out in Brooklyn, and wait for the smoke to clear. Someone was after her, alright, and by then they were watching me, too, so I had to go underground. Someone wanted to kill the both of us but it wasn't her husband. They were part of the network responsible for at least a dozen other disappearances that I'd been investigating."

"You mean its true?" And I explain, briefly, what Chambers told me, the internet entrepreneur, that is. "There's been a series of these disappearances? There's a Mr. X? There's a serial killer on the loose on the net?"

"Yes," the agent says, "it's true. But it's much worse than that."

"How could it be worse than that?"

"There's a killer stalking the internet, but this Mr. X isn't some lone looney; he's not just some kooky psychopath, some creepy sex fiend who lives in a basement apartment with his mother's stuffed corpse. No, this Mr. X is much more dangerous and organized and carnivorous than that. He's a professional. He's a businessman. He's a capitalist."

"I'm afraid I'm not following."

"What this Mr. X does is acquire internet personalities, sometimes legally, sometimes illegally, just like Mr. Chambers does, and then he resells them to the highest bidder, also like Mr. Chambers does. But Mr. X does something that makes these web personalities far more valuable to his potential clients than Mr. Chambers ever did. How Mr. X does this is the real problem, how he does this is murder.

"You see," Chambers continues, "Mr. X offers his clients the ultimate monopoly on these personalities and auctions them off to the highest bidder. After building up the most intimate profile possible—video, personal papers, medical records, online activity—a complete portfolio of that person in all his or her infinite human richness, Mr. X then, depending on the vagaries of the game of which these individuals are unknowingly subject, like game pieces on a Monopoly board, has that person murdered, driving their value through the roof. Among certain very rich and very jaded aficionados, the trade in these personalities is considered quite a thrill. Among certain very powerful and very bored individuals, collecting and trading dead web identities is considered a thrill like collecting art was once considered a thrill. What we're talking about here is collecting real-life human lives as if you were playing a video game. What we're talking about here is pure evil. We're talking about a community of online serial killers, soul-collectors, mass-murder hobbyists and each one of them without a drop of real blood on their hands.

"You're telling me these people are *gamers*...but that they're playing with real human lives?"

"And worse of all, the people who are behind this game are the kind of people that you'd expect to be stopping it. They are the same people who are supposed to put a stop to such things. They are, to put it simply, among the richest and most powerful people in the current structure of power."

"I might have believed this before when I was insane," I say, staring at the chunk of grey loaf on the end of my plastic fork; it looks almost blue under the fluorescent lighting. "But now, after being brainwashed into sanity, I have to admit, I'm having a hard time believing it anymore."

I'm putting it mildly, of course, I'm trying not to hurt his feelings or incite him into some kind of bipolar rage. Chambers is taking my skepticism with good cheer, though, like he's come across doubting Thomases like me a few hundred times before in his life. Falsely encouraged by his unexpected patience, I suggest that what he's saying makes him sound like he belongs in a lunatic asylum himself. I suggest that maybe, just maybe, he's mistaken and that he didn't infiltrate this place undercover, but was sent here to get well, just like the rest of us.

"You seem like a nice guy," I say, "maybe you should join me after lunch. There's going to be square-dancing in the gym!"

He doesn't rise to the bait. He swabs up the last of his gravy with the last of his dinner roll, pops it into his mouth, and simply says, "I have a message for you, Mr. Molloy." He swallows. "From Norma."

There's that word again. That word that feels like a sunflower made of razors blades just opened inside my chest. I feel more cold tears spilling down my cheeks.

"Is this some kind of test? Are you *trying* to drive me insane? Is that it?"

"She wants to see you again."

"Please..." I choke out. "Don't..."

"I'm not kidding. She ran off with me, it's true, and left you in the lurch. Sorry, dude. All's fair in love and war, right? But, go figure, she's had a change of heart. All she can talk about is you. She wants to see you again. Are you up for it? You don't have to answer right now. Think about it. There's still some time. But not too much time. You've got until four p.m. Country Crafts."

Sure enough, that afternoon he catches me in the hall outside the craft room during our fifteen-minute break.

"The choice is yours," he says, nodding towards the doorway conspiratorally. "You can go back in that room and spent another half-hour making flowers out of pipe cleaners or you can bust out of here with me, save the world, and rendezvous with the love-of-your life. So what's it going to be, sport?"

The escape plan is pretty preposterous, even as fictional escape plans go. Among other things, it involves the hoarding of drugs only pretended to have been swallowed, loosened screws on window grates, large canvas laundry bins, heating ducts, stolen lab coats, the release of hundreds of experimental lab rats, sympathetic insiders,

and, naturally, fake beards. It's doomed to failure, any idiot can see
that straight off. To prevent leaks, fears, doubts, and reasonable
second-thoughts, it's being sprung right this very moment.

"Let's go," Agent Chambers says.

I say, "Right now?"

He says, "Right now. This is it. No time like the present. Live in
the moment. Seize the day. Let's rock'n'roll."

As it happens, this is the plan's final phase. After a quick
change in a nearby supply closet, I'm in work overalls and heading
out to the back gardens supposedly to water the extensive strawberry
fields and gather the ripe fruit for that evening's mock strawberry
shortcake surprise. Chambers is accompanying me, dressed in a
guard's uniform. He's whistling, strolling, hands in his pockets,
nodding right and left, whether we're actually passing anyone or not.
The impression he's giving off is that he doesn't have a care in the
world. There's no skulking, sideways glances, or suspicious shuffling
of feet. The image he's creating is the perfect disguise for everything
and anything. The disguise he's wearing is the one that says, *I'm
wearing a uniform. I'm someone. I belong here.*

He looks, by the way, nothing like he looked last time I saw
him, but I'm used to that by now. Clean-shaven, hair trimmed to a
steely buzz-cut, he looks every inch the prototypical law-enforcement
agent. Minus the ratty bathrobe, you can see the wide shoulders, the
perfect posture, the suggestion of washboard abs. But, most
importantly of all, his blue eyes are clear and bright. They are the kind
of eyes that inspire confidence and attract followers. It's the
unmistakable look of someone who knows where he's going even if
he's going straight off a cliff. He's strolling along, whistling, eyes
glittering. He's radiating the kind of confidence and sense of purpose
that I've never felt for a single solid hour, not once, not in my entire
life. His attitude says, *I know where I'm going and I have the authority to go
there.*

He's crazy, I have to keep reminding myself. He looks so
goddamn irrepressibly normal and in control I can't let myself for a
second forget that he's totally insane even as we pass unchallenged
straight through the back door. It's cold and crisp in the free air, the

sky is clear, and the stars are glittering, tiny and sharp as rodent teeth. Under our feet, the frost crunches. Is it even conceivable that strawberries are growing this time of year? I have no clue. I have no idea what season we're in and as I'm marching double-time to keep up with Agent Chambers' giant, parade-ground strides, I'm not afraid to say I'm afraid to even ask him.

Passed the strawberry fields, past the pasture, the pasture wire, the copse of trees, passed the old barns and stone silos, through a drybed creek, up a hill, down the other side of the same hill, we reach the highway and an idling unmarked grey van waiting for us on the shoulder. The door slides open, we get inside, and off we go.

"Have some hot coffee," says Chambers' accomplice, a suicidal paranoid I recognize from the day-room. She hands me a paper cup and notes my hesitation. "It's the real stuff, don't worry, no medical additives." She winks and I think that what I first mistook as a wrinkle might be a lobotomy scar. She says, "100% Starbucks."

Looking over at Chambers, I see him dialing up internet access on my laptop. I wonder where he got my old machine from, but right now, that really seems the least of my many concerns. I sip the hot coffee, watching him. I say, "This is too easy. Can't you see that? They're letting us escape. This is all part of the plot. It's a set-up."

The machine hums as it connects, purring like a contented cat.

Chambers punches a few keys, waits for a site to download, and looks up at me with his glittering insanely normal eyes. "If you start thinking like that Molloy, they've got you beat from the start. If you insist on that kind of thinking, you won't do anything at all. You won't even get out of bed in the morning."

I say, "That sounds pretty good to me."

"Pshaw," Chambers says, and he really does say exactly that: *Pshaw.*

He spins my laptop around on his knees, all fixed and magically restored. All my hundreds of files and downloads listed in the hard-drive. But it's more than that, much more. I feel the old energy surging through my fingers as I touch the keys, opening email accounts, checking forums, scanning message boards. A tap on the touchpad opens up *nakedtrampolinebabes.com*. With a click of a single key, I'm watching passerby through a webcam set up at a Tokyo intersection. I'm everywhere and nowhere and exactly where I belong. I look up at Chambers in grateful awe.

"How…?"

"A gift from Ratking. He found a way to put the virus into remission." Chambers points to the heavens. "And a little help from above."

"God?"

"No. We've acquired our own pirate satellite. The important thing is, you're back online. It's not a cure, it's not forever, it's not even unlimited access, so use your time wisely. Welcome back from the land of the living. Congratulations. You're nobody again."

32. Road warriors, rest stops, and revolutionaries

I don't know where I am, but that's okay, that's hardly anything new.
We're driving down some look-a-like stretch of interstate or other.
All over the place I'm seeing big green signs with the names of towns
and cities that seem made up but familiar all the same. The names of
these places…well, there are dozens of places named the same thing
all over the place. Every state has a Jamestown or a Hillsdale or
something almost exactly like that. Whatever state you're in, you're
going to find a Springfield or a Westfield. You're going to find a
town with the word "lake" in it. Really, in the end, you come to
understand that it doesn't make any difference where you are: you
could be just about anywhere at all.

We're alone, Agent Chambers and I, for the time being. We
dropped the suicidal paranoid off in Minnesota at her parent's fishing
bungalow, or something equally improbable. She studies herpetology
at a community college in St. Paul, Chambers informs me,
conversationally. "That's snakes," he adds.

"I know. I know." I'm hardly listening to any of this. "Listen,
I've been thinking, and what you've told me is something no sane
person can possibly take seriously. A sex-and-murder scandal
involving some of the world's most powerful people, protected by
the government, trading in fake girls, perversion, and virtual slavery
and all of it some kind of bizarre snuff game…"

"So? What's your point?"

"My point is it's unthinkable."

"I take it you aren't a student of history."

"I don't just mean unthinkable as in horrible…I mean it's flat-out preposterous."

"What does that prove?"

Then he tells me what it proves. What it proves, according to Chamber's twisted conspiracy-theory logic, is that everything he's saying is 100% true. What better way is there to keep something hidden than to state it openly in all its outlandish improbability? What better way is there to keep anyone from taking something seriously than to make it something you'd only come across in the pages of a book labeled science fiction? No one believes the government would protect powerful people playing games with innocent lives and that's precisely how they get away with it. No one believes they'd allow top secrets to be seen every night on channel five at eight p.m. on the *XFiles*, so that's exactly where they put them. No one believes that actors playing roles are doing anything but pretending, anyway, so what better way to discount the fact that what they're doing is acting out reality? This way, if anyone claims to actually believe what they're seeing, what's the first thing that everyone else says?

That sounds like something you see on television.

Miles and miles and miles of the same crap rolls by the window. I don't even know how long we've been driving at this point. For all I know, we might be on another planet by now.

Chambers says, "Governments have learned a lot since the days of Stalin. Concentration camps aren't necessary any more. Mass graves are history. The best way to control dissidents isn't to round them up on trains and send them to barren wastelands anymore. You don't need pogroms, mass executions, crematoriums. Who can be bothered rounding up people in the middle of the night? Who needs the logistical headache of staging mock trials. It's a lot of work. All you really need to do is to make your opponents look ludicrous. All you need is to ridicule anyone who knows the truth.

"You don't need to go *boom*. You don't need to go *rat-a-tat-a-tat*. The most effective weapon of governmental control on the face of the planet goes *ha-ha-ha*. Hitler isn't necessary in the 21st century. We have Jerry Springer. We have Geraldo. Ridicule and shame are more effective silencers than any posion gas."

And this is how it goes as we cross the American night on the run from just about everyone as far as I can tell, or, maybe, just as likely, no one at all.

Whatever state we're in now, I realize I've been in a state of shock ever since Naomi left me. Over and over again, for months, I've been replaying our last conversations in my head. Like an assassination film, I keep replaying what happened to see if there's something I didn't see before, something I missed. I'm trying to spot that second gunman. I'm trying to peer around that grassy knoll. And now, unexpectedly, like the answer to a prayer I stopped praying, I was going to see her again.

It was a miracle.

After another few hundred miles of this, Chambers says, "I don't know about you, but I better make a pit stop at the next rest area. I need to take a leak. I need a burger deluxe and a soft drink. How about you?"

I say, "I need a Vicodin. Super-sized."

I'm not really hungry, and I really can't understand how Chambers can be hungry either, not at a time like this, when everything is up in the air. Sitting in a booth at an Arby's or a Roy Rogers or a KFC or whatever, he's munching away at some kind of oozing bacon double-meat hullabaloo and I'm pretending to be nibbling on a badly microwaved chicken burrito gas-wrap. Outside the window, across the parking lot, minivans and busses are zooming passed going God knows where at this ungodly hour of the morning. There are a few other customers scattered around the place, hunched over formica tables, desperately wolfing down whatever they can before hitting the road again. Like us, they can't afford to wait more than three minutes for real food. They have no time for someone to break a real egg in an actual frying pan.

There's only one thing I'm thinking about, only one thing I want to know.

"When do I get to see her?"

"Who?"

"Norma. Naomi. Nada."

Those security cameras, I'm thinking, they aren't really trained on the french fries like they seem. They're not really focused on the cash registers. They're watching *us*. They're probably relaying images of all of us, everyone in the place, to FBI headquarters, or the NSA, or Homeland Security, or, more likely, some agency no one ever heard of. There's probably arrest warrants, APB's, dragnets, roadblocks, all that stuff, in the very near future of everybody ordering a roast beef sandwich or Double Cheese Burgeroo. I'm thinking, *the minute we leave this joint we're all screwed.*

"About that," he says around a mouthful of McWhammy. He licks the secret sauce off his fingers. "Well there's something I should tell you…"

I don't understand. What I don't understand is why the police don't just raid all these late-night eateries and arrest the whole seedy lot of us all at once. What seems fairly obvious to me is that anyone scarfing down a fake ranch-style chicken sandwich at four in the morning by the side of an interstate, anyone doing something like that can't possibly be up to any good. There must be a catch somewhere, I'm thinking. I'm beginning to think that maybe this is all some kind of elaborate trap.

He says, "The fact is, I stretched the truth a little about Norma."

"You what?"

"I told you something I figured you needed to hear. You know, to motivate you. You were terribly unmotivated back there."

I say, "She doesn't want to see me?"

"Well, I don't know that I'd go that far. I'm sure if you showed up, she'd be cordial."

"You lied?"

"Now that's a little harsh."

"What the hell would you call it then, Mr. Sensitive?"

"When you build a home, you use a hammer to drive a nail. When the nail is driven, you put the hammer down. You live inside the home. The home is real, so is the nail, so is the hammer."

"What the hell does that mean? Since when did this become a Home Depot advertisement?"

"It means I built us a little place, safe and snug, that we could both inhabit while we figured out what to do next."

"You lied."

Chambers shrugs. "A home, even if it seems to be made of stone, is only temporary. Does that make it a lie?" He lifts his hands up as if in benediction, as if blessing the fast-food place, everyone in it, the interstate outside, the night, the crappy food, the whole goddam screwy situation. "Can it all really be a lie?"

"Where is she?"

"Honestly?"

"Yeah, don't build me any more houses."

"I don't know."

"What do you mean you don't know? You ran away with her."

"Well, the fact is, I was planning to run away with her. She disappeared before I could get to her. I don't know where she is or who has her, but I'm gambling that whoever has her wants you, too. And they won't harm her until they get you."

"Me? Why the hell would anyone want me?"

"Maybe they want your services."

"What services? I can't do a fucking thing right for anybody."

"It's just a hunch. I could be wrong. I hope not, because if I'm wrong, we're shit out of luck."

"I don't understand," I say, and I'm not just talking about these "services" I can provide, but all of it, everything, but most of all Norma. "Everything seemed to be going okay," I say. "She told me she loved me. She told me she was having my kid. Then…pow…out of nowhere she up and says it's over. How can that be?"

Chambers shrugs, swallows a big wad of food with a big gulp of his super-sized soft drink. Washing down all that junk food, he says, "Maybe she was just pretending. Nowadays everyone is. Love is a house just like any other. You live in it for a while, and then move on. I used to live there, too, don't forget. So did a lot of other men."

I don't really want to hear the tough love and real-estate advice he's dishing out. I really don't want to believe the psychotic self-help for a broken heart that he's urging me to accept.

"Who's living there now?" I whine. "Huh?"   For the seven billionth time I say, "It's as if I didn't even really know her. Was it all just an illusion?"

Chambers, finishing up his McWhammy says something, but it sounds like this: "Mgrthweewgh."

He swabs his mouth with a little square napkin, eats a last french fry, gathers up his tray. He says, "Let's go. We've been in one place long enough."

Crossing the parking lot, climbing into the ratty van, waiting for him to start it, I'm thinking how easy it would be if the crackpots were right and a big black disk from outer space came out of the heavens, hovered over us, and just beamed us right out of this whole impossible situation we call our lives. Morosely staring through the bug-spattered windshield, I'm making a mental inventory of various ways to commit suicide.

If I were a praying man, this would be about the time to start saying a few "Our Fathers Who Art in Heaven." This is right at the point where you'd start in with a "Hail Mary" or two.

Right now is one of those moments when you look up into the totally empty starry forever and wish something, anything, were out there. I'm looking up into all that loneliness beyond the windshield and I'm thinking, there's *nothing* out there, absolutely nothing, no gods, no aliens, no intelligence, no *nothing*. I'm thinking, we're really alone, each one of us, we're all so goddamned hopelessly alone.

"What are we going to do now?" I ask.

Really, I don't expect an answer because I ask this question in the most abstract way of all. I mean it the way you say it when there really is nothing anymore that you can do, nothing anyone can say, nothing that will make anything better.

To my surprise, Chambers answers this impossible question from behind the wheel of the van. We've gotten back on the interstate and dawn is beginning to break.

He says, "We all have a weapon we can use to fight back. We all have a battle-station. I'll show you yours."

What he shows me is a room in someone's basement. We're in a "safe-house" in the suburbs, pick a suburb, any suburb, and what he's showing me is a little alcove behind an oil burner, way back in a damp and moldy corner. There's a desk, a chair, and a narrow cot. I see a white pitcher of water. I see a hole in the concrete floor that'll do for a toilet. There's a jerry-rigged electric bulb hanging from a cord dangling from the unfinished ceiling. On the desk, he's set up my laptop with a cursor blinking in the upper left hand corner.

Chambers says, "There you go. Everything you need."

Up above me, I hear whatever family lives in this split-level house going about their business; I hear the distant sounds of television, kids running around, mom making dinner in the kitchen.

All that normal stuff.

I say, "Everything I need for what? What am I supposed to do down here? Live like someone's crazy bachelor uncle?"

"Think of it as exile, as a retreat into the desert. You're going to return with a testament. You're going to write that book you've been pretending to write."

"A book," I say, "A book about what?"

That's when he shows me all the notes I've been making about this case. I have no idea where he's gotten them from. They're scattered, incomplete, nearly illegible, and they really haven't helped me figure anything out so far, but I'm thinking they might come in handy now.

I say, "But even if I manage to get it all down, no one will ever publish this incoherent ramble. No one's going to believe this bullshit. This isn't going to be anyone's idea of a Book-of-the-Month. Oprah's not going to pick it. I mean, there's no weight loss tips, no recipes, no celebrity revelations. There's a love story, sort of, without any real love in it. There's a mystery, but I can't solve it. There's just a lot of failure, heartbreak, and random violence. I can't make head or tail of any of it. You can't make money or improve your sex-life with what I've got to say. What I've seen…it's not going to make anyone's life any happier."

Chambers says, "We don't need anyone to publish it. No one reads real books anymore, anyway. This is the 21st century. Internet, baby."

And now I understand why everyone in charge of everything is getting so nervous. Now I know why there are cops, or rumors of cops everywhere, why everyone is watching everything. Now I know why there are listening devices all over and everything and everyone seems more phony and plastic and pointless than ever before.

The government, the publishing companies, the TV and radio networks—we don't need them anymore. We don't need their approval. We don't have to please teachers or editors or producers or policemen. The censors can go fuck themselves. Anyone can get online and say anything they want. With all the personal websites, live journals, message boards, storysites, chats, and blogs, you can log on and speak your piece and get twenty-thousand hits before they can close you down. They can't force-feed us that steady diet of media-manipulated lies. They can't make us swallow the same-old-thing because it's the only thing on the menu. That's what Mr. Franklin and those he represents are so afraid of.

Now I understand what Chambers is trying to tell me. Everyone's got a little piece of the puzzle. With every personal blog entry, bizarre sex fantasy, lunatic rant, we're forming the real picture of what we're up against. Now, for the first time in human history, there's a slim chance of escaping all the propaganda and lies and cover-ups. For the first time there's a slim chance that we're finally about to see what being a human being is really all about and what it's capable of. If, that is, we have the guts to take advantage of the opportunity. If we have the courage to stop faking it and tell the *truth*.

I look around at the basement office/battle-station with a new appreciation for the simplicity of it all. I say, "This is some setup. Very economical."

Chambers says, "You're an underground man. Like Dostoyevsky."

Then he laughs.

He says, "Well, except for the gambling, the drinking problem, the faith, and, of course, all the incredible talent."

Upstairs I hear commercials singing, children laughing, pots and pans banging. I hear the sounds of a family and a life I don't have. I hear what we all are on the surface.

I say, "Do they even know I'm down here?"

"Of course. They just don't really know who you are or what you're doing. That's what makes it safe for everyone."

I remember what Chambers said about houses and lies.

"So they're fake, too?"

"It's all a front, Mr. Molloy."

"For what?"

He winks. "For those who oppose the powers that be. Whoever and wherever they be."

Writing, writing, writing, I put it all down, all that I can remember of what happened to me, anyway, and then I just fill in the rest with whatever pops into my head. What we need to say is the truth about things, the things no one ever says, no one ever admits: the fantasies, dreams, reflections, terrors, desires, everyday psychoses that we pretend not to have when we pretend to be the way we've been told people are supposed to be. What I'm writing in the basement are just such things. But that's not what you're reading right now. What I'm writing at my rented battle-station I can't write here for reasons you'll shortly understand.

I write day and night, catching a few hours sleep in between, guzzling thermoses of hot coffee and munching sandwiches sent down by the housewife in the kitchen above my head. She periodically sends down one of the kids to put the tray on the fifth stair from the bottom and then he or she scurries back up.

Sometimes I hear the kids playing in the main part of the basement behind the plasterboard that separates my cramped, makeshift cubbyhole from their playroom. I hear the woman of the house come down to do the laundry. At his workbench, the husband sometimes fixes something or other.

I don't see much of any of them, but that's how it should be. I'm separated from normal people. They laugh, argue, do all the heartbreaking things real human beings pretend to do while they're trying to save the earth without even knowing it. Listening to them, sometimes I can almost believe it wasn't all faked.

Most of the time, though, I don't believe anything at all. What I do, instead, is type up and submit my report about what I've seen, no matter what, and these reports I send out daily all over the internet with a virus that Ratking devised before he went offline that was painstakingly mutated from the one that Mr. Franklin's people spread to our computers. It's a super-virus, as I understand, the bubonic plague of the Information Age. No one is immune. My posts attach themselves to private and corporate email, random links, message boards, everything. Every time someone clicks on something my report is popping up on their computer screen.

It's only a matter of time before I hear from him. Just as we've planned. It's only a matter of time and it doesn't take much time at all.

All the while I'm writing I leave a chat window open just in case. All the time I'm waiting for his instant message. So it's no surprise whatsoever when I see the box open on my screen, it's no surprise the message that he sends me, or the nick that he uses.

It's Mr. X, of course, and the message he sends me is "Enough."

After a few not-so-idle threats about what he'll do to me, to my computer, to life as I know it, I tell him that there's only one thing I give a damn about. I tell him I'll knock it off if he gives me back Norma Blake Madsen. I watch the open message window for five, ten, twenty seconds. I feel my heart sinking fast. She's already dead, I think. It's too late. Then, in the open message window, these words appear: *Let's chat.*

Then these: *In the flesh.*

33. Lies, ripcords, and let's make a deal...

He looks like one of those sixty-five-year-old guys you only see on television soaps or in Tom Clancy action-adventure films playing the ruggedly handsome, ass-kicking U.S. president: the spitting image of what a sixty-five-year-old guy is supposed to look like in an ideal world, but never does. He's wearing a million-dollar suit and sitting across from me in a specially outfitted crop-duster flying somewhere above the big unrecognizable checkerboard states in the middle of the country. You can tell it's him: there are guards standing all around us disguised as an ordinary flight crew—each and every one of them ready at a moment's notice to throw themselves unthinkingly between him and a bullet. You can't buy loyalty like that. Oh no, you have to induce mass insanity in those who work for you.

He says, "I'll make this simple Mr. Molloy." He pauses for a moment, and then adds, "Well, sort of. You see, I'm a little upset with you. What I'm upset about is that you were telling everyone some very intimate details about our operation here..."

The plane hits turbulence, like heaven itself farted on us. Everyone but me looks pretty calm about it.

"You left me no choice," I say, when I regain my balance. "Exposure was the only weapon I had left."

"What is it that you expect from us, Mr. Molloy?"

"I want the truth."

He laughs and it's a genuine old-fashioned guffaw. Unexpectedly, I start laughing, too.

"The truth," he sputters, making comically helpless gestures, as if addressing an imaginary audience. "He wants the truth."

I'm laughing, but really, I'm wondering *just what the hell is so funny about that?*

"Mr X, I presume?"

He demurs. "No, not exactly."

"His representative?"

He looks embarrassed. "No, no. Not quite that either. I'm afraid not."

"Then who the hell are you?"

"I'm afraid I'm outside the alphabet entirely."

"Huh?"

"Putting aide false modesty, Mr. Molloy, you might say I'm X3."

"You're with the government?"

He says, "I'm a few layers above the government."

"What's above the government?"

"That's hard to explain. You see, I'm not so much a representative of anything in particular as an emanation of what can't be seen."

I do my best to ignore all that. "I thought I was going to see Mr. X. He's the one behind this. No?"

"Yes. But I'm the one behind Mr. X."

"I don't understand."

"Of course you don't. No one does. You see, people like Mr. X are basically businessmen, but in the worst possible sense, very powerful, it's true, but basically flawed."

"I'm still not getting it."

"Let me put it in terms that may help. Did you ever see a virus? You ever see a cancer cell on one of those science shows? You ever see a tick bloating up on a dog's ear? You ever see a vindictive ex-wife?"

I must have flinched.

"Ah," he chuckles, "I see I've hit a nerve. Well that would be
Mr. X. He has an appetite like that. Frightening. He wants *everything*.
That, by the way, is the true definition of evil, Mr. Molloy. Someone
who wants everything to the detriment of the whole. A parasite. We
all have to respect some limits. Mr. X, too. Well, I don't have to
respect limits, but that's another story. There have to be some checks
and balances. I represent the checks and balances. You might say I'm
a representative of the rules with a capital 'R.' I represent order. Life
can't exist without guys like me."

I say, "So you were watching the whole time? You waited for it
all to unfold?"

"Being who I am, let's just say I see a lot of things."

"Are you US? Is Mr. Franklin and his crew…are they your
agents?"

He chuckles, "That imbecile? Please. He's still caught up in that
either/or for-us-or-against-us binary program. That nonsense is so
old. It was so old back in the days of Zoroaster. Ultimately, take away
all the torture, kidnapping, brainwashing, demonizing, moralizing,
and incarceration and a guy like Mr. Franklin is no more harmless
than your average fifth-grade English teacher." He pauses for a beat
and adds, "I just made a funny, son. Let's hear a little appreciation."

"Ha ha," I say.

"That's better. Fact is, you can think of Mr. Franklin as a kind
of right-wing throwback, a reactionary crusader from the time when
there really were things like right and wrong, good and evil, US and
Them."

"Agent Chambers—the one I met in the loony-bin—he was
right then? It's all a conspiracy?"

"Conspiracy? You're still not seeing the big picture. We've been
preoccupying people with silly crap like this since…well…forever.
Crop circles, floods, cattle mutilations, black plagues, spontaneous
healings, stigmata, the Kennedy assassinations, walking on water,
UFOs, blah blah blah. What, you mean to tell me you never read
Orwell's *1984* in high school? Dammit…the think-tank is right: no
one ever remembers anything from eighth grade. That's the time to

tell people the plain truth and make sure it's completely forgotten. All those distracting hormones, I guess, better than any amnesiac drug."

"This is outrageous," I say, feeling outraged. "You mean its *all* one big conspiracy? And the conspiracy is that there is no conspiracy?"

He says, "Well, not really, but close enough. Why should that be any surprise? Everything and everyone is one, you know. Every fucking religious mystic from the beginning of time has said that, haven't they? Why do you think we burn them all, crucify them, incarcerate them? They all say the secret is right out there in the last place you'd recognize it...right in front of your nose."

I feel ashamed to ask it, but I just have to. I'll never forgive myself if I don't. I ask, "Are you God then?"

He winks. "Let's not get too metaphysical, but I appreciate the thought. Let's just say I am who I am. You know, I'm just a guy doing his job. But if you fuck around with me, you get zapped. I'm the limit of what you can get away with. I'm the one you can't mess around with. Not too many people get a glimpse of me. I don't make many unnecessary public appearances. All in all, it's usually not too pleasant to see me." He rubs his hands together. "So with all that in mind, let's talk turkey. Life's a game show, after all is said and done. Let's make a deal."

"Mr. X—I never get to see him?"

He holds up his hand and one of his assistants hands him a picture—an autographed 8x10 glossy. He hands it to me.

"Wait a second, I know this guy..."

If I told you who it was, you'd recognize him, too. You'd recognize him because he is very famous, very rich, and very dead. Or, at least he's supposed to be dead. I say as much.

I say, "I thought this guy was dead."

"He may have seemed dead, but when you have as much money as he does, you can buy a little extra time. Appearances are always deceiving, Mr. Molloy. I hate clichés, but you really can't judge a book by its cover. Or its title. Or even the story inside. Fiction, you know, lies. Ultimately, that's lucky for you. That's why you're here." To the confused look on my kisser he says, "Let me explain."

What the deal amounts to is this: I get to be left alone. They stop watching me anymore than absolutely necessary. They stop stealing time. They stop making buildings and friends disappear and other psychotic crap like that. They clear out of my apartment. I get to write my book in peace.

"You want me to continue my book?" I ask incredulously.

"Oh yes, Mr. Molloy. We want that most definitely."

"I don't understand."

"You see, we need stories to comfort people, to let them know that everything's going to be alright. People want things to make sense. If things don't make sense, everything as we know it breaks down. People like Mr. X don't make money. His customers become dissatisfied. People like me lose control. What we end up with is chaos and dissonance. What we have is a kind of galactic cancer that eats up the world. You see that, don't you?"

I say, "What you have is freedom. What you have is the possibility of something truly new."

Mr. X3 frowns. It's not a pretty sight; think earthquakes, landslides, battlefields on the morning after. "We don't want something new, Mr. Molloy. That's precisely the point. We just want different versions of the old. The old is comforting. The old preserves those in power. *I'm* in power."

"I see. But what has that to do with me? I thought my book was dangerous, that telling the truth would expose you."

"Some of the things that are important to us is that when your story eventually appears it appears in the fiction section of a bookstore, rather than on the front page of *The New York Times*. We'd rather see your story made into a movie by Paramount starring Tom Cruise than see it running on CNN. Narrative is the ultimate totalitarianism. You, Mr. Molloy, are going to write a story that makes *sense*, that fulfills people's expectations, which are their expectations because they are *our* expectations. You are going to tell a tale that structures people's lives, that controls them, that puts them back to sleep."

"But the slave trade in web personalities continues, the fake girls, the murders?"

"The rich have to have their fun, Mr. Molloy. Say what you will, it's a tough business running the world."

"That's unacceptable."

"Is it really? Well, war is unacceptable, too, and we have them all the time. Poverty, global warming, earthquakes, the exploitation of the Third World, it's all unacceptable and all of it is necessary to keep the world turning. The people who die you won't know. And the people you do will be saved. Some people always have to die, Mr. Molloy, that's just how it is. You have to ask yourself a couple of questions. Just who is important to you? Who is *real* to you? And who can you reasonably save? Do you want to save Norma?"

"You bastard. This is blackmail."

"I'd prefer to call it free-will."

"I want her back."

"Well, that's not quite what I offered. I offered to let her live. You see, she belongs to your pal, Chambers. Would you betray your friend?"

"What friend?

I think of Agent Chambers. He may have broken me out of the loony bin but I can see now that he wasn't doing me any favors by doing that. That didn't make him my friend. He was only using me as bait to get Norma back. And even if he were my friend, he said it himself: all's fair…

"I don't give a shit. I'm in love with her."

"Of course. But she's in love with Chambers."

"That's not true," I say. "She loves me. She said so."

"She changed her mind." Mr X3 shrugs. "A woman's prerogative, apparently."

"Can't you change it back?" I blurt in desperation, "get her to love me again? You can fix anything…"

"I'm sorry," he says, and even I have to admit that although I'm fairly sure he's been faking everything throughout this entire interview, the look of sympathy that crosses his face right now is one hundred percent real. "I'm afraid that's something even I can't do. Who the hell can figure out a woman, anyway? Fact is, she and Chambers have been in it together from the beginning. They were working in tandem. Chambers thought he was working a simple online prostitution sting, then he thought he was working a murder-for-hire case, but when he got a hint of what was really going on, who the players were, the agency wanted to shut him down. But the idealistic fool wouldn't leave it alone. Plus, by then he'd fallen in love with Norma. He thought he knew what was going on, but he was wrong about everything. The two of them set out to put the screws to Mr. X, which isn't a very good idea. When they finally realized the tiger they had by the tail, it was too late to let go. They had to make a run for it. But now they've brokered their own deal."

"Their own deal? You mean Chambers sold out too?"

"Everyone sells out in the end, Mr. Molloy. It's the only sensible thing to do. You will, too. You'll see. They agree to vanish, change their identities, and live care-free lives in total anonymity as a very rich couple. Mr. X gets his Nada Klone and his personality-slavery business stays intact. Mr. Knott and his stock-clerk concubine breathe a big sigh of relief that everyone seems to have forgotten about them, and that other Chambers stops having all those Al Capone-size tax problems he was about to start having that would have sent him to prison for life. Meanwhile, you get to live. Everyone gets something. You see how it all works out? That's why I'm so terrifyingly good at what I do."

"But that's not fair. I love her…"

"If this story were written entirely from your point of view, Mr. Molloy, it wouldn't be fair. It would be a real tragedy, I agree. That's the problem. You're thinking that this is a love story, but it's not. Well, it is in a way, but it's someone else's love story. This is your adventure story. This is your story of discovery. In the end, true love wins out, just as it always does, just not for you. You don't get the girl. Sorry. But it's not all gloom and doom for you."

"I know. I get to live. Jeez, thanks. Just what I always wanted. Listen, I don't believe you. I want to hear it from Norma herself. I want her to tell me herself that she doesn't love me."

"Wow, you're a real glutton for punishment, aren't you?"

"I want to see her one more time."

"I can give you ninety minutes with her. You can drive her to the airport."

"I want more."

"Take it or leave it, Mr. Molloy."

He says this with the finality of the last nail being driven into a gallows erected for an execution at dawn. The total despair I feel at this moment, well, somehow I'm sure he can feel it, too, wherever he exists emotionally, about one hundred billion light-years away from earth or anything human. I'd like to think that what he does next is an act of mercy. I'd like to think it was a gesture of kindness, a moment of grace in a universe utterly devoid of any of these things. I'd like to think so, but I'm not sure. Most likely it's just what it seems to be: a good old-fashioned bribe.

He says, "Look. I'll tell you what I'm going to do for you. I'm going to give you a number and I want you to write it down carefully."

Fishing around in my pockets, I come up with the usual effluvia: pennies, lint, spare keys, and assorted crap. I unfold a recent ATM receipt that shows I'm completely out of funds. I uncap a pen and take down the number he gives me.

"What's this?" I ask, "Some kind of secret code? An oversees phone number?"

"No. It's the winning lottery number in next week's New York State Super-Duper Megamillion Lottery. I think the jackpot will be twenty-seven million by then."

I look at the nonsense number I just scrawled on the slip of paper and I'm suddenly wishing I'd paid a lot closer attention, just in case. "You're joking, right?"

"Take a good look at my face. Do I look like I'm joking, Mr. Molloy?" His face, at that moment, looks like an open grave. I feel my knees wobble and my bowels get squishy. Mr. X3 says, "What do you think? Do you really suppose we let just anyone win those things? Do you really figure we just give away millions and millions of dollars willy-nilly to just any idiot who happens to guess a random number? Think about it, Mr. Molloy. Does that really make any sense to you?"

"I guess…I thought…I figured it was like getting hit by lightning. I though you had to be lucky."

He says, "There's no such thing as luck. That's hush money. That's money given to people who've got a certain…um…leverage. That's the price of silence. That's what *Sssssh* costs nowadays. You make your own luck in this world, Mr. Molloy. That fortune is yours on one condition."

"What's the condition?"

He says, "We want a happy ending."

I say, "A happy ending?"

He nods, "We like a happy ending. A happy ending keeps things going on the way they're going on. It keeps people on track. It keeps them content and…erm…happy, and we want things going on more or less the way they're going on. We want people happy and content. Isn't that a nice thing to want? Who can say that we're the bad guys?"

"You want me to lie."

"What's the point of telling the truth if it's only going to make people miserable? Why would we tell stories if they only bummed people out? What would be the point of *fiction?*"

"Do you think anyone will believe it?"

"That's entirely up to you, isn't it? But I'd hope they do, if I were you. For your sake." I feel another knee-knocking chill and this time it's not just because of his implied threat. Someone has opened the emergency door of the plane. "Now I'm afraid you'll have to excuse me. I have some other business matters to attend."

But when he doesn't get up like I expect, I realize that he's expecting me to get up. I do, and then it strikes me: I have nowhere to go.

"Get Mr. Molloy his coat." Mr X3 says to one of the flight crew.

Funny, I'm thinking, *I wasn't wearing a coat when I got here.* I'm about to say something to this effect when a stewardess walks up to me holding a vest with, presumably, a parachute folded inside. She helps me into the thing as I stare, momentarily uncomprehending, at Mr. X3.

"This is where you get out, Mr. Molloy."

"I can't...I...."

"Show our guest to the exit," he says, as two large men take me by the upper arms and propel me towards the open cabin door. I'm digging my heels into the floor, weeping, sweating, sniveling, begging for "just a second." I explain my fear of heights, my tendency to faint, my terror of falling ten thousand feet. Mr. X3 is unaffected. He sits pat.

"Oh, stop making such a fuss. Just remember to pull the cord, Mr. Molloy. Just remember not to panic. After all, it would be a real shame to have an accident now."

I'm in the plane's doorway, staring over the edge, barely able to hear anything over the drone of the engines. The clouds, the whole world, lies under my shoes. *He's bluffing*, I've been thinking up to now. *He's just trying to scare me.*

I'm only half right.

I scream over my shoulder. "But how can I trust you? How do I even know this parachute is packed?"

"What choice do you have, Mr. Molloy?," he screams back. "Oh my, you'll have to pardon me," he chuckles into his fist again, "I'm about to make another funny. You're just going to have to take a leap of faith."

I'm howling bloody murder now as the brutes holding my elbows tighten their grip, preparing to lift and toss me into the void. This isn't a bluff.

"Is this what you call a happy ending, you bastard," I wail back into the wind that's slapping me silly.

Mr. X3 yells back, "You tell me!"

And that's it. I'm suddenly running in space, but instead of going anywhere, I'm falling. I'm falling straight down. I'm falling and falling and falling and I hope I never reach the bottom because when I do it's going to be *splat*. But I will. I will reach the bottom just like everyone else. I know I will. I'm no exception to the law of gravity any more than I am to any other law. I'm in one of those situations where the only thing you can do is grit your teeth and hope for the best. Oh yeah...and remember to pull

...the fucking
...rip
...cord!

34. Love, Thunderbirds, and sayonara...

I'm falling from the heavens, feet-first, towards the unforgiving earth below. I've got the rip cord in my hands and it hasn't done a damn thing since I ripped it. *It's murder*, I'm thinking, plain and simple; they threw me out of the plane to get rid of me. I'm going to be spread out over thirty-five miles of red-state farmland. There won't be a trace of me left, not a toe-knuckle. I'll be pulverized into fertilizer. I'll feed next year's corn crop. Well, I reason, at least my life will have served some purpose. That's the kind of rationalization you go through as you fall through the sky at two- hundred-twenty-miles-per-hour. Not that I'm taking this with any dignity, mind you. No, I'm facing death just as I always feared I might: screaming and weeping and cursing in abject shit-in-my-pants terror.

If I knew anything at all about being thrown out of planes, though, I'd have known that nothing happening was exactly what was supposed to happen after pulling a rip cord...for a little while, at least. For up above me, everything is happening just as it's supposed to happen, just as it usually does. The parachute is unfolding, which means it looks like its just spilling uselessly out of its pack, and then a few moments later I'm jerked upwards in the harness and floating. Goddammit, I'm floating! I'm floating back down to earth like an angel, like a baby, like I'm being born all over again.

I land in the parking lot of a diner off the New Jersey Turnpike, sweating and laughing and practically pissing myself I'm just so plain thrilled to still be a solid. I shuck off the parachute harness and stagger towards the shiny metal eatery.

She's sitting in a booth casually smoking a cigarette. She's sitting in front of a poached egg she's not eating and a coffee she's not drinking. I slide into the red leatherette seat across from her. I look down at the placemat for a moment to collect my thoughts and I see advertisements for nail boutiques, dog-washing services, funeral homes, car washes, stuff like that. I play with a fork. I feel like I'm maybe fourteen in the presence of my first serious crush. I'm calling her Nada Klone, by the way, even though I know very well it's Norma Blake Madsen sitting across from me, the woman I knew as Naomi Blake, and whose image I know was sold to provide the physical reality of an X-rated woman who doesn't exist. The woman sitting across from me now, whoever she really is, wears a black leather bustier, black leather skirt, artfully torn black fishnet stockings, and red platform sandals with little padlocks on the ankles. There are chains and clips and rings and all sorts of other shiny paraphernalia hanging off her short leather motorcycle jacket. There's a peaked cap. There are fingerless black lace gloves. In short, she looks like the spitting image of Nada Klone, or what Nada Klone is supposed to look like, if she'd ever actually existed, if she hadn't been an X-rated fabrication based on every man's favorite wet dream.

"I'm in disguise," she explains, answering my unasked question, one of them, anyway.

Finally I look up. I say, "So this is where everything gets resolved?"

She shrugs. She says, "I guess so."

Sitting all around us, the people hunched in front of their hamburger specials and eggs ala mode are the usual plants made up to look just like typical real people caught in the long middle of a journey between here and there, en route to nowhere. They have the look you see on the faces of most everyone all the time in malls, in offices, in supermarkets. It's the everyday look you see on each and every one of us as we hustle our way through the long boring days from the cradle to the grave. Every eye in the place is on us, more accurately, *on her*. As usual, I'm just a prop.

I reach for the menu. Falling from heaven has given me quite a hearty appetite in spite of myself. But Nada puts her hand on the menu, holding it down.

"There's no time." She slides a set of keys across the table. "Our getaway car is outside. We can talk on the way to the airport."

Ah, that Nada, always the romantic. I look out the window and spot our ride immediately. It's a convertible Ford Thunderbird, red, of course (we're in disguise, after all), vintage, sitting among the usual Toyotas, Hondas, Jeeps, Acuras, and whatnot.

"Well then," I say, suddenly wanting to see nothing so much as Nada sitting beside me in the passenger seat of that hot cherry convertible. "Let's get this show on the road."

As we race along I-287, I'm looking at the scenery blurring past when I'm not looking at Nada: refineries, swamps, cities, car wrecks, hitchhikers, gas stations, all of it, like the whole world has been vomited up. If you go fast enough, I'm thinking, it almost makes sense. *Almost.* I press the gas to the floor, leave a state trooper disappearing in my rear-view like he was going backwards. He doesn't come after me. It's just as I expected. This is all going according to somebody's plan.

Even going this fast, the interstate looks a lot different than I can ever remember it looking and I'm guessing that's due to all the new construction they're always pretending to be doing. Nada and I haven't spoken more than twenty words in the last hour or so and that's mainly my fault. Being so close to a woman I've been seeking for so long, who I've loved so much, and missed so badly, a woman I'll have to say goodbye to forever in less than thirty minutes, has thrown a hitch in my usually relentless capacity for idle chit-chat. It's given me a case of world-class stage-fright.

"So you and Chambers," I say, and miles pass. "Chambers and you."

Nada's got a smile on her face like she knows a secret she's not telling. She's doing something sexy with the toothpick between her sexy white teeth. She's unlocked her heels and she's got her fish-netted bare feet up on the dash and she's wiggling her toes around. She casually licks her thumb and wipes away a smudge on her scarlet pedicure. I grow an instant hard-on. We're driving east on 278 or west on 287, one of those damned roads that look exactly alike coming or going, heading for JFK International Airport. Nada's got a map spread out on her lap and she's looking at it, maybe she's looking at it, it's impossible to tell what she's actually looking at behind her big dark movie-star glasses. She says, "Bear right up ahead. Take the next turn-off."

I screech down the exit ramp, my belly in my throat. "The two of you were in it together all along?"

"He was working under cover and found out I was a target. He figured he could use me as bait and I figured I could use him as protection. Once we learned we could use each other, it was kismet. We fell in love."

All that is interesting, but it's not what I want to know, not really. All that is just circumstance, it's not the answer to the mystery. Time's running out, and she's got a ticket for Frankfurt in less than eighteen minutes, and if I don't get her on that plane in time the megamillion lottery number in my pocket is null and void, and I don't get the girl, the money, nothing, zilch, zip, *nada*. Instead I get a whole lot of trouble from people I don't want a whole lot of trouble from. I get killed, presumably. People I know and love start to disappear from the face of the earth and it's all my fault. I lose, in other words, but in the worst possible way. So I stomp on the gas and force myself to blurt it out. The one question I've been dying to ask her all along. "Why? How could you possibly do this to us?"

Nada Klone turns towards me just a little bit, showing a little more than half her beautiful face, like a gibbous moon, her sexy mouth impaled on the toothpick like a ripe wet strawberry, and I don't think utter density has ever been more seductive. She says, "Do what?"

I say, "*Throw away everything we had.*"

But what's rapidly becoming clear even to me is that we had nothing to throw away; fact is, as far as Nada Klone is concerned, I was just as imaginary to her as she was to any of the many men who fell hopelessly in love with her. When I say "we," I'm really talking about "me." When I talk about throwing away everything we had, I'm talking about throwing away what I had—or thought I had. If I were in love, I was in love all by myself, because one thing is for certain and it's this: *Nada Klone doesn't love me.* Not if you consider love to be any of those things we've always been told love is supposed to be. It's pointless to tally up the things Naomi-Norma-Nada did and said, because none of it equals up in the end. And that's the real problem; in that is the way that madness lies. You spend your life futilely trying to make things add up that just don't. Life ain't math folks, x+z doesn't equal y. Maybe that's what Mr. X3 was ultimately trying to tell me. Maybe that's what love, life, God, all of it is in the end: this *problem* that just can't be solved and doesn't make sense no matter how you look at it.

"Things change," Nada says, and I know this is as close to an explanation as I'm ever going to get. "That's how it goes," she shrugs, and I know that's as much of an apology that I can reasonably expect. "Don't be such a victim," she says, turning away, and I know that's all the sweet talk I'm going to hear.

Looking at her now, I might as well be looking at an image on a screen. I'm looking at someone who doesn't see me at all.

I say, "You realize you're going to spend your life with someone who doesn't love the real you at all. This..." and I gesture towards this sexual mirage sitting next to me in the red Thunderbird, "...it's not *you*. He's in love with a fantasy."

She says, "What is *me*, anyway? Why can't I be this person just as easily as anyone else? He desires this and I desire to be desired. That may seem like a kind of solipsistic definition of love, but hey, so what? Maybe it's all just a big lie, maybe *that's* the truth, but is that really so wrong? I'll try to be what he wants me to be...who doesn't try to be what someone else wants? Who doesn't love an illusion? What's love, anyway, but that?"

And I realize that whoever I thought Norma Blake Madsen was, she's not the woman she is now. Or rather, she's sometimes that woman and sometimes not, sometimes she's here and sometimes she's there, blinking on and off, kind of like quantum physics. She's been pretty unstable all along, but who isn't? She's been a little bit crazy from the get-go, but ditto what I just said. And maybe she's right, after all. What's love at the end of the day but a negotiation of needs? And isn't that enough?

I say, "What about our baby?"

She says, "It doesn't exist anymore."

"Since when?"

"Since shortly after I decided it wouldn't exist anymore."

"I see. So that's it? You get on a plane and go to Frankfurt and then disappear to parts unknown and I never see you again?"

"Yeah, I guess so."

"And that's okay with you?"

She says, "Sure."

"Well, that about says it all. I guess that's it then."

"Cool beans."

There are a lot of other things I'd still like to ask her, but I can't quite find the words, and besides, what's the point? There are a lot of matters I'd like to settle once and for all, but I know that I can't really trust a single word she says. She's just a dentist's estranged wife on the surface, but to me she's like Helen of Troy, Mona Lisa, and the Sphinx, all rolled into one. She's the enigma at the heart of everything, in other words, a woman, but so much a woman that I have to wonder if she's really a real woman to me at all. Maybe, like everyone else, I'm just imagining the woman I love and not seeing the real person behind the illusion at all. Maybe there is no real woman behind the illusion and that's what love keeps us from seeing. Maybe the love-of-my-life is nothing more than a fake girl, after all.

Dropping Nada Klone off at JFK with less than five minutes to spare, I help her with her luggage and say a hurried goodbye on the run to Terminal B. I breathlessly tell her that I'll always love her, that she can contact me anytime, that I'll always want to hear from her, even if it's five, ten, twenty years down the road, how everything else might change, stars burn out, galaxies collapse, but that my love for her won't end and I guess I really mean it while I'm still saying it, but I know deep down in my heart I don't.

She's right, everything changes.

Even with the best of intentions.

In the meantime, I'm watching how she's turning heads with every step, every step coming quicker, until she's running in her stacked heels away from me and into the arms of a man in a black trench coat. It looks like the real Chambers this time, FBI undercover agent, adulterer, blackmailer, revolutionary, lunatic, who the hell knows who he really is, who anyone really is, and what difference does it really make to me anymore anyhow?

There's not much more about this scene that I remember. Frankly, there isn't much more about it that I want to remember. Walking back out of the terminal, crossing the street, heading for the parking garage—I just assume I do all these things. I'm on remote control. I'm like a robot—a robot with tears rolling out of its eyes. Putting the red Thunderbird convertible into gear, I roar out of that concrete hell of arrivals and departures they call an airport, but that can also be called a giant concrete metaphor for life itself, and get back on the interstate. What I do remember is flashing the finger at a honking cab behind me as I sit at a green light and watch Nada's plane rise softly into the clouds. I also remember getting hopelessly lost trying to find my way back to Manhattan. I remember thinking, "I don't give a shit if I ever get home."

"Hello?" I call out timidly when I open the door to my apartment God only knows how many hours later. It's hard to explain how I can tell but I can tell that the place is empty, that whoever's been living here with me in secret for the last several months has packed up and moved out. The place is a mess, but it's the mess I made, not a pen put down or a can opened that I didn't put down or open. For the first time in I don't remember how long, I can walk around the place with my ding-a-ling dangling and not feel vaguely embarrassed that someone is watching.

On the card table my laptop is up and running and back to normal. Whatever virus I had, it's all completely better now. The word processing program is open, a mug of hot coffee is steaming, a yellow Post-It note stuck to the mug says, *Welcome back.*

Pulling out the chair, I sit down. I roll up my sleeves. I crack my knuckles. Resting my fingertips lightly on the keys, I take a deep breath. I can't put it off any longer.

It's time.

It's time to get started on that happy ending.

I grit my teeth.

This is what I write:

35. Magic, good luck, and Happy New Year...

Five, four, three, two, one, we're all counting down. What we are all counting down is the last five seconds of the year. It's a New Year's party in a small apartment on York and 78th. There's quite a crowd packed into the place and I'm standing by a bookshelf with a bottle of Sam Adams beer and wondering if I know anyone in this room because I have no idea how I got invited, or what I'm doing here. But this is the party the person on the cell phone they "mistakenly" gave me back at the police station invited me to and I had nowhere better to go so here I am at the stroke of midnight. As the last five seconds of the year get counted down to zero, we're all watching the big screen TV against the wall as the famous Times Square ball slowly descends.

There's a girl standing just to my left who looks vaguely familiar. She's laughing, smiling, shouting out the countdown to the new year like everyone else. All around me the faces are bright and happy and full of hope and excitement for nothing in particular, just like they were last year, and every year before that. The girl turns to me, maybe sensing I'm looking at her, and she smiles even more broadly. She's from somewhere, I can't place her pretty face, her laughing eyes, her shapely little body.

She says, "Do I know you from somewhere?"

I say, "No I don't think so. Not really. But it sure as hell seems as if we know each other from somewhere, doesn't it?"

If she hears me at all over the general party hub-bub, the blaring music, the shouting of the countdown, I can't really tell. But she doesn't turn away and she's smiling that smile that always melts something inside me in spite of myself, that smile that says, *I know who you are,* but just as well might be saying, *You know who I am.*

Over the music I shout, "What's your name?"

And yes, I'm half-hoping to here her say, *Naomi* or *Norma,* but she doesn't. She says something else, and does it even really matter?

She asks me my name and I tell her the usual nonsense and then on the television the ball touches down and everyone shouts, *Zero!,* and the confetti falls, and *Auld Lang Syne* starts playing and everyone starts kissing and everyone is crying because we're all one year older and no one is any wiser and nobody is who they really want to be and nobody ever will be, but we're all hoping this year it will all be different all the same.

I look at the television and I see the new date glowing in lights on Times Square and my first reaction is, *They made some kind of mistake.* I turn back to the girl who's still standing next to me, jumping up and down on the tips of her toes, clapping, all excited for really no reason, and I say, "Did they make some kind of mistake?"

And before I say another word she shouts, "Happy New Year! Happy Two thousand and blah blah," by which I mean she says the year they have in lights on Times Square, the year it apparently is, the year that was supposed to be the year I just finished living.

And I think, *That bastard,* but I'm grinning.

I'm thinking, *That son-of-a-bitch,* but I'm laughing. He gave me back a year. *He gave me back the year stolen by US.*

"Happy New Year," I say to the girl beside me, the girl who's been all the girls I've loved so far, except this time I'm thinking that she might just be the one, the *real* one I kept thinking she was all along, the one who won't turn out to be faking. "Happy New Year," I say, and this year I really mean it.

We kiss, we talk, and she inevitably asks, "So what is it that you do?"

I say what I always say.

I say, "I won the lottery."

She smiles that smile I've loved all my life. Fact is, she hasn't stopped smiling that smile since I met her. If you could distill that smile, if you could put it into a syringe, you'd have the cure for death. She says, "The lottery, huh? You must be very lucky."

I don't change the subject, I don't quickly ask her what she does. I don't rush off and get another drink.

This time I just stand there. This time, whatever time it is, all time seems to stop. I think about Nada for a moment, about Naomi, about Meeah, about all the women I've ever loved in my life, and suddenly the fact that nothing means anything, and that we're all interchangeable and unreal to each other doesn't necessarily seem like it has to be a bad thing to me. Maybe it's even a good thing. Maybe it's what keeps us in the game no matter how many times we lose, that chance to go for that one in a million shot, no matter how many times we miss.

My heart, if there's anything left of my heart, is pulling itself magically together from out of ten thousand shards that don't even fit together anymore, cracked, trembling, susceptible forevermore to breaking all by itself. It's a miracle. A single breath could shatter it.

I hold my breath.

I say, "Yes, maybe I am." I can hardly believe my own ears. I'm looking at the love-of-my-life and for the first time it occurs to me, "Yes, goddammit, maybe I am very lucky, after all."

FAKE GIRLS 322

Final words...

So it's a happy ending after all, sort of. I mean, if I keep telling the story long enough, it'll end up just like all real-life stories do. Everyone will get old, get decrepit, start falling apart, croaking. People will fall out of love, resentments and cynicism will take over, everyone will end up bitter. Accidents will happen, strokes will start hitting, lumps will start growing. I don't want to see Meeah Soo die, or Ratking, or Naomi, or dad, whoever he might be. I don't want to lose Mr. Knott or Todd Sprocket or even any of the various Chambers's. I don't want to see any of that happen, but I will, it'll happen, so let's just end the story right here before anything too bad happens, before I give anything away. Let's remember it all just as it is at this moment, because that's all we have, that's what all the wise guys say, anyway, all those Buddhas, bodhisattvas, gurus, and Zen masters.

My advice, in case you're asking for it, is to keep your options open, be fluid, be flexible, don't let them define you, name you, number you, hem you in.

Be nobody.

Be nobody for as long as you can possibly take it.

Just glide beneath the surface of things for as long as you can. And then come up. Come up holding your *real* name between your teeth like a knife.

But don't tell anyone I said that.

What I'm doing now is winking. What I'm doing now is giving you the "thumbs-up." What I'm saying to you is basically all I can say before I send you on your way.

The game's rigged.

Nobody wins.

What I'm saying is, *Good luck...*

Don't miss these other exciting titles
charting the no-man's land beyond
contemporary literature

AFTERHUMAN PRESS
...what's next in books

Afterhuman
by Michael Cross

The Maniac Manifesto
by Nick Caligari

Hardcore Romeo
by Mark Nadja

For more information and free previews of all our books please visit
our website at www.afterhuman-press.com

www.ingramcontent.com/pod-product-compliance
Lightning Source LLC
Chambersburg PA
CBHW021455240626
47154CB00002B/377